Silence. Except for our quickening breath. The quiet made it worse – the anticipation of noises, unspeakable in the offing. I wanted to fill the quiet with my voice, but I dared not.

Nina said, "It feels like I'm underwater. I can't breathe."

We heard something then – a gnawing sound, like tissue being bitten and sawed apart.

We rushed to the top of the stairs.

A large room. Faint, lead-colored light over our heads. The air felt cool and drafty, the floor wet. My shoes slipped as if I'd walked out onto an icy pond. But this was no pond, and what lay obscenely before us was no injured animal in need of kindhearted rescuers.

It was far more hideous.

ARKHAM HORROR™

The LAST RITUAL

S A SIDOR

ACONYTE

First published by Aconyte Books in 2020

ISBN 978 1 83908 013 5

Ebook ISBN 978 1 83908 014 2

Cover art by John Coulthart

Distributed in North America by Simon & Schuster Inc, New York, USA

Printed in the United States of America

9 8 7 6 5 4 3 2 1

ACONYTE BOOKS

An imprint of Asmodee Entertainment Ltd

Mercury House, Shipstones Business Centre

North Gate, Nottingham NG7 7FN, UK

aconytebooks.com // twitter.com/aconytebooks

"The smoke banked like fog, and the opening of the door filled the room with blown swirls of ectoplasm."

F SCOTT FITZGERALD, "THE RICH BOY"

CHAPTER ONE

"The last time … ?"

Alden Oakes turned away from the window, staring coolly at the cub reporter who had paused with his pencil raised above the pad. Oakes had avoided his questions deftly so far, employing a defensive combination of small talk and awkward silences.

"I thought we might start there," the reporter said, prodding. He had a deadline.

Alden nodded and resumed pacing inside the hotel suite. "Strange weather we're having. First a dense fog, then blowing mists like gigantic gauzy veils. Now here comes the rain. I didn't need to open this contraption all the way here from the train station this morning." He tapped the window with the umbrella he was using like a cane. The reporter had noticed the famous painter suffered from a slight limp. "The air is strangely mild for midsummer. Don't you agree?"

"It beats the heat," the reporter said. He wasn't interested in talking about the weather, but whatever got his subject to relax and open up to him was worth a try.

Alden gazed out at the gloom as if he were trying to decipher shapes in the clouds.

"How does it feel being back at the hotel again?" the younger man asked, poking again softly, wondering if this afternoon was going to end up being a big waste of time. Usually, there were two ways to handle it. Either you pushed the subject harder and risked losing them, or you went all quiet and let the pressure of no one talking do the trick. He hadn't made up his mind which way to go yet.

"The doorman tipped his cap like we were old acquaintances," Alden said.

Rain hissed and slithered down the glass.

The reporter decided. He had spent hours trying to pry stories out of tight-lipped people in places far less pleasant than the luxurious Silver Gate Hotel. He could afford to kill a little time here in the comfort of a pricey room. So he dropped his pencil on his notepad and pushed back from the hotel room desk, letting out a gentle sigh. Though compact, the desk setup was more comfortable than his cluttered cubby at the *Arkham Advertiser*, where he was forced to share space with a sports reporter, a habitual snacker who left coffee rings and doughnut crumbs on everything. If the artist wanted to play coy, he'd wait him out, saying nothing. He gazed past the painter at the dim, graying view of downtown Arkham.

Alden pushed off from the window and smiled. He sat stiff-backed on the loveseat, his hands resting on the crook of the umbrella gripped between his knees. Leaning over, he switched on a lamp, casting light into the room which was growing noticeably darker despite the noon hour. "Ready?"

"Yes, Mr Oakes, whenever you want to get started." *Victory!* He snatched his pencil.

Resigned, Alden sank into the pale green velvet sofa cushions, closing his eyes. "The last time I saw the Silver Gate Hotel it was burning. I was burning too, or my jacket was, before an Arkham fireman tackled me to the ground, rolling me in the grass to smother the little fires climbing my back. I escaped with my life, as they say."

"You're a lucky man," the reporter said. Now that the ball was rolling, he just had to keep it going. He might get a decent story out of this yet. After all, the tragic and suspicious fire at the Silver Gate had been the biggest news story in Arkham last year. But Alden Oakes was considered only a minor part of it, a local celebrity footnote. A celebrity *painter*, no less.

"I'm sure some people might consider me lucky," Alden looked at him slyly.

The young man frowned, confused. Would he have rather had his bacon fried?

Alden went on.

"This suite we're sitting in, the one I've booked for this homecoming of mine, survived the catastrophe intact. It suffered serious smoke damage. The whole place did. But you'd never guess that judging from the building's current appearance. The bricks scrubbed clean, fresh from the rain, the lobby's glossy marble floor shining like a giant chessboard, and those vases full of maroon heirloom roses and white calla lilies. Such a transformation! Yes, they worked a real miracle bringing this hotel back into operation in a little over a year."

The reporter began scribbling notes. "The grand reopening gala is scheduled for tomorrow. Are you surprised the hotel owners invited you?"

"Why? Because of the rumors? My confinement?" Alden's voice rose. "Nothing was ever substantiated. Innuendos and idle speculation. The press planted theories to sell more papers. People like you." He checked his anger, pushing it back under the surface. "Others influenced them, of course. The doctors said I needed rest. I suffered from physical and mental exhaustion. No, I don't feel guilty about what happened to the hotel. But I'll admit it was a surprise to receive the invitation. Who are the owners, by the way? Do you know?"

The reporter shook his head. "It's a damned secret. The management company runs day-to-day business. But the legal paperwork is vague, a pyramid of companies, mostly European. Taxes are paid by an anonymous land trust. That's all I could dig up–"

"Don't bother digging. You won't find anything." Alden waved. "It's not important."

"But they wanted you here."

"My presence was demanded." Alden sat forward. "I just finished a gallery showing in New York. I have no real home any more, not in America. I was debating returning to France, or spending a few months in South America painting frogs and orchids along the Amazon. I'd gone as far as hiring a paddleboat with a small crew to ferry me into the jungle."

"Yet here you are," the young man said, shaking his head, incredulous. A trip into the Amazon jungle! Now there was a place where stories were ripe for the picking. They must be hanging from the trees like banana bunches. A journalist could write a big, fat book about it. "Why would you skip a trip like that, if you don't mind me asking? I'd jump at the chance."

"Adventure doesn't require an exotic locale. Only the proper spirit is needed..."

What the heck did that mean? Well, the young reporter

wasn't here to argue about foreign travel plans. "Keep talking, Mr Oakes, I didn't mean to interrupt you," he said.

"Not to worry. What's your name again?"

"Andy. Andy Van Nortwick."

"Well, Andy, let me ask *you* a question. How old do you think I am?"

Glad that the artist's mood had improved, Andy screwed one eye shut and appraised his subject. Oakes was slender, his pale coloring bordering on consumptive, except for a penny-sized, raised scar dotting his left cheek. He wore a pencil mustache. His hair receded in a sandy blond wave curling back from a high aristocratic forehead. And he dressed strictly top drawer, a tailored London suit. But his eyes gave it away. They looked watery and old, crowded by lines of worry, sleepless nights, and regret. "I've never worked at the carnival or anything, but I'll guess you're right about fifty. That's a nice round number. Fifty it is."

"I'm twenty-nine. My birthday was two weeks ago."

The reporter's face reddened. "I'm sorry, Mr Oakes. I didn't mean any insult to you."

Alden brought out a gold cigarette case and a banjo pocket lighter. He offered a smoke to the reporter. Then he lit both their cigarettes.

"That's what adventures do to a person, Andy."

Alden winked and settled back on the sofa. He exhaled a plume of smoke into the suite. Andy felt embarrassed. The *Arkham Advertiser* reporter kept his eyes glued to his notepad. He'd been writing for the newspaper for less than a year. Before that he had been delivering them on his bicycle. He was eager to be writing any story more momentous than Mrs O'Reilly's dog gone missing after chasing the milkman off her porch. He silently cursed himself for being so raw. A real dope. He wasn't like the cynical veteran ink slingers, with their grimy fingers stuck in every political pie. They wrote stories as favors or payback. He had no secret agenda. No one was pulling his strings. Not yet anyway. He only wanted to tell the truth. When he looked up again, Alden's expression had softened toward him.

"It wasn't easy walking in this place after what happened to me here the last time," the painter said. "My heart was thumping when I checked in at the front desk and got my key. They've got the elevator operator dressed up like a phony palace guard. So strange. I almost pitied the poor old guy sitting there on his stool."

"I saw him too," Andy said, smiling. "I'll bet it gets boring sitting in that box all day, riding up and down."

"Agreed," Alden said. "Is it me or do the hotel staff seem terribly cheerful to you? I wonder how many of them worked here before the fire. I arrived early to avoid the rush. Most of the invitation-only gala guests aren't getting in until this evening or tonight. As the elevator car rose, I fiddled with my room key, caressing the brass fob. It's shaped like the Silver Gate façade but in miniature. Here, take a look." Alden slipped his room key from his pocket, tossing it to Andy.

"It's heavy," Andy said, before giving it back.

"The fire stopped on twelve. The firehoses never reached this far." Alden tapped the number on the key. "1481. My room for tonight. I entered and hooked the chain behind me. Only smoke invaded 1481 the night of the inferno. Plenty of it. Sniff about I did, once I locked myself inside. Like a basset hound following a scent trail I got down on all fours, but detected nothing more than laundered bed linens and a whiff of lemon oil wood polish.

The new carpet feels different, spongier than I recall. They've repainted. The replacement color is horribly bland, less rich and creamy than the original. Your average person wouldn't notice the difference. But I do. Demolition might have been a better option. Start over from scratch. I suppose it all came down to cost. They've chosen to try and cover things up, but the residue is still here, lingering beneath the surface. Hints and echoes. Before you knocked on my door, I smelled smoke in the bathroom. I was *sure* I smelled it. Fleeting, but distinct, not the scent of cigarettes but acrid, choking fumes... I investigated but failed to discover any lasting trace of it, only a bleachy residue rising from the bathtub. Funny."

The reporter couldn't help but take a deep breath.

"You don't smell anything now, do you, Andy?"

"Not a thing, Mr Oakes."

"Maybe it's playing tricks on me," Alden said. "The hotel, I mean. Or, maybe, something else...." The painter seemed lost for a moment, unfocused; his head tilted as if listening for a muffled, distant sound. But then he returned. "The furniture appears solid, elegant yet standard: a bed, dresser, and nightstand. The cozy sofa and chairs, that neat little desk where you're sitting writing out my story. My version of the events as they transpired... what happened to me..."

"What *did* happen to you? It was more than a bad fire, wasn't it?" Andy's eyes sparked.

"You'll make a good reporter someday, Andy. You have the nose for it, as they say. I wonder if you'll believe me if I tell you everything I saw, everything I know is true."

"Give me a try." Andy tapped the ash off his cigarette and licked his dry lips.

"I've got a bottle of gin in my bag," Alden said. He stood up quickly and moved to the closet. Taking down a red crocodile suitcase and setting it on the luggage rack, he pulled a small key from a necklace he wore under his shirt and unlocked the catches. From the case he unpacked a bottle of bootleg gin, a shaker, and a pair of glasses. He left the case open. "Hand me that ice bucket, would you? Thirsty?"

Andy found a full ice bucket sweating on the nightstand. He brought it to the painter.

"I don't drink on the job," he said. "My boss wouldn't like me breaking the law."

"Admirable," Alden said. "But the martini is for me. Ginger ales for you are in the desk drawer." Alden tossed him a bottle opener. When both men had their cold drinks, they settled back in their seats. Alden raised his martini for a toast. "What shall we drink to?"

"Truth?"

Alden shook his head. "Too much responsibility. How about, *my side of things*?"

"To your side of things," Andy said. He sipped his ginger ale.

Alden took a long swallow of gin. "That's all I can tell you, really. All any of us ever can tell, in the end. Nina would agree. She'd like you."

"Who's Nina?" Andy asked.

"She's my best friend," Alden said. "I'll get to her eventually. She's a big part of what this puzzling business is all about. A writer, too, my Nina, 'Alden, if you and I don't tell people what's going on, who will?' she'd say."

"She sounds like somebody I'd like to meet."

Alden smiled wistfully. "Nina isn't here to help us right

now. Words are her strength, mine being colors… pencils and brushes, paints, canvas. She would've been much better suited to be your source. But you've got me instead. Let me know if you get hungry. We'll order up room service. Oysters Rockefeller and shrimp cocktails. Put it on the hotel tab."

"Swell. I've never eaten like a rich man before."

Alden set his martini down to light another cigarette. He clicked the lighter dramatically and said, "My curious reporter friend, I'll do everything in my power to set things out right. The dreadful truth of the events as they really occurred, even the unbelievably scandalous details and most gruesome, loathsome facts. But you must know that it all started for me well before that frightful night at the Silver Gate Hotel."

Andy's pencil moved mechanically across the blank page, filling in the lines.

So, Alden began his tale.

CHAPTER TWO

The summer before... well, around two years ago now, I was watching a hot sun set into a cold glittery sea when I heard someone calling my name across the beach at Cannes.

"Oakesy!"

Now, my proper name is Wilfred Alden Oakes. But my father will always be the only Wilfred Oakes, renowned industrialist and philanthropist, et cetera. Everyone else calls me Alden. Except for one person. So I knew, before I saw him stepping through the long shadows stretched out on the sand, that it was Preston Fairmont walking toward me with a martini glass gripped in one hand and the other waving as if he were trying to hail a cab.

"Oakesy! Over here! I can't believe it's you. What are you doing in France?"

I was sitting in a wicker chair beside a small slatted wood table at a beach café, resting my legs after a day of climbing the winding cobbled lanes of the old quarter, Le Suquet, in search of untapped inspiration. Preston grasped the chair across from me and pulled it free from the beach. A bag containing my brushes and paints popped out of the seat but did not spill. Preston removed it from sight. Jubilant and tan, he sat down, beaming.

"What are you drinking?"

"A rose cocktail," I said.

"Splendid."

Preston caught the eye of the waitress. He had a manner about him that service people always noticed. He exuded money. The waitress slid another coaster onto my table.

"*Voulez-vous quelque chose à boire?*"

"I'll have one of these," Preston said, pointing to my drink.

The waitress nodded, smiling, but Preston was already looking away from her at the deep blue waves, the people lounging on the sand, and lastly, as she departed our company, at me. Despite my surprise at seeing him, I was instantly reacquainted with his aloof charm.

"How are you, Preston?" I said.

"Glorious, I've spent the day... I don't know... walking? I never tire of this place."

"Staying long?" I tried to sound neutral. It had been a while since we last talked, and the gap was not entirely by accident. Preston and I shared a lot of mutual background and friends. I preferred the illusion that I was unique in the world. He made that more difficult.

He shook his head. "I leave tomorrow. Sailing in the morning. That's why it's so perfect that I've seen you just now. I've been trying to reach you. You are desperately elusive, Oakesy."

"I've been here all summer," I said, squinting, shading my eyes.

"At the beach? It's no wonder you haven't had an exhibition in ages."

His comment casually found a way to bruise my pride.

Preston's cocktail arrived.

I ordered another and requested the check, hoping to measure our encounter to the most enjoyable length. "Painting isn't all getting and spending. Learning the craft takes time. I've grown this year, but finding my own style has been more difficult than I first anti–"

"Artists throw the best parties," Preston interrupted. "I'll bet you've been to a few."

Preston Fairmont was no amateur about throwing parties. At college he became a Miskatonic University legend. He'd started out at the University of Chicago, but his lack of seriousness as a student caused his parents to want him closer to home. So, reluctantly, he transferred to MU after a year. When we roomed together as classmates, he was still in his hosting infancy and busy establishing himself, keenly assessing maneuvers in the social terrain. During the Great War we talked about dropping out to join the navy because we liked their uniforms. The girls did too, or so we had surmised. There was something romantic yet viscerally tangible about the sea. It's the same reason I've always enjoyed painting in seaside locations. Well, neither of us volunteered to fight, and the war ended the autumn following our graduation. By then Preston was a connoisseur of the party scene and a host of epic renown. I dabbled on the periphery of such events, more comfortable spending my time slapping paint on canvasses in a studio or lugging an easel around outdoors.

"Why were you trying to contact me?" I asked.

"I'm embarrassed to say."

"Impossible," I said. Preston had an innate confidence bred into him. "I've never known you to feel that emotion."

"You'll see when I tell you why."

"Go on."

"I'm getting married." Preston smiled sheepishly.

"Congratulations! That's nothing to be flustered about. Cheers!"

I genuinely felt happy for the old boy, but the joyous surge was quickly throttled.

"To Minnie Devane," Preston added.

The empty glass squirted out of my fingers, tumbling off the table into the sand. Luckily its replacement was due any second. So here was the sticking point. Minnie Devane had been my on-again, off-again college girlfriend, my fiancée and ex-fiancée, my inspiration, the first woman I ever thought I loved. Now, I could write a book about Minnie, but if I did, I'd have to burn it before I was arrested for violating the Comstock Laws. Not that Minnie herself was obscene. See, she was like a piece of broken mirror. Small and shiny, and if you weren't careful she'd leave you bleeding. She reflected back places in yourself that were better left unexamined. I fell for Minnie because she had a smart, sassy way of talking and a wild, fast, shimmery way of whipping herself around a room so that everybody felt charged up. She was all heat and energy.

Sometimes that energy exploded. And people got hurt.

"You and Minnie?" It seemed so impossible, and then, even worse, so obvious.

I picked up the glass and dusted it off.

"Ain't it grand?" Preston said. His forehead beaded with sweat. Dark patches stained his shirtfront. He kept folding and unfolding his arms. His hands were like a pair of birds he was trying to keep from flying away. I noticed his color draining off, like a man about to faint. Was he *that* nervous about telling me? I hadn't thought my opinion mattered to Preston.

"When's the big day?"

"Oh, not until next summer. I've got… We have a year to plan," he said.

The shock of the news still reverberated, of course. I nearly felt concussed. But I was having a hard time coming up with a good reason to object or even to feel bad. I liked Preston. And I liked Minnie. Why shouldn't I be happy for them?

"I don't know if you're looking for it, Preston, but you have my blessing," I said.

The more I thought about them as a couple, the more I saw how they fit better than Minnie and I ever did. I was too solitary to match their robustly sociable personalities.

Preston and Minnie. Linking them up like that would take time to get used to.

"Oakesy, that's real swell of you. I'm relieved." He didn't look relieved. He was scratching his shoes back and forth under the table, peeking occasionally to witness the progress of his dig. He looked worse than when he dropped the big wedding bomb on me. Was there something else? "You're a champ. We hoped you wouldn't be too sore."

"I'm glad you found each other. Honestly, I think I really frustrated Minnie. The lonely artist, I guess, living inside his own head. In an imaginary world. 'But it's always raining in your world,' she'd say. 'That's the trouble.' Maybe I was just too peculiar for her."

"That's what she told me."

Did she now?

Frankly, Preston and Minnie were the kind of people who

typically did as they pleased. If they were inconvenienced, they might try to patch things up to see that things would go smoother for *them*. But they were hardly the type to lie awake at night wondering about the impact their actions had on bystanders. I felt sort of honored in a weird way.

"Minnie and I are hoping dearly that you'll come to the wedding. It's in Arkham."

The unexpected invite dizzied me. Certainly, I might get used to the idea of my old flame marrying a college buddy of mine, but did I want to be there to see it happening?

Preston glanced past me over my shoulder. The corner of his mouth twitched in an anxious half-smile. I turned to see what he was looking at. It was a woman in a floppy sun hat with a pink ribbon. Either because Preston had been staring, or because I turned abruptly, she concealed herself, lowering the hat's wide brim to avoid our further attention.

He reached over the table and grabbed my wrist. His look was pleading. I felt sorry for him. "Please say you'll be there," he said. Why was he acting so desperate?

"I'll come to the wedding." I had time to adjust, and he wanted me there so badly.

His face stretched in an elastic, white grin. "That's terrific! They will be so happy!"

"They? Who are *they*?" I asked, confused.

Preston paused, then shrugged. "It's just Minnie and me. No one else."

"Now what about that woman sitting behind me? With the sun hat?" I thumped his shoulder. "I saw you smiling at her." Here I wagged my finger. "Minnie will expect your complete attention and strictest devotion, if you haven't discovered that already."

Preston swallowed dryly. "Well, she's the only one for me."

"Good man! Come next summer, you shall worship the goddess Minnie!" I joked.

"Ha!" His loud exclamation startled the beachgoers around us.

The waitress finally came with our drinks. After I signed the check, I pretended to drop my pen accidently so I could get a second, better look at the woman in the floppy hat. But she was gone.

While I was bending over, I happened to glance under the table. During our conversation, Preston had slipped off one of his white bucks and drawn something in the sand with his toe. A cup-like shape balanced on a triangle. Inside it were two ovals. Next to the cup, and less distinguishable, he'd scratched a three-pronged fork.

How truly bizarre, I thought.

As I tried to make sense of the upside-down symbols, Preston dragged his foot through the sand, obliterating them. Initially he'd come on so very Preston, but now I was noticing his unease. Perhaps this impending marriage really did shake his pillars. Minnie had that effect on some people.

"When are you planning to head back to Arkham?" Preston asked me as I sat up.

"I have no formal plans. I'll be in France for a short while. I was hoping to make a trip along the Spanish coast. My mother wants me home for Christmas. Why do you ask?"

"Minnie and I are throwing an engagement party. No date yet. Probably at my parents' house in French Hill, or maybe at the Lodge. We'd like you there. We have a lot of new friends who'll be attending the wedding. You need to meet them first.

Fascinating crowd. Bohemian types, right up your alley. Arkham has a vibrant art scene these days, or so Minnie tells me."

"That sounds intriguing," I said. Since when did bohemians flock to Arkham? "What kind of arts do they practice?"

Preston's skin turned a clammy gray. No longer the tanned picture of good health, he gulped his drink and began sucking on the ice. I worried he was suddenly feeling unwell.

"Are you all right, chum?"

"One too many escargots last night, I'm afraid," he said, wiping his damp forehead.

"And a few too many bottles of bubbly to chase them?"

Preston smiled. "You know me, old friend."

I thought I did.

He asked me to consider a return to Arkham in the fall. He and Minnie needed to start planning for their wedding bash. And weren't the fall trees beautifully colorful around our New England town? Couldn't I find something worth painting closer to my birthplace?

"In any case, get yourself home before all the leaves are gone," he said.

"I'll try my best."

My answer seemed less than satisfactory to him, but we shook hands (his felt like a cold thing washed up on the beach) and said au revoir.

Our waitress swung by, and I ordered an absinthe.

My nerves felt jangly, my inner wiring frayed. For no real reason, my senses felt as if they were set on high alert. It was as if I were living on only coffee and cigarettes.

The water flashed with intricate, metallic-seeming patterns. I noticed one sailing yacht anchored out in the bay, closer to the beach than any of the others. She wasn't the biggest. Her slim white lines lay just above the water like a bobbing shard of ice.

Quickly, on an impulse, I grabbed a pencil and pad and began to sketch her.

Out onto her foredeck stepped a figure visible only in silhouette. Sexless, ageless, viewed at this distance and in the failing light, it might have been any person on the planet. I knew not what drew my eye to it. But I could not look away. The figure glided along the yacht's length. It must have been a sailor carrying ropes, I told myself. Long tendrils looped from the central body and were cast off into the sea. The figure appeared to vibrate. Trick of perspective. The water's reflection was at play with the abundant shadows. My mouth felt dry, tasted of salt. A ripple of nausea passed through me like a sound wave traveling from the middle of the bay. My hand trembled as I traced long, unbroken lines onto the paper, attempting to capture the oddity I saw.

The horizon divided into layers: dark blue, indigo, purple, violet, and smoked gray.

The Bay of Cannes became a sheet of glass.

Those ropes, if they were ropes, retracted. The figure elongated, growing taller by half. This sailor, or fisherman, this distortion of a human form also wore something on its head.

Huge spikes, in the fashion of a crown, a dark cluster of bayonet-like appendages.

That's what they looked like, anyway.

Then the light changed, and soft black fuzz seemed to sprout from the air itself. The yacht became a normal sailing vessel at anchor among dozens of others.

I saw no one onboard.

Night had arrived. I looked around me as if I had been sleeping and wakened in my chair. The corrugated sea came alive once more with twinkling lights mirrored from the cafés and hotels ringing the shoreline. People were talking, sipping aperitifs or cups of coffee.

Normal.

Whatever peculiarity had passed briefly over the bay vanished.

I contemplated the spot where Preston had been talking to me less than an hour ago. He might have been a mirage, a conjuration, a product of my imagination animated in a dream. I picked up my bag from the sand, then stood to put away my sketchpad. I swayed, feeling lightheaded. Was it the liquor? The onset of a fever?

Too long in the sun, I concluded.

I walked back to my hotel in a daze. Falling on my bed, I didn't even bother to undress but slept straight though until morning. I woke instantly at daybreak. The room smelled stuffy, but I felt revived, energized. I might've looked like hell, but, boy oh boy, was I humming. After my breakfast I told the hotel manager I wished to settle the bill. The idea came to me that I must leave Cannes at once. I had no obligations but to myself, so I followed this unexplained urge, curiously compelled to see where it might lead me. I bought a map of Spain and arranged to rent a car. I gave myself through the month of August to prepare for my return to Arkham. If someone had suggested to me, when I went down to the beachfront for a drink by the sea, that I was going be altering my plans and heading circuitously back to the USA early, well, I just might have believed them. But if they had told me that the reason would be a wedding invitation from Preston and Minnie, I would have laughed in their face.

Clearly, I might have said no and stayed in France. Sometimes I've wondered what my life would have been like if I had. Would I be where I am today? And the rumors that inevitably follow me, what would it be like to live without hearing them? The horrible deaths, everything we saw at the Silver Gate event that night, everything that emerged in the unwholesome chaos...

But such thinking is beyond pointless.

I said, "Yes."

And nothing that followed will ever be changed.

CHAPTER THREE

I drove along the coast, saying goodbye to France mile by mile. I had little in the way of luggage, and art supplies took up most of the space in my sleek yellow Renault. I drove dangerously. I never was a particularly good driver and have no sense of direction.

Somewhere between Toulon and Marseilles my map flew out the window and the mountain winds kited it into a ravine. How could I get lost? I kept the ocean to my left and drove on, snaking my way through the stony massifs until it got dark. I looked for a place to get a hot meal and a soft bed for the night. There were no villages to be seen. My eyes burned with fatigue. I considered pulling over to catch forty winks, but the back roads were far too narrow. I didn't want to wake up pasted to the grille of a speeding delivery truck.

To occupy myself I entertained thoughts of Arkham.

Why had I left? What had I missed? How would the city look when I got back?

I was born in Arkham. My family was rich and socially prominent, although my parents were getting older and Wilfred, my father, had turned over much of his company's management to his younger associates. He made most of his money in metallurgy and chemicals. I never understood the specifics of what his Northside factories produced, nor did I care to learn more. Father's life appeared unbearably dull to me. He ranked the arts somewhere below sports and marginally above children's games. I knew the war had been good for the company, good for my family, as horrible as that sounds. My mother, Pearl, had her charity work. She wasn't overly concerned with helping actual people. Her causes leaned more toward public places like parks and museums. I don't fault her too much. I am certain my passion for painting was born out of wandering bored one evening into an exhibition hall during a fundraising dinner. The paintings leapt out at me! Such colors! I really *saw* them for the first time, and I trembled. It was like a religious epiphany without any religion. Or, I suppose, my god was art. In that instant I decided the direction of my life. *I must do this*, I thought with a zealot's clarity. I will make beautiful things. I wanted *my* work to hang in museums. I wanted people, like my mother and her friends, to organize fundraisers to hang pictures I would someday paint and, in return, I'd help people escape their dreary, tedious lives. Conveniently, I'd discovered a way out of the suffocating future that lay ahead of me.

Visions of Arkham flooded my brain for the remainder of my drive, and before I knew it, the world turned blue, then golden, and finally, an almost blindingly sunny white.

I was not seeking out any singular or heightened experiences in Spain. I wanted simply to relax. I settled in a rooming house at the center of a fishing village like many others that exist along the coast. I visited churches and strolled the steep, winding streets, lost in a maze of picturesque dwellings. Like much of the Mediterranean, the buildings I passed were whitewashed with red tiled roofs and tall windows shuttered against the sun's rays during the hottest hours of the day. Cats of every stripe and color napped in the shadows and eyed me with lazy indifference. I moved more slowly and felt myself adjusting to my old roommate's unexpected announcement of what was certain to be Arkham's social event of the year. I warmed to the idea of seeing Minnie and Preston together, and attending their fabulous parties. It would be good to go home again.

Although I was obviously a foreigner the villagers did not stare at me, but neither did they ignore my presence. When engaged they were uncommonly polite. I ate my meals in restaurants, devouring bread, olives, and plates of various small, oily fish, guzzling bowls of gazpacho, often imbibing a glass of Andalusian sherry before slouching off to a soft bed. My condition became one of blissful isolation. Language was like a cage I carried with me everywhere I went. I spoke no Spanish. No one I met spoke English. But I discovered that a mix of French and pantomime was all I needed to get my meaning across.

I completed more paintings there than I had in three months at Cannes.

While they were good, they lacked something almost palpable, as if the real subject had wandered away just before I started to paint. Haunted by absences. I put them away.

Preston was accurate when he alluded to my lack of artistic progress. It was true. I hadn't had an exhibition in ages. I had reached a point of stagnancy, a sluggish creative limbo where my talent and I sat together like a stale married couple who lacked the energy to argue. The truth about my artistic gift is that if I had been born a little better or a little worse, then my life might have been easier. I was never going to be one of those artists who sit in tattered overcoats selling their paintings at weekends on the street in the South Shore of Kingsport. I had no hustle, no salesmanship. I was born rich, so there was always money. Slumming seemed false. My skills revealed a mastery of technique. What I lacked, and what I desired, was originality. I was a copier, an imitator of the painters who came before me with superior vision. I felt like a fraud. I had concluded that the malady I suffered from was an absence of inspiring subjects to paint. Determined, I left Arkham bound for Europe. Once there, I was drowning in history, museums, and galleries, cloyingly surrounded by other artists doing the same thing I was. What new contribution might Alden Oakes possibly make? Where was my vision? It was a self-pitying view, I know, and like all self-pity it quickly grew tiresome.

Even to me.

So I brooded.

I painted realistic representations of fields, forests, and seashores. Though technically excellent, my work was hollow. I hated each of them, piling the canvases in the corner of a shed I rented from a peasant farmer, only to find later that it had a leaky roof and the paintings I stored there were ruined. There seemed no rush to produce more. I avoided the company of other artists and found myself forsaking the smoky coffeehouses and noisy, cheap cafés. Preston was right about the parties, but I didn't go any more. Still, I held out one last hope of discovering an ideal subject that would unlock my inner potential. The world would have to pay attention. Finally, they would see that I had something unique and powerfully beautiful to contribute to the world.

Such were my daydreams.

One day I decided to leave the village and venture south to Barcelona.

Did I ever get to Barcelona?

I don't *think* so. I know that sounds peculiar, but I've mentioned my horrible sense of direction. I might have reached the lesser known outskirts of the city, or gotten myself sidetracked into an oddly secluded neighborhood. I saw no La Rambla, no Gothic Quarter, or Basilica de La Sagrada Familia, in fact no famous landmarks at all. It occurred to me that I might have mistakenly paid a visit to a completely different town. The architecture had an overcrowded ramshackle quality, not at all what I anticipated seeing. I had gone to the place where I expected Barcelona to be. But no signpost told me definitively whether I ever arrived there. The streets through which I drove had the industrial character of a metropolis. One bizarre thing was this: whichever road I took, I always sensed I was driving downhill. Even when I attempted to backtrack, the Renault pitched downward as if I were trapped in a funnel.

I saw lots of soldiers.

They marched past me in groups, or they lingered in pairs. I never spotted one out walking alone. Their uniforms were tannish yellow, and they wore soft peaked patrol caps with maroon armbands. I couldn't tell how the civilians felt about them, but they made me nervous with their blank expressions and casually thuggish attitude. I looked for a friendly, clean-looking hotel. Everywhere I stopped I was told, "No vacancies." When I asked for recommendations, the clerks indicated there were no rooms to be had in the city.

I parked in front of a bank, thinking I might go inside to exchange some francs and ask the teller to recommend a hotel. I'd enquire offhandedly if this branch was indeed in Barcelona proper. I never had a chance; when I tried the doors, I found them locked.

I cupped my hands to the window.

Deserted, lights out. Nobody home.

It was a weekday. I was sure about that when I left the fishing village.

I lit a smoke and took a stroll. Noting the particularities of the street, I made sure I'd be able to find my car when I returned. Three roads met, forming six corners. A star-shaped island with a dry fountain occupied the center of the intersection.

I went up for a closer look.

Under a layer of foul green water, coins filled the fountain. Curious, I rolled up my sleeve, dipped my arm into the basin, and scooped up a handful of coins. A film of yellow slime covered the coins, which were unpleasantly warm, like little fingertips grazing my palm. I scraped away a bit of scum with my thumbnail. I'd never seen such strange currency. If these were *pesetas*, they must have been very old indeed. The coins lacked any numbers whatsoever. The symbols found there were worn smooth and difficult to recognize, but they depicted mythological beasts unfamiliar to me. I dropped them back into the filthy water. Perhaps it was a local custom to make wishes and toss these peculiar old coins. This fountain had a statue in it at some point; now it was missing. Only the empty pedestal remained. Gazing outward from the font, I surveyed my directional choices.

"Eeny, meeny, miny, moe…"

I picked one of the six streets and started walking.

No shops were open for business. I saw few people. When I passed them, they looked away. With regularity along the avenue there appeared large, dangerous, open holes in the pavement; the air wafting out of these pits smelled of sewage. Puzzled and alarmed, I wondered why they were not covered, reminding myself to use caution on my return journey.

Multiple stairways leading underground offered another clue that I had reached a city center of some size. I assumed they connected to an electrified subway. I knew of no catacombs in this region. But the station entrances bore no names that I could find. The only things differentiating one stairway from another were primitive-looking symbols carved into wooden panels above their subterranean thresholds. Upon closer inspection these hackings seemed to be graffiti, the handiwork of an artistic hooligan with a pocketknife. They reminded me of an exhibit of ancient druidic runes I'd seen once at the Miskatonic Museum.

Locked iron gates were drawn across the stairways.

If they were used for transport they, like the banks, were closed.

The deeper into the neighborhood I explored, the more I noticed the buildings around me falling into obvious stages of disrepair, their architecture looking less structurally sound. Fissures creeping along the buildings' foundations and cracks in their facades had me speculating that the city had experienced a recent earthquake.

The entire scene spoke of disintegration. This could not be Barcelona!

I had arrived during the early evening, and now, a couple of hours later, the sun plunged in the west. Light cut through the alleyways like gold bayonets. I turned at an intersection, always checking behind me to remember a key detail or two. For example, up there was a headless manikin dressed in a red cardigan, leaning forward against a dusty second floor window. Here, glass blocks frame the etched word *Farmacia* over a doorway. Farther on, rows of brown boots are standing to attention on a rack inside a cobbler's dimly humble shop. I planned to follow this trail of breadcrumbs back through the urban forest.

Crimson streaked the bruised sky whose unraveling bandages were merely clouds.

I heard voices, many voices, talking excitedly.

So I followed their sound.

Crack!

A gunshot?

I froze.

Then a volley of loud explosions. A scream. People laughing.

A woman in a black and white ruffled dress ran diagonally across the street ahead of me. She glanced over her shoulder, smiling, I thought at me, but then a young man with curly black hair and a guitar on his back emerged, chasing after her.

I tailed them to a plaza.

Here were the dwellers of the neighborhood. Long tables and kitchen chairs ringed the plaza and branched down the intersecting streets. In the center of the plaza towered a pyramid of old furniture, wood scraps, and even an old, peeling door. Families sat around the tables drinking wine and eating. Children ran everywhere. A man touched a fat cigar to a fuse in his fist and tossed the firework high in the air near the pyramid.

Crack!

The children screamed, laughing, and ran away.

It was a summer festival. I had heard about them from associates in France. It was common to see midsummer bonfires around the solstice throughout Europe, dating back to medieval times or, perhaps, earlier. Many had their roots in ancient pagan rituals. Harmless, good-natured fun said to be effective in repelling evil spirits. Who but the bitterest killjoy could argue against burning pyres and drinking through the night with friends until dawn?

I must've stumbled upon a local custom, I thought. Before I could question it further, the young woman in the black and white ruffled dress offered me a glass of sangria, which I accepted, as her beau whisked her away to listen to him play his guitar in the shadow of the pyramid. I noticed the soldiers mingling with the civilians. It seemed they came from these families. The resemblances between them were undeniable. So any worries I had about civil unrest died there, as I sipped my sangria and smoked, wishing I'd brought a sketchpad and my pencils. Someone offered me a chair. As I sat down, I discovered my glass being refilled. Such hospitality! Waiting for night to fall and the festivities to begin… that is when I first heard mention of the name Juan Hugo Balthazarr. Oh, I didn't hear it strung together like that, but in whispers, an insectile buzz that infected the crowd. "Balthazarr, Balthazarr, Balthazzzaaarrr…."

Could they be speaking of the most shocking living painter in the world?

No, I told myself. It must be a common name in these parts.

Yet I wondered…

Juan Hugo Balthazarr was a Spaniard, born in Barcelona. He was rumored to live there still, inside the walled, crumbling ruins of a Gothic monastery. As I looked around, I convinced myself some of these people at the tables might be his relatives. But no, it couldn't be.

Could it?

Balthazarr was acknowledged, most notably and boisterously by himself, as a genius destined to save the twentieth century from irrelevant art. Renowned as a relentless experimenter, he drew, painted, and sculpted with incredible energy and stamina, often said to spend days, or even weeks, without sleep in order to complete one of his outrageously fantastical visions. Critics either hailed his works as revolutionary or vehemently despised them, but all agreed his creations were as breathtaking as they were indescribable. Yes, there was something of Goya in them, and of those medieval painters who conjured torturous scenes in Hell. But Balthazarr's influences remained hard to pin down. Gustave Doré's woodcuts and engravings. The Dadaists and Cubism, of course. Currently, he was a major force in the Surrealist movement. But he was always his own artist. Incomparable, prolific, and a young man, barely older than I was. How I envied him! If only I could harness the talent I felt I had within me, if only I might push it into the world with such confidence, style, and gusto.

People were turning their chairs to stare down one of the streets.

I looked too.

I had seen only one photo of Balthazarr who, despite his growing worldwide fame, disliked having his picture taken.

He was tall and well-known for his athletic physique and long forked beard. I glanced over the heads of the festivalgoers but saw no one resembling Balthazarr. What a shame! If there was one artist in the world whom I admired, it was him.

They said he painted portraits of his darkest dreams. He possessed a perfect memory of everything that ever happened to him, both awake and asleep. Some claimed he was a seer.

Others derided him as the Devil incarnate.

I met a man in Paris, an English muralist, who swore Balthazarr kept him hypnotized for three whole days. Eventually he woke from his trance standing naked on the ledge outside a Moroccan hotel room window with a scorpion in one hand and a bag of semiprecious gemstones in the other. He dropped the scorpion and traded the gems for money to buy a ticket back to London. When I asked him if he held a grudge against the painter he laughed, saying it was the best weekend he couldn't remember in his life. Then he told me that Balthazarr still followed him.

"How do mean 'follow'?" I said.

"Oh, I see him, usually in reflections. Mirrors or windows, the surface of a pond. Never straight on, mind you. Always behind me, he lingers. That beard, and those eyes! When I turn, he's gone. I don't think he's menacing me. He's keeping me company. I only wish he'd stay."

I thought of no reply at the time.

The muralist seemed a bit mad. He had taut, unhealthy yellowed skin, and I noticed he wore two different shoes. One brown, the other black. His fingernails were overgrown and stained from nibbling red pistachios which he kept in every pocket of his jacket and trousers. I heard later that he'd been found drowned in the Seine. But I don't know if that was true. He might've gone home to England. He was quite a character. The kind you might believe anything about if someone told you. Anyway, he insisted that Balthazarr was a mesmerist and he could, if he chose to do so, bring a roomful of people under his power without them knowing it. Part of me loved every wild detail, and didn't care if they really happened or not.

The sound of drums echoed from one of the narrower streets, growing louder. People rose from their chairs and formed a circle in the plaza around the pyramid of items to be burned in the bonfire. I went with them. The noise was deafening as the drummers entered the plaza. They wore rustic costumes. Though simple, they were effectively frightening, a combination of hooded robes and masks made from human hair, dyed red yarn, and grotesquely painted smears of silver, copper, and gold on rough, blackened wood. It was surprisingly easy to believe that instead of people, the drummers were subterranean goblins. The sort of creatures that might've lived down wherever those iron-gated stairways led! They must've worn stuffed gloves to make their fingers appear so crookedly misshapen.

The crowd cheered and clapped.

Round and round the drummers circled the pyramid.

Finally, a tall figure in a silvery robe emerged holding a torch.

"Balthazarr! Balthazarr! Balthazarr!" the crowd chanted.

Caught up in the spirit of things, I joined them. A group rushed in from the rear, blocking my view. Feeling annoyed, I shouldered my way through the throng. "Excuse me. I'd like to see," I said, in English and to no effect. They refused to step aside. I pushed harder, not caring.

"I want to see Balthazarr! Let me see!"

Finally, I broke through to the front.

There was no way of telling who the tall figure really was, because over its head it wore the most startling full-head mask, fashioned like a black sunburst. Each of the daggerlike rays sparkled silver, as if dipped in stardust. The face was round-cheeked and grim, its mouth and eyes thin slits through which the wearer could observe without their identity being revealed. My pulse quickened. Deep interest and anxiety mixed in my blood.

The mask must have weighed an absolute ton. Yet the wearer bore it naturally without a sign of physical strain or restriction.

The robe, I realized, was composed of small mirrors, each no bigger than a playing card, and shards of broken glass secured with wire twists sewn onto a background of dark material. They flashed as the tall figure turned, bending at the waist and touching its torch to the base of the pyramid. The wood pile had to have been soaked in gasoline. That was the only logical explanation for the roar and explosion of flames that climbed higher than any of the buildings in the little street plaza. The tall figure tossed its torch into the conflagration.

The heat caused me to back up and shield my face.

But the other revelers drew nearer.

I don't know how they stood so close.

I felt my skin tighten as it does after a bad sunburn. The drummers marched and banged their instruments louder than before. The crowd swayed and began a chant in a tongue I did not recognize, but it certainly wasn't Spanish.

"*Ebuma chtenff! Gnaiih goka gotha gof'nn! Fm'latgh grah'n ftaghu grah'n!*"

Over and over they repeated... I dare not call them words, but these gross utterances.

"Balthazarr! *Hafh'drn!*" someone cried out.

The tall mirrored figure lifted its arms.

I do not know if I am particularly sensitive to heat. Never had I noticed any delicacy in my skin or nerves. Yet, in this plaza, at this moment, I became terrified that I might begin to burn. That my flesh might melt, sliding off my bones. It sounds ridiculous, but the pain transfixed me. My spine felt as though it were hardening, the fluid inside converting to steam. My marrow bubbled. My panicked brain kicked like a lobster dropped into a pot of boiling water.

Did I hear my bones snapping? Or was it the sound of firecrackers?

Firecrackers, it must be. I watched a belt of them writhe on the plaza floor. A second team of performers entered the circle around the flaming pyramid. This group was nimbler than the drummers. They frolicked and skipped, running up to the crowd and touching them. Why did it make my stomach lurch to see this? The nimble goblins brandished spinning sparklers held aloft on long pikes. As they approached me, I saw the ends of the pikes were three-pronged forks like the one Preston scratched with his toe in the sand under the table. White-sparking wheels spun on the tips of the prongs. I could not move or look away.

A goblin pushed a wheeled cart to the tall figure who stooped, picking something up.

Two puppets?

They had to be puppets, or large floppy dolls. The first was dressed as an adult man and the other as a woman. What unwholesome effigies!

The curly-haired guitar player strummed his guitar. The young woman with the ruffled black and white dress danced, not in any traditional way, but as if she were possessed.

The tall figure raised the puppets. A man's deep voice spoke through the mask.

"*Ebuma chtenff! Gnaiih goka gotha gof'nn! Fm'latgh grah'n ftaghu grah'n!*"

The crowd squeezed closer to the flames. Someone shoved me ahead. I tried to protest, but my throat was paralyzed. The guitar player thrashed the strings. The dancer flung herself to the ground, and then it was like an invisible hand jerked her body up again.

On the edge of the flaming pyre, I saw a painting propped in the flames.

The crowd pushed me in farther. The temperature was unbearable.

It was a painting of a city…

I strained to see the painting better. But flames licked over it. The canvas burned.

The tall figure, whose mirrors repeated images of the inferno, lifted the man puppet and the woman puppet… was one of them wailing? He muttered in that awful tongue-defying language. The intense heat must have made those puppets wiggle and worm.

"*Lw'nafh. Lw'nafh. Yuyu-Va'bdaa!*"

He spit the final words from his mouth and cast the puppets onto the pyre. His heavy mask slipped. Under it, I thought I saw the end of a long, forked beard.

He put the mask back in place.

"*Yuyu-Va'bdaa! Yuyu-Va'bdaa!*" the crowd shouted.

Facing them now, his resonant voice boomed out like an almighty drum.

"*YUYU-VA'BDAA!*"

They pushed me closer. I breathed in the harsh smoke from the pyre.

Then all was blackness.

CHAPTER FOUR

The child's poking woke me at noon. I opened one eye and immediately shut it. The sun, aiming like a sniper through the steeple belfry of a church, blinded me. I shaded my eyes and tried again. The boy smiled, approaching cautiously with a half-burnt stick he had used to prod me from my slumber in a kitchen chair. He was dressed as the male puppet had been during the festival.

I sat up and felt the contents of my skull sloshing like a pail of curdled milk. I was hot, my sweaty shirt peeling from my skin. In my lap rested a sweet-smelling pitcher of macerated fruit, which proved to be the remains of the night's sangria. I set it on the ground and used my shoe to push it away. A fly escaped the pitcher, buzzing past my cheek. My wicked head ached. I had drunk too much, and what lay in my stomach threatened to reappear.

The boy jabbed me in the knee with his stick.

Behind him came the sound of giggling. From under the tablecloth, a little girl of approximately the same age rushed out and stood beside the boy. Her dress matched the female puppet.

"*Buenos días*," I said.

"*Buenas tardes*," the girl corrected me.

I nodded. My tongue twitched like a dying lizard. I had exhausted my Spanish vocabulary for the day. Remaining as motionless as possible, trying to move only my eyes, I surveyed the wreckage of the plaza. Like me, there were other sleepers lying across chairs and under the tables. The cigar man who had lit the fireworks snored like an old tomcat in the doorway of a butcher's.

The pyre had burned to ash. Smoke flavored the air. I attempted to stand and saw the error of my judgment. Daggers cored my eyes. I fell back into the chair, nearly tipping over. The children found this entertaining. Elbows resting on my knees, I held my broken head and tried to piece together the tattered scraps of my memories concerning the festival. The families eating and drinking. Drummers. Goblins twirling sparklers. Pyre burning. The puppets. The tall masked figure with the forked beard. The portrait of a city in flames–

Poke, poke.

The boy was holding a glass of water out to me. His chin quivered. His eyes were a beautifully clear, sugary brown.

"*Agua*, señor?"

Parched, I took the glass with both hands and drank. After swallowing greedily, the smell of sulfur hit my nose, and then came the revolting taste of mold and an oily residue. I spat the water in my mouth back out onto the plaza. Coughing, gagging, I stared into the glass. Green and tan globules floated in the warm liquid. It looked like the water from the coin fountain.

The boy and the little girl laughed and ran across the plaza, screaming happily.

I wiped my mouth with my shirt cuff.

Slowly, I approached the ashes.

No amount of sangria would've triggered a hallucination of the grand appalling ceremony I had witnessed. Or so I presumed. I kicked through smoldering embers. Under the scrim of dust, I perceived the outermost markings of a diagram drawn in chalk. I knelt beside the cinders. Whatever this design was, the bonfire pyramid had been built upon it.

Two large charred footprints were scorched into the plaza stones.

The tall figure with the full-head mask and the forked beard had left them.

I rubbed my grizzled jaw.

What exactly had I seen last night? Under oath, what could I testify to in a court of law? Had there been a crime committed? A double sacrifice?

No.

The events might've been a festival after all. I might've drunk too much sangria. Evidence supporting a more sinister theory was scant. You can't jail people for having an odd dialect. Sure, they acted bizarrely, even scared you. Ever been to an Arkham gala party?

The cigar man groaned as he rolled onto his other side. A hot wind blew. I was a stranger here. Who was I to question their traditions, however disturbing they might appear to my alien eyes? How much of it was my own fantasy? I can't honestly say. Suddenly, I was overcome with a strong urge to return home. I wanted to feel that old familiar strangeness I knew so well. I needed to see Arkham.

It was surprisingly easy to find the Renault. The streets were deserted, and someone had covered the sewers. I dreaded navigating a route out of this city. But this morning I got lucky. I discovered a backstreet that connected to an avenue I hadn't passed on my way into town.

Soon I came upon a highway.

At the first crossroads I spotted a sign with an arrow pointing in a direction away from where I'd come that read: BARCELONA. So I suppose I never visited *that* city.

I started back to the fishing village.

Travel is a liminal state. In such states the mind is often vulnerable, even fragile. Suddenly I was panicked with a sense of being adrift. What was I doing here? In Spain, and in the universe? These questions attacked my head as I drove.

But it might've only been the worst hangover of my life.

I assured myself that I would feel better once I got back to Arkham. Seeing the faces of people whom I recognized; friends, acquaintances from my past, my family, even my old dog, Thorn, would offer me comfort and stability. A solid New England rock under my feet.

Get thee home, Alden, a soothing voice said to me.

I packed my bags, changed my ticket, and did as I was told.

CHAPTER FIVE

"Sir, Mr Alden… sir…?"

A bony hand grasped my arm. The coolness of the fingers penetrated through my silk pajamas. I recognized their icicle touch. It was Roland, our family's ancient butler.

The hand shook me.

"Uhh… hm… grrr…"

"Sir, are you awake?"

"No." I pulled the blankets to my chin.

"You have visitors, downstairs."

"Send them away. I am entertaining no one this morning."

"It's Mr Preston Fairmont. Miss Minnie is with him. They say you are to lunch together."

Alarmed, I flipped up the edge of my sleeping mask.

"What time is it?"

Roland consulted his pocket watch. "Very nearly noon."

I threw off my blankets and jumped up. The room was dim. Thunder rumbled the house. Wind and rain slashed at the red maples in the courtyard of Oakwood. Our family's Italianate mansion perched near the top of Arkham's historic French Hill, where its architecture stood out among the Huguenot and

Colonial-inspired residences like a tiramisu in the window of a Paris patisserie. Oakeses were never shy about being noticed in a crowd.

"What day, man? What damned day is it?"

I tore free from my pajamas. My bare foot landed in a puddle on the floor. My bedroom's doors swept inward from the balcony, the draperies darkened from the rain.

Roland's white eyebrows wrinkled. "It's Monday, the 20th of September… in the year of our Lord 1925… You've been home for a couple of weeks. You should be adjusted."

"Why are those blasted doors wide open? There's a flood in here."

"You insisted they be kept that way last night, sir."

"I did? And you listened to me?"

"You made me swear to it. You said the rain helped you to sleep."

"Well, obviously I was correct."

Roland handed me a wool suit and a pair of two-tone Oxfords from my closet.

"Thank you, Roland. You know how confused and cranky I am before breakfast."

"And lunch."

I nodded, buttoning a fresh, purple-striped shirt. Roland had dealt with my habitual lateness since I slept in a crib. I was an only child. Roland was the closest thing to a much, much, *much* older brother that I had. While traveling in Europe, I had missed him more than I had my own parents. That isn't saying much. We had been through a lot together, Roland and I. We shared a fondness for each other's sense of humor and amusement at our, often uncomfortable, social predicaments, although

Roland had to be careful to keep his opinions secret in order to maintain his position in our household. I ran no such risks. Roland's clear blue eyes twinkled merrily at me.

"Stall them, will you?" I sighed. "I'll be downstairs in a minute. Make coffee."

"I brewed the Ethiopian Harar you prefer. A cup is ready when you are."

"You're a godsend, Ro."

Without so much as a smile, he shut the door.

"Minnie! How long has it been? You look scrumptious as usual." I took her hand and kissed the knuckles. "What enormous jewelry you're wearing. I nearly chipped a tooth."

"Oh, Alden! Preston outdid himself. He must've brought this gigantic diamond over the mountains on the back of an elephant." Minnie's jasmine perfume filled the foyer as fully as her mellifluous voice.

"Without a doubt, your beau has spent many nights astride prodigious beasts," I said.

Preston shared a look of horror with me over the top of Minnie's head.

But Minnie was ignoring both of us as she admired her betrothal ring.

Roland entered silently as a wraith and announced the coffee's readiness.

Minnie jumped at his presence behind her.

"Join me for a coffee before we venture into the elements?" I said, holding out my arm. She linked up with me. Her free hand clasped onto Preston.

Conjoined, we followed Roland.

Minnie pulled me down, whispering, "Your manservant gives me the creeps. There's something sepulchral about him."

"Oh, Ro's a good egg. Recall that he never once reported your late-night presence in my bedroom to my parents."

Minnie nodded in acknowledgment of Ro's discretion and gave me a squeeze in memory of former times spent in each other's company. In the drawing room, I pulled out a chair for her. Roland brought in a silver cart with a coffee urn and sweet treats. The gray rain beat tiny fists at the windows. Wind, catching in the throat of the fireplace, groaned. Preston acted distracted. He sipped his coffee and paid no attention to the nuptial details as Minnie ran through them. I guessed he'd heard the plans dozens of times. Perhaps he was feeling trepidatious, anticipating the big day. He appeared dashing as usual, but distant, a tad cool. Minnie, on the other hand, glowed. I'd never seen her so animated. Movement enhanced her the same way stillness improved others. No painting I attempted of Minnie did the woman justice. It always felt somehow *less*. One needed to meet her in person to experience her enchantment. Aside from the fact of our broken engagement, I had always liked Minnie. I found I still did.

"Preston, tell him about the tickets," Minnie said, slapping him on the knee.

Preston woke from his trance. "Oh, of course, the tickets… it's a surprise. We want you to come with us. As a gift for returning from France ahead of schedule."

"Tickets to what?" I said.

"Tell him, tell him," Minnie squeaked with joy.

"Houdini," Preston said. He reached into his jacket's inner pocket.

"The magician?"

"What other Houdini is there, silly," Minnie said.

"He's having a show here in Arkham. We're going. And you're going with us."

Preston handed me my ticket.

"Why, it's for tonight. At the Ward Theatre," I said, taken aback.

"Afterward we'll go backstage and meet Houdini himself," Preston said.

"Well then…" The idea of spending the rest of the day with Preston and Minnie raised personal alarms. I didn't want to be a third wheel. On the other hand, I'd always hoped to catch a Houdini show. Denying Minnie was also inadvisable. "…I'd love to join you."

Minnie clapped her tiny hands together. "I shall be the envy of every woman in attendance," she said.

"You always are, darling," Preston said.

They kissed.

I studied my ticket. "It says it's a three-part show. I wonder what the parts are."

Caught up in Preston's tweedy arms, Minnie ruffled her fingers through his hair.

"Illusions, Escapes, and Exposing Frauds," she said, breathless.

"Illusions, Escapes, and Exposing Frauds," I repeated, tenting my fingertips and touching them to my lips, as one does while contemplating deep, philosophical conundrums.

"The show is a bit of fun and games. Nothing too serious," Preston said.

"I was only thinking you two might want to pay especially close attention. The lessons you learn may prove helpful after you are wed."

They both laughed.

"Oh, Alden, how I've missed you! You are the perfect antidote to the Arkham gloomies," Minnie said. Parting her lips revealed the intriguing little gap between her front teeth.

"I hope you didn't miss him too much," Preston said, frowning.

I was about to interject something clever when Thorn, my blue greyhound, bounded into the room. He was irresistibly drawn to Minnie and tried to climb into her lap.

She fed him a butter cookie. "Oh! May we take him out with us for lunch?"

"There's a bistro right around the corner where Thorn is a welcome guest," I said.

"I'd love to walk him," she volunteered.

"Be my guest." I fetched the dog's leash from the wall peg.

"While we walk, you tell me all about your time in the Mediterranean. How was it?"

"Hot, interesting, boring… strange."

Minnie smiled. "We're going to have so much fun together this year! Did Preston tell you? Our engagement party will be on Halloween. Doesn't that sound positively bloodcurdling? There are so many fascinating new people for you to meet, Alden. Arkham is changing. Don't laugh, it is. And things are heating up. Remember how hard it was to find a good party years ago? Everyone was still down because of the war and all that dreadfulness. But now it's gotten to be really fun again."

"Who doesn't love fun?" I said, as the three of us crossed the threshold into the chill.

Houdini did not disappoint. He executed the famous East Indian Needle Trick and his own diabolical invention of the Water Cell

Torture, which had us gasping for breath in the balcony gallery of the Ward Theatre. Every escape and trick went off without a hitch. The illusionist also took time to debunk the methods of the Spiritualists and other hoaxers. His message was that one may talk to the dead, but the dead never talk back. During this portion of the show, I happened to scan the crowd below us, and to my great astonishment I swore I spotted Juan Hugo Balthazarr sitting in the front row, near the middle of the stage. I did not have the best angle to confirm if it was indeed him, but when the man leaned forward intently, the resemblance to the photo I had seen of the Spaniard was striking. He had a forked beard and was a head taller than his seatmates. And there was no mistaking the animosity apparent in his brutal visage. It was as if he harbored a personal hatred for the debunking Houdini.

Minnie had fallen asleep against Preston's shoulder during this part of the act. But by the end she was awake again. Preston had remained riveted throughout.

"You enjoyed the show?" he asked me.

"Very much so."

He couldn't have known my excitement also stemmed from a possible sighting of Balthazarr in the theatre. This might be my chance to meet the famous Surrealist! I searched for him in the post-performance hubbub. But nowhere in the departing crowd did the tall man with a forked beard appear. Perhaps I was wrong and Balthazarr had never been there at all.

"Ready to head backstage?" Preston asked us.

Minnie nodded enthusiastically. "They call him the Handcuff King, you know."

"Careful. He might lock you up," I said.

"Then saw you in half, darling." Preston pointed. "Through

those heavy curtains, there's the door to the backstairs. Lead the way, Oakesy. If we run into security, I'll just tell them I'm a Fairmont. We saved this place from closing. They had a dreadful run, some play about a Yellow King, and people literally died. Which is sad because I heard the play was quite excellent. Who can ever understand the dramatic arts?"

I found the stairway and headed down, with Minnie and Preston pressing in close behind me. The farther I descended, the darker it grew. In the blackness at the bottom, I tripped on the final stair, falling forward against a steel door. It burst open. A narrow hallway. Closed doors on both sides. One weak light bulb dangled from the ceiling by its wire. On the floor, a birdcage filled with white doves. I had crashed through the door so hard that it hit the brick wall behind it, sending a boom echoing down the passage. The doves beat their wings.

I was about to ask Preston if we were in the right place when one of the doors opened.

A head stuck out.

Houdini himself peered at me from around the corner. His intense eyes shone in the semidarkness. Minnie and Preston poured out from behind me, laughing.

Minnie gasped. "Is that him? The real McCoy?"

"Not the McCoy. But if you prefer, I am the real Houdini."

He stepped forward and bowed.

Houdini was not a big man, but compact and solidly muscular. Even in his shirtsleeves, he utterly commanded whatever space he entered. We bowed back to him in reply. He wore a towel around his neck, but on him it appeared a mysterious accessory rather than a cloth to wipe away his sweat after a physically punishing exhibition of his skills.

I remained speechless, paralyzed. But Preston was less awestruck.

"May we visit with you? We have backstage passes," he said.

"Of course, please join me in my dressing room," Houdini said.

We were surprised to find him alone.

He shut the door and squeezed past us.

"My wife, Bess, has gone out to see about our dinner. Please sit, won't you?"

The small room was dingy. A threadbare carpet covered only part of the scuffed floorboards. There was a musty smell and poor ventilation. With the three of us gathered around the magician, I felt cramped, bordering on claustrophobic. Houdini didn't seem to mind. He reclined on a chaise longue, drinking from a glass of ice water.

Now that we had special access, we didn't know exactly what to do.

An awkward silence settled.

Preston coughed.

"I hope you're enjoying your trip to Arkham," Minnie said.

"I love performing here. I have many fans. They are thirsty for magic," Houdini said.

Again, the silence. An unseen clock ticking. Footsteps in the hall.

My tongue loosened. "You have a true zeal for exposing charlatans," I said.

"Vultures," he said. "They prey upon the weak, the grieving. It is an insult to my intellect and yours. I'll fight them. I have offered a $10,000 reward to anyone who professes to have so-called supernatural powers and can prove to my satisfaction they are not conmen. No one will ever claim it. Yet I keep an open mind. I like surprises. 'Show me,' I say."

There came a firm knocking at the dressing room door.

"Excuse me," Houdini said.

He moved around us to greet his new visitor.

Preston leaned into Minnie and me. "Perhaps he might do a few card tricks for us."

I shook my head. "He's already given us a show we'll never forget. We should go."

"At least he can sign our programs," Minnie said.

Preston agreed. "We should have something to remember this night."

"I, for one, will never forget it, whether or not he gives us anything more."

Houdini was talking in hushed tones with his visitor. Suddenly he cried out in pain and staggered backward, bumping into Preston who grabbed the magician around the shoulders to prevent him from collapsing to the floor.

"What happened?" Preston said.

"Why, he's paler than a ghost," Minnie said.

I rushed to the doorway and looked out into the hallway, in time to see the quickly retreating figure of a tall man in a silk top hat and cape disappearing into the shadows.

"You! Stop right there!"

The tall man half-turned. I saw the forked beard. The same person I had been studying in the audience. The one I swore was Juan Hugo Balthazarr! I started after him.

"Balthazarr? Is that you? What is going on here?"

But the tall man kept walking, never breaking his stride.

"Alden, help us!" Minnie shouted.

"I don't think Houdini is breathing," Preston said. "Get a doctor!"

Despite my desire to pursue the phantom, I returned to the stricken illusionist.

"Where am I supposed to find a doctor, Preston?"

He shrugged. Houdini's head lay in his lap.

The magician's eyes were locked on some far-off distance. His mouth fell agape. It was as if he beheld an unnamable terror stalking him, one from whose clutches he could devise no escape.

"Houdini! Houdini!" I shook him.

Then he drew in a deep breath like a man who had been saved from drowning. "I am stabbed. Low, on my right side. The fiend has put his knife into me."

Preston and I searched but found no wound ... no sign of any bleeding...

"You are whole," I said. "I cannot see any injury."

Houdini prodded himself, at first gingerly, and then with greater force. He checked his fingers for the red evidence of a wound. "Amazing! I *felt* the blade slicing through me. Like a jolt of electricity! That devil placed his hand on me and spoke in a language I've never heard before. I understood not a syllable. Yet I swear he was killing me. Wait. He did say one thing I understood. As he cut into me, he said, 'Tell me, sir, if this feels real enough.'"

"Did you recognize him?" I asked.

Houdini shook his head. "He was a stranger."

I hesitated to use the name of Balthazarr. I had no proof at all. None.

Sitting up, the magician slowly regained his strength.

"Shouldn't we call the police?" Minnie asked.

"What crime has been committed?" Preston said.

"This man's been assaulted," I said.

"He looks fine now to me. Maybe it was simply a prank," Preston said. "A trick."

With our help Houdini stood. He brushed himself off, checking his lower right abdomen again. "Your friend is right." He squeezed my arm. "I received no damage. And my attacker is long gone by now. I only need to rest."

It was then that Houdini's wife, Bess, arrived. We told her of the incident. While she was alarmed to hear of the baffling encounter, her husband assured her he was feeling normal again. We parted. I felt no small degree of embarrassment when Preston and Minnie presented their programs to the illusionist for signatures. Houdini was friendly and obliging. Holding up his pen, he asked me where my program was. I had it in my pocket but told him I left it in my seat.

"You can sign it the next time you're in Arkham," I said.

"Yes, I will. Thank you for your assistance," he said.

We were about to exit when he exclaimed, "Hold on!" We turned in unison to see the escapologist digging into a lumpy sack behind the chaise. He found what he was looking for.

"Please let me offer you a token of my thanks."

Houdini held out a pair of handcuffs.

As I reached out to take the shackles from him, he snapped them on my wrists.

I struggled to pull them open, with no success. The thick iron bit into my flesh.

"What's the trick?" Minnie asked.

Houdini showed us his empty hands. "No trick. Put out your

palm, my dear." Minnie obeyed his instruction. He covered her hand with his closed fist. Then he opened his fingers.

"The best way to open a lock is to have the key."

He deposited it into Minnie's hand, and she squealed with delight. After some teasing, she put the key in the locks and liberated me.

I rubbed my wrists.

Houdini clapped me on my shoulder.

"I will treasure them always," I said, pocketing the cuffs.

My friends and I left the Ward Theatre. The rain had stopped, but the night air was thick. A fog blanketed the city. Downtown, the gaslights flickered like torches afloat in space.

I imagined the tall, bearded man out there in that fog.

Watching us.

Tell me, sir, if this feels real enough.

I shivered. The evening had unnerved me. That man couldn't have been Balthazarr.

Could he?

It was a year later, on Halloween in fact, that the Great Harry Houdini died after a show in Detroit. Doctors determined the cause of death to be peritonitis secondary to a ruptured appendix. Subsequent rumors blamed a Canadian college student who allegedly punched Houdini in the gut days earlier. Houdini's last reported words were, "I'm tired of fighting."

I'll bet he was. He'd had that curse growing inside him for months. I'll leave you to form your own opinion on the matter. I know that I have mine.

CHAPTER SIX

By mid-October the Oakes family mansion was proving to be too confining for my parents and me, despite our habit of keeping to divergent schedules and occupying separate rooms. One morning, Roland brought me an envelope on a silver tray – inside, a note from Mother.

> *Most Beloved Alden,*
>
> *You know that your father and I adore you and are deeply pleased to have you back at Oakwood with us! Yet we can't help but wonder if you mightn't be still happier with companions your own age who are cheered when they hear you knocking about the house regardless of the hour. Of course, you may remain if you so choose, and we would be nothing but delighted if you did. But mightn't it be better for all concerned parties if you were to seek other viable options?*
>
> *With much Support and Encouragement,*
> *M and F*

"Well, isn't that just great? She's giving me notice, Ro. I am to vacate the premises." I always was conscious of being in the way of my parents. Such was the warmth of Oakwood.

I suppose I should've expected this.

Snowy-haired Roland, ever my silent comforter, stood beside my desk staring out into the red maples of the courtyard. The scent of smoldering leaves lifted like sacrificial incense into the sky as the gardeners winterized the grounds. Out back stood a cast iron and glass building shaped like a small Gothic chapel – my mother's greenhouse – where she rotated pots of African violets, regulating their sunlight, checking for aphids, thrips, spider mites, and mealybugs, dipping her pinkie into the soil, monitoring whether it was too dry or too wet.

I scribbled a note on the back of Mother's stationery.

> *Dearest Mother,*
>
> *I will begin my search immediately. If nothing surfaces, I've heard there's a "deluxe" vacancy at Ma's Boarding House. Close enough for you and Father to walk over and join us boarders for a plate of Ma's famous homemade stew!*
>
> *– A*

"There," I said. "That'll just about stop her heart." I folded the note in half and tossed it on the tray. Mother loathed teasing, all humor, really. "I will be going out, Ro."

Roland pivoted away from me. He paused before leaving.

"Shall I call you a cab?"

"No, thank you. I'll walk. Do you have today's paper? I need to get a new place."

"I will fetch it from the study. Would you like the Boston papers as well?"

"Start with the *Advertiser*. Tell me, Ro, how does one find lodgings in this town?"

"Carefully I should think, sir," he said. "I've lived at Oakwood for eons. I hardly recall what it's like to stay anywhere else. But I'm glad for it. A person hears stories…"

"What kind of stories?"

"Oh, horrible ones… peculiar happenings, disappearances, strange murders that even the most seasoned police detectives can't explain. Mutilated bodies floating in the Miskatonic River and down along the train tracks. There was a pair of lovely young dancers who went missing. Later their bodies were found burned… It's quite appalling if you think about it." He smiled, toeing the threshold with his pointy black boot. Roland did relish a good gruesome tale.

"I'll keep only happy thoughts in my head as I go about my apartment hunting."

"An excellent idea," he replied. "It pays to stay positive."

He grinned and was gone.

After a few minutes, I was running my razor over my soapy jaw as Roland slid the paper under my door. I toweled off and picked up the news. I heard a curious scratching outside in the hallway and opened for a look. Thorn wandered in.

"What's the latest in Arkham, Thorn?" I threw myself across the bed and began leafing through the *Advertiser*. Thorn slumped at my feet with a deep sigh.

My father had read the *Arkham Advertiser* back when it was still called the *Arkham Gazette*. At first, his goal was to see his name in the paper as his fame grew as a businessman. Once he was rich, he spent more time keeping his name, and his companies, out of the paper. He was no fan of the current paper's editor-in-chief, or the "nosy fiction writers," as he called their team of muckraking investigative reporters. But he paid for a subscription so he could read about his rivals, chuckling at their misfortunes and damning their triumphs with a spoonful of his daily morning grapefruit. Between bites of buttered rye toast, he'd punctuate his perusal of the news with exclamations of "Lies! Nitwits! Horsefeathers!" and an occasional rhetorical question, "Who gives these fools jobs?" and "Why waste the ink?" Also, I think he just liked to complain.

I'd skimmed through most of this morning's edition and was about to chuck everything but the classifieds on the floor when a story on the back page caught my eye.

Sculptor Killed by Crumbling Gargoyle

Arkham, MA, October 13th – Artist Courtland Elias Dunphy was killed yesterday morning at the All Saints Roman Catholic Church of South Arkham while taking measurements for the replacement of a gargoyle statue on the northwest corner of South Church's roof. Witnesses say part of the statue broke loose from the building, causing the artist to lose his balance and plunge to the sidewalk below. Dunphy moved to Arkham from Wisconsin last month after winning a nationwide competition sponsored by an anonymous donor to furnish South Church with new statues. "Court was a sensitive soul and a fine sculptor. I only wish he had more climbing experience before undertaking this job," said Father Michael Cryans, South Church's pastor. Dunphy leaves behind no known relatives.

"How perfectly dreadful." Maybe this was the kind of strange and horrible story Roland mentioned. For no good reason, I flashed to the bizarre festival I had attended in Spain. The figure with the full-headed mask like a black sunburst. And the fire. The painting of a city in flames. As quickly as the vision came, it disappeared. I couldn't figure out why I'd thought it just then. I leaned down to scratch Thorn's head. "You were an unlucky fellow, Mr Dunphy." Thorn shivered and with a whimper curled himself up around my ankles.

"You're right, Thorn. I promised Roland only happy thoughts."

I paged through the classifieds and found nothing.

I decided on a whim to take a stroll around the city and see if anyone had a sign in the window declaring a room for let. I dismissed the idea of buying a house. I'd been roaming Europe for months, and I wasn't ready to sink my roots down. Staying in European hotels while traveling gave me a sense of freedom I'd come to like. I could pick up and go whenever the mood struck. Thinking about doing that in Arkham was different. Everyone I knew here either still lived at home with their families, or were married and starting a new family of their own. I was aware of a few dedicated bachelors left from my college days who now roomed together, but they were as close as married couples, and I didn't want to intrude upon their domestic arrangements. No, it wasn't the idea of moving out that bothered me as much as the fear of not moving on, of getting stuck again in the stagnancy that haunted my time in Cannes. I had taken out the paintings I did in Spain after I resettled in my studio at Oakwood. They were good. Better than the half-starts and failed projects that came before. But they still lacked something. It was like they were waiting for another piece to arrive.

So I put them away.

I hadn't painted anything since getting back to Arkham.

Such was the rambling direction of my thoughts when I looked up to see that I was standing in front of South Church, the scene of the terrible accident where Courtland Dunphy died only a day ago. My feet had carried me to the spot, almost automatically. The brain is an odd organ indeed. It operates at depths science has yet to plumb. Some portion of my consciousness had driven me here. Could it be a coincidence? I dismissed that outright. I'd read about this case. Now here I was. Did I burn with curiosity on an instinctual level of which I wasn't fully aware? Or had something else guided me? A mysterious impulse?

I gazed up at the steeple and realized I was on the wrong side of the church. Here were the front doors securing the narthex, but Dunphy had tumbled off the back end, behind the sanctuary. No gargoyles perched on this section of the roof. The angle of the sun made the stained glass redder, as if it were seeping blood. My morbid imagination! I tramped onward, crunching dead leaves along the side lot of the church. As I turned past the sharp corner of gray, vertical stone, I was surprised to see another person, a young woman, loitering over the scene of Dunphy's demise. She was casting her eyes downward.

I had time to watch her before she noticed me. She cut a smart figure in an olive wool dress and black cloche hat snugged over her bobbed soft curls. She'd been crouching at the edge of the walkway with her fingers stirring a leaf pile. As she rose, she noticed me and cried out, startled, her slender ankle bending awkwardly and tipping sideways at the lip of the cobbled walk.

"Oh, shh–!" she said.

I rushed forward and grabbed her wrist to steady her.

"Sorry," I said.

She pulled herself free from my grip.

"You shouldn't sneak up on people. It's rude," she said.

"I wasn't sneaking."

"Well, creeping then," she said.

Her eyes were nut brown, so too was her hair, and both looked dark under her hat. She lifted her chin to see all of me, and she couldn't help but appear haughty and annoyed as she peered down her nose. At her full height, she stood a good two inches taller than I did.

"I beg your pardon," I said. "It wasn't my intention to surprise you."

"Why are you poking around at the back end of this church?"

"Why are *you*?"

With narrow eyes, we stared at each other.

She went first. "I came to inspect the scene of a man's death."

"I did as well," I said.

Our exchange led to another round of staring.

This time I broke the silence. "I read about it in the *Advertiser*. I was curious."

She nodded.

"Well, I knew him," she said, with the faintest hint of superiority.

"You knew him! I'm so sorry. I feel terrible for you."

She shook her head. "I didn't know him well. We were acquaintances. We said hello when we passed each other in the mornings. He was dedicated to his work at the church." She gestured toward the building.

I looked up, and here I did see gargoyles hunched like stone raptors on the corners of the structure. My mind made quick calculations, and yes, a plunge from that height would most likely be fatal. My stomach flipped in a sympathetic sensation of falling.

"Was he a religious man?" I asked.

"I should think not," she said. A smile curled one side of her mouth. "Art was his religion, I think. We never talked about philosophies. As I said, we were acquaintances."

"I am much the same."

"An acquaintance?" She frowned and cocked her head to one side.

"An artist… a painter." I made an embarrassing flourish with an invisible brush.

"Oh," she said. Her lips were dark red. I wanted her to talk to me more.

"How about you? Are you an artist?" I asked.

She looked away. "No, I write here and there. Bits of things. Small pieces…"

"Writing is an art."

"Not the way I do it. At least that's what I'm told. Mostly by men," she said.

"You can't always listen to what others tell you. Especially men. They are weak creatures. Believe me, I know. I'm one myself. There's little we understand. Only we can't let on how lacking we are, or others of our kind will attack us. Listen to your muse, I say."

"That sounds ancient and fantastical."

"Like gargoyles?" I pointed to the rooftop.

"Like the Greeks."

"Oh, them," I said. "Do you have something in your hand?"

"I might," she said.

"I know you do. I saw it when I snatched your wrist. A stone, maybe? Is it a clue?"

"A clue to what exactly?"

I shrugged.

She opened her palm and showed me a limestone cone, pitted and rough-looking.

"Gargoyle horn," she said. "See how it's sharp and whiter on this side…" She touched the thick end with her fingernail.

"It's broken off from the one up there, do you think?" I squinted, trying to focus on the rooftop gargoyle. He looked older and dirtier than the church he sat upon.

"Courtland must have grabbed hold of it before he fell," she said.

"You found it where?"

"In these leaves." She gave the pile a soft kick. "I guessed this was where he landed. Bang! He hits the walk. His hand relaxes. Opens. The horn rolls away. Or he lets go as he's falling. Anyway, the horn doesn't get very far. The detectives missed it, I didn't."

"What makes you say he landed right here?"

She walked in a semicircle. "Look, there's dried blood between the cobblestones."

She crouched while I kneeled. She's a cool one, I thought, poring over the details. Maybe she wants to be a crime reporter. It takes a certain detachment if that's your beat.

"I think this was his head. Feet off that way. Arms out like this." She showed me how. It looked like she was praying, supplicating to an ancient demigod. We were close. I felt her breath brush past me. It was chilly outside, but I felt warm. "That has to be his blood. They scrubbed the stones but not in between. You can see dried soap bubbles where it drained off in the mud."

It hurt me to look at her, but I didn't know why. Maybe there was too much to take in all at once, an urgency to soak everything up so I'd never forget.

"Don't you think that's blood?" she said.

There was rusty purplish black residue gummed into the cracks. It made me queasy to think how much liquid probably leaked out of the man. Had he died instantly? I wondered. Or did he lay here watching it all go running out of him like beer from a shattered bottle, the foam of his life escaping as he hissed? I shivered. "I don't know what dried blood looks like."

"It looks like that." She got up.

I followed her lead, dusting off the knees of my trousers.

"Why are you here collecting horns and thinking about death on this autumn day?"

"Boys aren't the only ones who get to be curious. Girls want to know too. I could ask you the same thing. In fact, I will. Why are you here? Do you like sneaking up on people?"

"I told you, I wasn't sneaking. I was out walking. I don't know what drew me here, to be honest. What are you going to do with that horn?"

She studied it. Rolling it contemplatively between her hands. "I think I'll keep it."

"Shouldn't the police have it?"

"Why? They're the ones who left it here. There isn't even a crime according to them."

"Are you interested in crimes?"

She stepped back and studied me. "What if I were?"

I shrugged. "Everyone has a passion. It's spooky... that horn. You're keeping it?"

"Yes," she said, defiantly.

"A sort of lucky charm?"

"Some luck it brought to Courtland. I think it will be a reminder to me, a warning."

"Warning about what?"

She thought for a moment. "Be careful of what you grab." She put the horn in her pocket and started to turn away. I was afraid she was leaving.

"Listen, I like talking to you. I passed a diner back there about a block. If you've got the time, maybe we could get a coffee and talk some more?"

She shook her head. "No, I'm late for an appointment. I only meant to stop here for a moment." She was backing away from me, a little suspicious but smiling. Not afraid.

"How do I know we'll meet again?"

"Arkham is a small place. I'm surprised how often people and things… overlap." She opened her eyes big, as if she'd said something mildly shocking and was trying not to laugh. I wanted to hear what her laugh sounded like. "Goodbye," she said.

She waved to me.

"Goodbye."

She walked briskly around the corner. I hadn't asked her name or told her mine.

I ran after her but I was too late.

The South Church's side lot was empty except for blowing leaves and crooked trees.

CHAPTER SEVEN

"Roland, there's a goblin in the bushes." Mother twitched the drapery. "Roland!"

Turning from the window, she surveyed my costume as I reached the bottom of the staircase. "What are you supposed to be?"

"I'm Pagliacci." I modeled my baggy shirt with its giant, ruffled black collar and pompon buttons, and the sad, droopy spectacle of my pants. My long hat might've doubled for a chef's pastry bag.

Mother's face remained blank. "The clown? From the opera? But you can't sing."

"That's not the point. It's a costume party, not a singing competition."

Roland materialized from wherever he went when we didn't need him.

"Ma'am, you summoned me?"

"Dispose of those trick-or-treaters." Mother ordered.

"Yes, ma'am." Roland picked up a wicker handbasket full of Abba-Zaba bars from the end table and went to the door to pass out the Halloween candy.

"It's only one day a year," I reminded my mother.

"One day too many. What a nuisance! Youths trudging onto the property like vandals. We feed them for free! It's not civilized. But people will talk if we don't answer our door."

Mother adjusted my pompons, checking on me like one of her African violets.

"Found a new home yet?" she asked.

"No." I sighed.

"Have you looked in Uptown? It's where all the Miskatonic U students live."

"I know where they live. And I'm not a student any more."

"Of course not, dear. Don't snap, I'm only trying to help," she said.

I caught sight of myself in the vestibule mirror. I'd painted my face with greasepaint, only using white except for the twin blackened pits of my eyes. A sad clown, indeed.

"Where is this party you're going to?"

"At the observatory. Preston and Minnie's engagement party? I told you about it."

"See! You *should* find a place to live near Miskatonic, Aldie. Ask around. Preston might know of the perfect property for a bachelor. His family has more connections than the New York subway." She stepped back to assess me. "There! You look quite operatic."

Another flurry of low-level knocks jarred Oakwood's stately door.

"Roland!"

Mother's expression softened. She squeezed my fingers briefly, and then let go.

"I wish only the best for you, my little Pagliacci."

"I know you do." In her own distant and cultivating way, she cared about me.

"Enjoy the party!"

Preston and Minnie's engagement soiree would, of course, have to be a costume party. They'd rented out the Gerald Warren Astronomical Observatory on the Miskatonic University campus. I'm sure everybody thought it was strange when they got their invitations. The observatory wasn't open to rentals as far as I knew, but like my mother said, the Fairmonts had connections. Fairmont dollars flowed into the Miskatonic coffers, and they could party wherever they wanted. Tradition said that rules didn't apply to the Fairmonts, or people like them in Arkham. I knew that it was true because I was one of those people.

I had the cab driver drop me off on the edge of campus. I didn't want to wait in a long line of cars and partygoers making a big show of their entrance. Not really my style. I'd rather come in on foot, at my own pace, and get a look around before I went in. This used to be my crowd. Now I hesitated, wondering if we'd outgrown each other while I was away.

I was late, of course. The party had already exceeded the confines of the observatory. The untrimmed, but mostly dead, grassy yard behind the small building was filled with ghouls and witches in pointy hats sipping bourbon-spiked punch. A live jazz band played "You'd Be Surprised!" and the singer did a good imitation of Eddie Cantor's jokey, nasal delivery. Orange glowing tips of cigars and cigarettes bobbed in the shadows under the arching warlock limbs of the black cherry trees which spread wide, as if to welcome them. A cherry sweetness tinged the air. It mingled with smoke from a bonfire burning in a rough stone circle near the back of the property, where demons paired off with ghosts or a menagerie of animals, real and fantastical, for more private assignations. I would not be the only clown in attendance at tonight's festivities. My costume choice proved to be popular with both sexes. But I was the only Pagliacci. I smoked a cigarette and came in through the back door. My throat was parched, and I needed something to keep my hands from hanging idly at my sides. The punch bowl was out of glasses, but I found an abandoned one on top of a bookcase, wiped it with my sleeve, and filled it.

I couldn't spot Preston or Minnie. Arkham hadn't been my stomping ground for a couple of years, but I was shocked at how few people I recognized. I chalked some of it up to their clever disguises, but I knew it was more than that. I'd been out of circulation for too long. The social turnover in Arkham wasn't what it was in Boston or New York, but my current state of dislocation had me feeling suddenly old and, like Pagliacci I suppose, more than a bit confused.

The band announced they were taking a break for a few minutes. They reminded everyone about the banquet laid out in the hallway. I wasn't particularly hungry, but I had nothing better to do, so I checked out the hors d'oeuvres.

The revelers weren't interested in eating. I found myself alone in the hallway, poring over deviled eggs, tomato aspics, skewered meatballs, crudités, oysters swimming in a pond of melting ice, fruit salad, stuffed mushroom caps, and shrimp cocktails with most of the big crustaceans picked out. I grabbed a handful of roasted mixed nuts and was crunching them when an old man with a long Whitmanesque beard emerged from the stairway.

He eyed the table with curiosity.

My mouth was full, so I greeted him with a nod.

"My wife, Bernadine, used to say that if you put out a spread of food and scientists are anywhere around, they will soon discover it. I don't like parties. But it seems this gathering has moved on. All these leftovers will go to waste, won't they? That is a terrible shame," he said.

I'd finished chewing. "Go ahead. Fill up a plate. My friends paid for this fête, and they won't mind. There's plenty. Most of them are too busy drinking."

The old gent was surprised by my offer. "Thank you. My wife said I never eat enough when I'm here. 'Head in the stars,' she told me. I get caught up in my work and forget."

I reached for more nuts. Although the hallway was empty, the observatory felt horribly warm from all the bodies bustling through. I saw why people had drifted outside.

"Doesn't your wife want you home for dinner?"

The bearded fellow smiled sadly. "Not any more."

"Given up, has she?" I asked, jokingly.

"No, she died."

Now I felt stupid and awkward, wishing I'd skipped the nuts and followed the others into the backyard. "Please forgive me," I said. "I'm sorry about your wife."

"Not to worry." The scientist went on filling his plate. "I'd rather talk about her than forget how lucky I was. Norman Withers." He held out his hand. "I work upstairs."

"On the big telescope?" I asked, feeling less embarrassed, as we shook.

Norman nodded. "In the lab, too. That's where the real discoveries are made. Reviewing the data. Deducing what the numbers mean. Even so, sometimes I see things I wish I had not."

"Like what?"

I was intrigued. I drained my glass of punch, wishing I had more.

"Oh, lately there have been gaps… perturbations… unexpected deviations."

"Sounds almost spooky when you put it like that."

"The universe is mysterious," he said. "Yet, based on years of research, we know where certain objects are. We can predict their locations. Map them out. They appear and reappear like clockwork. But when I look up and they're not all there…"

I had a feeling that maybe the professor might not be "all there" either. But he seemed nice enough, if more than a little lonely. I'd never had much interest in the sciences, but I liked unexplained mysteries.

He leaned against the wall and devoured a deviled egg.

"Couldn't it just be a mistake?"

"A hiccup in the data?" he asked.

I nodded.

"Yes, it's theoretically possible. I've gone over the measurements, recalibrated my equipment… There's nothing wrong with the telescope. But one too many hiccups…"

"Perhaps you should try holding your breath?" I kidded.

"I wish it were that simple." Norman finished eating his food. He took a second pass at the banquet table and reloaded his plate.

A server came by with a pitcher of the "holiday" punch and poured me another glass. I happened to glance out the back door and spotted Preston waving for me to join him. I was ready to say goodnight to the astronomer when he spoke up again.

"This fellow, Hubble, has argued an earthshattering theory,

pardon the pun. Those swirling clouds of dust and gases we call nebulae are, in fact, distant galaxies. The Milky Way is but an eddy in a constant whirlwind. We're spinning like a hurricane on a vast, dark ocean among a staggering number of other hurricanes. Churning, round and round. Our sun, worshipped for millennia and over which gallons of sacrificial blood have been spilled, is but a dingy, minor star. You see, the cosmos is a frightfully bigger place than we ever thought."

"And we humans are…"

"Living on a speck of grit," he said.

Feeling small, slightly dizzy, and apparently insignificant – I gulped my punch.

Norman was obviously a learned man, but in that moment he had the wild, glassy eyes of an asylum patient. Exhausted, haunted. And I'd be lying if I said he hadn't scared me.

The piano player started playing "Fascinating Rhythm."

I tried to find a silver lining. "Life may be Earth's only claim at uniqueness," I said.

The musicians played louder. People were rushing back inside to see the band.

"What if it's not?" Norman said, "What if life is not unique? Who knows the immense sizes and irrational shapes our 'neighbors' might take? They may be our competitors or even our enemies. How will they deal with us when they arrive? We could be at their mercy."

A bowlegged man dressed as a faun, complete with panpipes, leapt up onto the band platform. He planted a pair of fake deer antlers on the piano player. The faun slyly pranced away. It was all in the intoxicating mood of chaotic good fun. The crowd loved it. Not missing a beat, the piano player sang:

"*Got a little rhythm, a rhythm, a rhythm*
That pit-a-pats through my brain;
So darn persistent
The day isn't distant
When it'll drive me insane…"

Dancers kicked their legs, threw their arms in the air, and shook themselves. A tray of glasses hit the floor, shattering. A woman screamed in mock terror. The pianist hit the keys in a frenzy. It grew hotter in the room. The windows fogged up. Everywhere, people howled with laughter, enjoying what surely was the swankiest party of the year.

I shouted my last question to Norman.

"Tell me, professor. Do you really suppose we aren't top dogs in the new cosmos?"

Norman's eyes narrowed. His gray eyebrows bristled. Gently, but with a degree of urgency, he nudged me into the corner under a candlelit sconce. I soon realized he wasn't concerned with me but instead was staring at the floor along the wall next to the table's edge.

A brown beetle scuttled from under the baseboard.

He crushed it flat.

The old man chuckled. "We might just be the cockroaches."

Holding up his leg, the astronomer regarded the gooey insect remnants sticking to his boot sole, before wiping them off with a napkin and tossing the paper into the trash.

CHAPTER EIGHT

After Norman returned upstairs to his lab, I walked to the back entrance to get a breath of fresh air. I was leaning against the doorjamb, lighting a cigarette, when Preston approached me from behind to shout in my ear.

"Was that Methuselah you were talking to?" Preston asked.

I jumped as if I'd been hit with a jolt of electricity, dropping my cigarette in the grass.

"Don't do that!" I said.

"Sorry to panic you, Oakesy. You seemed lost in deep thoughts. I wanted to make sure you were having a good time."

"I'm having a fine time when my friends aren't shocking the hell out of me."

Preston bent over. "Here's your Lucky back."

I picked a bit of turf off my cigarette and stuck the tobacco between my lips. "It wasn't Methuselah by the way. His name is Norman. Norman Withers."

Preston joined me on the threshold. People had to walk between us as if we were standing guard. They nodded cordially at Preston and gave me odd glances as if they were trying to figure out who I was, or maybe if I belonged.

"Never heard of him. Must be from Minnie's side."

"Norman's not from either side." I blew out a plume of smoke. "He's a scientist. Works here at the observatory, studying the heavens. He's an intriguing fella. I don't think he talks to outsiders much. By outsiders, I mean non-academics. He had a lot to say."

"Oh, about what?"

"The cosmos. Deviations floating around up there. He painted an alarming picture."

"Funny old bird." Preston slipped a flask from inside his jacket and took a slug before he passed it to me. "Well, I hope he was having a good time too."

"That's some fine whiskey." I said, wiping my lips. I felt a comforting warmth, like a cozy campfire aglow inside me. "Canadian?"

Preston winked. "You have a good palate. But you should. You're a painter!" He looked drunker than I first thought. Eyes red, collar askew. A spot the color of dried blood stained his cuff. His clothes smelled like patchouli smoke. "What do you think of this crowd? I know people, Oakesy. Wonderful new people. Soon enough you'll get to know them too."

To me they didn't look very different from the old people we knew.

A cluster of merrymakers – arms linked or hugging tightly as if they'd been cast off the *RMS Titanic* and were clasping together while they waited for the rescue boats, slippery hands grasping slipperier hands – attempted to pass between us.

"We probably should move," I said. The slow crush had me backed up on my tiptoes.

"My party, Oakesy. I'll stand where I want. But you're right, as usual."

They knocked me against the door frame while blasting a mixed chorus of "Let us through!" and "Gangway!" as they passed us. A happy, absolutely sozzled stampede that posed no real threat to anyone but themselves. The next morning their hangovers would arrive overly bright and shiny, clanging pots and pans, marching into their bedrooms as the morning sunbeams cut into their skulls: so many weekend actors in smeary makeup and gaudy rented wardrobes. Preston enjoyed a high status with this crowd – his guests, his *new people* – so I bore the brunt of the bodily pressure. I'm making it sound more unpleasant than it was. What I felt mostly was a thrilling, though fleeting, symbiosis with the others, as if, however briefly, we became a composite creature. Palpable energy surged through the whole group with a crackling power. Preston's Canadian hooch was good, but not good enough that my head was humming louder than the jazz band. It had to be something else at work here.

Preston followed the crowd back inside.

I felt like I needed more air. As soon as I took two steps away from the building, my clown pants began to hang low on my left side, and a heavy weight brushed against my thigh. I reached into my pocket and withdrew a broken piece of limestone carved in the shape of a curved horn. It came from the gargoyle at South Church. Doomed Dunphy's last handhold.

When I'd figured out what it was, I looked up to see the woman I'd met in the churchyard. Now she was standing in the smoky, yellow flickering of the party's bonfire.

I couldn't make out the details of her face, but I knew it was her. She had one leg raised up, her bare foot resting lazily on a tree stump, and there were ribbons hanging off her. She was watching me, the corner of her mouth hooked in a smile. Chin out, head back. I saw that much. So, I walked over. You would have too. Hell, any man would have, possibly a few women as well. Not ribbons, I decided. *Bandages* – that's what they were supposed to be. They wrapped around each of her legs and her torso. She wore a short, nude-colored dress under them. Unraveled bindings trailed from her wrists. Assorted metallic bangles were stacked nearly halfway to her elbows, catching the firelight. Around her throat she'd taken a piece of shroud and tied it in an ascot knot, as if it were the chicest couture. Her head, free of encasement, was topped simply by a small gold crown with an aqua stone set dead in its center. She'd straightened out her bob. The color was a shade darker than I recalled, but maybe the night was doing these things to her, or to me. She looked knowing, yet expectant. Kohl rimmed dramatically around her big, luminous eyes. Bordeaux lips, wet teeth. A person waiting for something, perhaps something owed? Not harmless, not by a mile. Those piercing eyes were capable of shocking and showing outrage in the same instant. *I never want this woman angry at me*, I thought. She's the kind of lady who might stab you with a pair of scissors if she figured you deserved it. Or she might die for you. It all depended.

On what exactly, I wasn't sure.

I tried my best not to look too eager. I'm sure I failed miserably.

"Who are you?" I asked.

She acted insulted. "You mean you can't tell?" She took the cigarette holder from her right hand and clenched it between her teeth. Then, very tall, arms stretching high overhead, she twirled. "I'm an Egyptian mummy."

"But your face isn't wrapped."

"Would you wrap this face if it was yours?" She blew smoke at me.

"I can't say I would."

Her gaze fell to my hand. "What have you got there?"

"I think you know," I said.

"I don't." She was playing a game now.

What was she doing at Preston and Minnie's party? Was she one of the new people?

"You put this in my pocket." I showed her the gargoyle horn.

"I did? My, my, that was awfully presumptuous of me. What business do I have going in your pocket?"

"Let me decide that."

"I'm not making any promises," she replied. Her hands were dusted with a golden powder that sparkled whenever she moved. There were traces of it on her cheeks and chin, from when she had touched her face. Her feet were bare, also gold. I saw a pair of black heels she must have kicked off in the grass behind the stump. She had no drink, but I smelled gin.

"Why give this to me?" I asked, pointing the end of the horn at her. My hand glittered now too.

"To remind you of the unfortunate reason we met," she said.

"Courtland Dunphy?"

She stuck out her lower lip. "He lived across the hall from me. Not for very long, though. He'd recently arrived in town. Did I tell you that before?"

"No, you only said you saw him in passing."

"Court was the serious type, all business. He had a kind face.

You know he wasn't the first. There have been quite a few. He was only the latest."

"Latest what…?" I wasn't following her. I thought I was for a second. But I wasn't.

"The latest death… suicides, murders, missing people… It's practically an epidemic."

"Oh," I said. "I heard about them. But I've been out of town so I'm still catching up."

"I'll cross you off my list then." She turned away to light another cigarette.

"What list?"

"Of suspects," she said, offering me a smoke.

Before I could accept her offer, a hooded monk lunged out from the shadows carrying what I took to be a beer keg over his head. Finally, I recognized someone I knew from the old days. It was Clark Abernathy, another of my college classmates, costumed as Friar Tuck. He wasn't carrying a beer keg but a gnarly log, which he tossed on the bonfire. *Craaack!* Sparks exploded into the sky. The black cherry tree branches were lit up. Their fleshless, ghoulish arms hovering above us, making witchy signs over a boiling cauldron.

Clark hadn't seen me. I thought about calling to him.

But I was in a conversation, you see.

"Arkham's always borne its fair share of tragedies," I said. "I've chalked most of them up as legends and rumors. This town likes to tell stories."

"Not all legends and rumors," she said. "These things really happened. People died."

"What are the police doing about it?"

She scoffed. "Nothing. What did they do about Court?"

"I thought what happened to Court was an accident."

"Was it? Court had a premonition a bad thing might happen to him."

I blinked in surprise. "Did he tell you that? I thought you didn't really know him."

She took the horn from me. "I don't really know you. But if you were feeling under threat? I'd pick up on it," she said. "For instance, I could tell if you were scared."

"And am I scared?" I looked right into her eyes.

"Definitely." She smiled. "Anyway, I think something in that church killed Court."

"The gargoyle?" I was puzzled, but intrigued now.

"The gargoyle literally did kill him." She arched her eyebrow, challenging me to argue. When I didn't, she continued. "I don't mean it came to life. That's goofy. I'm talking about a more subtle force. What made Court go up there? Why was he standing so close to the edge? You know it rained that morning? The roof was slick. The gargoyle was scheduled to come down in a week. Its removal had been meticulously planned. They were bringing in scaffolding, ladders, ropes and pulleys; a safe, logical system. Court never told anybody he was going up there. Father Michael didn't even know. Court had his own key to the church. Why did he grab that horn? Was it for balance in a moment of panic? He knew the gargoyle's condition. He'd inspected it many times. Was his fall simply chance?"

"One might call it fate." But I was beginning to understand what she was poking at.

"Or, maybe, just maybe… it might be something else."

"Like a curse?"

She shrugged. "I prefer to call it an *intelligent influence*."

"You mean someone, or something, made him do it?"

"Oh, damn, here she comes."

I looked through the bonfire flames and spotted Minnie approaching.

"There's my favorite clown," Minnie kissed my painted cheek. She wore a sequined gray leotard. "If you're wondering, I'm a peacock." She turned around so we could appreciate her colorful iridescent plumage. "Have you seen Preston? He was supposed to join me for a duet with the band, but I can't find him anywhere."

"Last I saw him, he was heading inside with the crowd."

"Uggghhh. When was that?"

I shrugged. "Five minutes ago."

Minnie frowned. "I do hope he can remember the words to our song." She paced around the fire, her eyes searching the murky yard for her misplaced beau. "Preston has gotten to be such a worry wart lately. The smallest bump in the road and he startles. I'd think he was cheating on me, too, the way he slinks off without telling me where he's going. Keeping odd hours. A regular Count Dracula. He barely sleeps a wink, even when he's not with me. It's the wedding, I'm sure. We're both terribly excited. But I swear he'd frighten me off if I didn't know the real him. Preston is not one to be bothered. Alden, you lived with the man. He usually takes life as it comes, right? And to Hell with tomorrow."

I nodded. "A cool cucumber is what he is. He looks fine to me."

"Well, he isn't," Minnie said.

What I didn't say was that Preston didn't worry about

tomorrows because somebody had always taken care of his, ensuring he'd be given his choice of the best money could buy in all the things life had to serve up. It was impossible to imagine any true harm coming to him. From birth, he'd led a privileged, boyish life. Maybe he thought that was ending.

"Well, I'd better go find him." Minnie marched off. After she rounded the fire pit, she paused – her head swung back – to ask a parting question of me. "Who's your shy friend?" But she wasn't really asking, only being polite. She didn't wait for my answer.

"Who *is* my shy friend?" I said. "You never told me your name. I'm Alden Oakes."

"Nina Tarrington," the mummy queen said.

We exchanged bows.

"Nina Tarrington. Where have I heard that name before?"

"Preston was going to marry me once, too."

If I'd had a drink, I'd have spit it out into the flames. God, I thought, she's telling me the truth. Now I remembered that Preston was engaged to a Nina Tarrington. A Boston woman. Her father was a publisher who owned a newspaper chain. They'd butted heads, Preston and Nina, and fought constantly. Ultimately, the wedding was called off only days before the ceremony. A wild tale accompanied the news. Something about a sword and a wrecked sailboat. Champagne bottles smashed; a man lost tragically overboard.

"You're *that* Nina Tarrington?" I said.

"See, I told you people overlap in Arkham."

"We certainly do."

"Alden, now that we know each other better, do you think you could find me a drink?"

"I'll do my best."

"What more could a woman ask?"

I held out my arm, and Nina took it.

"You know, I was engaged to Minnie. That makes you and I related, I think."

CHAPTER NINE

"You and Minnie? Knock me over with a feather. We must learn from our pasts," Nina said.

"I plan to do just that." We were returning from a trip to the punch bowl. I raised my cup in a toast. "Here's to learning!" Nina clinked her cup with mine.

We entered the observatory library, which appeared cozy at first, but upon further exploration revealed a warren of nooks and tome-packed aisles that curved around one whole side of the building. People wandered in and out, but no one stayed for too long. For a library it was awfully dim. The room's electrical lighting wasn't working for some reason. I thought it strange, but wiring in Arkham was sometimes a spotty business. Turning the library switches did nothing, leaving us with the moonlight to guide our way. Nina and I found a secluded corner. She curled up catlike on a cracked leather brandy-brown wingback. I perched on a lowboy bookcase filled with scientific pamphlets. Everything was looking very nineteenth century, very Victorian. The music from the band thumped like a heartbeat in the walls.

"What were we talking about?" I asked.

"Outside, before Minnie came over? I was telling you about the unexplained deaths."

"That's right. Arkham's had a run of bad luck lately."

Nina's gaze narrowed. "It's more than bad luck. I think the incidents are connected."

"To what?"

"To each other, for a start," she said.

"Heavens! Do you have any proof of this theory?"

I scooted my bottom back onto the bookcase and bumped into something behind me. It was an orrery depicting our solar system: the sun, planets, and all their moons. I picked it up. The cool brass apparatus resembled a faceless automaton juggling semi-precious orbs in its spindly arms. Gears moved inside the glass dome which formed its base; quite a mesmerizing clockwork model. It reminded me of Norman the astronomer's cosmic lesson.

But I set it aside to listen to Nina.

"I've dug up a few things," she said. "The big picture's still fuzzy."

"A series of murders? That's gruesome." The mood in town seemed dark these days.

"They weren't all murders. Some were suicides."

"That hardly makes it better."

"I agree," she said. "There's been an uptick in missing persons cases too. We can presume a few of those will turn out to be suspicious deaths. And I've come across a couple of other oddities. What the coroner calls 'deaths by misadventure.' But they're far from ordinary accidents."

"Like Court Dunphy's plunge from the South Church rooftop," I said.

"Precisely. My research is leading me to hypothesize an underlying pattern to these deaths. If not in method, then in flavor. They share the same… unique design."

"That 'intelligent influence' you mentioned outside." Now normally, I wasn't drawn to the macabre the way Roland and, apparently, Nina were. But I liked puzzles. However, this puzzle appeared too weird and obscure to feel real. Then I flashed to the bizarre street festival I'd witnessed in Spain. Perhaps the world *was* weirder than I knew. Yet I worried Nina might be more deeply eccentric than I first thought. Would Houdini's debunking have made her angry? I hoped not. I was a fan of logical earthly solutions. "If the design is the same, that might suggest a designer, a unifying personality behind it all. Like an artist compiling a body of work. Do you suspect a hidden force is behind these fatal events?"

Nina considered my question. "Not always hidden. Some of the deaths were violent homicides; people committed them. However, their motives may be… highly unusual."

I breathed a sigh of relief. At least she wasn't talking about vengeful ghosts.

"I'm so glad to hear you say that," I said.

"What do you mean?" She frowned at me.

"These mysterious deaths are like puzzles. They present us with a challenge, and I do like challenges. Maybe I could help you solve them?"

She straightened out her legs. "I never asked you for any help."

Don't blow this, Alden, I thought. "Perhaps, you'd like, what's a good word, a kind of *collaborator*? Someone to talk over the crimes with. Another mind in the mix. A teammate?"

"How would you assist me?" She raised her eyebrows, quizzical.

She had raised a salient point to which I had no ready reply.

"I don't know exactly." I had no investigative experience. I was an artist.

"Well, then." Nina slid to the front of the wingback seat as if she were getting up.

"I have a good imagination," I said, quickly. "I'm a visual thinker. What if you describe the murders, and I'll picture them in my head. Maybe I'll see something useful?"

After a skeptical tilt of her head Nina settled back in her chair again.

"I guess it's worth a try," she said.

"Oh, I think so." Maybe it hadn't started out entirely that way, but now I really did want to hear about these unexplained cases. I wanted to see if I might contribute something.

Nina drew in a deep breath. "Dr Juliana Silva was found hanged from a lamppost in front of St Mary's Hospital in Uptown. She was visiting Arkham from her home in Rio de Janeiro, Brazil. An expert in contagious diseases of the Americas. She traveled here for a year of teaching. A nurse arriving to work her morning shift discovered Dr Silva's body."

"Hanged overnight at the hospital. It wasn't a suicide?"

"Dr Silva's hands were tied behind her back. She was swaying six feet above the sidewalk. No one saw or heard anything. No signs she fought off an attacker. She was still wearing her stethoscope and eyeglasses. She had purple witchweed flowers stuffed in the pocket of her exam coat. Those flowers are not easy to come by, but they grow nearby at Hangman's Hill. Dr Silva was known to take walks there in the daytime, but never at night."

I closed my eyes, concentrating.

Like a sketch, the scene began to develop, stroke by stroke, in my mind's eye.

"Flowers pilfered from a potter's field… Her killer knew where she went for walks. Maybe they picked the flowers knowing she liked them. And used them to lure her." My mental sketch showed a bouquet, an outstretched hand, a length of rope concealed behind the strangler's back.

"Hmm… so she didn't run or fight because she didn't see the killer as dangerous." Nina's voice betrayed her surprise. "I hadn't thought of that. She was killed quickly?"

"I haven't any idea. Go on. Tell me another one…"

"Udo Ganz, union organizer. His body was discovered floating in the Miskatonic River near the docks." This time there was a tinge of anticipatory excitement in her recap.

I opened my eyes. "Hardly much of a mystery there. My father is a local business owner and he hated Ganz, as did most of the industrialists in Arkham. There's a crime there to be sure. Sadly, I don't think it's unusual if a businessman's hired goon drowned Ganz."

"Except he wasn't drowned."

My dull reaction switched to bewilderment. "Beaten to death?"

Nina shook her head. "Mr Ganz had his skin peeled off in one piece. The folded-up flesh suit was mailed to the *Advertiser* on ice. With a note explaining that Ganz had to die. Several elaborate tattoos covering his chest and back made the identification easy. A confidential source told me Ganz had scaled back his union agitating because he was receiving bribes from the same business owners he'd battled for years. In other words, he'd sold out. But union members didn't know. His funeral devolved into a pro-

Labor riot. Factories were set on fire. Equipment destroyed. The police arrested over fifty protesters."

I decided not to draw a mental picture of the skin suit. Nina's facts made Ganz's hellish demise plain enough. How could a person commit that crime unless they were insane?

"You have more cases, right?"

Nina nodded. I closed my eyes again.

"The Galinka sisters, Mary Lou and June, perished on the Unvisited Isle. A Boy Scout troop out on a Saturday canoeing excursion discovered their charred bones."

"Oh, my butler told me about this one! They were dancers?"

"That's right. Say, you knew about Ganz and the Galinkas. Maybe you're the missing connection between these deaths?" she teased.

I hoped she was only teasing.

"Ha ha … Just because I know names doesn't make me guilty. Continue, please."

"The twin sisters owned a dance studio where they taught ballet and the latest modern steps. They had vanished after a Friday night recital. The twins were renowned for their cheery, vibrant personalities. Witnesses reported seeing 'a wall of flames' on the island early Saturday. The reports were ignored by the police who figured it was a hobo campfire."

Behind my eyelids, I saw a ring of trees around a blaze. Twisted orange flames licking the sky. Dancers in the dark. "These murders all happened last year?" I was shocked.

She stared at me. "No. That's in the last six months. Go back a year, you can add another half a dozen unsolved bizarre deaths. Each one stranger than the last. My favorite? At the train station, a drifter's body turned up in a boxcar. Throat opened ear to ear by a switchblade knife. The knife clutched in his hand. Not a drop of blood left in him. Or on him. Or anywhere else in the boxcar."

"How did the police explain that?"

"They didn't." Nina threw her arms up and the scent of Chanel No.5 enchanted me. She ran her fingers through her short, slick hair and gazed out the window at the pale moon.

"Look there," she said, whispery.

I looked.

"No. Not at the moon, silly." Nina blew a gentle breath toward the dusty windowpane.

A spiderweb trembled in a corner of the window.

Where a delicate spider balanced on the swinging threads.

Waiting. Watching.

A shiver crawled over my skin. "All this bloody-minded talk has me tragically sobered up. I plan to address this issue without haste," I said, offering Nina my hand.

We navigated a trail through the stygian, labyrinthine library. The air smelled of mildew, old books, and dust. Nina stopped abruptly. "What's that noise?"

I listened. "I don't hear anything. We're almost to the door."

"The door is the other way." She stopped again and tugged me back.

We were in a very dark aisle, and I began to think she was correct. "Maybe I'm not looking for a door. Ever consider that? Maybe I'm exploring." I turned, hesitating among the oppressive shelves. Which way was the damned door? I squinted without it doing any good.

"Some explorers get lost and are never heard from again," she said. From behind me, she grazed my neck lightly with her fingernail. Then I felt her warm fingertip press down.

"Maybe I want to get lost. That's been my plan all along."

Now we stopped talking. I turned to her.

But I could hardly see anything. Silhouettes.

Nina came closer, so our faces were inches apart. Were we going to kiss? The music from the band had gone quiet, though I swore I heard the blood pumping in both our hearts.

Soft murmurs.

Her face swiveled away from me. "What *is* that noise? I'm not kidding, Alden. I hear people. Two voices, I think." She tipped her head to listen better. "Talking. You hear it?"

"It's just us," I said. "Isn't it?"

But it wasn't just us because I could hear the low voices now too. They sounded… funny. Guttural, deep, and thick. But hissing too, filled with fricatives. I felt an unpleasant creeping chill, like a cold, damp knuckle gliding down my backbone.

"It's coming from this way," Nina said.

I flicked my banjo cigarette lighter so we could see better.

Just under our chins, Nina approached a shelf housing leather-bound, astronomical textbooks and star charts, an English translation of Copernicus's *De Revolutionibus Orbium Coelestium*, and a battered tome entitled Morryster's *Marvells of Science*. Quickly but quietly, she unloaded the musty, thick books, piling them in my waiting arms. Once she'd cleared the space, Nina stuck her head inside the vacant cubby.

"They're behind this bookcase," she said. "On the other side of the wall."

"You still hear them?"

"Shuush!" She pointed into the cubby, then nodded.

I snugged myself beside her for a listen.

I held my lighter's wobbly flame up, although there was nothing to see.

There were only sounds.

We leaned forward together.

Voices! Yes, I heard them more clearly inside here; the space made a kind of acoustic amplifier. Voices talking in rhythm, a cadence, as if reciting prayers. Alarmingly close.

Nina held up two fingers.

I nodded in agreement. Two people talking.

She whispered, "A man and a woman."

"Yes. I hear the same."

Almost musical, yet discordant, a harsh pattern. If these were words, they made no sense to me. I could hear them well enough now, but their meaning remained cryptic. I might've even called it gibberish, but despite my lack of comprehension, the utterances were affecting me. I felt uneasy, nauseated. My muscles ached as if I had come down with the flu. We were hearing a sort of chaotic language, nonsense sounds, disorganized but repetitious.

"Yoohoo? LA. Pada," I tried to recreate what I heard.

"Something like that. Not quite," Nina said. "They're saying it over and over. You? You? *Fapada. Vadada? Rabada?*"

The source was frustratingly close. What did the words mean? Who were the talkers?

My brain stirred. A thought in my grasp slipped away. I'd heard something like this language before. But where? Gregorian chants? No. A Dadaist poetry reading?

I smelled a sudden acrid burning. My thoughts derailed.

"What's that horrible smell?" Nina asked as a flame reared up next to her like a darting snake head. "Fire!"

Nina pulled out of the bookcase. The amber serpent of flame

followed her. It had coiled itself around her left arm.

Nothing so exotic as a flaming serpent.

In my distraction I had accidently ignited one of the mummy bandages dangling from Nina's wrist. Jerkily, she waved her blazing arm. I grabbed the clown hat off my head and smothered her combusting bindings with my floppy chapeau. The flames quickly snuffed out.

The burnt bandages were a crumbly black mess.

Reluctantly, I struck the wheel of my lighter. Nina's skin appeared slightly pinkish.

"Are you hurt?" I felt terrible, responsible, foolish.

"My skin feels hot but not burned. Don't worry. I'm fine."

When we bent our heads toward the bookcase again, the voices had fallen silent.

"Damn! They've gone," Nina said, disappointed.

"The energy has changed. It's as if I can feel their absence. Do you feel it too?"

She did.

Nina insisted that we had to search for the room beyond the bookcase. I agreed. We began by inspecting the hallway, but found no doors on that side. All the second-floor accesses were locked. We went outside. The area of the building in question had no windows. I wondered if it was storage space. The dome of the observatory loomed above the yard.

"We have to find a way in there," Nina said. "What if someone's stuck in a closet?"

"That doesn't seem likely."

"I need to know where those voices came from."

I fetched us more punch. The alcohol made our quest more feasible.

"Well, we do know one possible way in. Don't we?" I said.

Nina wrinkled her forehead. As we sipped, I watched her eyes grow wide. When she grinned at me, I knew she'd do it. "We're going to need tools."

"And more punch," I said.

The party was enjoying a second wind. The band returned to the stage after a refreshment break. Using the distraction to our advantage, Nina and I returned to the library. We were alone this time. Hurriedly, we blocked the doors from inside to avoid the need to explain our peculiar destructive activities. Having discovered an unlocked janitor's closet, Nina procured a hammer and a sturdy mop handle. She weighed these in her hands.

"Hammer first, then the stick. Are you sure you want to do this?" I asked.

"Fairly sure." She handed me the mop handle and gave the hammer a practice swing.

"Fairly sure or *sure* sure?"

"I'm sure. Let's do it. Preston can pay for the damages later. He owes me."

Experimentally, I rapped my fist inside the empty bookcase, noting the hollow sound.

"Ladies first?"

"I would stand for nothing less."

Nina bashed the hammer through the back of the bookcase. The wood was old and dry. It made a splintery crunch. I jabbed with the mop handle, clearing a wider hole. Even with the band bashing in the other room, I couldn't believe no one heard our demolition.

We discovered a void where there should have been a solid wall.

Like Howard Carter inserting a candle into Tutankhamun's tomb, I slid my hand into the gap, tasting strong musky incense, and something more metallic and far less pleasing.

"Alden, there's something terrible in there. I feel it." She touched her stomach.

"I fear you're right." I had the awful sensation of turning in a forest and feeling lost.

"We've gone this far," she said. "No backing down now."

I didn't argue.

I was preparing to yank out the bookcase, when my grasping fingers entered a notch behind the bookcase's crown molding. It felt like a latch. I popped it.

The bookcase swung free – a hidden doorway: that old gothic trope.

Side by side, Nina and I followed the tiny flame of my lighter into the vault.

"Look at that. It isn't a room after all," I said.

"A secret staircase. Where do you think it goes?"

"One way to find out."

"These stairs are quite narrow," she said. "I'll follow you."

"Oh, thanks!"

I went up one step. Nina was right behind me, her hot hand pressed firmly to my back.

"This might be the closest I've ever come to being frightened," she said in my ear.

"I'm well past that point. We don't know what's at the top of these steps."

The stairway was utilitarian; its wood painted all black. Above us, a soft gray rectangle of space awaited our arrival. I kept seeing bulky imaginary forms oozing into view.

Silence. Except for our quickening breath. The quiet made it worse – the anticipation of noises, unspeakable in the offing. I wanted to fill the quiet with my voice, but I dared not.

"That iron smell is blood. Isn't it?" she said.

"I believe so." Why did the blackness ahead seem to shift to red?

No. It was black.

Nina made a tiny choking sound at the back of her throat. "Keep going."

Five stairs higher and we took them without hesitation. I paused halfway to the top. "We could turn around." There was a pressure now ahead of us and behind. It felt as solid and real as the stair treads under our feet. The pressure pushed. "There's no shame in that."

Nina said, "It feels like I'm underwater. I can't breathe."

We heard something then – a gnawing sound, like tissue being bitten and sawed apart.

"Do you think some poor animal got trapped?" she asked.

"And it's chewing its leg off?"

"Go! However bad, I need to see it," she said. "I can't take it. This wondering."

We rushed to the top of the stairs.

A large room. Faint, lead-colored light over our heads. The air felt cool and drafty, the floor wet. My shoes slipped as if I'd walked out onto an icy pond. But this was no pond, and what lay obscenely before us was no injured animal in need of kindhearted rescuers.

It was far more hideous.

CHAPTER TEN

The unclothed corpse of a man: awash in blood, shockingly headless.

He lay on his back in a glistening red pool. Arms and legs stretched wide like a stranded starfish, with one key difference: his missing body part would never regenerate. The crimson stain spreading underneath him crept to the edge of the stairs. It was a hard struggle whether to stare at him or to look away. I was transfixed and repulsed in equal measure.

Could this be a particularly well-staged Halloween prank? A bit of artful drama?

The raggedy flesh, the glistening ring of exposed cervical spine told me, "*No.*"

This was not a clever prank.

My stomach lurched a little then, and the whiskey inside wasn't helping. Looking away, I found myself observing Nina's face as she comprehended the extent of the horror we had stumbled upon. Her unblinking eyes. Mouth falling open, then the sharp intake of breath.

"What the *hell*…?"

I was about to suggest we go back the way we came, when it occurred to me that the executioner of the unfortunately deceased individual on the floor might still be in the room with us. I did not want to offer the killer my unguarded back.

I swiveled around, my nerves on highest alert.

But I saw no one.

As I stated, the room was large. But it was also open and uncluttered by much furniture. An attacker would have had trouble finding a hiding place, unless they were a contortionist or very, very small. Nevertheless, when I located a switch on the wall, I quickly turned it.

Nothing happened.

Then I remembered the electricity was out in the library. Were these rooms on the same circuit? And had that circuit been cut here, intentionally, in preparation for the act of murder? Despite the impediment of unavoidable darkness, I knew exactly where we were.

Above the body loomed the observatory's most famous attraction, its huge refractor telescope; like a giant metal finger, the narrow end pointed at the headless body. Next to the body stood a wheeled set of steps which the Miskatonic astronomers ascended in order to peer into the telescope's eyepiece. Each wide step served double duty, providing a bench seat for any extended study of the galaxy. "Someone pushed these steps here," I said. "They're far from where they belong."

"The murderer must have done it," Nina said.

"They had plenty of room for killing. Why move things?"

Nina crouched beside the mutilated remains. "See here? Beneath the blood there are markings drawn on the floor. Do you think they're scientific?"

Most of the design was obscured by blood and the corpse. Judging from what remained visible, the dead man lay atop a diagram made of interlocking angles and circles. I bent and dabbed my finger, smudging one of the lines but avoiding any blood. I rubbed my fingers together and sniffed. "It's chalk. I doubt an astronomer drew it. To what purpose?"

"What if the astronomer is also the murderer?" Nina asked. She stood and walked over to a lab table slashed by the shadows. Gazing skyward, she pointed. "That's where the draft is coming from." The observatory's shutters were open. The moon entered through the slit in the dome roof. Nina found the nub of a candle stuck to a table. "Toss me your lighter."

I did.

Candlelight mixed with moonlight, but neither made the sights less dreadful.

"The blood is so red," I said. "And so… everywhere." I gulped sourly.

While I was feeling close to being sick, Nina appeared unnaturally calm.

"I wonder who he is?" she said, returning to the body.

"Doesn't any of this bother you?" I said. "It's all rather graphic and, well… authentic."

Nina shrugged. "I've seen dead bodies before."

"Where?"

"When I was a girl my father had a preoccupation with criminality. He was a newsman and an amateur sleuth of sorts. He took me to crime scenes. Fresh ones. I know it sounds abnormal, but I liked going with him. Seeing Boston's underbelly. It was exciting. I inherited my sordid interests from him. Daddy bought a newspaper, then a few others. We stopped roaming the streets together. Where do you suppose this man's head has gone?"

"The killer took it?"

"Yes. We heard the killer, didn't we? Separating the neck joints moments before we arrived. How did they get up through the shutters with it? It's too high to jump. We were blocking the secret stairwell, which must be a shortcut the astronomers use to get to the library. Going out the main door leads downstairs to the banquet table. It would be too risky."

We could hear the muffled noise of the partiers below us.

Nina's mention of the banquet put me in mind of Norman Withers. "Good heavens! Nina, let me have that candle."

I studied the body closely.

"What is it, Alden?"

I passed the candle flame along the length of the body, careful not to drip any wax. "I met a Miskatonic astronomer at the party tonight. Talkative fellow. Long beard, lively eyes – details which won't help us here. He was working upstairs in this lab. I feared this might be him. But, no." I leaned away from the corpse. "This guy is too young and portly to be the same man. Even lacking a head, he can't be Norman Withers."

"Good news for Norman," she said. "I wonder who…"

A small scuffling noise called my attention to the far corner of the room. A rat?

I do not like rats, though I suppose they were the least of our potential problems.

Still, a rat makes a person feel crawly. Maybe vermin smelled the blood?

An astronomy lab is not the ideal place to find a decent weapon. We had left our hammer and mop handle downstairs. I picked up a slide rule from the table. "Come with me."

"What are you going to do with that?"

"I want to make sure we're alone under the dome."

"And if we're not, you'll take measurements?"

I ignored her jibe. Candle in hand, we made a thorough inspection of the room. I know this may sound callous, but once the initial shock of the gruesome murder had settled in, it was easier to appreciate the inspiring size of the grand telescope we were circumnavigating.

"It looks like Big Bertha. Doesn't it?"

Nina shrugged. "I can't really say. I've never seen a howitzer in person."

"In photos it is impressive." I pointed to an iron track circling the room. "The dome rotates around on rails. Ropes and pulleys move it. That one hanging by the opening controls the shutter. Hey, look! Is that blood on it? The killer must've been covered with the stuff."

"You seem to know a lot about this place." Nina examined the stained cable.

"I visited here on school field trips when I was a kid." Now that we had checked the room thoroughly, I was feeling less threatened by an impending attack. "I think we can say, with some confidence, that the killer has fled. It's time to call the police."

Nina pursed her lips, tapping one knuckle against her chin.

"Do you really think that's wise?" she said.

"A man's been murdered. What other choice is there?"

"How will we explain ourselves? Our discovery of the body, for instance?"

"The police will understand." I was not eager to involve the authorities. People of my class generally prefer to handle life's unpleasant and socially embarrassing events less formally. But here was a decapitated man! "They'll know the right way to handle this."

"That has not always been my experience." She paced nervously. "We should think this all the way through. The body will be found tomorrow at the latest. There's bound to be cleaners coming in after the party. Either way, it won't help him." She tipped her head at the corpse. Then she sighed deeply. "I'll just say it. I don't want to become a suspect, Alden."

"A suspect?" I didn't understand. "Why on earth would *you* be a suspect?"

"I've had trouble with the police… in my past." She looked frightened.

I was curious to know more, but I could see that she was reluctant to tell me. If I pried, she'd clam up. So I lit two cigarettes and passed one to her. We smoked silently in the semi-dark. The two of us. Just thinking. I was waiting for her to make up her own mind. Did she trust me enough to say anything more?

Nina stared at the opening in the dome and watched the smoke escaping. Her big eyes came around to meet mine squarely. "Do you remember when I told you about Udo Ganz's funeral? How there was a riot afterward and protestors were arrested? I was one of them."

"You were picked up at a political protest?" That didn't seem so bad.

"It was more than a protest. But I didn't go for the politics. I went to have a look at the crowd. Maybe I thought the person who killed Ganz might show up. I don't know what I was thinking. That I'd just look at them and somehow know? Maybe it was a fantasy I had of solving the murder. Pretty soon the march turned serious. Out of control. Bottles thrown. Threats and insults traded back and forth between the protestors and the cops. I got caught up in the crowd. I couldn't slip away. Carried along in the river of bodies. The police rushed us. It was terrible. Fists and clubs flying. It felt more like a boxing match than a mass arrest…"

"Nina, I'll make the call to the cops. When they get here, we'll both have to talk to them. There's no avoiding that. But we can stay together. If there's any problem, anything at all, I'll phone my father's lawyer and have him out here tonight. Nobody gets hurt."

Nina hugged me.

I turned my head as we embraced, trying not to see the body in that lake of blood.

"Alden? There's more…"

"More?" I pulled back but held onto her shoulders.

"Just a little."

"Go on."

She turned sideways and started pacing again as she relayed her story. "When the Galinka sisters were discovered on Unvisited Isle? After the story came out in the papers and everywhere people knew what happened? That day, I borrowed a boat. A leaky old rowboat I found tied up on the shore. I rowed out to the island to see things. For myself, you know? Well, the boat belonged to this grubby fisherman. I thought it was abandoned! But he went to the police station and told them I stole it. They raced out with half a dozen big police boats because they thought maybe the person who took this fisherman's boat might be the one who started the fire and burned up the bones of those poor

Galinka girls. The cops ran up on the island waving their guns and clubs like wild men. They looked crazy! And when they saw me, I ran too. I tried to get away from them because I was scared. How far could I go? They chased me, high and low, blowing their whistles. I only went out there looking for clues…"

"They arrested you again?"

She nodded. "Handcuffed me. Took me to headquarters. Made me sit in a cell for hours. I explained the whole situation to them. But they acted like I was lying. They dug up my arrest sheet from the Ganz riot. They made me promise to stop investigating things on my own. Leave the police work to us, they said. I promised I would so they'd let me go home."

"And they said if they ever caught you out at a crime scene again…"

"They'd lock me up for a long time. Long enough that people would forget me."

"The joke's on them. I can't imagine ever forgetting you." I wanted us to kiss then, if only a dead man weren't lying there on the floor. Nina looked at me quizzically. Had she misheard me? The trace of a smile said she hadn't. Surprised. That's all. Honestly, I was too.

We agreed that I would say I broke into the telescope room on my own. I'd been taking a whiskey punch-induced nap in the library and heard weird noises beyond the wall behind the bookcase. I'd gone into the hallway and, when I couldn't figure out a way into the room, I grabbed whatever tools I could find in the janitor's closet. I was half-drunk. I thought somebody got themselves trapped inside the wall. I could sell it. The police wouldn't care about that part when they saw the body.

Nina would not be any part of my story.

I watched her disappear down the secret staircase.

She vanished into the dark.

I was about to go downstairs and place my call to the cops when I noticed a row of coat pegs on the wall. Hanging from one of the pegs was a brown hooded robe. A monk's robe. I lifted the robe off the peg. Where had I seen this same rustic getup? The spiked punch must have dulled my brain. My mind was drawing a blank until I spotted the thick wooden staff propped in the corner. Friar Tuck!

This was the garb of Robin Hood's tonsured companion.

Clark Abernathy! My old college classmate. He'd chucked that fat log on the bonfire in the backyard while Nina was filling me in on Arkham's string of unexplained deaths. If this was his Halloween costume, then Clark....

We had been acquaintances, never friends. But Clark was a member of my college group of companions. The Abernathys were new money; rough around the edges, eager to please. Ruddy, freckled, and prematurely bald, Clark could be depended on to hoist a bottle of ale, or a dozen. He liked to toss around the ole pigskin and wrestle his comrades into submission on gym mats. Clark was a legend of the dining hall, regaled for his bottomless appetite. By himself, Clark once consumed a stuffed saddle of lamb, three creamed onions, a tray of cinnamon buns, and a Nesselrode chestnut custard pie in a single sitting. The post-collegiate years lured him away from the gymnasium but not the dinner table. His father was grooming him to take over the family's sporting goods empire. Likable Clark was a born salesman. Clark's rise to sporting goods fame had followed right on schedule. Until tonight.

I returned to the body.

During our junior year Clark took a drunken spill off a bicycle onto the railroad tracks. He gashed his knee badly, requiring several stitches and the temporary use of a crutch. I remembered because I was the one who drove him to the hospital that night. I saw the doctor stitch him up.

My lighter flame located the pink scar on the corpse's knee.

Clark's knee.

Poor old Clark. He never did harm to anyone. Yet he ended up like this.

I resisted the urge to cover him with his frock. I didn't want to spoil any evidence.

Instead, I went downstairs to call the police. I'd find Preston first. Clark was his friend and a groomsman at his upcoming wedding. I wanted to tell him before the cops did.

Poor old Clark.

"Oakesy, I can't talk to you privately right now. I'm in the middle of a party! Minnie, darling, come here!" I first thought Preston had come to his party without a costume, but now he was wearing a purple felt top hat with a piece of paper pinned to it that read, "In this Style 10/6." He held a cigar in one hand, an inch of ash about to plummet off its tip, in the other hand he clutched a gin martini poured into a huge china teacup. Partygoers danced around him.

"Preston, Clark Abernathy is dead," I said.

"That's not possible, Alden. I just saw him not an hour ago. He's here at my party." Preston sipped from his martini.

Minnie materialized out of the crowd and rushed to her fiancé's side.

"What is it, my Mad Hatter?"

"Alden thinks Clark is dead. Tell him he's wrong. The boy has had too much punch." Preston fell deeply into a high-backed chair, offering Minnie his knee for a seat. She borrowed his cigar, filling her mouth with smoke, blowing a series of rings at the ceiling. Preston watched her, his eyes hooded with prideful possession, before returning his attention to me. "Now, Oakesy, where have you been?"

"Upstairs, under the observatory dome. That's where I found Clark. We need to call the police," I said, exasperated.

"You're joking! Oh, Alden!" Minnie howled.

People began to drift to our corner to see what they might be missing.

"Please come. I'll show you," I said.

In the background, the trombone player blew a sad vaudevillian solo. Preston rose and put his arm around me, dropping copious ash on my shirt. "Now, now. Oakesy, you're obviously upset. I hate to see that. We'll go with you and clear up this misunderstanding." He turned to the gathering crowd. "Everyone, wait here. We have a private matter to resolve. Minnie, I might need your support." They stood up. Wobbly in each other's arms.

"We should call the police," I said.

Preston looked at me with genuine affection. "You're too damned serious, chum. It's probably a prank. Clarkie loves to pull a good one. These are all my friends here tonight. I'm not about to summon the police and have them hauled away to jail for drinking. Now, how about we three go under the dome and chew out Clark for his poor taste in humor?"

Preston snatched a candelabra from the table. Minnie grabbed onto Preston.

And I led them toward the stairs.

"There's a lot of blood. Prepare yourself."

Preston's expression grew serious for the first time. "Blood?"

"Someone cut off Clark's head. They've taken it." My words sounded insane to me.

Preston looked uneasy. "You'd better go first. I've got a weak stomach when it comes to body fluids. It must be a joke. Don't you see? It can't be real. Fake blood. I'll take Clarkie to task for it. He shouldn't scare my friends. It isn't fun at all when a person takes things too far." In the hall, Preston strode to the door, grabbing the doorknob, twisting. "It's locked."

"There's another way," I said. "A secret passage through the library."

"Secret passage, did you say?" Preston arched an eyebrow.

"Oooh, I like the sound of that," Minnie said. "A touch of Poe!"

I led them to the library, but the doors wouldn't budge.

"We blocked the doors from inside. I forgot."

"Who's we?" Preston asked.

I wasn't going to mention Nina. "It's not important. Maybe if we pushed together?"

We pushed. The doors moved enough for us to squeeze through. Inside the library, I showed them the bookcase and the hidden entrance it concealed.

"What's happened here?" Preston asked.

"Sorry, I'll pay for it. What I must show you is inside and up," I said.

"You're lucky we didn't call the police. You'd be arrested for vandalism," he said.

Minnie forced her way to the front. She peered into the

ragged hole I'd made with Nina, then she spied behind the door into the gap. "It *is* a secret passage. Preston, please don't scold him. This is going to be the most memorable party I've ever had." Before I could stop her, she raced into the opening, her tiny feet thumping up the stairs, feathers brushing the walls as she went. Preston ducked through, chasing after his bride-to-be.

"Wait! Wait!" I tried to caution them. But it was of no use. I had lost control of the situation. *Where was Nina now?* I wondered. I hoped she was on her way home, safe and sound. Reaching the top of the passage's black steps, I followed after Preston and Minnie.

Preston's candelabra glowed, torch-like.

It stopped near the telescope.

I caught up, out of breath. "I'm sorry, Minnie. Preston, I should've warned you what to expect. How bad it really is. No one should ever have to see a thing like this."

"See what?" Preston shone his light on the floor. He pushed aside the wheeled set of steps. He lit up the astronomers' ladder. Walking around the room, he proceeded to illuminate the ropes and pulleys, the work tables, and the rails that circled the dome.

"There's nothing here, Oakesy. Nothing."

Preston was right.

Clark's body was gone.

I thought I must be losing my mind. But there could be no mistake. Here was the very spot I stood with Nina. I crouched and touched the floorboards.

Minnie went over to her beau, and he gathered her in his arms.

They're standing where Nina and I stood, where we nearly kissed not a half hour ago.

Where was the body? Where was poor old Clark?

"Wait. Clark was dressed as Friar Tuck. He had a robe. A staff."
I ran over to the coat pegs. But his costume was gone. I wasn't
making things up. I wasn't that drunk. Was I? No. And I wasn't
alone when I found Clark either. "Nina saw him too."

"Who?" Preston said.

"Nina Tarrington."

Preston looked gobsmacked. "By Zeus! I haven't heard that
name in ages. What's gotten into you, Alden Oakes?" Preston
wasn't angry with me, confused was more like it. Puzzled at
my erratic behavior. "Maybe you've had one too many. That
Canadian hooch has your head in a spin, my old friend. Sit
down. We'll find you some water or hot coffee. Are you feeling
ill? Does he look ill to you, Minnie?" Preston drew Minnie tight
against him.

He put the candelabra up near my face.

I winced at the brightness.

"He's very pale," she said.

I did feel sick. My head banging loudly. The light bothered
me. I pushed it away.

"He said he saw Nina. Did you hear that, Minnie? Is she even
back in town?"

"She was here tonight. At your party," I answered.

"Here? I don't think so." He stared at Minnie. "Can you
imagine her showing up?"

"You saw her with me at the bonfire," I said.

Minnie looked surprised. She shook her head emphatically.

"My *shy friend*, you called her."

Minnie thought about it. "The mummy girl?"

"Yes. Mummy queen. Nina *was* here. She and I discovered
Clark together."

"I don't think that mummy was Nina, Alden," Minnie said. "Clark's not here either. I haven't seen him. His father called to say he'd hurt his back playing polo and he wouldn't be able to make it tonight. Isn't that right, Preston darling?"

Preston nodded. He looked like he felt embarrassed for me. Pity welling in his eyes.

"Nina was here. She absolutely was," I repeated. "Clark was here too."

Talking mostly to myself. I couldn't have dreamed the whole thing up. *That* was crazy. Crazier than what I thought I'd witnessed in Spain. Rituals and sacrifices. This was Arkham, and I know Arkham. That's what I tried to tell myself.

"Go home, Alden." Minnie pulled a sad face. "Preston, have your driver give him a lift. He looks so very tired."

"I'm not tired. I'll walk home." Is this what cracking up feels like? But I wasn't cracking up, was I? No, I'd had too much to drink perhaps. Got a taste of some bad bootleg that scrambled the inside of my head. It would clear up soon. In the morning I'd be myself again.

"The air might do you some good," Preston said. "Do be careful. Arkham can be dangerous at night."

I searched outside for Nina. Maybe she was hiding somewhere nearby, watching for the police cars to pull up, sticking around just to see if I'd made it out unscathed.

I checked for her by the fire pit. The fire was dying. I tried to pick out any trace of that hefty log Clark tossed in the flames, but everything was embers. Ashes.

No sign of Nina anywhere.

So I left.

CHAPTER ELEVEN

Ever walked home late at night and thought someone might be following you? I don't mean muggers. I had a few of those on my tail in Europe, looking to roll a drunk and steal his pocket money. As a man, I've never had the same worries women deal with whenever they hit the streets alone, particularly at night. I'm talking about something different. What I mean is someone is following you, and only you. They haven't picked you as a random target or a victim of bad circumstances. They wanted only you from the start, because you are you. This was a specific brand of stalking I felt that night. Somebody wanted me, Alden Oakes, badly.

But I'm getting ahead of myself.

I left the observatory in a bad mood. Minnie was right about my feeling tired, but I was experiencing more than that. I'd had my head messed with. I was furious. If I had been pranked, I wasn't getting the joke; nothing about it felt humorous. I saw that oozing neck stump and it was not fake. Clark was dead. But how had they erased the crime so quickly? It was like magic. Something Houdini might've pulled on his audience. But with

Houdini's act, the audience was in on the game. They knew they were being tricked. That was half the fun of it. My experience finding the headless man left me confused, worried I might be losing my mind. Not really, though. I wasn't insane. Mostly, I was angry at myself for having been manipulated. Who had played me? Who killed Clark?

Why?

After checking my cigarette case and finding it empty, I walked down Crane Hill feeling fidgety. Restless. A carload of Miskatonic U fraternity boys swept past, hurling out insults and impinging my clown heritage and the marital status of my parents at the time of my birth. I gestured at them, immediately regretting it when their car pulled to the curb at the next corner. Several dark shapes exited. They were waiting. I am no stranger to fistfights, having spent enough of my youth at boarding schools and, later, in gritty, illicit barrooms where the masculine pecking order is maintained. I avoided violence when possible. Artists by nature tend to be a hot-tempered, impetuous lot. I was guilty on both counts, though I hoped maturity had improved my judgment. The car moved on. I felt a surge of relief. The boys had simply relieved themselves, leaving a puddle on the sidewalk and a trio of empty beer bottles littering the grass.

The night air had grown wet. Cold fog snuck between the buildings, snagging like cobwebs on the hedges and trees. Without thinking, I found myself veering west. Going downhill to the river. The sludgy black Miskatonic flowed on, mistakable for tar, its odor hardly less noxious, though fishier.

At the apex of the bridge crossing the river at West Street, I paused. I didn't need to travel this way. My house was on the same side of the Miskatonic as the university. But I wanted time to cool off. The river had always been a good place to think, at least during daylight. I never came here at night. Huge warehouses hunkered behind me. Warped piers wandered into the water like suicides. Only a few boats were docked tonight. Scores of gulls slept on the birdlimed warehouse roofs. A tangled pile of fishing nets lay heaped against a brick wall like a formless blob, oddly sparkling under the lights, as if it were covered with a thousand tiny, winking, jeweled eyes. I couldn't imagine eating anything that lived in this polluted sludge. Waves hung dirty lace collars on the pilings. A thick layer of muck the color of leeches sprouted everywhere the water lapped. I caught a darting movement on the dockside: a rat. *Ugh.* I couldn't help but think "*Plague!*" whenever I saw one skittering by. This plump specimen went about its business, paying no attention to me.

Out over the water, squatting in the middle of the river, was the reason I had come here. The Unvisited Isle. The place where the Boy Scouts tramped their boots upon the charred bones of the Galinka twins, and where the police nabbed Nina after her excursion in the pilfered rowboat, if she was to be believed. Why shouldn't I believe her? Because Preston and Minnie told me she wasn't in attendance at their party? I knew she was. I talked with her, and stumbled onto a dead man with her standing at my side. Drunken Preston and Minnie were unreliable witnesses. Though I'd been drinking too, of course. I knew what I had seen. It was absurd to think otherwise, to question myself would be to question my very sanity. I wasn't ready to do that. Honestly, in retrospect, I was only a little drunk.

Squeaking off to my right…

Two more rats were having a polite conversation about the quality of leavings on the shore this clammy Halloween night.

Woolly fog collected over the water. I turned up the collar of my clown shirt. To my left, on the other side of this moat, ran the Boston and Maine Railroad tracks, the same site where a collegiate Clark had dumped off his bicycle and split open his knee.

I thought about what Preston had said.

Obviously, I wished Clark were still alive.

Only, I knew he wasn't. True, I hadn't spoken to him at all during the evening prior to his demise. I didn't verify the identity of Friar Tuck. But the man in the monk suit looked just like Clark. Maybe a little more jowly than how I remembered him. Surely it had to be him.

Chattering...

A line of rats now – a night patrol I guessed – advanced along a warehouse loading ramp. The pageant of them sent a chill into me. The docks are notorious for rats, but seeing them in action was repulsive. Their hungry eyes bulged with intelligence; those pale, hairless tails like dirty pulled roots bobbing above the alley, suggesting pestilence. No creature of this Earth should instill a reaction of pure disgust. But I was no philosopher or saint. Rats gave me the willies. I sidestepped farther along the bridge until I was a decent distance away from the rodent activities.

I needed to find Nina.

But where to look for her?

I knew she lived wherever Courtland Dunphy was staying when he perished.

It shouldn't take much research to locate her. We needed to talk. Had she barged her way into Preston and Minnie's party uninvited? That was brazen but forgivable. Perhaps her curiosity had gotten the best of her. She seemed to have that problem on a regular basis. Driven by a need to know. I respected that. More importantly, I wanted to tell her about Clark's missing corpse. In all the excitement it hadn't occurred to me before, but I felt certain that he belonged on Nina's list of recent eerie deaths in our city–

What were those rats doing?

I peered into the hazy light surrounding the warehouses.

That heap of fishing nets. The rats were jumping into it. One after another. And they seemed to be disappearing. It had to be an optical illusion. The number of rats going in was startling. Where were they vanishing to? There must be quite a tasty treat nestled down in that jumble of knotted twine to make them dig themselves in so deep. Something rotten and delicious, and no doubt delectable. I shivered again. I swore I heard the rats chewing.

The sound reminded me of the gnawing noises we'd heard in the observatory.

When Clark's head was removed.

Rats?

No, it couldn't be…

Had they absconded with his body *and* cleaned up afterward?

I laughed. The boom of my voice on the otherwise silent bridge was alarming. I had always entertained notions about individuals who laughed loudly at their own thoughts.

Yet, here I was.

The pile of netting shook. I figured that was possibly natural, given how full it was with inner rats, but what struck me was how unnatural it seemed, a quivering, vibrating, jittery pile of woven–

Those tiny jeweled spots on the nets, at first I thought they looked like eyes, well, now they seemed to act as eyes, because the blob of nets lifted itself off the ground and stood on two sloppy... legs... and the net creature... walked away from its resting place against the wall... Its amorphous head, which sported more eye organs than the rest, swiveled to face me. I swear it looked out over the slick water and picked me out where I leaned on the bridge rail in the fog.

And it beckoned.

I know, I know. How could that be? Impossible, you say. But I tell you, a snarled roll of netting separated from the bulk of the shifting, permeable mass. It was an arm! The arm waved to me. I startled, and then my startlement stretched out into a sense of queasy panic.

Come here, Alden.

I gasped. Words! It used words! With my sleeve I wiped at my face, thinking somehow the fog was altering my vision. Clearly, my eyes were strained. I must've had something in them. Residue. A salty drop of sweat. Contamination from an unknown source. Perhaps a wisp of toxic fog drifted off the rippled surface of the Miskatonic. A smear of distortion from... what exactly? I had no answer. Despite my rubbing, the sight before me did not alter for the better. No. It beckoned again.

Come closer, Alden. Don't be afraid. I've something to show you. Now, listen to me.

I heard it speak. It had no mouth. But I heard it talking to me. Uttering words in a warm, syrupy baritone that was so soothing, so utterly charming. You'd put your trust in this voice. Although, I wasn't sure where it was coming from. The net blob was responsible, but the sounds were emanating from everywhere at once. They assailed me from all directions.

That's good. You keep walking. I'll wait right here for you.

Keep walking? What did it mean by that?

With a sudden, snapping realization, I perceived that I was nearer to the blob. I looked down. My feet shuffled slowly, but doggedly, toward that... knotty thing. Good heavens! I was obeying it without knowing what I was doing. I forced myself to halt. My hand shot out, grabbing the iron bridge rail for support.

"No," I said.

Why do you forestall the inevitable? Who are you to challenge me?

"Who are you?" I shouted.

You know who I am.

"I... I don't..."

You do know. I am no one. I am you, Alden. I am no one and I am everyone.

"That makes no sense. Leave me alone."

You called me. I always come when I'm summoned. You wanted to see. See me, Alden.

"I never called you. Even if I did, it was by mistake. I'm telling you now to go away." My voice sounded weak, as if I were losing the ability to resist. Or worse, the desire.

That is one thing that will never happen. No one turns us back after calling. No one.

It pulled at me then like a magnet that attracts flesh and bone. I felt my body being sucked toward that mound of eyeball-covered, rat-filled, fish-rot-stinking, fibrous threads.

With two hands I grasped the bridge. My fingers slipped on the wet rails. I tightened my hold, my knuckles turning whiter.

The net blob sighed. Its breath of putrid water and vile, greasy mud enveloped me.

If you will not come to me, I will come to you, Alden. I will come for you. We will. All of us. You see us now as you wished, and you will join soon. All makes one. You. Us. In the stars…

It dragged itself along the dockside; the mass of old nets trailed cork floats, broken clamshells, sprigs of decomposing weeds and algae yanked from the Miskatonic's riverbed.

I screamed. Cold sweat ran over me like chilly water scooped from below the bridge.

Was there no one else on the docks at this hour? Nobody guarded the warehouses? Not a single bug-eyed, beleaguered bookkeeper who labored at this late hour with his coffee and cigarettes under a desk lamp? I guess not. Because I screamed my throat raw, yet no one came to my aid.

We are no one. We are coming for you.

The net blob hitched itself along, hauling forth its girth with maximum effort. It shambled onto the bridge. How sluggish it was, but how impressively persistent. The smell overpowered me. Every breath was a taste of slow-cooked garbage, featuring entrails, ripe and green. A halo of flies buzzed around it, ignoring the cold to feast on morsels hidden in its collapsing chambers – its honeycomb of well-aged slimes – slurping at the lumpy, fecund jelly of its malodorous taint.

The lights on the bridge shone through the blob. Inside, the rats tumbled round as if they were spinning on a wheel. Somehow, I knew the swirling energy of their lifeforces fed and propelled this monster. The motion of their rat bodies animated its horror.

If the blob were to consume me, then I would power it like the rats did.

I was not about to let that happen.

I let go of the bridge.

The blob opened its arms and ballooned hugely to catch me.

Be with us. One of us. Be one with us.

I let it pull me close, but in that final instant before its hug would snag me inside its ropy folds, I sprang across the bridge. My muscles strained. Teeth gritted. Rebounding off the rails, I lost my breath in a rush but landed on my feet behind the monster, where its mysterious attraction exerted no pull on me. Go! Run! I told myself. My panic charged me with energy.

Up the hill on West Street I ran.

I did not look back until I reached the Miskatonic University campus grounds.

There I paused, bent forward, resting my hands on my thighs and gulping fresh air. The fog thickened. My view toward the river lay in obscurity. In fact, it appeared as if the fog were advancing out of the river channel and into the city above. The swirls moved too quickly for my comfort and gave me new apprehension. If a pile of old fishing nets could become enlivened through the ingestion of rats, might the fog be vitalized and inspirited? Was this no ordinary weather event but some previously unknown manifestation of a sentient, uncanny phenomenon?

"It's only fog," I said. Only fog...

I made a point to turn my back on it, resuming my journey homeward, this time walking, not running. I tried to talk down my fear. I had to regain some control. Steadfastly, I refused to turn around and acknowledge the heavy dampness in the air. To occupy my mind, I attempted to explain my weird encounter with the net blob. How could I explain it?

It's Halloween! I tried telling myself. You saw a ghost! Wasn't it quaint to think that?

There are no limits to what the mind will do to cast doubt on its own experience of the bizarre, but only after the physical threat is removed. How quickly we reverse our opinions in order to count ourselves among those who are labeled as sane. The inner conversation hammers away at firsthand observations in favor of mundane solutions. Alden, you merely saw someone in a very clever disguise. More University students playing pranks on a lonely drunk stumbling by the river. Students can be awfully clever. What did you *really* see, Alden? What did you hear? You aren't ready for the asylum yet, are you?

I saw a net blob monster, and it knew my name.

Oh, ho ho… who's going to believe you? It was foggy, you admitted that. You'd been drinking quite a lot. You thought you saw a dead man tonight. I think maybe you'd better get yourself home in bed and under the blankets. Take another look at things in the clean light of morning. See if they don't look quite so ominous and dreadful. You got yourself spooked. Good and spooked. Well, one thing led to another and, in the end, this is a classic case of the carried-aways. You panicked, plain and simple. You're a creative type, right? Now see, your excellent and fruitful brain started feeding you the most outlandish ideas. You know what you should do? You should go home and paint. You haven't painted in a while, have you? Anything since you got to Arkham? No? This is your brain giving you inspiration. It's breaking through that wall you put up without knowing you were doing it. Isn't this exactly what you asked for, Alden, old chum? A bolt right out of the blue of good, old-fashioned inspiration. Sure, it was fantastical and well, frankly, weird. But who's to say that's not what the doctor ordered. The Surrealists you admire so much are weird. Maybe you're like them. They have crazy dreams and visions. That's what you had tonight. You weren't asleep. But maybe you were just a little, and you had yourself a waking dream. Don't question it. Or fear it. Paint it, my boy. Go on! Paint it!

CHAPTER TWELVE

I awoke in my bed the next morning and took a hot bath to wash off the greasepaint and any remnants of the night. Steam filled the bathroom. I sank to the bottom of the claw-footed tub, my eyes and nose above the waterline. I soaked for a long time, thinking about all that had transpired at last night's party, and after. When I climbed out, I dried off with a soft, gold towel, digging my toes into a gold velvet rug. All things considered, I felt remarkably well-rested. I was hungry for breakfast. I wiped off the mirror. Shaved. Then I dressed in my painting clothes – a pair of frayed, color-spattered canvas pants and a tan chamois shirt. I put on a pair of moccasins and went downstairs to my art studio. The studio was brick-walled and drafty. I built a fire in the fireplace, tossing in a few birch logs. Roland must have seen me, because he soon visited, delivering a pot of coffee, my favorite chipped mug, and a plate of scrambled eggs and buttered rye toast. I thanked him. Now I was ready to work.

I started the way I usually do: a rough sketch. I broke out my charcoals and a pad of newsprint, whipping through a dozen quick compositions, getting a feel for the best perspective – how much, or how little, to show of my encounter on the bridge. Choosing angles, I settled on a view across the Miskatonic toward the docks. I avoided oils and grabbed my watercolor box. I fixed a board, stretching a sheet of handmade paper, wetting the paper with a sea sponge, securing it to the board using butcher's tape. I leaned the finished board against a wall near the fireplace so it would dry faster. Meanwhile, I planned out my palette, the tubes of cool, earthy colors I'd be using, and a couple of my favorite sable brushes. I kept it simple. When the paper was dry and ready for painting, I picked up a sharp pencil and sketched in the river, the low arc of the bridge, the crooked fingers of the docks. I omitted myself from the picture. I also left a pyramidal blank space halfway up the bridge's span.

I closed my eyes.

Transporting myself backward in time to the night before.

When I saw it again, I took the whole thing in at once, the way you swallow medicine.

I opened my eyes and drew what I had seen there lurking in the fog-draped dark.

Then I put down my pencil, picked up my brushes and paints, and got to work.

By late afternoon I had something that almost satisfied me. I stepped back, walking away for a break. I munched the cold eggs and toast. But I wasn't hungry any more. I'd drunk all the coffee. Loyal Roland had brought me a second pot. I poured a cup, trying to keep my mind quiet and empty from outside thoughts. I only wanted one thing in my head: my ill-formed counterpart on the bridge. I opened the French doors that led out to a pea gravel turnaround and our garages. I smoked three, four, cigarettes. Feeling rejuvenated, I went back inside and looked at the painting I had made.

It wasn't perfect. No painting is.

But I didn't hate it.

It was… close… very close to what I had witnessed last night.

The nighttime docks, pools of curdled light, the river like a sheet of corrugated tin.

Shambling up the bridge: a hideous creature fashioned of nets and fish parts and multiple eyes; the lights shone through it, rats wheeling around inside.

A tangled arm lifted, beckoning to me.

Yes, this would do for now.

I cleaned my brushes, shut the French doors, and left.

Once I'd made the first foray into processing my strange experience on the span over the Miskatonic, I felt I had to find Nina again. I needed to see her. To talk. I wanted to tell her everything that happened after we parted, and to ask her a few questions. Had she crashed the party? Where did she go after she left? Did anything peculiar happen on her walk home? It took me under two hours to locate Courtland Dunphy's building. I'd started down at the South Church rectory, where I went searching for Dunphy's address. The pastor was friendly and no dummy. I spotted him outside the church, smoking his pipe and admiring a pair of crows bathing in the rectory's stone birdbath. I still had my painting clothes on, but I wore a black wool overcoat on top of them, so they weren't obvious. I had exchanged my moccasins for boots. A flat cap kept my head warm. I walked up to the priest.

"They say crows are bad omens. Don't they, Father?"

"God made crows. Just like he made you and me." He removed his pipe, smiled, and asked if I might help him carry a trio of flower baskets inside the sanctuary.

"Sure thing, Father Cryans. You keep up this place by yourself?"

He handed me the heaviest basket. After opening the side door, he wedged it with his foot and took up the other arrangements. "Call me Father Mike. I manage what I can and pay for what I can't. The Lord sends me helpers. Forgive me, but have we met before, Mr…?"

"Rose," I said, caught off guard. I didn't want to use my real name. "Sonny Rose."

"Welcome to All Saints, Mr Rose."

I cringed at my improvised alias.

After the door closed, the hush of the building settled over us. We walked along the communion rail. The priest genuflected. I did the same, not wanting to give offense or rouse any suspicions about my visit. The thickly sweet perfume of roses surrounded us.

I never liked the fragrance of roses. It made me feel vaguely sick.

"Please set those in front of the altar. Now, what can I do for you, Mr Rose?"

"I'm a friend of Courtland Dunphy's, a fellow artist. I wonder if you have Court's address on file. A problem's come up. Having his address would help me solve it."

"You don't know where your friend lived?" The priest poked at the roses, drawing out a bruised bud before stepping back to recheck their appearance. The nave of the church was dim and shadowy behind us. To our right, votive candles burned in a cast iron stand holding tiers of red glasses below a radiant gold crucifix. Scents of damp stone, lemon-oil wood polish, and frankincense lingered. I stepped aside to give the priest a little more room, and my heel stuck in a puddle of wax drippings that had dried on the marble floor. I lifted my shoe while I deposited a few coins into the votive stand offering box. I took a taper and touched it to one of the votives and then moved my flame to one of the unlit candles.

Bowing my head, I offered a silent prayer. *Let this man give me what I want.*

The good father waited for me to finish.

"We'd meet up for coffee and pie," I said. "At a diner. I never visited his apartment."

"But you knew he lived in an apartment?"

"He talked about it. Complained it was small, you know? Artistic commiseration." I was about to blow out the taper, when I noticed the wax drippings on the floor had been spilled in a definite pattern.

A three-pronged fork.

Beside it was another drawing. This one showed a spiked crown, formed by a cluster of wavy-bladed bayonets. A star symbol hung over them both. The star was flying through space, trailing a row of diminishing dots behind the tip of its long, daggered tail.

The pictographs were not the accidental result of spillage, but an intricately fashioned tableau. In the devotional area, the church marble tiles were rusty reddish-hued. So the drawings seemed to boil out of them like hallucinogenic mirages spawned in a scorched desert wasteland. It required an extraordinary amount of self-control for me not to gasp aloud.

My head was spinning. My vision zeroed down to a small, claustrophobic aperture.

"Courtland never struck me as much of a complainer. He told me his place was rather roomy for one person, as I recall."

His unexpected recollection jolted me. I tried to remain outwardly impassive.

The priest blinked at me like a storybook owl over his reading glasses. Plenty of patience this priest had. I suppose it came with the job.

"Ahh… well… you caught me, Father. Maybe I was the one complaining to him."

"Are you feeling unwell, Mr Rose?" he asked.

I shook my head to clear it. But that only made the sudden dizziness worse. The church seemed to be resting on a giant gimbal, where it commenced rotating and tilting like a stomach-flipping carnival ride. I wiped nervous sweat from my forehead and hoped the priest wouldn't notice my unease. Lowering the taper once more, I confirmed the shape of the wax design. "A bit dizzy maybe. The smell of flowers gets to me sometimes. I'll be fine."

"Are you sure?" Father Mike asked.

I gave a small affirmative nod.

He walked away and found a watering can in a closet behind the altar. He started watering the plants, in no hurry.

"You were the one who found him. Is that right, Father?"

I dropped my head and chipped my heel at the wax, hoping I was being subtle enough not to draw the priest's attention to what I was doing. My leg tingled, all pins and needles.

"I was. Unfortunately, his soul was gone. By the time I got to him he was ice cold." He picked a few brown leaves off the altar cloth and put them in his pocket. "Feeling better?"

"What do you think happened? Up there." I pointed to the rafters above us.

My head was clearing; the room steadied. I'm fine if I don't look down, I thought.

The priest stared at me.

It was my turn to be patient.

He rubbed his chin. "Rainy that day. But the roof is flat where Court was. The rain had stopped, too. He shouldn't have fallen. I was in the church when it happened. All those windows were open. Yet I never heard him scream. Can you believe it? You'd think a falling man seeing the ground coming up at him would cry out. His scream would be involuntary. Court broke his neck when he hit. Died instantly, they told me. I can't explain it."

"Me neither." But what if seeing a strange sign made Dunphy as dizzy as I was a moment ago? What if an invisible force drove him out onto the ledge? Red light streamed through the stained-glass windows. The ruddy beams flooded down into the church pews. "The landlord is selling off Court's things to pay the missed rent. He didn't have any family."

"An orphan," the priest said. "Court shared the tale of his lonely childhood with me."

Orphan? That was news I hadn't read. The inside of my mouth tasted sour. It was difficult to swallow. Poor Dunphy. Even more tragic than I thought. What exactly had he gotten when he won that contest and came to Arkham? His luck changed from bad to worse.

"As a fellow artist, I want to make sure he isn't forgotten.

Maybe we can exhibit his works. Give him one last show." I had told white lies. I'm sure lying to a priest carries extra penalties if anyone upstairs is keeping score. But what I said was partially true. I *didn't* want Dunphy forgotten. Maybe he'd never get a final gallery show. But if his death was a crime, he deserved justice. My body started quaking. What was going on with me? My throat jerked like I was about to cry. But these spasms weren't from emotion. I checked my boots. My heel was caked with that damned white wax. I couldn't wait to get it off me.

"Nobody deserves what Court got," I said. My lips were twitching.

Smiling kindly, the priest stepped toward me, grasping my shoulder. The man felt sorry for me. Maybe he thought I needed saving. Maybe he was right.

"Sonny, I'm glad to hear that. Let's go to my office. I'll look up the address."

At Schoffner's General Store, I bought a bottle of ginger beer to quench my thirst. I was on the correct street, but it was hard to find any numbers marking the shabby houses and empty storefronts. The evening sky dimmed to plums and oranges, and as the sun set, the wind promised to turn knifing cold.

Rivertown.

Dirty red bricks and the cold, oily shimmer of the water flowing below.

I blew on my hands to warm them.

There was a man on the sidewalk tending a small charcoal grill, roasting chestnuts. I bought a bag. Too hot to eat. I peeled their skins and watch the steam. The man wore fingerless gloves, and three of his fingers were missing. He had an eyepatch and a pucker of scar tissue high on his cheek. He bent to retrieve more chestnuts from a bag he stored inside a child's red wagon. His movements were stiff, as if his joints needed lubricant. He wasn't old. Maybe he'd have been a class or two ahead of me had we gone to the same school.

"Sell many chestnuts?"

"I do better at the holidays. Around Merchant is always hoppin'. It pays to start early." He scored the chestnuts with a paring knife, testing the heat of the coals against his knuckles before adding the nuts to the fire. Using a long spoon, he stirred them on the grill.

I didn't see anybody else on the street. Where did his customers come from?

"How's business by the river?"

"This place is as decent as any, except for where the nicer shops are. But the cops chase away street peddlers like me. I can get into the Merchant District closer to Christmas. Some of them blue boys are all right. Couple of those fellas know me. We fought the Huns at the Marne."

That explained his old injuries. He'd been to the war and lost years and blood there. I was lucky I hadn't joined the navy with Preston. Our bodies were still young and whole.

"I'm Alden," I said, holding out my hand.

"Christophe," he said.

And we shook.

"You move to the neighborhood recently?" Christophe asked.

"What makes you think that?"

"On account of you're a painter by the looks of those splotches on your pantlegs. But you got money for a nice wool coat and polished boots, so you're not a housepainter. You're an artist. Other artists live around here. Never seen you before, so you must be new. How am I doing?"

"Right on target."

He nodded. "I thought so. Just 'cause I got one eye don't make me blind."

I guessed my coverup wasn't enough to fool the observant chestnut man. That had me wondering what else the vendor might be noticing while no one paid attention to him.

"Anything strange ever happen here?"

He eyed me cautiously, as if he thought I might be attempting a joke and failing miserably. "Depends what you mean by *strange*. Arkham's no stranger to strangeness, is it?"

"Can't argue with you there. I grew up on French Hill."

"Ah, French Hill hides her oddities better than the rest," Christophe said. "The Colony wears her peculiars like a badge of honor. She's proud home to an assortment of human curiosities. All shapes and sizes. They grow wild on the riverbanks. Boy, they sure do."

I frowned. "What's the Colony?"

"You're standing in front of it. The big building behind you, that old Georgian mansion. It was abandoned for a decade. A real rathole. About a year ago, they converted it to apartments. Must be fifty people living there. Those fixed-up houses next door? They're part of it too. The whole block got a fresh coat of paint. It's an art commune they call New Colony. Or just 'the Colony' for short. They're inspiring each another, I hear. Hell, some nights they sound like they're inspiring themselves pretty good. They live together, eat together. Do everything together, if you catch my drift." He shook his head wistfully.

I did catch it. The chestnuts were popping open, turning black from the fire.

"You ever see a tall woman with dark hair and eyes? High class and knows it?"

"Can't say I have. Must be a remarkable lady."

"Her name is Nina."

"I don't know their names. I only sell chestnuts to them."

"It was a longshot. Thanks anyway. Somebody's bound to know her if I knock on enough doors. She lived across the hall from this sculptor, Dunphy–"

"Maybe Calvin knows her. Hey, Calvin!"

The chestnut seller was motioning to a light-skinned black man walking on the other side of the street. He had short hair and no hat. His canvas jacket was too light for the weather, and his hands were stuffed deeply into the pockets of his faded dungarees. He hesitated to cross the street at first. It was obvious that the reason for his hesitation wasn't Christophe. It was me.

But he came across.

"I thought you don't know names," I said to the street vendor as the man approached.

"I know Calvin. You don't need to worry about him."

"Who said I was worrying?"

Christophe cackled.

"Boy, you been worrying ever since you walked into Rivertown."

Calvin ambled up, and Christophe passed him a bag of chestnuts, free of charge. I watched as Calvin scanned up and down the street. The rumble of a large engine and the grinding of gears resonated behind us. He tensed as if he was preparing to bolt. Around the corner, out of the dark between streetlights, a boxy, dirty white seafood truck emerged. He watched until it passed. His feet were never still, and his eyes moved constantly, but the rest of him stayed poised like a middleweight boxer, ready to duck or throw a punch. I wondered what had him so jumpy.

"Calvin, right?"

I held out for a handshake. But the man just looked at me, terrified.

"How do you know my name?" He flexed his shoulders.

"Easy, Calvin. He heard me calling you. That's all," Christophe said.

"You never said my last name," Calvin said. "How do you know me, stranger?"

His free hand went into his pocket. He had a knife or gun hiding in there, and I had no interest in finding out which, or in seeing if he knew how to use them.

"Last name? I never said anything about a last name." Then I put it together. "Oh, your last name is Wright. Like the flying brothers? That was a coincidence. But if it makes you feel better, I'll tell you my name. I'm Alden Oakes. I live up on French Hill. I'm looking for somebody. A woman who lives around here, I think. Now, her name's Nina Tarrington."

I opened my coat and found my cigarette case. Calvin's hand stayed hidden. I put a smoke between my lips and lit it, no real hurry, hoping my fingers didn't twitch too much. Then I offered the case to Christophe and Calvin. They decided to join me. We stood there smoking. The tension ran off like juice out of a steak when you cut it. I didn't want to think about cutting meat and oozing blood, so I kept on talking. Calvin didn't trust me, and I wasn't sure if I could trust him. But I asked anyway. "You ever heard of this Nina?"

"No."

"How about Courtland Dunphy? He was a sculptor who was working on the new gargoyle at South Church. Is this the address for that building over there?" I showed him the scrap of notebook paper where Father Mike had written Dunphy's street number.

I didn't have to wait for an answer, because I could tell by the way Calvin tucked his chin and shifted that he did know Dunphy. He knew he was dead, too. Because Calvin's face turned as gray as the ash on the end of the coffin nail drooping over his lower lip.

"Yes, I knew Court." His gaze broke away quickly, not wanting to lock eyes.

"That's swell. The lady I'm looking for lives across the hall from him."

He pointed at the Georgian mansion. "Third floor."

"The Colony, see?" Christophe said. "Your lady must be an artist too."

"She's a writer," I said. "So, maybe."

"Calvin here is an artist's model. Aren't you, Cal? That handsome mug of yours." The vendor laughed and struck a pose. "He's always finding one job or another to keep the wolf from the door."

"Is that right? And you live in the Colony?" I asked.

Calvin shook his head. "I stay there sometimes. But I work down on the docks. I load the Burdon's Fishery trucks with the daily catch. Started there this summer."

"That's why you smell like a mermaid!" Christophe pinched his nose. "Whee-ew!"

"There are mermen swimming in the sea too," Calvin retorted, cracking a smile and tossing a hot chestnut at the street vendor. "What do you smell like, Chris? A hobo's campfire?"

I said a quick goodbye and left them standing there, two men joking with each other.

But as I opened the front door to New Colony, I glanced back. Calvin Wright was staring at me, hard. His sunken, dead eyes holding their connection with mine longer than they had during our conversation, and I felt the full weight of his fear. I wasn't sure what had him scared. But whatever it was must've been awfully close.

Because I felt the fear crawl inside me until it became my own.

CHAPTER THIRTEEN

My first impression of the Colony was that it needed better lighting. The hallways were gloomy. The carpeting suggested a dusty aubergine. Ornate wallpaper intimated a floral trellis. But a second glimpse told me no, there were no flowers here, only the serpentine motif of a writhing, tubular organism that threatened to squirm off the wall if I glanced away for an eye-blink. Outside, one saw three symmetrical stories of red brick and a slate roof. Each floor had seven windows, except the first which traded its middle window for a door crowned by a triangular pediment. Two chimneys topped the roof at either end like rooks on a chessboard. Inside, I expected to see a well-lit space, but partitioning of the apartments had created a maze of cramped passages instead, chopping up the common areas into smaller morsels. It was twilight. But indoors, night had already fallen. The windows appeared thicker than normal. Light seemed to have difficulty passing through. Luminous pendant globes dangled from the ceiling, emitting auras the color of cod liver oil. Come to think of it, an unctuous fishy essence permeated the old mansion. Stationed on the banks of the Miskatonic, perhaps it had an earlier life as a fish house. I went up to the third floor, looking for Nina's door.

She lived at the end of the hallway. Before knocking, I turned to inspect Courtland Dunphy's door. Paneled golden oak. In every way it mirrored Nina's. I tried the doorknob.

Unsurprisingly, it was locked.

From behind me came a loud click and a whoosh of fresh air.

"Oooh!" a voice cried, startled.

I spun on my heels.

"Alden!" Nina said. "What are you doing here?"

"Finding you. How's that for amateur sleuthing?"

She leaned out in the hall checking to see if we were alone.

"Come inside." She ushered me into her apartment. Shut the door, locked it. Beneath a Mackinaw coat, she was dressed in men's tweed knickers, thick argyle socks, and a pair of dark oxfords. She'd tucked her hair under a newsboy cap, a cashmere scarf draped around her neck. From a distance, I'd have taken her for a college man. Up close, she was Nina.

"Heading out for a stroll?"

She ignored my question. "How do you know where I live?"

"I told you, I was sleuthing. I needed to see you. A lot has happened since we parted."

"Did the police make an arrest for the murder?"

"No. There were no police, because there was no body. And I know whose body it was. An old college friend of mine named Clark. Clark's body disappeared."

Nina looked astonished. "Disappeared? That's impossible."

I wandered deeper into her apartment. In one corner she'd arranged a comfy reading nook: Chesterfield club chair, torchiere lamp, and a carved mahogany belly dancer balancing a pebbled amber glass ashtray on her head. I sat in the armchair. "I thought so too. But when Preston, Minnie, and I returned to the scene, we observed no signs of a homicide."

"This is a most strange development, Alden." She began to pace about the room.

She unbuttoned her Mackinaw coat. I thumped the chair for her to sit next to me.

"What's also strange is that Preston told me you weren't even at the party."

She squeezed in snugly beside me.

"Oh, did he?"

"He swore to it. Hadn't seen you in ages, or so he claimed."

A bitter smile crossed her face. "Preston would say that. Let me guess. Minnie was there when you said this to him?"

"She was," I confirmed.

"Preston's no fool. He wasn't about to start an argument with his fiancée over me."

"Minnie said she didn't recognize you, even though we talked to her at the bonfire."

Nina pursed her lips. "Minnie and I have never met. I only know what she looks like because I observed her once, leaving Preston's house at a late hour. *She* was the one leaving."

"You were doing what…? Loitering outside?"

She ground her hip against mine. "I happened to be in the neighborhood. Walking."

"Hmm. You did say Arkham's a small town. Are you going for a walk now?"

"Yes."

"Where?"

"Out." She left it at that.

"Acting cagey, are we?" I tried to make it sound light, yet I was terribly curious. When I'd taken my last walk, it hadn't exactly turned out well. I was worried about Nina.

Her spine grew rigid as she sat up. "I don't have to tell you anything."

"Now you sound like you're talking to a policeman." Did she not trust me?

"Well, you're being nosy like one. If you must know, I was heading over to the observatory to investigate. I left in a hurry last night. Remember? Daylight feels safer."

So that's why she was dressed up like a Miskatonic U student. I had a fresher location in mind. "It happens that real monsters were out roaming after hours. I found one lumbering down at the docks. Not too far from here, in fact." I waited for her reaction.

She twisted, staring at me. Intrigued. "You are being too mysterious. Spill the beans."

"I was followed last night. Stalked. The thing that stalked me has invaded my brain. I can think of little else. I'm not sure if it was an elaborate collegiate prank or if I dreamed it up in a drunken haze. But I've spent all day painting the impossible thing I saw."

"What do you mean 'impossible thing'?"

I told her about what had stumbled toward me on that overpass in the dark. The rats and the net blob. Sentient fog rolling off the river. I left out none of the weird aspects. To my relief, she didn't laugh at me or question my grip on sanity.

She simply listened.

Her face provided no hint at what she was thinking. Nina is a modern woman, I told myself. A Bostonian. Educated and independent. That means she believes in reason. But I wasn't sounding very reasonable right now, was I? At the party, I'd been worried for a moment that she was too eccentric for me. Now I was concerned that I might be the overly imaginative one. A painter who sees visions of fishing gear dancing in the moonlight! When I finished relating my fantastic tale, would she ask me to leave and never return? With some trepidation, I reached into the pocket of my overcoat, removing a folded sheet of newsprint. "This is a sketch of the thing I confronted last night. I have a painting of it at home I'd love to show you, but this is the… the substance of it… its hideousness… Words fail me, but here's what I saw."

She took the paper carefully by the edges as if it were an ancient scroll she needed to decipher. Her mouth falling open in astonishment as she studied the portrait. Quietly, she handed the drawing back to me, walked to the door and opened it wide.

I stood. "Look, I know how crazy this sounds. But you were with me at the observatory. You told me about the bizarre events occurring in Arkham. Those unexplained disappearances and deaths… then we found evidence of a ritualistic murder! I hoped if anyone would believe me about the bridge, it would be you. I guess I was wrong."

Her head tilted as she watched me, a look of puzzlement, but she said nothing.

I stepped toward the open doorway. "I'll be going now."

"You mean *we* will be going." She sounded rather firm on the topic.

"We?" It was frustrating enough to feel scoffed at. I didn't need to be flummoxed too.

Now Nina did laugh. She touched my arm. "Oh Alden, I'm not asking you to go. I believe you. Don't you see? There might be a connection between the chimera you met on the bridge, Clark's missing body, and the crimes I'm researching. At least, I'm eager to find out if there is. I trust you feel the same way?" She raised her eyebrows, awaiting my answer.

"I do," I said.

I don't know which was greater, my relief or my determination to forge ahead.

"To the river!" she cried.

"The river!" I rejoined. How could any two people be so invigorated by strange and dark occurrences? Yet here we were, and out the door we went.

But we didn't get very far.

Before we'd reached the stairs at the end of the hall, Nina stopped, glancing over her shoulder. Something was tugging at her curiosity. "What's the matter?" I asked.

"I was thinking about Court's apartment," she said.

"What about it?"

"Do you want to look inside?" She raised her eyebrows and plucked at a loose thread on her Mackinaw's belt. "Maybe there's a clue that will help us."

"You haven't explored the premises already?"

"Until now I lacked the nerve."

"I find that hard to believe."

"We aren't always as bold as we intend to be," she said.

"Fair enough. But the door's locked. I tried it when I came up."

"Locked doesn't mean impossible." Nina reached into her right argyle sock and pulled out what looked like a handle made of animal horn. She touched a brass button and a very long slender blade shot forth. "It's a Frosolone stiletto I purchased in

Rome. Useful for a lady who walks alone and goes places others say she shouldn't. I can open doors with it." Nina dashed back down the hall to the Court's door. "Keep watch. I'll be inside in a jiffy."

I blocked the line of vision for anyone coming up the stairs.

"Are you sure you're not a criminal?" I asked.

Nina inserted the point of the stiletto between the door and the frame. She slid it down until she found the bolt. The tip of her tongue poked out of her mouth while she deftly worked the blade around. "Think I've got it."

I heard the bolt spring back into the doorjamb. "You're secretly a cat burglar, aren't you? Stealing precious diamonds around the globe while the good citizens sleep."

Nina smiled as she twisted the doorknob. "Beginner's luck." She retracted her switchblade and slipped it back into her sock without looking. "Shall we?"

I made one last check of the hall for witnesses. Nothing. All was quiet. "This part I *know* is against the law."

"We are working for a higher purpose," she insisted. "Do you think the Arkham police really care about Court's death? Will they do anything to solve it?"

"I suppose not."

"There, you see! We're better suited for the job. And we care."

I followed her into Dunphy's vacant rooms. Instinctively, I reached for the lights.

"Leave them off." She covered the switch. Her hand was hot and as soft as a velvet glove. "What if someone sees the glow under the door? Or a cop walking by notices the window and remembers this unit isn't occupied any more. Pull the curtains, let the moon in."

I did as she said. I tugged the curtains aside. It was a clear night. The moon was a jack o' lantern starting to rot. Stars, like seeds, sprayed in the sky. New Colony's backyard had a nice view of the Miskatonic. Across the water, I saw the railroad tracks. The headlamp of an oncoming train swelling, irradiating the ditch weeds and mud, the sluggish river. The train whistle shrieked.

Even though I saw no one, I backed away, trying to stay out of sight.

"Alden, take a look at this."

I followed Nina's hushed voice behind a lacquered Chinese screen covered with dragons. I jumped. Nerves jolted and tingling. We weren't alone. Hairs raised on my arms. My temples were pounding like a headache.

Nina kneeled on the floor of what was clearly Courtland Dunphy's studio space.

I smelled clay and saw newspapers covering the hardwood boards. Two crates filled with rags and sculpting tools set against the wall.

What had me frightened was a short naked man crouched on a pedestal behind Nina.

He had wings.

Moonlight sliced the studio in half. Nina and the man occupied the center, in and out of the shadows. Neither of them moved. Two cone-shaped horns curved up out of the man's forehead. His skin was pale gray-green.

"I know him," I said.

Nina swiveled toward me. The edge of her cap masked her eyes.

The naked man stared blankly ahead.

"I met him outside of Schoffner's. His name is Calvin Wright. He told me where Court lived." I walked over to the clay statue to inspect it closely.

Dunphy was a talented sculptor.

"It is a smaller version of Cal! He modeled for Court," Nina said. "They worked on the South Church gargoyle. But this can't be the church's replacement, they need stone."

I touched the surface of the clay, admiring the smooth curves and muscular lines. "This is a full-scale model. The final limestone block would've been too heavy to keep in the apartment. Court must've rented another place for his carving." I noticed a second, much larger – but empty – pedestal beside the Calvin gargoyle. "I wonder what was standing here. It's been removed, obviously." There was a stained canvas tarp bunched on the floor. I picked it up and spread my arms. "Big, whatever it was. Dunphy kept it covered. Guess he didn't like what he saw of his other work-in-progress. Did he ever mention working on a side job?"

"No." Nina was opening and closing drawers. She went exploring in Court's spartan bedroom. A neatly made bed and a night table. Against the wall, a bookcase filled with weeksold *Arkham Advertisers* and a Gideons' bible. There was a closet. She struck a match and poked her head inside. She blew out the match before it burned her fingers. She rummaged through the hanging clothes. I heard a jingle. "I found Court's keys," she called out.

Nina backed out into the bedroom.

I pointed to the night table. "What's that?"

She struck another match. Finding a stout black candle, she lit it. Its warm bloom revealed a carving on the tabletop. Only the outermost edges of the design remained visible, a few tantalizingly suggestive dashes and sinewy curlicues bordering on the arabesque; the rest had been gouged completely away. Deep furrows clawed into the table. Blond woodchips littered the floor next to the bed.

"Look! It says something on the wall," Nina said. She picked up the candle and moved it over the pillow on the bed, revealing a square block of letters chiseled into the plaster above the spot where Court would've laid his head each night.

MONSTER

DREAMER

NO MORE

Around the letters was the outline of a house with two chimneys, like rooks on a chessboard. "It's New Colony," I said, feeling myself getting excited. "One letter to represent each of the windows. The blank space is the front door." I lifted the pillow. Underneath I found a chisel. I hefted the tool. "Makes a nice weapon. I wonder why Dunphy thought he needed it."

"Who was he afraid of?" Nina said.

"Or maybe we should ask *what*." I flashed to the rats inside the net, lurching toward me. "Maybe monsters haunted his dreams. Those words might be a kind of protection. Warding off the creatures that chased him when he slept. '*No more…*'"

"Do you hear that scratching?"

I listened.

Faintly, I *did* hear something. Scrape-scraping without rhythm. It continued on. Not a dog or cat caught behind a door. Nothing frantic about it. Measured, deliberate strokes. "It isn't in this room. Is it coming from outside?"

We cocked our heads to listen.

A loud crash exploded in the other room. The sound of glass breaking...

I already had the chisel in my hand. Nina pulled out her stiletto.

We ran into the studio.

"Where's the statue?" I asked.

"It's gone."

"How can that be? The thing was made of clay. It was heavy."

Sure enough, we had heard glass breaking. The window was smashed... outward. No pieces on the floor. Something had gone outside. Whatever it was had been in here with us. My hand was sweaty on the chisel. Heart hammering. I looked down into the back lot. Shards of glass sparkled on the grass.

Nina gripped my elbow. "There! Across the river. On the tracks!"

The gargoyle crouched, looking right at us. Its eyes glowed red-hot in the washed-out moonlight. It raised its hand slowly, waving steely claws in our direction.

"It can't be! It... just... can't be real. Impossible." I felt a rumble in the floor.

A Maine freight loaded with lumber was barreling down the tracks.

"The train's headed right for him," she said. "It'll hit Calvin!"

"Whatever that winged fiend is, it's not Calvin... not even human."

How could we look away?

We couldn't.

A second before the engine made mincemeat of that gray-green monster, the gargoyle pumped its powerful wings and flew up to the smokestack. Grabbing hold, it flattened its body – a streamlined demon – and crawled on its belly over the hot-as-Hell boiler, the sandbox, and the steam dome. When it got to the cab roof, it spun around, sitting up. The gargoyle threw its head back. Although we couldn't hear it, I knew it was laughing at us, whooping madly as it rode the southbound like a bronco-busting cowboy out of Arkham.

CHAPTER FOURTEEN

After we watched the gargoyle disappear, we stayed there by the shattered window, not thinking any more about who might be seeing us. Not thinking, period. I knew we were in shock; numbness filling up our bodies like sand, weighing us down, making us move slowly, think slowly. I couldn't believe what I'd witnessed. Yes, I'd seen the net blob come to life and harass me on the bridge, maybe it even planned to swallow me up like it did to those greasy river rats.

But this encounter felt different.

It was much worse.

Maybe because I couldn't doubt it. I didn't have the luxury, if that doesn't sound too funny. Because we were both there together, Nina and me.

And the two of us couldn't be crazy.

"That really happened. Didn't it?" she asked, not in a whisper, forcing her voice to sound firm. Nina was taller than I am by a good two inches. She had an athlete's confident posture. Her physical strength was never in question, but this was not a purely physical threat we had confronted. Our reality was under attack.

"Yes, it did. I don't understand how, or why. But it happened as surely as I'm still standing here with you. We're in a rehabilitated Georgian mansion on the banks of the smelly old Miskatonic River in Arkham, Massachusetts. My family's lived around this moldy old town since before the Revolutionary War. I was born here. Tonight, the moon is putrid but it's still shining. Not a cloud in the sky… and we're both real. We are here."

"I'm shaking. Can you feel me?"

I hugged her tightly. Our hearts thundered. "I feel you as surely as I've felt anything."

"You're shaking too, Alden. So this is no dream."

Not a nightmare. Reality. Our solid flesh was proof of that fact. Knowing this didn't make things better. Dreams are something that end; you wake up and they're finished.

Yet, even abject terror in the face of monsters reaches a lull over time. You manage somehow to get past it. The panic fades to background terror, a jumpiness. But it's no less a threat once it gets behind you than it was when you faced it head-on. The lingering sense of the monstrous becomes worse than its actual presence. It surrounds you, and fills you with an inescapable pressure that builds and wrecks you inside and out. It's personal, an invisible invader who might manifest at any moment. Expectation of evil is your new sickness. The worrying eats at you like acid. You and the monster become one thing, and that feels like the dirtiest trick of them all.

We were only beginning to learn this lesson in fear. We weren't experts.

Not yet.

Her arms, my arms, loosened our holds on one another. We spoke in gentle looks until we found the power of language again. We breathed. The shaking subsided. From outside the broken window came the soft hoot of a screech owl. The grumbling motor of a fishing boat headed out for a night's catch. Cars passing. The chuckle of the river flowing over rock bars. In the distance, a dog howled.

"Why didn't it attack us? Why are we alive?" she asked me.

"I don't know," I said. "We should get out of here."

Nina fixed her cap on her head. "One more look around before we go. This might be the only room in Arkham we know of that has monsters."

We scoured Dunphy's apartment. This time with the lights on. It was when we were leaving that we found the message. It couldn't have been more obvious.

The gargoyle had scratched it on the inside of the door so we wouldn't miss it.

CALvin RiTe
NinA TArrinGTon ALL Den Oaks
WiLL Die by the HAnd of the ONe who CALLs the
FALLing sTAr Thru The GATe
TwsTer of The CoiL
The Un-Sun
yoOYUVABDAA

"He isn't much of a speller, is he?" I said, joking to hold my fear at bay.

"Except for that gibberish at the end, he gets his point across."

Below the words was a series of symbols which were becoming familiar to me. Part of me was happy to see them. They helped to pull the pieces together. Figures I remembered from the Mediterranean coast. Wax drippings on a church floor. Now this.

"What are you doing?" Nina sounded as edgy as I felt.

"Looking for paper," I said.

Inside a drawer I found a sketch pad and a charcoal stick. I tore off a couple of sheets and held them up on top of the etched symbols. "Help me. Here."

"What should I do?"

"Press the corners down. I'm making a rubbing. I've seen these signs before."

I passed the stick over the newsprint. Symbols began showing up on the page like a secret message. "This one's a fork with three prongs. I've seen it the most. Then there's a spiked crown. Not always the same when it shows up but close enough. Here's a shooting star. That's new. But I saw it earlier today. This last one looks like the letter U balanced on a triangle. Maybe it's a cup? With two ovals inside. That's the one I saw when all this started."

"Where did you see these signs?"

"At South Church. In wax spread on the church tiles. I think they might spell out a kind of curse or something. When I looked at them, I felt funny in my head, like I might faint." I was almost finished with my copying. "Tear me off another sheet, would you, please?"

"Do you think someone used them on Court? To make him fall?"

"They might've. I wouldn't have wanted to feel disoriented on the roof. It reminds me of a festival I visited in Spain. Oddest thing I ever attended. The principal player wore a spiked crown. These forks were present too, carried around a bonfire circle by little goblins. People *dressed* as goblins, I assumed. Strange fiesta.

Pagan. Very ritualistic. They burned effigies in a mock sacrifice. Massively unsettling. Boundaries were crossed. It left me feeling strange for days." I saw him again, the tall man in the full head mask. The crowd chanting. Then I saw Balthazarr in another crowd, sitting in the front row at the Houdini show. Was that really him, there and backstage? Why was I thinking about Juan Hugo Balthazarr now?

"Ritual sacrifices!" Nina drew me back into the moment. "That *is* creepy."

"Careful. I want proof that we can show to an expert when the time comes."

"Who's an expert on this?"

I shrugged. "I don't know. Perhaps we can find out."

I completed the last of the rubbings.

"Alden, I'm frightened. Human killers are one thing. Supernatural monsters take things to another level entirely. That gargoyle isn't supposed to exist. Should we stop?"

I checked the copies I'd made to see if they were legible. "Look, I'm scared too. It would be insane not to be. I thought you wanted to look for the net blob. To discover any connections to those unexplained deaths. But if you say you want to quit-"

"I'm not saying 'quit.' Only let's think things through. After the gargoyle... reading this message... I don't know if I want to know more. What are we getting ourselves into?"

"I haven't the foggiest. But we have to keep going, Nina."

"Why?"

"Because the first time I saw these symbols was on the beach at Cannes. Preston drew two of them in the sand with his foot." Saying that out loud felt peculiar. A kind of betrayal.

But who, or what, had I betrayed? Balthazarr leaped into my

mind again. I saw images floating in the air of Dunphy's room. Mirages of infamous Balthazarr paintings. Fantastical creatures. Physics-defying acts. The world tearing itself apart, melting and shredding. Provocative. Unnerving. To live in that man's mind had to be a cosmic adventure. The images faded. I hadn't really seen them. They'd come from my memories of his paintings. My stressed brain projected them in the air like shadow figures on a wall.

Nina shook her head. "You sound utterly mad. What's Preston got to do with this?"

Preston. I shook off my fuzzy thoughts. "I don't know how he fits. But he must. Maybe it's like automatic writing. Turn the mind off and let the body draw. He didn't realize what he was doing. It originated in his unconscious. Maybe he'd seen them somewhere. They obviously made an impression. I plan to ask him. Tell me something. What is the Colony?"

Nina frowned, puzzled. "It's an artistic collective. This is the Colony's home."

"A commune? Like Barbizon, or Byrdcliffe in New York?" Why was a gargoyle statue coming to life here? Dunphy was an artist. Isn't bringing art to life what artists do? It felt like I'd taken hold of a string. But I couldn't see what was on the other end of it yet.

"I suppose it's the same idea. A special place for creativity. What are you getting at?"

I wasn't quite sure myself. But I kept pulling on that string. "Why do you live here, Nina? Where do you fit into the picture? Who invited you to the bohemian village?"

I saw the anger flare in her. The muscles of her jaw pulled taut. Her eyes narrowed.

"I applied. I'm as much of an artist as anyone here. As much as you, too."

"You're not a novelist, playwright, or a poet. You don't write for a newspaper. Who's familiar with your work? Who sent you the invitation?"

Nina reined in her anger and thought back. "I received a letter from the Colony Board of Judges. They said I'd been recommended." The weirdness of it struck her for the first time.

"Who recommended you?"

She walked to the shattered window. Looking out at the night. Seeing her reflection. "They never told me. Recommendations are kept confidential from the applicants, they said. I'm writing a study of crime in Arkham. Chronicling Arkham's social decay. I've had a few excerpts published as articles in journals. I figured someone influential read one of them and liked it. I want to write a book. That's what I've been doing here since I arrived. It's my project."

"What better way to keep an eye on you and your project than to bring you close, where they could watch you. I'm not threatened by you, Nina. But who is?"

She brushed her fingers along the broken glass hanging in the window. "What you said about Preston a minute ago, did you mean it? Do you think he's involved in this madness, these events?"

"I can't say. But he knows more than he's admitted. He's acting bizarrely. At first, I thought he was spooked by the upcoming wedding. But I think it's more than that. Something is eating at him. He wants to tell me, but he doesn't know how."

"Preston was the one who got me in here," she said, defeated. "I'm sure of it."

"What do you mean?"

"When I applied to join New Colony, he greased the skids. He made certain my application was approved." She jerked away from the glass. She'd cut herself. A drop of blood welled up. She popped her injured finger between her lips.

The light in the apartment felt too harsh. The shadows, too dark.

I was lost. I felt as if I'd been rolled down a hill in a barrel. What was she saying? Which way was up? Preston and New Colony? I didn't follow her implications.

"What does Preston have to do with whether you're Colony-approved?"

"It's his money that paid for it. Or his father's, to be more precise. Fairmont Senior. Along with someone named Carl Sanford. They bought this block and transformed it. They're behind the New Colony Foundation. They decide who gets in and who doesn't. It's a confidential process, very hush-hush. Cloak and dagger stuff. The Colony Board of Judges allegedly decides, but it might be one or two people. Who really knows?"

I laughed, but the noise I made was hollow. I couldn't believe what I was hearing.

"I figured Preston never gave a damn about the arts."

Nina came closer. "If it was his idea that I move to New Colony, if he invited me, then what does that mean? I only wanted to write my book. I never questioned being here. I like it here, Alden. The people I've met don't feel weird to me. But..."

"But what?" I asked.

She gave me a look of grave recognition. The broken window gaped behind her.

"Who invited you to return to Arkham, Alden?"

I folded the rubbings and slid them into my coat pocket.

"We have to talk to Preston," I said.

Nina nodded. "First, we need to warn Calvin. According to that door, he's in as much danger as we are. The gargoyle wasn't an assassin. He was a winged messenger."

CHAPTER FIFTEEN

On the street, Calvin and Christophe were long gone. I looked back across the road at the Colony mansion. Lights glowed in the apartments. On an unseen phonograph, King Oliver and his Creole Jazz Band were playing the Dippermouth Blues. It looked so normal from the outside. Just a nice building where people lived. Except I knew it was different. These people were all artists, handpicked by a mystery cabal. Monsters appeared in their midst. Perhaps I was being overdramatic.

I regarded Nina. "Why would Preston's father sponsor an art commune?"

"Don't know," she said. "He never discussed art while we were together."

"I feel like we have some of the pieces, but we aren't putting them together in the right order. There's no money to be made at the Colony?"

She shrugged. "If an artist sells anything, they keep the cash. It's basically a charity."

Our steps carried us along River Street toward the docks. Soon we'd pass the Unvisited Isle, winding up on the West Street bridge, where I'd had my supernatural encounter. Ramshackle private residences yielded to warehouses and vacant lots. Fences and padlocks. Garbage dumped where no one cared to look: bags of rotten onions, paper waste, a collapsing pyramid of concrete chunks. In a mud patch, a French Provincial dining set waited for guests who would never arrive, unless they were ghosts. It reminded me of ancient ruins.

"The Fairmonts might be profiting in other ways," I suggested.

"How do you mean?"

"Well, maybe it's a place to hide cash, or launder it through the foundation's finances." I wasn't sure how closely Preston monitored the family business and its lawyers.

"Now you sound like a muckraker," Nina said.

"What I'm talking about is buying influence. Making connections they couldn't forge through legitimate channels. People like the Fairmonts pursue money the way roots seek water. My mother says they're connected to everything happening in Arkham. Preston's father is a big wig at the Silver Twilight Lodge. And Carl Sanford is the biggest wig of all. My father's a member, but he never goes, as he is the crankiest curmudgeon in New England. Preston told me *his* father practically lives at the Lodge. He hounds Preston to get more involved, for the sake of their family business. Well, the Colony might be another tentacle of the Lodge reaching into the community. If they control the art scene, no one else does. They decide what's popular. They pick the hot artists in town who get all the attention. Then again, it might be the infamous vanity of Arkham's upper crust. Legacies and all that jazz. Or it might be a scheme we can't even imagine." I threw up my arms in frustration.

"A scheme for what? Taking over the world with art?"

We laughed at that idea.

"Maybe old man Fairmont doesn't want people making anything ugly associated with his fair city. Dragging down its reputation. That's something my mother always says to me. 'Alden, why don't you try painting pictures that people want to look at. Beautiful things. Things that make everyone feel happy.'"

"You don't do that now, do you?" Nina linked her arm through mine.

I thought about the paintings I had attempted in Spain. How an unnamable quality haunted their periphery, hovering just beyond the canvas, affecting every shadow and brushstroke.

"Wait until you see my net blob." Now the unnamable had moved into full view.

"Not pretty?"

I considered her question.

"Depends on your taste, I guess. If you like vampires, ghosts, and ghoulies, then you might love it. Have you seen what the Surrealists are doing? Automatism is a technique they use. You create without thinking. André Breton called it the '*Dictation of thought in the absence of all control exercised by reason and outside moral or aesthetic concerns.*' Pick up the pencil, or brush, or whatever's at hand and draw… paint… just go. No plans. No authorial censor. The Dadaists did it too. You give up control. Chance takes over. The psyche shows itself, unfiltered. They're trying to release the subconscious mind from its prison. Order brought us the war. Chaos might bring peace. I find it exciting. Much of their new work is astounding. There's this fellow from Spain, Balthazarr, who's transcendent. A truly modern explorer. Tapping the inner cosmos of human existence. Uncaging dreams, letting them run loose in the world."

She squeezed my arm. "Nightmares are dreams, aren't they? I'd rather not meet mine when I'm awake. You know mediums and Spiritualists do the same thing. Open themselves up to the spirit world. They let entities pass through. I find it eerie." She shuddered. "I don't want to know what might be lurking inside of me."

"Well, I do."

From the twist of her lip, Nina was about to say something sarcastic, when she froze.

"Is that your blob?"

She pointed with her chin to a pile of fishing nets heaped on the docks. The streetlamp shone on them like a spotlight. It was as if a danger had crawled up out of the waters by its own power and lay asleep on the warped boards. A venomous snarl of sea snakes, perhaps.

"I can't be sure if that's the blob I saw. Nets look alike. But it could be..."

"We ought to make a closer inspection." She took a few baby steps. "I can't believe how nervous I am about a stinky ball of twine." She edged up closer. But not very much.

I found a boat hook, forgotten against the warehouse wall. "I'll give it a poke."

Hesitation makes unpleasant tasks worse, so I strode up to the net and skewered it. Nothing happened. I stabbed harder, swirling the hook around for maximum damage.

"Hey, you there! What d'you think you're doing?"

It was a night watchman. He must've spotted us from his post inside the warehouse.

"What should we do?" Nina asked.

The watchman was a hulking type. He was marching right for

us. His boots boomed on the boards. He aimed a flashlight in our faces. It was a blinding slap across the eyes.

In his other hand was a baseball bat. He was snapping it around. Quick wrist snaps that would crack a bone, knock loose a few teeth. My hand went involuntarily to my jaw. I liked my bones and teeth the way they were.

"The hell you think you're doin'? This here's private property." He snapped the bat.

"Get ready," I said to Nina. I hefted the boat hook like it was a javelin.

"Ready for what?"

I threw the javelin right at the flashlight.

"Run!"

There was a clatter, a meaty thump. The flashlight rolled away, casting its beam wildly on the stained waves. Colored orbs floated in my vision, the aftereffects of the light blinding me. Out there in the dark, the angry watchman was picking himself off the boards.

"Why, you sonofa…" he began.

I didn't stick around to hear the rest. I ran for the warehouse. Nina was ahead of me. Inside the warehouse doorway, I could see the hut where the watchman spent his shift. A cup of coffee and an *Adventure* pulp magazine, his pushed-back three-legged stool. I waited to see which way Nina would dart.

Left.

She went around the corner of the facility, vanishing into the dimness between the buildings. If she was going left, I chose right for my escape plan. I hoped it would be an escape, because the watchman was going to exact his revenge on me, *if* he ever caught me. My legs pumped. Thighs burning. My overcoat flying out behind me like a cape. The watchman was puffing, chugging away at my back. Suddenly, he lunged for me – a wide hairy-knuckled mitt swiping at my flappy coattails. Luckily, he didn't grab any material.

My move knocked him off his rhythm.

I veered close to the warehouse wall zipping by my left side. He followed.

"Gaaahhh…!" He grazed his shoulder inside the siding.

A shaft of brightness ahead: Main Street. Then I saw what I needed to get away from my pursuer. I slowed down a tick. Enough for him to think I might be hesitating, deciding which way I wanted to cut when I reached the roadway. He grunted, digging down for one last charge. And as he did, I rolled off smoothly to my right.

He had no time to see the trash barrel.

He ran full force into it. Can and man becoming one thing launched into space, then smashing down on the pavement. All the air blew out of the watchman in a low groan.

Out of the corner of my left eye, I saw Nina emerging from the other side of the warehouse. I switched direction and followed her up the middle of Main Street. She geared down so I could catch her, and we turned up Garrison, not stopping until we hit the campus of Miskatonic U. We collapsed on a bench outside the library. Trying to catch our breath.

Laughing. Tears rolling down our cheeks.

She climbed right up to me and filled her hands with my overcoat lapels. We were in the middle of campus, but the campus was deserted. Library closed. No one out but us.

"He was going to kill you!" she shouted.

"But he didn't."

She kissed me.

"You're crazy," she said. "Reckless man."

"I'm not the one who carries a stiletto in my sock."

We kissed again, longer this time. I reclined on the bench and she lay beside me.

Nina propped her head on my chest.

The air steaming from our mouths.

"I don't sleep," she said.

"What?"

"I'm an insomniac. Have been since I was a girl living in Boston. That's why I always liked going out to crime scenes with my dad. Bad things always seemed to happen to unlucky people at night. He couldn't sleep much either. The house would be quiet, and I'd be awake, just hoping he'd get wind of some news. We could go and look. Find the story. Well, I can't lay around nowadays. Knowing no one's coming to get me so we can go see something sensational and exciting. So I take walks on my own. I look at the world asleep. Nighttime can be beautiful. The best time, really. Quiet, mysterious. It's when I think about solving those terrible crimes in Arkham. I've visited all the crime scenes at night. By myself."

"Maybe you can show them to me, if you like. We can visit places together."

The skin on my neck suddenly touched a cold metal part of the bench.

"You're shivering," she said.

She opened her coat and closed it around us like a pair of wings.

We stayed like that for a long time.

CHAPTER SIXTEEN

It was a few weeks later, while enjoying a scrumptious white-tablecloth breakfast, that I confronted Preston with my knowledge of his involvement with New Colony. We were dining at the Harvest, the Silver Gate Hotel's finest restaurant. This was the first time I'd ever visited the hotel. In terms of Arkham's historic grand hotels, there are Silver Gate people and Excelsior people. The Oakes family had always been in the Excelsior camp. I'd seen the Silver Gate many times from the outside. The institution was, and is, a fixture in the city. How amazing that we'd never crossed paths before. I'd walked past the imposing façade always destined for another location. Passing by, often admiring the fine lines and impeccable profile from the street, I felt everyone I knew had been there before me. They all possessed a charming story of some unforgettable private party or a memorable night tucked away in one of the fashionable suites. But I had never partaken, not until this breakfast meeting with Preston. He must've chosen the restaurant and made the reservation, although I'm sure Preston never had to reserve anything in this town. He simply called up and asked for what he wanted, or, more likely had someone else call and use his name like a magic key to open any door, gaining access denied to the lower strata of the acknowledged social order – Those Who Must Wait. I was happy to approve of his choice.

"You've been to New Colony?" He smiled and took a sip of his freshly squeezed grapefruit juice. "What were you doing there?"

"Visiting Nina Tarrington," I said.

He showed no extreme reaction. A twitch in his right eyebrow, perhaps, as he swallowed. Nothing more. "How is Nina? Still a night owl?"

"She is. You might've confirmed that yourself at your engagement party."

Preston nodded. He didn't remark upon his previous denial of her presence at the fête.

"What did you think of the place?" he asked.

"The Colony? It's fine, I suppose. The hallways are narrow, the rooms a bit gloomy."

"Artists do better when they suffer. Or so I've heard. My father poured a bundle into saving that relic. He wouldn't shut up about the cost of the investment he was making. It was rat-infested, the foundation cracked and so on. That whole block of land wants to slide into the Miskatonic and float out to sea. Carl Sanford was the one who found it. They fixed it and turned it over to the bohemian set for fun. So Nina told you we're involved, did she? Well, that's true. For the good of Arkham. The Fairmonts have long held up their end of the bargain as far as local charitable causes go. My father always says we've made so many sacrifices." He sliced into his steak; a little blood ran out onto the plate.

"I've never known you to care about the arts." I lifted my rye toast, pausing midair.

Preston shrugged, chewed. A server approached with refills. He waved him off.

"I don't care for the arts, truthfully. I find my entertainment elsewhere. Thirsty?"

His question surprised me. I had coffee, apple juice, and ice water on the table.

"I'm satisfied."

Preston shook his head with mock sadness. "Oh, Alden. One must never be satisfied. It will kill you faster than anything." He motioned the server over and whispered in the man's ear. The waiter nodded and exited through the swinging door that led to the kitchen. "May I ask why you were seeing Nina? You have a growing interest in her?"

"We're fond of one another. Getting back to New Colony. What goes on there?"

"Art? Who knows?" Preston dismissed the query. "I never interfere. Here we go."

The waiter reappeared with a bottle wrapped discreetly in a towel. With a practiced twist he released the cork. A curl of smoke left the bottle like a djinn. He filled two champagne flutes and placed them on the table. Then he deposited the bottle in an ice bucket, draping the towel over it. No one in the restaurant noticed we were breaking the law. Or maybe they were used to it. The right last name and a pile of cash bought certain privileges.

Preston picked up his glass.

"To never being satisfied."

I clinked and we drank.

"How's Minnie?"

Preston rolled his eyes. "She's on the warpath about the number of fondues, or maybe it's the size of the wedding cake.

Possibly both." He rotated his glass, focusing his attention on the bubbles. "I can't keep track. But she isn't happy. We're thinking of moving up the date and having the reception here at the Silver Gate. Don't ask. Nothing's in stone yet. The Silver Gate always puts out a good spread. I'll credit them that." Preston tore away the towel and refilled our glasses. He seemed tipsy. I smelled whiskey on his breath when I arrived. Perhaps Minnie was right to be worrying about his mental state. He looked drawn, his eyes ringed and sunken. Was he still awake from a marathon night of cardplaying? "Let me give you a little advice regarding Nina."

I opened my mouth to protest.

He raised his palm. "If you're happy, then I'm happy for you." Here, he made a puzzled face. "But does Nina ever worry you?"

"How so?" I wondered where this conversation was heading. It didn't matter to me what he thought of my spending time with his ex-fiancée. I was curious about his warning.

"Nina has a vivid imagination. You've learned that by now. She likes to pretend. Gets you to play along. It's intriguing at first, a fun game. But she takes things too far. She loses her perspective and can't judge where the actual world begins. If you aren't willing to follow her then she gets …" He waggled his fingers.

"She gets what?" My voice was loud. I was perturbed by his butting into our relationship with his unwanted commentary. I scraped my chair back. Several heads turned.

Preston leaned forward and whispered. "She gets *serious*. Do you know, she nearly ran me through with a sword? That girl knows her way around a blade. She's a fencer. She can throw knives, and make them stick, too. I've seen her do it."

"What's your point?" If Nina knew how to defend herself, what did he care?

"My point is that you don't want *her* point between your ribs."

He smiled. I flashed to our college days, a pair of thieves watching each other's back. My anger receded like the tide pulling back from a beach. Here I'd come to confront Preston, and instead I felt like he was challenging me, but not out of malice.

"Thanks for the information," I said. Preston was too tipsy to note my sarcasm.

He refilled his flute. "If it all works out for you, I'd be thrilled. More for you?"

"I'm good." I covered my flute. Preston was drinking enough of the bubbly for both of us. I didn't want to talk about Nina any more. I didn't want Preston talking about her. But I wasn't ready to let the topic of the Colony drop, especially because I had a favor to ask of Preston. I didn't want his guard raised too high. I had to keep things friendly to succeed.

"Nina told me you might be able to influence acceptances to New Colony."

Preston ran a finger around the rim of his glass. "I would hope so."

"I want in. Can you do that?"

He acted surprised. "I'll talk to my father. He'll see things get done. It will be a step down from Oakwood. The Colony is little more than a glorified dormitory. Ahh… wait, let me guess. It gets you closer to Nina. See, you *are* playing her games." He shook his head, baffled. "The two of you are very rich. You know that, right? You could live anywhere. Paris? New York? But if you want to play artists starving in the garret, who am I to interfere? Was this her idea?"

"It was a mutual thought we had together." But it wasn't. Nina had presented the idea to me the night before my breakfast with Preston. I agreed because it solved multiple problems. I needed a new place to live, I wanted to be closer to her, and it aided our investigations. Yet I hated that Preston seemed to know my every move before I made it. Before I could stop him, he tried to refill my glass again. Champagne overflowed, fizzing down the outside of the crystal; a spreading stain darkened the linen.

"Oops… I'll have to see what's available for rooms." He sounded like a desk clerk. "The Colony might be full up at the moment. I wouldn't know."

"It isn't. There's an apartment right across the hall from Nina. Rooms previously occupied by a sculptor named Dunphy. He died recently."

Preston didn't blink at the mention of Dunphy's name, though he upended his glass, draining it. "We all die eventually, Oakesy. Oh, that reminds me. Guess who's missing. Clark Abernathy. Isn't that a funny coincidence? You thought he was murdered. Now nobody can find him. His father told me Clark probably ran off with a dancer he'd made acquaintances with at the Clover Club, named Diamond something. But I don't think he really knows. He seemed distraught. It's not like Clark to up and vanish. I hope he isn't in serious trouble."

Clark was well past his troubles. "Where's the Clover Club?"

"Oakesy, we need to reacquaint you with Arkham's nightlife." Preston drained the last drops of champagne into his flute. "It's the only thing stimulating about this place." How quickly had he killed off the bottle? He looked greener about the gills than the glass did.

"I appreciate your efforts on my behalf." I raised an eyebrow. "Are you feeling well?"

"Me? I'm fine, just dandy. It's the least I can do for a friend."
He hiccupped.

Preston shifted his gaze to the restaurant windows. A wave of
sadness and regret passed over him. Where it originated, I could
not say, but a hallucinatory alteration took place. I watched
Preston age rapidly in front of my eyes. His brow wrinkled,
cheeks sucked in; the patch of hair on his head thinned and
grayed, before settling on cottony white wisps. He looked like the
spitting image of his father. Was this a psychic vision of my friend's
future? Appalled and astonished, I held my breath. The immense
pressures of eventually taking up the mantle of the Fairmont clan
weighed heavily on Preston. His father constantly measured him
up, trying to groom him. One day soon he'd have to live up to the
task or be ground to paste by it. Or so his old man said. Preston
bent forward as if he were about to be sick. His eyes clouded.
The rapid transformation continued until all that sat across
from me was a jumble of bones inside a withered, yellow skin
sack. Before I could fully comprehend his evolution, the process
reversed itself; Preston quickly returned to the youthful – if
exhausted – man I recognized. I rubbed my own eyes, wondering
if something was wrong with *me*, or with the champagne. Had we
been drugged? Was the alcohol contaminated with a toxin? The
illusion passed like a slow-waking dream.

Preston coughed.

"Are you sure you're in decent shape, Preston?" I was checking
myself too.

"Right as rain," he answered with a tired half-smile.

I offered him a cigarette from my gold case. We smoked in
silence, then he snapped his fingers at me and said, "There's
someone you should meet. I fetched him at the train station this

morning. He arrived after a long, arduous journey."

"Do you pick up strangers at the train station often?" I said in jest.

"Colony business, to be precise. My father suggested I play the part of welcoming committee."

"Who's the visitor in town?"

Preston pushed back his chair. "He's coming toward us right now." Preston stood and smiled, beamingly. A golden boy displaying all his breeding and charm despite his inebriation. He was motioning emphatically to someone. *Join us, come join us…*

The visitor entered the room behind me.

I turned in my chair.

Preston stepped around our table to receive his guest. Etiquette required me to stand and greet the man. He must have passed behind one of the restaurant's pillars, because I saw no one. Preston appeared dazzled; I might've been a mustachioed hussar on horseback, still he wouldn't have noticed me.

"Pres-TONE! My new friend!" An accented, unmistakably masculine voice impacted us. I felt it as much as heard it. His chic figure arrived. A gust of brisk air accompanied him.

First, I saw his outstretched hand. Long fingers, lean, a network of thick veins visible under the skin. A craftsman's hands, strong and knowledgeable. Preston's pale digits vanished inside the other's grip. He pulled Preston in close and embraced him, thumping him on the back. He was taller than us. Dressed like a raven. Hatless, brunet. He used a chrome ornamental cane. When they parted, the visitor pivoted to face me. It was like opening a high window, the danger.

"Juan Hugo, this is my old friend, Alden Oakes. Alden, meet Juan Hugo Balthazarr."

"Good to meet you, Alden." The artist bowed. His forked beard was luxuriant.

"I am honored." I could hardly breathe. Here was the living artist I most admired in the world. Standing right before me and offering his hand!

Like a blacksmith's vise, he crushed my fingers. It was all I could do not to wince.

"Alden's a painter too. Just back from Europe. He couldn't keep away from home."

"Ah, you are an Arkhamite. I am finding your city most enticing. A dark confection."

Only then did he release me from his dominating clutch.

"I hope you enjoy your visit," I said, rather pathetically. My hand was hurting. The vision of Balthazarr hurt too. He overtaxed the senses. Too vivid, too loud, too aromatic. None of these were unpleasant, but in combination the effect was an intensity unleashed upon the hapless experiencer. I'd never been awestruck until that meeting at the Harvest. If Balthazarr was excessive, he induced the countereffect of making you feel lacking. My flaws suddenly became my very essence. I wanted to run and hide. But his power of attraction prevented me from that.

"Already, my trip has proved fruitful," he said.

Everyone in the Harvest watched him. They tried and failed to look away. He demanded attention; and when you were around him, you surrendered to him gladly, paying your respects. You knew you were going to tell your grandchildren about the time you saw Balthazarr, what he did and said. The encounter scorched itself into your memory with a psychic branding iron.

"Juan Hugo is our first ever artist-in-residence at New Colony.

Some Lodge members thought bringing in a master would inspire others to reach for the stars. Does it inspire you?"

"I'm speechless."

"Oh, we must loosen that tongue. I don't want silence. I want exchange." Balthazarr draped his arm across my shoulders. He smelled of saddlery and cigar boxes. Opium incense.

Now that I was seeing him up close and in person, I was sure it wasn't for the first time. "You know, I think we've met before. In October. The Houdini performance at the Ward Theatre? You were backstage visiting Harry Houdini's room. Preston, you remember."

Balthazarr showed confusion. "Impossible. I arrived in town a few hours ago. Before that I was in New York, but only for a short stay. I crossed the Atlantic on the *RMS Aquitania* last week. You see, we could not have met. A Houdini trick would be the only way," he quipped.

"You're thinking of someone else." Preston was irked by my apparent error.

I wasn't convinced I was wrong. Balthazarr's resemblance to the man in Houdini's audience, the one who accosted the escapist at his dressing room door, was uncanny. I tried to recover from my faux pas. "But I did see you in Spain, near Barcelona. At a festival."

"Yes, yesss… now you are talking about my homeland. I was born in Catalonia and have a house by the sea. The festivals are as old as they are exquisite. When were you there?"

I told him, and his expression changed to a frown.

"No, I am afraid you are amiss again. I have been living in London for most of the last year. I haven't visited home, this breaks my heart, in two years. You remind me to return as soon as I have the opportunity. Tell me, how did you like the festival? Was it exciting for you?"

"Very," I replied. "Unlike anything I ever witnessed before."

"You see." He swiveled to Preston. "I told you. No one can resist Spain."

Preston grinned and nodded. "I will have to take Minnie there."

"Maybe for your honeymoon," Balthazarr suggested.

"Maybe," Preston said, noncommittally. "We've finished eating. But would you join us for coffee?" He looked at the dreary weather. "It's nasty out there."

The Spaniard politely declined the offer. "I have an appointment. And I am not afraid of the elements. I brought a cape. Back home I climb the mountains in rain or sun. My mother says I am like a wild beast who always wants to be outside. Sleeping under the stars."

We parted company.

After Balthazarr left the room, several guests concluded their meals. The atmosphere of the dining room deflated. Nothing tasted as delicious as it had previously. Preston and I asked for our coffees, but it was like sipping bitter brown water. I felt run down, vaguely feverish, as if I were catching a cold. We smoked and watched the room depopulate.

Sleet ticked at the windows.

"What do you make of him?" Preston asked. "Our friend with the forked beard."

"Balthazarr's a genius. He knows it. The world knows it."

"He doesn't intimidate you?"

"He intimidates the hell out of me. I don't feel competitive with him because it's no contest. I'll never be a Juan Hugo

Balthazarr. But, coincidentally, my work has taken a Surrealist direction as of late. It started with a watercolor I did a few weeks ago, right after your observatory party. I've switched back to oils. Feels like I'm stumbling in the dark. But it's worthy exploration. I'm going places I never dreamed of. Or all I did was dream of them. Now they're happening on canvas. The work's good. I'm going somewhere… I don't know where yet…"

"Perfect timing, then. You take advantage of this opportunity with Balthazarr, and it can only boost your career." Preston ground out his cigarette in a saucer. "I'll be inviting him to my bachelor party. You're coming too. It's after the New Year. Minnie's got us booked through the holidays. We're visiting every damned mansion in Arkham for one social function or other. I've always loathed Christmas."

"Old humbug." Smoke leaked past my teeth. I reached into my jacket for my pocket journal. I leafed through the pages. "Do I have the date of your bachelor party? I can't remember." I unscrewed my pen. "Did you say you're moving the wedding date?"

"Minnie and I are impatient. Why wait until summer? Decisions will be finalized soon. As far as a bachelor party goes, I'll pin it down. My life is so planned out right now. Allow me a little spontaneity, will you?" He slumped back in his chair and shut his eyes.

"You can improvise like a jazzman. Kid Fairmont hammering at the ivory keys."

He stared at me from two sunken pits. "We'll have an old-fashioned boys' night on the town. A real bash. You and me… and all the rest…"

By the time the events of that ill-conceived boys' night ended, neither Preston nor I wished we had been there to see it. But by then it was too late. The die was cast, the play made. The cigarette girl wearing that sparkly red and gold skirt, catching everyone's eye….

What occurred on that ghastly night, lurking the back alleys and secret rooms of Arkham's underbelly? What did Balthazarr really do? A parlor trick, an illusion, or something much worse? Once we realized the level of horror, we couldn't stop it from happening. The blood… everything came bursting through the wall… guns barking, bullets flying… the screams of men and women running for the exits… fleeing an earsplitting roar from beyond.

But I'm getting ahead of myself.

CHAPTER SEVENTEEN

By the time I arrived at Oakwood after breakfast, the sleet had turned to snow. Whiteness sugared the evergreens, the walk, the hip roof. Barren trees framed the house. I'd pick up a few things, then be out again. A quick turnaround. I hadn't been spending much time at the family hearth lately. Mother was tense because I hadn't moved out yet. That would be changing now. When I entered, Thorn greeted me. Mother was less sanguine. She passed specter-like, silently gliding at the back of the hall, her head turned to note my arrival. I didn't call to her with the good news. I'd tell my parents once I had official word from the Colony that Dunphy's apartment was mine. A few days at the most, I figured, after Preston made his calls. Father wasn't home; he'd absconded to New York to meet with his brokers.

I wiped my shoes and went upstairs. Thorn weaved in front of me. He loved to romp in the snow, the sight of snowflakes made him giddy. Inside my rooms, he dashed to the window and stood up with his paws on the sill, checking if the snow was still swirling. It was. He looked over his shoulder at me, his sad gray eyes pleading.

"All right, I'll take you for a walk. Let me change my clothes."

Thorn's tail wagged.

Roland had my walking clothes ready, hanging on the closet door. The man scared me sometimes with his prescience. He'd looped Thorn's leash on the door handle. I grabbed a satchel stuffed with toiletries, clothes for the weekend, and my sketchbook.

"Come on, boy. I'll show you our new digs."

We descended French Hill, taking a circuitous route. Thorn and I needed our exercise. We cut through the Miskatonic campus. Thorn loved it when the college girls would stop to rub his ears and praise his handsomeness. The quad was empty, and I couldn't guess why until I remembered it was the week before final exams. Everyone was inside, studying. I always loved taking tests. I performed at my best under pressure. Lack of urgency is what plagued me. Sloth and procrastination were my nemeses. If the net blob and the gargoyle did anything positive, they spurred me to get to work. I had painted a life-size canvas of the winged creature riding the train, and, frankly, the sight of it disgusted me, not because the demon was hideous but because it made me realize how I'd wasted years of my life painting anything else. I was born to midwife monsters! As much as they lit my creative fires, I was happy not to have met up with them again. Except in my dreams.

Nina and I were both suffering from frequent nightmares. I was perpetually back in Spain, having the tall, masked man toss me on the pyre or goblins fork out my guts. Nina dreamt she was Dr Silva swinging under a streetlamp. Another night she'd be roasted at the stake side-by-side with the Galinka sisters. Following our run-in with the watchman, I steered clear of the docks. Brave Nina ventured down there on her own in the daytime, inquiring as to the whereabouts of Calvin Wright. Calvin seemed a key to things. He knew Dunphy and had a familiarity with the Colonists. And there was the matter of a living gargoyle flying around town with his body and face. Maybe he could help us. But he'd disappeared. People at the Burdon's Fishery icehouse claimed he quit working there. No one at New Colony had seen him for days.

I spotted Christophe selling chestnuts outside the shops in the Merchant District, but he claimed he hadn't talked to Calvin since introducing us. In the meantime, he added a string of sparkly silver garland to his red wagon, and a fake white beard and elf's cap to his head.

"You're looking festive," I said, handing over coins.

"God bless us, everyone!" He winked at me.

"What's the scuttlebutt?"

"It's cold on the corners and hot behind locked doors."

"What's that mean?" I picked at my bag of chestnuts, trying not to burn my fingers.

"Means I'm freezing my caboose." He dropped his voice to a whisper. "There's trouble brewing in whiskey town. I hear a war's about to break out between rival crews."

"Gangs?"

Christophe's face screwed up. "Ya think I'm talking about knitting circles?"

"I don't often mingle with the criminal element."

"Who you kiddin', pal? Arkham's built on dirty money. Dig under French Hill if you don't believe me."

I thought of all my father's friends and how they'd "made" their fortunes. His point was well-founded. "Do the bootleg wars have to do with Calvin lying low?"

"I never said Calvin was lying low. Only I haven't seen his strong jaw lately. A man could make a pile of dough with those rum-running river boys. Dangerous dough, though."

The Merchant District looked safe and golden on a crystalline wintry night. Customers expressing holiday cheer. Children frolicked around a faux manger. A string quartet played "Silent Night" outside Lunt's music store. Rosy cheeks and red noses were a symptom of the temperature, not illicit drink. It was hard to imagine a gang war in the offing.

"What's the reason for the war?" I asked.

"You don't listen. I said, 'I hear a war's about to break out' and that's not the same thing as predicting that one will. Here's what I can testify to. Everybody's nervous. It's like they caught some bug and they're passing it around so the whole city's infected. The atmosphere is heavy. Could be a real thing. Or it might be something floating around like smoke. All I know is I smell it. Rotten things are coming. Maybe Calvin tasted it on the wind and left. Who can say?"

Who, indeed?

That conversation had taken place a few nights ago. If the Colony was connected to gangsters, I didn't see how. Art and violence are two different things. One's fantasy and the other is real. Artists like Balthazarr depict scenes of horror. But they were colorful fantasies.

Violence in a painting isn't real.

No one ever died at the wrong end of a paintbrush.

Thorn menaced a couple of Miskatonic squirrels, and I tugged him away. We left tracks in the fresh snow leading to the Colony. He didn't growl at the old mansion. Maybe I expected he would sense evil in the air. I was superstitious that way. Instead, he made friends with Portia and Delilah who lived together in a corner unit on the first floor. They were sculptors like Dunphy, but they'd arrived after his fatal fall. Portia replaced him on the South Church gargoyle project. Delilah was her apprentice. Nina knew them better than I did.

The three drank tea together.

"Alden, who's this?" Portia asked from inside her fur-trimmed hood. The women were headed out. I'd interrupted a chat they were having as they stepped out the door.

"Thorn, my trusted sidekick."

"Your puppy is awfully cute. But we were hoping you'd bring Juan Hugo around," Delilah replied. "Him we're just dying to meet."

Portia gave her a stern look which she ignored.

"You've heard about Balthazarr already?" I asked, surprised. How did they know?

"It's all over the Colony. The notorious Spaniard has arrived," Delilah said.

I petted Thorn's side. "What makes you think I am acquainted with Balthazarr?"

The women looked at each other, passing silent messages.

"We heard you visited him at the Silver Gate," Portia said. "This morning…?"

"Is it true?" Delilah asked, eagerly.

I was taken aback. News spread fast in the commune. I needed to be wary of that, as a rule. Privacy would be a luxury forfeited. "In fact, it is true. But I don't really know him."

"Surely, you do," Delilah said, as if I were playfully deceiving them.

"Will you introduce us?" Portia was trying unsuccessfully to contain her excitement.

I decided not to fight their assumptions. "Well, if the opportunity arises…" Though I was hardly in any position to be escorting Juan Hugo Balthazarr around New Colony. "We have a mutual friend, Balthazarr and I. Simple as that."

"We'll all be friends before too long, I expect." Portia measured her words.

"All makes one in the end," Delilah said.

Portia shot her a look. It *was* an odd way to put things. Yet somehow familiar…

In any case, I didn't want to disappoint them. "Next time I see Balthazarr I'll invite him to come for a visit."

Delilah said, "You don't need to invite him. He's been with us from the very star–"

Portia elbowed her roommate in the side. "We know him by his work, she means."

Straightening, Delilah acted as if she hadn't felt the blow. But she clammed up. When she spoke, her voice sounded tight, breathless. "Can't wait to meet face to face."

The women had me bewildered. But I liked them and wanted to appear amicable, especially since they were Nina's friends. "I don't know about Juan Hugo, but you'll be seeing a lot more of me in the future. I hope to be moving in soon." They were underwhelmed. Apparently, I was small potatoes compared to a world-famous Surrealist.

"Uh huh." Delilah said. She and Portia moved off, waving.

"Be seeing you!" Portia called out, sounding like an enthusiastic, but poor, actress.

The two women crossed the street. Heads tipped together in hushed conversation.

Maybe someday I would be famous enough to excite people,

to make their eyes brighten as I passed. To want to meet me. I needed to get used to living among groups again. I'd forgotten how it was since leaving college. In Europe, I chose to live off on my own.

I went up to Nina's apartment. She opened the door before I knocked.

"My, my, what're you dressed up for?" I said. "It's too early for a night out."

"Hello, you two." She kissed me and scratched my dog behind the ears. She wore a shiny black dress that had silver teardrops sewn on; her Mary Janes had rhinestones glued to the straps and heels. Silk stockings. I'd never seen her so done up. She ushered us in.

"I have news," Nina said.

"Me too. But you go first. Is your news good or bad?"

"Good, definitely."

"Mine too."

She poured two whiskies to celebrate. Thorn curled up on the rug by the fireplace. We drifted to the living room. It was all terribly domestic.

"I found Calvin Wright." Nina's eyes glittered, proud of her success.

"Great! Where is he?"

"Staying with friends in Easttown. He's got a new job. Been busy, working."

"In Arkham all along." That made things easier. If he'd left town, we were doomed.

She gulped half her whiskey. "His employer is a bootlegger. Calvin unloads trucks. They're taking the shipments off fishing boats on the river."

"Is that where you got this? It goes down smooth." I flopped onto her sofa.

"Somebody bought me that bottle. I've been out all night at a speakeasy." She waved me off when I furrowed my eyebrows, showing concern. "It was perfectly safe. Listen, Calvin wants to talk. I told him Court's death might not be an accident and that the gargoyle isn't in his apartment any more. He knows something. More than we do. I warned him that he might be in danger." She kicked off her shoes and sat down beside me, massaging her feet.

"What did he say when you told him the gargoyle came to life?"

"I left out that part."

"That's a big part, Nina." I sipped my drink. "You met him at a speakeasy?"

"I had a lead on the Galinka sisters. Apparently they were dancing at the Clover Club to make extra money. I ran into Calvin making a delivery at the club. Our conversation was less than private. So I had to be careful. We can speak freely when we meet again to share what we know." A log popped in the fire. Thorn startled, then heeded the grate suspiciously.

"What exactly do we know?" I swirled my whiskey. Drank it. Added to the glass.

"Something you said earlier got me thinking. I have a theory," she eyed me, tentative.

"The more I think, the more confused I feel lately. Please, I need enlightenment."

"Remember when you were doing the rubbings?" She put her feet back on the floor. "You mentioned 'ritual sacrifices'."

"I saw one in Spain. A reenactment of sorts." I thought about my dreams: the tall man in the mask, the two puppets, a crowd chanting around a pyre. Was it only a reenactment?

"What if the deaths in Arkham are part of a ritual?" Nina watched me, waiting for a challenge. She held her chin out. She'd been examining the crimes on her own for so long that sharing her private theory felt like taking a risk. I was more intrigued than judgmental.

"A ritual for what?"

She shrugged. "Rituals serve many purposes. To worship, to remember… what else?"

I sat forward, trying to think. "Well, maybe… to call something?"

"Yes! Sending a signal for someone, or something, faraway to receive."

"So the crimes are repeating this call?" As the whiskey warmed me, the idea was starting to make sense. But it felt like holding a live fish. I feared it might wriggle away.

"Not repeating, so much as amplifying. Think of it like a radio transmitting more and more powerful waves. Each murder sends the call out stronger than the one before…"

"Until at last something picks up." I felt a victory, short-lived. "And does what?"

"I don't know." She sighed. "Perhaps they find a way to answer?"

"Or they show up." I had a sick feeling in my gut. The net blob. The gargoyle. Were they harbingers? If they were, then whose arrival did they herald? What was hurtling relentlessly toward us? "Tell me the name of the place again. Where you met Calvin last night."

"It's called the Clover Club. Why?"

"You're the second person to mention that place to me today."

"Who was the first?"

"Preston."

"Preston?" Nina acted surprised. But Preston always knew where the best parties were. He'd be intimate with Arkham's speakeasies. For the first time I wondered how well Nina got to know Preston during their time together. I'd had the opportunity to see the part of him that was attracted to the underside of things, the part interested in forbidden pleasures.

"We had breakfast. He told me Clark Abernathy is missing. Clark's father said he might've run off with a dancer from the Clover Club. A woman named 'Diamond,' he said."

"Alden! The Galinkas used fake names at the club. Ruby and Sapphire. Not Diamond, but close. Do you think Clark's dancer was one of them? Did they know him?"

"It's a possibility. Although the sisters have been missing for some time… but if Clark only recently tried to see her, he might not have heard. We *know* he didn't run off."

"News stories of the murders didn't list any aliases. There really might be a connection." She stood up. "We have to talk to Calvin. He's going to be at the docks today."

"The docks? I'd rather not go there. That watchman might remember me."

"We'll be careful. We must see Calvin. He told me something else about a famous artist coming in to lead things at New Colony. He seemed disturbed. I don't know why."

"The artist is Juan Hugo Balthazarr," I surprised Nina again. "I met Balthazarr this morning at the Silver Gate. He makes an impression. Bigger than life. Preston introduced us."

I filled her in on the details of my morning with Preston.

"Let's go," she said, finally. She ran into her bedroom to change her clothes.

"Where're we going?" I called from outside the doorway.

"Calvin said he'd be able to meet us a half hour from now. There's a boat due." She opened the bedroom door. "Say, I never asked you. What's your good news?"

"I'm moving in across the hall." But there was no time for us to celebrate.

Instead, we were going to talk to a man about monsters.

CHAPTER EIGHTEEN

I was worried about showing our faces at the docks. The snow offered obscurity. The docks remained busy regardless of the inclement weather. Longshoremen hauled crates back and forth from the ships to the cavernous warehouses. We were just a couple out walking their dog. Thorn provided a cover story, but we weren't having any luck spotting Calvin. The snow hurt as much as it helped.

We were ready to turn uphill and leave the dirty river behind when a voice called out.

"Hey!"

I froze, recalling the watchman and his wood bat. We wouldn't be so fast running down a slippery alleyway. The shape I saw was a man. Too narrow to be the bulky guard.

"Alden," he said, approaching.

Calvin manifested out of a gust of snow. I couldn't help but check if he had wings. Fortunately, he didn't. He smiled at us.

"Miss Nina." He tipped his head. He wore a knitted cap, a heavy sailor's coat.

"Calvin. I'm glad you were able to come," she said.

Calvin offered his hand for Thorn to sniff.

"You're a fine-looking dog," he said, as he petted my hound.

"Where can we talk?" I asked.

"Follow me." Calvin led us between two warehouses. At the back corner of one building was an unmarked door; he opened it, and we went inside. Calvin pulled a string. A weak bulb. Plank walls. A table and two benches covered with idle pocketknife carvings and cigarette burn marks. The air was stale with men's sweat. Butts and refuse littered the floor; it hadn't been swept out in weeks. A frightened mouse skittered past with a breadcrust.

"Lunchroom," Calvin explained.

"You eat in here?" Nina asked, repulsed.

"Not me," Calvin said. He picked up a broom from the corner. "I don't work here any more, remember?" he said. "I'm along for a ride today. We can talk. Anybody comes in, that changes. We'll have to go someplace else."

"How's your new boss?" I asked.

Calvin shrugged. "A boss is a boss. What'd you want to talk about?"

"How do they sneak the booze out?" I asked, curious.

"Under the fish. Not every truck. I saw them doing it when I was shoveling ice for Burdon's. Then I discovered this other opportunity. Some of the fish trucks take a detour."

I dug out a cigarette, holding out the open case to Nina and Calvin.

"As long as I get paid." Calvin leaned on the broom and put a cigarette between his lips. He raised his eyebrows. "Are we here to chat about running whiskey, or is there something else?"

"Something else," Nina said.

I lit their smokes. "But if it's tied up with bootlegging…"

Calvin picked tobacco off his tongue. "Everything's tied to bootlegging in this town. That's where the money's at. And the police, too. I don't need trouble with them. Nina said this was about Court." He watched me, remaining wary.

"It is," she assured him. "I think ... well, *we* think it all might be connected, somehow. The speakeasies, a recent string of strange deaths, and the odd clues we've uncovered so far."

"Probably is connected." Calvin exhaled, tired. "Court didn't even drink. He was too damned serious. At the end, he was acting truly bizarre. Having crazy dreams every night."

"Nightmares?" I asked. "We're having them too. Nina and I. We're getting scared."

"The dreams scared him too. He'd wake up covered in sweat. Couldn't focus. I was worried about him. He'd mumble nonsense to himself while we worked. He thought he was being followed."

"Was that all you did together?" I asked.

"How's that your business?" Calvin's suspicion of me was turning hostile.

"None of it's my business. I'm trying to figure out where everyone fits in the puzzle."

He cooled. "We were friends. Court was too caught up in his art to enjoy more."

I left it at that.

"The gargoyle, the stone one. Do you know where Court kept it?" Nina asked.

Calvin was surprised by the question. "He rented out a garage, not too far from here. The gargoyle was in there. I assume it still is."

"Was Court working on something else? Another sculpture? When we found the clay model of the gargoyle in his apartment, we saw a bigger pedestal. It was empty," I said.

"Nothing I know about." Calvin shook his head. "What's going to happen to that clay gargoyle? It has sentimental value to me. I'd like to buy it if it's for sale."

Nina and I exchanged glances. We had to tell him. No way around it.

"You won't believe this," she started, hesitant, but needing to plunge on. "Dunphy's clay gargoyle came to life." When Calvin made no reply, she continued. "It crashed through the window and flew across the river. We *saw* it ride out of Arkham on top of a train."

Calvin laughed. Waiting for us tell him the rest of the joke.

But we didn't have a punchline.

Understanding our seriousness, he staggered backward as if he'd been physically struck. He sat on a bench, sucking his cigarette and rubbing his chin. His eyes moved back and forth like a man putting together his own puzzle, sorting the pieces out, in the same way we'd done. "It really came to life?"

"It did," I said.

I reached into my pocket and took out the folded rubbings I made from Court's door. I passed them to him.

"What's this?" He seemed afraid to look at the papers.

"We found a message carved on the inside of Court's door. The gargoyle wrote it."

"It wrote something?"

"I made a copy. Words and symbols. Our names are written there. Yours too."

Calvin's hands were shaking as he opened the papers. He spread them out flat on his knees. Ash tumbled onto the newsprint. He didn't bother to brush it away. Concentrating.

"You *are* in danger," Nina said. "We all are, as you can see. That's why we need your help. Together, we might have a chance against whatever evil force is at work here in Arkham." She sat next to him and touched his hand. "Can you help us? Will you?"

Calvin was stunned, and silent.

"What do you know about the Colony?" I sat on his other side. The stark room was cold to begin with, but a new chill creeped in. Bone deep, awful. A palpable presence.

Calvin crushed out his smoke. "I know these signs. I've seen them before."

I jumped up. "Where did you see them? Do they mean something?" I took the paper. Shook it. I turned it around so he could see. "See, here. This one looks like a star. Is it a star?"

Calvin's shoulders dropped. He slouched forward like a prizefighter in his corner between rounds. His breath quickened and grew shallow. "It's called the Falling Star. I've heard others call it the 'Un-Sun.'" He wiped his dry mouth. "They are calling to him."

"We thought they might be trying to make contact. What is the Un-Sun?" Nina asked.

Calvin was twisting his neck, trying to clear his head. Suddenly, he looked exhausted.

"The Gate will open soon," he said. "They'll try to bring him through…"

"Who'll try?" Nina asked.

Calvin bit his lip. "I shouldn't tell you more. Get away. Stay far away. Leave town if you must… you're sure the gargoyle wrote this? He wrote… my name?"

"Yes, all of our names. We need to know what you know. Over the last months several people have died in Arkham under unusual circumstances. Nina and I think it might be a ritual. Dunphy was one of those people. Now we're seeing monsters pop up in town."

"Monsters? Others like the gargoyle?" Calvin looked to Nina to confirm my words.

"We think so," she said. "We've witnessed two for ourselves."

Calvin closed his eyes. He rubbed at his chest. Then his eyes opened and he steeled himself. He pointed to the three-prong fork. "This is their sign. A pitchfork. They've been searching for a leader, a sorcerer to open the Gate without getting them all killed in the process. This mark is the sorcerer." He tapped the spiked crown pictogram. "He might be the Twister of the Coil. I don't know that title. But the sorcerer wears the crown. And they unlock the Gate. The cup with the two eggs in it… I've never seen that figure. A sacrifice, maybe?" Calvin got up. His skin looked slack and gray, as if he'd lost a lot of blood.

"How do you know about this?" I blocked the door. I couldn't have him leaving, and he looked like a man ready to bolt. "Are you one of them?"

Calvin shook his fist in the air. "I'll never be one of them! They killed all that was important to me!" Anguish contorted his face. Hot tears came. But he was not ashamed.

"Who are they?" Nina draped her arm around him as he lamented.

He shuddered. "I don't know. Not exactly. I've been chasing shadows on two… no, three continents. There's more than one group. *That I know about.* They are aware of each other, but not always. It is… very complex. Cults are active in Arkham. They have members inside New Colony. I can't prove my suspicions… not yet. I came to stop them. And I will!"

"I don't understand," I said, frustrated. "Are these secret cultists worshippers of this Un-Sun? Is it a star in the galaxy? Are they sacrificing to the Sun like the Aztecs?"

"They are not like the Aztecs. They do not build. They have no society, no religion but destruction. Their goal is annihilation. You said you saw the gargoyle alive. Well, it was never alive. Animated, yes. But not alive. Did it still look like me? The face?"

"Yes," Nina said.

He gasped. "Sorcerers can copy life. Take a being or an object and control it, like a puppet jerking on a string. But who holds the strings? I've heard they change themselves. Walk around like your twin, a perfect double. It comes before they possess you. Each step is a higher display of power. Masks, all of them. Lies. If it's gone this far… they're close to something big." Calvin surveyed the squalid room, talking to himself as much as to us.

"Slow it down." I grabbed him by the shoulders. I needed to make sense of what he was saying. "You said they have members in the Colony. So which ones are doing it? Not Nina. Or Dunphy. Where did you see these signs?"

"The Black Cave. The signs are there. Painted on the walls deep in the cave. Old paintings. But paint was added to them… *fresh* paint. Wet, bloody smears on the rocks. We heard voices chanting when we moved the hooch… They always come at night… in their cloaks. We can't go back there. Who'd want to? The other boys in the gang ignore it. Keep silent. *Get away from there, son*, they tell me. *Come up to the cave mouth.* But I need to see for myself… under those robes and hoods… they're not human. We have to do something before it gets too–"

Thorn began to whimper.

I knew of a place in Arkham called the Black Cave. Calvin couldn't mean that. It was a minor geological site. Unworthy of a city plaque. Hardly the stuff of sinister machinations.

The lunchroom door burst open.

The doorframe filled. I'd have known him even if he didn't have that ball bat gripped in his right hand. His face was a granite block. But the granite had flaws; a row of stitches crawled along his forehead. Purple wedges under both eyes, and his nose was swollen, bending to the left. When he spoke, it sounded like he had a bad cold.

"What the hell is this, now? A church meeting?"

Calvin snatched up the broom. "I'm just cleaning up. These folks are leaving."

The brute stared at me. "Don't I know you?"

"No, sir. I don't believe we've ever been introduced. My name is Johannes Vermeer." I held out my hand, but he didn't take it.

Thorn growled. I wrapped his leash tighter in my fist.

The night watchman pointed his bat at my dog. "I'll bash his brains out."

Nina slid between us and the guard. "We were hoping to buy a fish for our dinner. I have such a taste for winter flounder in a lemon butter sauce. Johannes was trying to procure one."

The watchman's gears turned. "You can't buy no fish here."

"Off the books," Nina said, smiling. "You can do just about anything off the books."

He wouldn't budge from the doorway. His smell was beer breath and Tres Flores hair tonic. "If it was a fish you wanted, why are you back here jawing with these bums?"

"She opened the wrong door," Calvin said. "The lady's lost–"

"I ain't talking to you." He poked the barrel end of his bat into

Calvin's breastbone. "Say, I thought you quit here. Went to work for O'Bannion."

"No, I've been sick is all." Calvin coughed. "Flu, likely."

"Flu?" The watchman backed off a step.

Calvin kept his hand on his chest, ready to snatch the bat. "I'm feeling much better now, though."

"Huh. Tell your story to somebody that cares." He snapped his attention back to me. "I do know that cocky mug of yours. You ever take a tipple down at Donohue's?"

"Me? No, no. I'm a teetotaler. Nothing stronger than a root beer for me."

"Shuddup." Softly, the watchman appraised us, rocking on his heels. He slapped the bat into his palm. It made a meaty thump. "What am I going to do with you?"

"You're going to let us go." Nina threw back her shoulders, moving ahead and taking Thorn's leash from me, ready to slide around the guard. "I've had quite enough of your games." Her free hand disappeared into her pocket. I wondered if the stiletto was hidden there. Was she about to shiv him?

To everyone's shock, the watchman turned to let her pass.

"Good day. Hope you find your fish." He touched the bill of his guard cap.

I went next. Not looking at him. Keeping my gazed fixed on Nina's back as she retreated into the swirling snow with Thorn. After I turned out of the doorway, I let out a sigh of relief and breathed in the crisp, metallic flavor of snow. The waters of the oily Miskatonic rolled in the distance. A fishing boat coasted into my view as sailors moved about the pier, securing its moorings.

Calvin will be behind me.

He'll duck past this overgrown galoot, and we're home free.

Just keep walking. Not too fast or too slow.

You made it.

That was the last thought I remember having before the sky fell on my head, and I watched as a star exploded – a spray of gold sparks – fluttering as they fell in the snow, and the Miskatonic overran her banks, flooding around me, cold, inky black, pulling me down, down, down into its blank heart, a void, and me caught spinning like a snowflake, melting to nothing.

CHAPTER NINETEEN

I woke up under a pile of mackerel. I tasted blood. Not theirs, mine. I tried moving and found I couldn't. Not without a sledgehammer pain squarely smacking my forehead. I puked.

"Easy there, fella." An invisible hand pushed me down. Unfriendly? I couldn't tell.

Another voice. "He's awake. Hoo-wee! Stinks worse than today's catch."

"At least he's not dead. Naomi wouldn't want us bringing in a dead guy."

"No, she wouldn't."

"Nina," I sputtered. My mouth and throat burned, like acid. "Where's Nina?"

"I don't know who that is, boyo. But she ain't here. Keep still, or I'll tie you up."

"You don't need to tie him. He's half dead, poor sap. What a walloping he got."

I let that assessment sink in. Where was I? How did I get here? Ah, yes. The watchman and his bat. I kept my eyes shut because when I tried opening them, scissors stabbed in between them. I wiggled my fingers and toes. At least I wasn't paralyzed.

Cold, I was so cold. I felt like another fish on ice. Limp as a rag, twice as wrung out.

Was this death? When your body gave up and your soul slipped over the brink, is this how it was? The truck hit a bump and jolted me out of my stupor. Someone was moaning.

Me. That was me making a pathetic, gurgling, clubbed-seal lamentation.

I clenched my fists. My fingers dug into scoops of ice. I opened just one eye a slit. Not too bad. There was a man beside me sitting on a Burdon's Fishery crate. They'd tossed me in the back of a Burdon's truck. We were probably taking one of the detour routes Calvin talked about. Delivering contraband whiskey smuggled into Arkham in the bellies of those ships moored at the docks. Riding uphill, the engine growled. Tires spun. Downhill it eased off, but the brakes made a racket, grinding. Axles squealing. Mackerel were sliding around me as the truck negotiated uneven ground. My guess: a dirt road, the ruts clogged with snow and ice. The wind screamed outside the truck, pushing it with each strong gust. The driver was being careful not to end up nose-down in a ditch, because he wasn't headed to any fishery, and losing his shipment might cost him a few years in the slammer, or his life. Through half-lidded eyes, I assessed the man to my right. He was eating an apple, cutting wedges with a short knife, sliding them off the blade into his mouth. Freckles, short red hair. A white man. So it wasn't Calvin.

The driver – the one who called me half dead – didn't sound like Calvin either. It was the voice of a teenager, a farm boy.

Of course, that didn't rule out him being a killer. These two might both be killers, I thought. The night watchman wasn't around. That counted for something.

I went to sleep again. No dreams. Nothing. I was on, then I was off, like a switch.

I don't know for how long.

But when I woke the second time, the truck was parked up, its engine off.

I was alone. My back was wet. I picked up a handful of red ice. I rolled onto my side, thinking I might be sick again. But the nausea subsided. I propped myself up on my elbow. I touched the back of my head. My hair was gummy, my fingertips red. The side of my neck sticky with blood. *My* blood, I realized with a sickening thud. Wide-open, dead moony fisheyes stared at me from the bed of glistening ice – my unlucky travel companions, sleeping the sleep you never wake up from. Hours ago, this school of blue mackerel was swimming in the ocean, making their way in the salty world. Gutted, they were bound for somebody's Friday fish dinner. At least I was still swimming. I had a fighting chance.

The big cargo door was open a crack.

I sat up. My head pounded. I waited to see if it would quiet down.

I looked out.

Men talking, smoking. At work. If I was a ghost, then this was going to be a terrible group to haunt. They looked too tough to scare. Scars and muscles. Just like the dock workers, they hauled merchandise. Illegal merchandise. Loose bottles clinking until they packed them away in crates lined with straw. They were getting the liquor ready to ship out again. I smelled coffee brewing, and spotted a pot chained to an iron tripod over a campfire. There was a kettle over the fire too. Clam chowder by the smell of it. But I wasn't feeling hungry, not that anybody was asking.

My head was a little quieter. Why had they brought me here? Blood trickling from my broken noggin was more pink than red when I dabbed it again with my fingers. The bleeding had slowed down. I didn't go searching too high on the top of my head. I was afraid if I reached up there, I'd feel a crack in my skull, bone chips, and wads of gooey brain.

This way I could almost pretend it was a bad hangover.

Give it a few hours and my normal self would return. Shamed but intact. No permanent damage. Nothing that couldn't be fixed with a meal and sleep. I scooted half out of the truck. Legs dangling. I felt like a broken clock. My springs sprung. The minutes I heard ticking by were my pulse, and it wasn't keeping regular time.

I put ice on my tongue to rinse out the foul taste. Gritty, but better than before.

I sucked. Spit. I mopped my brow with my wet sleeve.

When I checked the interior of the truck, I found the booze was already unloaded.

Just me and the fish left behind.

So long, I thought. Here's my stop, boys. Fare thee well.

I hopped out. Nearly ended up flat on my back again. My legs were rubbery, like the bones were going soft and bendy inside. *Shit*. I was dizzy to beat the band. I held onto the truck.

We were in the backwoods somewhere. A curious cardinal was watching me from a pine. I looked around toward the other end of the truck and saw a hole in the side of a hill.

What had Calvin called that place where he saw the symbols painted?

The Black Cave.

Like I said, I'd heard about it growing up in Arkham. But I'd never been there.

Was this it?

Hand over hand, I made my way to the front bumper, out of sight of the men.

Sure enough, the truck was pulled up to a cave. Inside the cave mouth, torches burned. Off to one side stood several copper pot stills, and stacks of firewood for heating up the pots. Above them, a natural chimney formation in the rock let the smoke out. Distillers worked at night to avoid attracting attention. But nobody had been distilling whiskey here lately. The equipment appeared to be stored away. Instead, the cave acted as a kind of warehouse for shipping and receiving barrels and crates of illegal alcohol smuggled in via the docks. The men were working outside the cave today, emptying the Burdon's trucks of their hidden cargo and repacking bottles to fulfill orders waiting on pallets in the snow. Here was a band of pirates divvying out liquid treasure. But the truck I arrived in was parked away from the action. Nobody was bothering with me for right now.

Where were Calvin and Nina? What did the night watchman do to them? I didn't want to think about it. They were smart. Maybe they got away…

I tried standing on my own. Wobbly. But I didn't fall right over like a bowling pin. I stumbled into the cave. I had to stare at my feet to make sure they did their job properly. I bumped into a wall. Or two.

It was darker here. Better for my battered brain. I shuffled in the sandy soil.

Then it was hard rock under the soles of my shoes.

Rock on every side. I ran my hands over the surface of the walls like a blind man.

"Where the hell is he?" a voice said, from not too far away.

"I left him right there. Out cold. I swear to God. I put my hand under his nose to make sure he was breathing. He couldn't just up and go, I'm telling you. Down for the count he was." I recognized the second voice. He was the guy who rode in back with me.

"Well, he isn't here now. Go find Freddie. Maybe he took him somewhere. Go!"

"You got it, boss," said the voice I knew.

"Get back before Naomi hears about this. She'll put both our asses in slings."

I listened to one man walking away. The other climbed into the truck and then jumped out again. I put one foot in front of the other and kept going farther into the cave.

Darker and darker.

It smelled like the sea when the tide goes out and things are left to die on the beach. But I didn't care. It felt good being back there in the blackness. I was protected. The cave floor ramped downward. I kicked something solid that rattled and fell over. Rolling.

"Freddie! Hey, Freddie, that you back there?"

I had to keep low in the dark. If they found me, who knew what they'd do. I wasn't about to go and find out. I knelt on the floor and felt the shape of the thing I'd kicked. Smooth, cool glass. Scratchy metal. When I shook it, liquid sloshed around inside.

I smelled fuel.

A lantern!

I tucked it under my arm and felt my way until I turned around a corner.

It took me a little while to dig my lighter out of my pocket and get the wick lit in near total darkness. When it blazed, I put the cover on and covered it quickly with the flap of my coat. The man standing by the truck, the one who asked if I was Freddie, couldn't see me unless he came deeper inside. My only choice was to explore the cave.

The passage turned to the left. So I did too.

Lifting my light, I continued down the ramp and came to steps chiseled in the rock.

Down I went.

The swinging lantern and the shadows on the bumpy walls didn't help my dizziness.

But I tried to look straight ahead, and I still was climbing down.

A helluva lot of steps this cave had. I had to sit for a while and rest my head on my knees. The effort of walking had my head pounding again. I don't know how long I sat there, quietly. But then I thought I heard footsteps and voices murmuring. Not behind me, where the bootleggers were likely searching for me by the cave mouth, but in the opposite direction, ahead of me.

Deeper inside the subterranean cavity.

I held up the lantern.

Movement… maybe… a piece of the darkness darker than the rest… separated.

I stood up and bent forward, trying to see more. But it was no use. I had to keep going down to make sure.

Eventually I got to a sort of landing. It was as wide as a dance hall. At the far end were more stairs, and I didn't want to walk any more. I was feeling tired. Sleepy. And the blood was pumping from my head wound again. I had to wipe my neck a few times with my wet sleeve. I thought about curling up on the landing and taking a little nap. *When I wake up again, I can go back, or I can take those steps going down.* That's what I was telling myself when I saw them.

I don't know how they got behind me.

But there they were, huddled by the wall with a fire, not yellow-orange like my lantern but encased in a greenish glow all their own.

Three figures in cloaks, like monks.

I remembered Clark Abernathy in his Friar Tuck costume. I recalled how later, when we discovered him, he had no head. Sprawled out on the observatory floor, his neck stump chewed, his cloak hung up on a peg.

The three figures were bent over a little. Close to each other, their backs to me. One was finger-painting on the wall, one chanting, and one stayed silent but attentive.

"You, you," the chanter said. "You, you... you, you..." He said it over and over.

I walked up, more curious than alarmed, and raised my lantern. "Me? Are you addressing me, by chance?"

None of the three bothered to turn.

You, you... you you... you, you youyouyou...

It was as if he were a needle stuck on a record. He bowed slightly with each utterance.

I edged forward, feeling a sour gush of fear kick up inside me but not knowing why.

I tried the finger-painter. "What are you drawing?" No luck. I stepped back, irked. "What is this? A church meeting?"

I asked in a raised voice. My head really hurt. I'd heard that question somewhere before. Maybe I was making a joke, but my lines didn't even make sense to me. *You, you…* That sounded somehow familiar too but completely out of context.

The chanting petered off into gibberish.

"*Yuyu! Va-BaDAAAHHH!*" the chanter shouted in a finale that startled me.

The odd phrase echoed in my mind, bringing back thoughts of other voices, the ones Nina and I overheard through the wall in the observatory library. Somewhere else as well. Spain? Was that where I heard these alien sounds the first time?

Never mind, because they finished what they were doing. The finger-painting, chanting, and staying silent were over and done with. They stepped away from their work. The chanter, who was in the middle, was much taller than the other two. The finger-painter was quite short, like an older child, but you could tell by the way they moved they were no child. A petite woman? Their hoods were pulled low, hiding faces. The green light and my light joined on the landing. There were markings on the floor I hadn't noticed before.

Lines. Angles. It reminded me of a geometry problem. Find the missing angle. I recalled the design chalked on the floor under Clark's body.

"You ready to talk now? It's rude not to answer when someone speaks to you," I said.

The one whose job it had been to stay silent responded.

"It isn't time for you yet. Go back." A man. He spoke with a slight German accent.

"Back where?"

The one who had stayed silent pointed up the steps toward

the cave opening. I was shocked! His hand and arm had no skin, just wet muscle and sinews, a network of throbbing blood vessels pumping. I should have been terrified, but I didn't feel that way. I was numbed.

"I'm too tired for that now. After I sleep," I said. "It's a long way to daylight. Trust me." I gestured with a sweep of my fortunately skin-covered arm.

"You're injured," the finger-painter said. No child's voice. Feminine, speaking in a hoarse whisper, as if her voice box had been injured. "You have blood on you," she rasped.

"You do too. See?" I shifted my lantern to show the finger-painter her bloodied hands.

The tall chanter in the middle came forward. The green light around the three came out of him. I say "*him*" because the shape had big shoulders, and it stood like a man with its legs spread far apart. The light spiked out of his head like a crown, and green spikes ran down his spine, reminding me of reptiles I'd seen poised on zoo rocks, with their flicking, forked tongues.

"Alden, you are important. Most important. We need you. Please, listen to us." I can't say it was a man's voice. More like a god voice that went through me so that I vibrated. All their voices sounded odd and dreamy. The chanter touched my shoulders.

The pain in my head vanished. I was tingling.

"Are you helping me?"

"Yes," the three said together in a single combined voice.

"You're my friends?"

"Go back, Alden," they said. "We will call you when it is time."

Then I saw the landing was crowded with cloaked figures. There was hardly any room for me to move. Two of them were dancing and leaving sooty footprints on the stone. They lifted me up on their shoulders and carried me up the carved steps. I wasn't frightened, though I should've been. But they felt strong and sure, marching me back to the cave entrance. My lantern was gone. I don't remember where it went, but I didn't need it. We had the eerie swampy green light, and they all knew the cave better than they knew their own homes. Why did I think that? I don't know. But it felt true. I was so light in their hands. It was like I floated above them. Their humming – did I tell you they were humming or chanting or doing something that I could feel, buzzing around me like a swarm of bees, not to sting me, but to save me? – their noise, it relaxed me. Like machines more than bees. A kind of staticky noise that made me sleepy. I wasn't asleep, and I wasn't awake either. When the humming static, or whatever that sound was, when it stopped, it did it all at once. The silence afterward was total. I was lying on the cave floor, near the light from the sun outside, on the rim of the shadows that lived in the cave forever. Not on the hard rock but on the sandy soil, on my back.

My hands were folded across my chest.

"There you are," they told me inside my head, comforting me.

There you are.

CHAPTER TWENTY

"There you are!"

Boots stomped toward me where I lay, dazed. A leather toe prodded me in the side.

"You awake? Or faking it?"

"Man, he ain't faking it. Look at all the blood. His skin's as white as a fried egg."

"I don't know, Freddie. He tricked us before. Boss was mad he wasn't in the truck."

Freddie, who sounded like he was the farm kid that drove the truck, defended me from his partner's accusations. "He probably fell out and crawled in here like a sick tomcat. He's tricking exactly nobody."

"Let's get him up."

Somebody took hold of my legs.

Freddie said in my ear, "C'mon, buddy, you need help for that busted head of yours." Hands under my arms, he lifted me. The men carried me out of the cave, past the parked truck, and over to a table constructed of planks laid across a pair of sawhorses. A tarp corded between two pines tented the table.

I was groggy, nauseated. Freddie looked every bit the rangy teenager, sporting a tousled thatch of hair, the faint hint of a moustache, and a jacket two sizes too large. He ladled out a cup of hot chowder, setting it on a stump beside the table. Then he propped up my head, pressing a canteen to my cracked lips. "This here's water. Drink some if you can. I got tasty soup waiting when you're ready. Doc Unger is coming to inspect that knot on your pumpkin. Boy, that guard feller got you good. I wonder what you did to make him so angry. Doc will fix you up. He's a real steady operator for a dope fiend."

"Stop mothering him," his partner said.

Freddie looked at my eyes, which were getting slowly better at focusing. "Winston's ornery by nature, but he's all bark, no bite. Pay him no mind."

"I'll chomp on both of you," Winston said, snapping his raggedy, tea-colored teeth.

"No, he won't," Freddie assured me.

Winston stood under a corner of the tarp, smoking the shortest, fattest cigar I ever saw. I sipped from the canteen. The water's cold made my teeth ache.

"You want to try sitting?" Freddie asked.

I nodded. He pushed me up. The snowy bootleggers' camp tilted and rocked as if it were built on a platform at sea. But then the motion settled down to a tolerable balance.

"Where're the monks?" I said, slurring my words. But I made myself understood.

"Why, he's been to the pearly gates and back." Winston laughed, slapping his thigh.

Freddie watched my face closely, looking for signs of ongoing impairment.

I didn't feel chipper, but I knew I wasn't brain damaged. I gave Winston a hard look.

"I think you might've had yourself a vision," Freddie said.

I shook my head, which was a mistake.

"In there." I pointed to the cave. "Way at the back. People in robes."

Winston stopped his smiling and gaped at Freddie, then back at me. "You best stay out of there. And don't tell nobody you saw people in robes inside the cave. That's off limits." He chewed on his cigar. It had gone out. He took it from his lips, contemplated it, and put it back. Freddie went to the stump and held up the cup of steaming soup.

"No thanks," I said. "You eat it. My stomach's feeling queasy."

"Suit yourself." He drank half the cup, wiping his mouth with the back of his hand.

"Why am I here?"

"He's a philosopher," Winston quipped.

"The watchman from the docks? Remember him? He clocked you when you weren't looking," Freddie said. "That's what Calvin told us. Well, Cal, he didn't like that. He fed that head-knocker some bare knuckles. Cal couldn't hang around after that. He stuffed the guard in a trashcan and asked us to bring you here for Doc to patch up. Said he'd hitch a ride here as soon as he could." I'd have preferred a trip to St Mary's Hospital over this gutter medic they kept mentioning. But I understood Calvin's instinct to keep things off the books.

"What about the woman with the dog?"

"We didn't see no woman," Freddie said.

Winston nodded in agreement. "No sir, no dolls or dogs on the docks today."

Where had Nina gone? My anxiety was interrupted by a new source of unease.

"Here comes Doc now." Freddie looked past me. "Make no mention of his wig."

"What wig?" I asked.

"Shush," Winston said, putting a finger to his lips and waving at me to pipe down.

"What have we here, gentlemen?" Doc Unger said, in lieu of a proper introduction.

I was glad they warned me not to mention the man's hairpiece. Because if they hadn't, it surely would've been the first item on my conversational list. As best as I could determine, Doc Unger wore a seventeenth-century French wig in the style of the Sun King, Louis XIV. It was a glossy mass of curls that fell to his shoulders and perched upon him like a slightly snarled, snoozing pet.

"Our boy here suffered a blow to the head from a wooden club," Freddie said.

"Did he now?" The faux courtier set his leather bag on the ground. With firm but gentle pressure he turned my face away from him. His fingers delicately probed my injury.

"Is it fatal, Doc?" Winston asked, snickering. "Should we call a priest?"

"I think not." The real exam began then. I yelped in pain. Doc rustled in his bag. He numbed me, cleaned my wound, stitched me. Then he bandaged my skull, wrapping my battered crown in a gauze turban. He handed me a small brown bottle of pills for pain, two of which I swallowed immediately. And he added that I should drink fluids, but not liquor, and to rest for a few days. "The human skull is a natural helmet, and yours, luckily, has not been breached. Not for lack of trying, you dear hooligan."

After my treatment, I tried to pay him, using damp bills dredged up from my pockets.

He refused. "My work here is charity. For the good of society, I endeavor."

With that he exited, dissolving into the snow like an extravagant ghost.

"I've never met a doctor like him before," I said, astounded.

"Oh, Doc's not a real doctor. He was a patient at the asylum before he escaped. He does quality work. Long as he gets his dope, he's pleasant as can be. Keeps us fit as fiddles."

I thought about my sewed-up head under the turban, the fat numbness sitting on me like a giant snoozing spider. This formerly institutionalized man had put his fingers inside a rip in my head. I surprised myself by feeling less worried than impressed. Though that might have been the pills already at work.

Freddie refilled his cup from the kettle. Steam rose, a scent of the sea too.

"Want a little soup now?" he asked.

"Sure, why not? What have I got to lose?" Lunatic surgery relaxes one's standards.

"That's the spirit."

Even grumpy Winston appeared buoyed by the shift in attitude. "You really see monks in the cave?" he asked, earnestly.

"I did. They carried me back up the steps from down on the landing."

The bootleggers exchanged quizzical stares.

"What?" I asked. "What did I say?"

"There ain't no steps in the cave," Freddie said. "It's twisty back there, and it pitches down to the caverns that fill up when the tide's in, but no steps. No landing neither."

"But... but I was there," I said, thinking about my memory; how unlikely it really was.

"Oh, you got conked and went to dreamland. It's no big thing," Winston said. He fished a flask out of his coat pocket and, after taking a swig, offered it to me.

"Doc said, 'No liquor'." Freddie reminded him. He kicked snow at his criminal cohort. "But give me a taste, Win."

The two bootleggers drank, staring into the pines and falling snow.

"Strange life," Freddie said, finally.

I didn't disagree.

Darkness crept into the woods around the Black Cave. Winston and Freddie pointed out a gap in the pines and told me the Miskatonic River was less than a hundred yards right that way. Through the trees, I thought I could make out distant church steeples. So, we weren't all that far from the docks and the city. But I couldn't walk it in my current shape.

"The hooch goes out to a boat after nightfall. We load it on the beach," Freddie said.

"Does the booze always come in and go back out again?" My pain had reduced to a pounding, but tolerable, headache.

"That's called distribution," Winston chimed in.

"Rum-running boats ferry shipments down the river. A part stays here and goes to the O'Bannion joints. The rest leaves by truck, headed inland," Freddie said.

"The Clover Club? That's an O'Bannion place, right?" I felt recovered enough to join them for a smoke. "Naomi O'Bannion. She owns the place?"

The men nodded.

"That's one thing her family runs," Freddie said. "Quite a lady–"

"Don't say no more. He's a stranger," Winston cautioned. "No offense, mister."

"None taken." My new bootlegger friends lit torches and staked them in the ground so their fellow brethren in the whiskey trade could see their work. The other members of the bootlegging crew were off nearer the road. We were on our own. "I know a lady like that."

"The one you lost at the docks?" Winston asked.

"That's her."

"You called her *Nina*," Winston remembered my ramblings from the ice truck.

"Did somebody say my name?"

Nina glided out of the trees.

Freddie and Winston jumped like a couple of spooked squirrels.

I nearly fell off the table. Nina approached, red-cheeked from her hike in the woods.

"What the hell? She's a damned witch!" Winston pulled a pistol.

"Easy, fellas," Nina said. "I'm no threat." She raised her hands in the air.

"Where'd you come from?" Freddie said. Winston still had the pistol trained on her.

"Back there. Down by the river. After the watchman attacked Alden, I ran and hid in a toolshed. It was so abominably frigid, I thought I might emerge an icicle. When I worked up my courage enough to climb out, I saw Calvin in the alleyway looking for me."

"Calvin? Where is he?" Winston's finger hooked tight on the trigger.

"Point the gun down at the ground, please," I said.

He seemed unsure. He switched the barrel back and forth between us. "I don't know you. You sure as hell don't know me. Don't go telling me what to do."

"Easy, Win. Don't do nothing you can't take back." Freddie said.

I turned to Nina. "It's awfully good to see you. Where's Calvin?"

"We found a boat. Calvin rowed up to a spot on the banks and dragged the boat ashore. I raced up here to see if I could find you. You looked so lifeless at the docks."

I touched my turban of bandages. "Now I look like Rudy Valentino in *The Young Rajah*. It's nice to hear you haven't lost your skills as a boat thief. I do hope Calvin shows up soon." Boots stepping in snow. *Crunch, crunch.* "Ah, here he comes now."

Calvin pushed past a snow-heavy branch. A shower of ice crystals danced in the torchlight. A sweaty-faced Calvin smiled before his expression turned to surprise at the sight of Winston's pistol. "What's this? Winston, are you going to shoot me?"

Winston lowered the gun.

Freddie said, "Cal, you about gave us a heart attack."

Sensing the danger had abated, Nina rushed into my arms.

We kissed.

"You two should leave," Calvin said. "The current will carry the skiff into town."

"I can steer," Nina said. "My father had me sailing my own dinghy when I was ten."

"Can you walk?" Calvin asked, helping me down from the table.

"If I go slowly." I grabbed Calvin's thick forearm. "Thank you for everything. They told me you took care of that bat-wielding maniac. I owe you."

"After I took his club away, he wasn't so tough."

"We need to talk. Soon. I saw things in the Black Cave. Monks... well, they weren't really monks. It's difficult to explain."

Calvin looked at Freddie and Winston. They shrugged.

"We'd better go," Nina said.

I followed her through the pines to the black river, where Thorn, with his tail wagging, waited for us in the boat. Home to New Colony we went.

CHAPTER TWENTY-ONE

Two weeks later I finished moving into Court's old apartment. The property manager had cleaned the place out. He sanded the inside of the door and slapped on a new coat of varnish. If I peered from the side in the right light, I could still read the message and see the symbols the gargoyle had carved there. The three butchered names of Calvin, Nina, and me followed by the threatening ominous prediction.

CALvin RiTe
NinA TArrinGTon ALL Den OAks
WiLL Die by the HAnd of the ONe who CALLs the
FALLing sTAr Thru The GATe
TwsTer of The CoiL
The Un-Sun
yoOYUVABDAA

I read our names again. It dawned on me that, apart from the random capitalizations, the creature had gotten the spelling of Nina's first and last names correct. That's interesting, I thought.

Tarrington was the longest word, and the animated clay thing had even managed the double "r" bit, which might've meant nothing, of course. He'd succeeded with a series of double "l" spellings in the next line. Perhaps it was random chance; I was looking for clues where none existed. Or maybe he was more familiar with her Boston clan, or a namesake in another city. Or did Nina mean more to him? And to the Twister of the Coil? And the Un-Sun?

I set aside my ruminations about our names.

It was the last word that interested me the most. This *was* the word I heard from the tall monk in the Black Cave. *You, you... Va-BaDAAAHHH!* Something like it came to Nina and me through the library wall as well. I was convinced I'd heard it at the ritual in Spain.

But what did it mean? It might have been a kind of prayer or interjection.

Yet I suspected it was a name. So many of the words in the gargoyle's message were names: Calvin, Nina, my name....

The others were less clear: Falling Star, Twister of the Coil, and...

Yooyu Vabadaa.

It had to have meaning. Two parts. It felt like a name when I spoke it aloud.

I wanted to ask Calvin. He was vital to our solution. But where had Calvin gone?

Since that night we left the bootleggers' camp, we hadn't seen him. He never came to New Colony. We certainly weren't going to return to the docks. Nina tried to persuade me to pay a visit to the Black Cave. I wasn't ready for that. How could we go there without the risk of being shot by gangsters? I was sure we could find its location. We knew the side of the river it was on and how far from town. It was only a matter of picking the correct dirt road.

But no, it wasn't safe.

Calvin knew where to find us. We simply had to wait for him to make contact, as hard as that might be. I'd shared my idea about *Yooyu Vabadaa* with Nina. She agreed it sounded like a name. Beyond that we were stuck. Oh, we had plenty to keep us busy. But none of it related to Arkham's mysterious deaths or monsters. My head was feeling better. I was grateful for that. I had used up the pills Doc Unger gave me.

Nina and I mostly did what lovers do. Mother called it "playing house." All I knew was that I was in love for the first time in my life. Every scrap of evidence told me that Nina loved me too. We did make a cute couple, as Preston said. I hadn't seen Preston either lately, not since our breakfast at the Silver Gate Hotel. Preston never came down to New Colony. He was a silent partner.

Balthazarr had arrived at New Colony.

I wasn't the one who brought him around. He didn't need a handler. The man made his own way. The whole Colony buzzed with new energy. Our artist-in-residence, Juan Hugo Balthazarr, the Shocking Spaniard, was no wallflower. More like a carnival barker, combined with a one-man band and a living fireworks display. He had the instincts of a master thespian and the charm of a motivated salesman pushing the snazziest, gaudiest product in the world: himself. He knew how to attract attention. His artwork was brilliant, ground-breaking, and relevant to modernity like no other's, yet he still managed to outshine what he did with who he was, a true celebrity. He gave a few lectures, even taught a class or two. Mostly he talked. During one class I attended, he had us paint a communal painting. Each student added a brushstroke, a color, or a line scraped with a palette knife.

In the end, the painting itself was abstract. A chaos of styles.

"Do not think. Create," he said. "Forget logic… order. Tap into your elemental self."

I had difficulties. If I abandoned logic and order, then how could I pick up a brush?

When it was finished, Balthazarr had us gather around the canvas.

Around him.

We sat on the floor – like his worshipful disciples.

He lit a match and burned the painting.

I excused myself, suddenly feeling ill. I was back in Spain watching the pyre.

Christmas came and went. Nina and I bought a small tree. We tied red velvet ribbons on the branches. Put our wrapped gifts under its pagan branches. We drank eggnog and built fires.

I met the other Colonists. For the most part they were examples of types, and if you've spent any time around artistic communities, you'll likely know exactly what I mean. There were the brooding loners. You met them once, then saw them only from afar, or in passing. The society-seekers were the opposite, always around, even when you wished they'd stay in for a night. They spoke outrageous things into a crowd and watched to gauge the reactions. Drank too much, ate off other people's plates, smoked constantly, and you'd better keep a hand on your partner, or you'd find theirs in its place. They broke things, including themselves, and, bright as they were, the shine would not last for too long. This you discovered soon.

I know I must sound critical, but you misunderstand me if you think I didn't like the Colonists. They were my people. I was among my own kind. They were the crazy makers of art. Creators whose acts of creation typically involved an equal, or greater, measure of selfdestruction as a price paid. A self-fulfilling myth. They glowed from inside, like hot embers, and whatever color existed in Arkham only existed because of them. For the most part, as cohabitators, they were never easy.

Take Portia and Delilah, the sculptresses I mentioned before, who were our downstairs neighbors. They fought with each other. Screaming matches we could hear through the walls. At other times, they were so sweet and perfectly fitted to each other, you'd swear they were twins. But twins fight too, I guess. I liked them. Portia's new gargoyles were better than Court's.

"Do you really think so?" Portia asked me one frozen afternoon, while the ladies drank Oolong tea, after I'd returned from the bakery with warm doughnuts and a sour cream pound cake. Delilah and Nina were in the other room slicing up the cake, putting it on plates.

"That gargoyle could sit atop Notre Dame," I said. "*Très magnifique.*"

Portia nodded and nibbled at her doughnut, unsure whether to believe me.

That's one of the big problems with artists. We're inner people, despite the outer drama and colorful displays. Selfish by nature, consumed with our own visions and dreams. We alternate between delusions of grandeur and crippling self-doubt. It lures people, then drives them away. *I love you – I hate you. I love me – I hate me.* No wonder the world thinks us mad.

"I guess it could be turning out worse," she said. "How's your painting coming along? Do you have anything to hang in the gallery this weekend for New Colony's winter show?"

Balthazarr had insisted that we present our art. Permit ourselves to be judged publicly, so he organized a show. Everyone was thrilled… and equally terrified.

"I'm working on a couple pieces." That was all I wanted to share. *See? I'm like them.*

I had three completed paintings in Court's old studio. There was the watercolor I painted at Oakwood of the net blob shambling across the bridge toward me. Since my arrival at the Colony, I'd done two new oils. The gargoyle hopping the train, cackling with its head thrown back and wearing Calvin Wright's face like a mask. And my latest creation, an interior of the Black Cave: the processing monks in hooded robes carrying me aloft, the chiseled steps and knobby walls cast in a sickly greenish hue. I painted my damaged, bloody head, but my eyes were wide open, staring at the viewer, entranced. In the background, on one of the cave walls, small details: finger-painted symbols – smears of scarlet defacing the rocks – and angular geometric lines crisscrossed the landing, half-concealed in shadows. I made some of them look like the gargoyle's symbols I kept finding. I wasn't even sure what I'd seen on the walls of the cave. My memory was too foggy, the details already fading.

I hadn't shown this painting to Nina. Not yet. I told her it wasn't ready, but that was a lie. The painting was finished. I wasn't ready for her to see it, or anyone else. It was still too enigmatic to me. Had I traveled that far into the depths of the cave? Or was this canvas the cryptic hallucination of a shaken brain after it suffered a pummeling with a bat? Who knew?

I had a fourth painting, an oil I'd begun after the net blob's portrait, but I had abandoned this work. It showed the inside of the Warren Observatory, the telescope dome. Clark Abernathy's headless body ceremonially arranged on the floor. Preston and Minnie were there but facing away. I was pointing at the corpse, covering my mouth, horrified.

I'd pushed Preston's bachelor party from my mind, when one evening I checked my mailbox at the Colony mansion and discovered an invitation, unstamped, hand-delivered, waiting for me. I tore into the envelope as I climbed the stairs.

*You are cordially invited to a night of debauchery and excess
in celebration of the eminent departure of Preston Fairmont
from the domain of the unmarried into the bosom of his bride.
We shall convene in Independence Square at 11 o'clock
on the night of January 28th, 1926.
Bring nothing but your imagination. Expect nothing but
pleasure and future legendary stories.*

The invitation card was engraved on fine handmade paper. In the lower left corner of the card was a woodcut print that I recognized immediately as a never-before-seen design by Juan Hugo Balthazarr. Another abstract – stark black against the creamy paper – it hinted at the contours of a twisted limb, possibly botanical, but more suggestive of animalistic inspiration. The fleshy tip reached up like a decomposing finger from a cursed and diabolical grave; it sprouted from an ink splat.

Looping tributaries leaked off the page. I felt my heartbeat catch. First from seeing an exclusive, obviously very recent, Balthazarr creation, but secondly, something unnamable in the pattern drew my fixation and stimulated a sense of compounding dread in me.

"You're not dressed yet?" Nina's voice startled me from the top stair.

I nearly toppled backward. Regaining my balance, I quickly covered the invitation with its envelope. I *was* dressed. I just wasn't dressed for tonight's affair. We were headed to the opening of the New Colony's inaugural Winter Show.

"I have time," I answered, composing myself as I mounted to the third floor.

Nina wore a sleek red dress that clung to her – a second skin, smooth and shimmery as a salamander – radiating the spirit of a creature born in, and impervious to, fire. She tilted her head while affixing a pearl earring. "You'd better hurry. What have you got there?"

"It's nothing." I attempted to pass her in the hall. But the lady was faster.

While I reached for my doorknob, she darted in a slender hand and snatched the invitation from my grip. A laugh on her face, celebrating her quickness and victory, soon dissolved. She handed the invitation back to me.

"Do be careful about Preston," she said.

"How do you mean?" Was she worried on his behalf, or that he was a threat?

"Steer away from trouble. That's all." She went back into her apartment.

I went inside mine to get dressed.

When I came outside again, Nina was there, waiting in her furs.

She assessed me up and down and smiled.

"You look smashing," she said.

"Likewise. Care to take my arm?"

She did care to.

Ours was a short walk in the chilling New England air. The gallery showing was being held in one of the New Colony buildings, down the block from the mansion. This ancient house once belonged to an Atlantic sea captain who was lost, along with his ship and crew, in a freakish storm. Fully restored, the domicile provided a viewing gallery and hosting site for parties like the one we were attending tonight. Someone had lit the path to the front entrance with rows of long black candles set in wrought iron stands. Their flames twinkled brightly in the crisp stillness.

"How pretty," Nina said.

I nodded, gazing at the Indian teak double doors as they parted to receive us. This was my first visit to the "Sea Captain's House," as it was called within the Colony. While I had passed it many times, I had never been close enough to notice the detailed carvings on the doors. Now I read symbols there which resembled the spiked crown, the falling star, and the trident fork. Was I seeing these signs everywhere I looked because they inhabited my brain? Or did they encroach upon us?

I tried inspecting them more thoroughly after we crossed the threshold. But there was a rush to shut the doors against the wintry blasts. Our greeters blocked the carvings in question with their bodies. They asked for our coats. Still, I hoped for another chance to review what I thought I saw. A waiter carrying a tray of champagne swept past. Laws that ordered the outside world seemed suspended in the Colony. Or maybe Preston paid the police to look the other way. Nina captured two flutes, passing one to me. A cluster of artists, mostly other painters I'd met since joining the Colony, pressed in, offering a chorus of warm, boozy hellos and taking us politely, though firmly, by the elbows, ushering us into the confusing warren of rooms that served as the gallery.

Francine, a miniaturist, led the group. "They've done a fabulous job," she said, showing us a path to the hors d'oeuvres. "I don't know who ordered the food but it's the tops, I tell you."

She handed me a crab pastry.

Nina picked out a skewered meatball dripping with gravy, popping it into her mouth.

"The bar's through there." Francine gestured to the next room, its wallpaper crowded with tropical fruit and exotic birds. "There's a harpist plucking away upstairs, and a man playing pan flute. It's so luxurious I might die. Oh, get me a mint julep will you, dear?" She waved to Oscar who threw enormous pots on his potter's wheel, decorating them with ferocious jungle cats and popeyed monkeys swinging by their tails. Oscar waved back. "There are people with money here tonight." Francine jerked her head toward a couple in the corner, conversing with Dexter, an experimental sculptor. He liked to glue string to objects, layering the strings, varying colors and thicknesses. I doubted they would buy anything from him. I'd gone to prep school with the male of the pair, and he was strictly a fan of realism and female nudity. However, his wife I didn't know. The room was crowded. Overcrowded. I fought off a surge of claustrophobia.

"Quite a group," I said over the noise of multiple conversations going on at once.

"Lots of money," Francine said. "Hear it? *Chang, chang…* pockets of gold."

I turned to ask Nina if she could hear the money, but she was gone from my side. When Francine paused to accept her mint julep from Oscar, I slipped out into the foyer and spotted Nina's red curves halfway up a winding staircase, leading to the house's second story. She was smoking a cigarette and talking to someone. A man. She laughed at something he said, nodding dramatically and resting her hand on his arm, which in turn leaned casually on the banister. As Nina inclined to take a sip of her cocktail, I wondered briefly how she'd gotten a drink so quickly when the bar was packed, but then I saw the man had the same drink in his hand. I realized both that he'd offered the sip to her and that he was Juan Hugo. When he saw me looking up, he motioned for me to join them.

"The man I wanted to talk to," he said. His beard looked longer than the last time I saw him. It split at the end into two dark wedges. It was hard to keep from staring.

"Why are you looking for me, Juan Hugo?"

"Because you have the most beautiful date, and I must tell you I intend to steal her."

I said nothing.

He turned to Nina, white teeth smiling. "I think he believes me."

Nina held her chin up like she was balancing a china cup on her head. Amused or embarrassed? I couldn't tell what she was feeling. She took the glass from Juan Hugo and drank.

"I never believe anything. It's the key to my happiness," I said, taken by surprise.

Nina frowned.

Juan Hugo broke into laughter. "I am joking. Not about this woman's beauty but my intentions. I want to talk to you about your paintings, Alden. I've seen them. They are hanging in a room upstairs. Can we go there now?"

"We are free," Nina said. She didn't look at me, but she held out her hand. I took it.

"Let's go," I said.

"Excellent!"

Usually the crowd followed Juan Hugo wherever he went. They hung on his words for sustenance. Engaging him in conversation elevated anyone's status in the community. To have his full attention the way we did was the envy of every artist in the Sea Captain's House. It seemed peculiar how empty the upstairs hallway was; almost as if the others had been told beforehand to stay away, to keep their distance while Juan Hugo talked with us. It was crazy to think you were the center of everyone's awareness, that you as a couple were objects of their total absorption. Why did it feel slightly sinister? Even conspiratorial?

Yet that's precisely how it felt.

Balthazarr guided us to the room.

"This must have been a bedroom, no?" He considered the chamber. The walls and floorboards were strangely blacked. Shutters sealed off our view from the only window.

But it was the paintings we had come for.

My three paintings were the only artworks on display in the room. They were large, but still they seemed to float on the otherwise barren walls. Each painting positioned alone.

Every other room was a shared exhibition space. I didn't know if I was lucky or not.

Balthazarr approached my watercolor portrait of the net blob. He folded his hands across his chest and stroked at his beard with the fingers of one hand. "Here." He pointed to the blob. "Yes, yes…" He stepped back and took me by the shoulders, positioning me directly in front of my work. "What you did here, Alden, is extraordinary. I have never seen anything like it before."

"It marked a new direction for me."

"A new direction for New Colony!" Balthazarr clapped his hands. The explosive sound hurt my ears. "What to make of this one? A train to Hades? Don't tell me a word. The painting speaks for you. Never explain your paintings, Alden. That is not your job." On the adjacent wall, hanging separately and alone, was the vision of my experience in the Black Cave. Balthazarr framed his hands around the edges of the canvas as if he were trying to squeeze the ritual images together. "I feel like I was there with you. In this Black Cave. You are painting nightmares, whether you know it or not. Dreams. The landscape beneath the conscious mind."

"How do you know about the Black Cave?" I said, trying not to sound suspicious.

His arm struck out toward the wall. His finger indicated the white card with the name of the painting typed on it. "It is titled *The Black Cave*."

"Oh, right. So it is."

"But my favorite of your paintings is this one."

Balthazarr stepped over to the wall behind us. There was a canvas on the floor, facing away from the room, tilted against the wall. He turned it around. Then he hung it on a nail.

"What do you call this one? *Witness to A Ceremonial Beheading*?"

It was my unfinished depiction of the observatory's dome room. Clark's body lying on the floor. Preston and Minnie. My self-portrait refusing to deny the mutilated corpse.

"How did this get here? It's not supposed to be in the exhibition. It's unfinished."

"The incomplete condition is unimportant. It is finished, Alden."

"No, I abandoned it."

"It is a work of genius. If I were you, I would not change a thing."

Nina hadn't said a word.

"What do you think?" I asked her.

"We should listen to Balthazarr." Her voice had a flatness, as if she were hypnotized.

"There! You see!" He grabbed the back of my neck with his pincer hand. "I want to say it is my privilege to be in the Colony with you. To belong to this commune with *you*." He kissed my cheek with effusive affection. "What an exciting time to be alive and in Arkham!"

CHAPTER TWENTY-TWO

After Balthazarr left us alone to rejoin the party, Nina and I stayed there in the room. Outside, we heard the gathering regain its former volume, as if they'd hushed up to eavesdrop on our meeting with the Spaniard.

"He called you a genius, Alden." She held tight to both my hands.

"I know." I squeezed her and looked again at my paintings, one by one. "What do you think it means?"

"I think it means you're a genius, silly boy." She kicked the door closed and switched off the light. Did she feel, as I did, that my paintings were somehow watching us?

Nina and I kissed for a long time in that dark room. We couldn't see each other, but we could feel. Weirdly, I started imagining these amoeboid lifeforms crawling in the black air around us. Some trick of the eyes caused by the absence of light, no doubt. Like gigantic pseudopodal protozoans trapped under a microscope, the magnified apparitions constantly reshaped themselves. Slither and flow. Had I had not been otherwise preoccupied, I might've watched in fascination. As it was, my observations came from the periphery of my vision. The mirages shone iridescently as drops of oil in water do. There was a chance that at any moment someone might walk in and catch us. Short of breath, we paused for a laugh at the absurdity, the headiness and unreality of it all.

"Things are changing for you," Nina whispered.

"You're the cause of it. Surely you can tell that."

She nuzzled my neck, her warm breath tickling me, sending shivers.

"I don't mean that. I'm talking about your career. Things *there* are changing."

"Yes, that too." I stroked her back. "They really are. Aren't they?"

She laced her fingers in my hair and pulled me in for a last kiss.

"We'd better join the party before they find us," she whispered.

"Reluctantly... I must agree." I switched the light back on.

We repaired our states of dishevelment. At first, I detected what seemed to be a chorus of chanting emanating from down below us. Chanting! But it was only the end of some sea shanty type of song the attendees were finishing. An alien and unfamiliar tune, which the harpist and pan flutist both seemed to know, for they played in support of the voices. We'd worried about a romantic interruption for no good reason, apparently. The hallway stood vacant, eerily so. We felt a bit like a pair of children sneaking down to see what their parents are up to at the grownups' party. In any case, that was how I felt. How was it we hadn't been missed?

I followed Nina downstairs into the only room large

enough to hold all of the visitors. It must have been a dining room in bygone days; long and rectangular, with accesses from both ends, and a chandelier hung in the center where a table might've been. Despite the size, the crowd had packed themselves in. It was a ridiculous sight, like a game almost. See how many we can fit in here. The light fixture above looked like a dead spider flipped on its back, trapped in a chain web of its own fashioning. Beneath the spider stood Balthazarr beside a circular stand, atop which rested an odd golden bowl. He had a little space cleared out around him, but he was the only one. I almost turned back.

"You are here right on time, my friends." Balthazarr beckoned us closer to the action.

We proceeded to the front of the crowd.

In the center of the odd bowl, a thin spike protruded; it looked alarmingly sharp.

"What is this old relic?" I was amused by the ornately embossed basin, its outer shell decorated with rows of concentric circles aligned and alternating bands of hammered nubs.

"Alden, you jest. But do you know you are correct. It is a relic."

"Where's it from?" Nina said. She traced her finger along the rim of the bowl.

"I brought it with me from Spain. But it is much older than Spain herself. Are you aware that people have lived on the Iberian Peninsula for thirty-five thousand years? Before the Romans, Phoenicians and Celts lived there. Is this Celtic?" He shook his head. "I don't think so. More likely Phoenician. Its origin is mysterious. Suffice it to say, it is ancient."

"What's it used for?" I said.

One of the attendees chuckled behind us.

"It's a tub for taking bloodbaths," the man said, sounding intoxicated.

A woman shushed him. Balthazarr's stare grew hostile at the interruption. Two men slid quietly across the room and removed the drunken man.

"Hey, whaadid I do? I wanna watch. Aw, c'mon guys. Don't be sore. I'll be good from now on and keep my trap shut. Lemme go back. *Pleeease…*" But he did not gain reentry.

Balthazarr pointed to the hole in the crowd where the man had been. "In a way he was right. Though the gin has given him a flair for the overdramatic."

The crowd laughed.

"It does involve blood," Balthazarr said.

"Whose blood?" I asked.

"All of ours! We are going to swear an oath of artistic dedication. Of brotherhood and sisterhood. We are proclaiming ourselves New Colonists. To mark our bond with one another, we are going to give a symbolic offering of our physical selves. A drop of blood. No more. I don't want anyone fainting."

I felt unsure and glanced at Nina, but she was transfixed by the bowl.

The crowd laughed again. A nervous tension was building in the atmosphere, like a coming lightning strike. The crackling of electrically charged fields.

"You want us to cut ourselves, so we bleed?" Nina said. She didn't sound afraid.

"No, no, no. Not a cut. A simple quick tap on the end of this nail. Use your pinkie finger if you like. You won't even feel it, I assure you. The nail is so sharp. Then a drop in the bowl. A token act to represent our vital connection, our collective lifeblood, if you will. You'll be surprised how good you will feel once we have all taken our turns."

"Shall I go first?" Nina said.

"Please, yes. Unless you prefer that Alden takes his turn before you."

I said, "Maybe one of the people who came down earlier should do it." I was no fan of bloodletting. The bowl seemed unclean, though I couldn't pinpoint why.

Balthazarr stiffened his back. "I am offering it to you out of respect, Alden. Artist to artist. It is my bowl, and I want you to be the first. Think of it as a game we are playing. We will all have our chances. Please, don't insult me."

"I'll go first," Nina said. "I'm not afraid of a little blood." She pushed up her sleeve.

Balthazarr spread out his arms. He looked like a statue standing there.

"Your hand… I will guide you."

Nina stretched out her arm. I wanted to stop her. But I didn't. She'd be mad at me. It was only a little prick on the finger. Hell, I was pushing up my cuff and thinking about what it would be like when I went next. That might sound cowardly. But I felt very brave.

Balthazarr seized Nina's wrist and pulled her over the bowl. In a swift motion, he pressed her hand down and the end of her middle finger touched the ancient golden needle.

"Ow." She winced. "You promised it wouldn't hurt." Nina stuck her finger in her mouth and sucked the tip.

"See? I'll bet it's already stopped bleeding, hasn't it?"

Nina inspected her fingertip. "No. It's still bleeding."

Balthazarr was reaching for me. "Alden, it's your turn."

I hesitated. But I couldn't back out after my girlfriend went, could I?

Balthazarr took hold of my wrist. His fingers were like a shackle pinching too tight. I knew that I couldn't pull away from him if I wanted.

"I'd prefer to do it myself. If that's permitted."

He smiled. "By all means."

I tried not to stare too hard at the pointy thing. It looked worse the longer you stared. But you had to keep it in your sight, or you might end up impaling your hand! So, what I did is, I went sort of soft-focus. In the blurry haze, I reached for the spike. I tapped my finger down like I was checking for wet paint. The blood bubbled out, a swollen red berry. And I squeezed my finger with my other hand. The drop made a soft ping when it hit the bowl. I must've squeezed too hard because I heard a couple more pings. I put my finger in my mouth and tasted salt and copper.

After that, the line went faster. There was champagne making its way around the room on new trays. The waiters must've been hanging around until the made-up ritual ended. That's what it was really, a ritual. And like I had in Spain, I felt I'd witnessed something forbidden.

More than witnessed this time. I'd acted a part in it.

The blood offering wasn't the end, though.

Balthazarr had something more to give than blood. He offered his drops last. Last man standing, I thought. Because I felt kind of drunk even though I'd only had that one flute of champagne and now here was my second that I hadn't even sipped yet. But word went out that we were supposed to wait to drink this glass. Balthazarr was going to make a toast. Everyone who was a member of the Colony, and a few rich people who'd come to buy art (they gave their blood offerings too) paused. Balthazarr was like a conductor. We were the orchestra. The members of the orchestra looked a bit glassy-eyed, like I felt. I saw a spirit of sleazy debauchery traveling around the dining room like a secret. Mixed in with the alcoholic lushness was a glaze of lechery and a languid slothfulness, an overripe sense of gluttony and satiation. We were like a den of fat vipers, our bellies full of a fresh kill and our mouths dripping venom, slits for our eyes.

"Attention!" Balthazarr called out.

He tapped a spoon against the side of his crystal flute.

To my ears it sounded like a gong. So loud and piercing.

The vipers met his gaze.

Nina was at my side. The two of us slumped against the wall. Her hot fingers were playing with mine. I felt a desire to look at her, to do more than that. First, I had to hear Juan Hugo make his toast or whatever it was happening in the center of the crowded house party.

"Each of you has made a blood sacrifice to New Colony. This cannot be changed. We are linked, brother to brother, sister to sister, brother to sister, sister to brother. A commune with a single cause. To change the world."

"Hear! Hear!" voices agreed.

I mumbled along. But my lips felt fat. I touched my face. Hot and numb.

Balthazarr lifted his champagne. "New Colony!"

"New Colony! New Colony!" people began to chant.

"Success to our ventures! Merciless vengeance to our enemies! Power is ours alone!"

The crowd cheered.

I thought I hadn't heard the outlandish Surrealist correctly. Had he said, *"Merciless vengeance to our enemies!"* and *"Power is ours alone!"*?

The moment passed. My legs were weak. I braced my back against the wall.

Balthazarr said, "Drink, Colonists. Drink!"

We all did. Maybe it was the heat, the room being too close. My head was swimming. I thought drinking something might help. The champagne must have come from different bottles than the first round. It tasted metallic, a tad briny. The bubbles were slack, and the temperature grew so it was like standing in front of a furnace. I made a sick face.

Balthazarr smashed his glass flute on the floor.

We copied him.

My movements were automatic. As if my body mimicked what it saw.

Shards flying. Broken glass crackling under our best shoes. The harpist and the pan flute player began a peculiar melody. Dissonant and sour; their instruments had fallen grossly out of tune. But no one seemed to care. I felt both exhausted and frantically awake.

Balthazarr, after throwing down his empty glass, had not moved. Now he picked up the golden bowl from the stand and he raised it over his head. His deep voice rang out.

"Ebuma chtenff! Gnaiih goka gotha gof'nn! Fm'latgh grah'n ftaghu grah'n!"

He lowered the bowl, tipping it into his open mouth, and swallowed our blood.

The music grew louder and louder. Flutes and harps and unseen gongs.

I gasped for more air.

As the house and all its occupants fell into a dizzying and impenetrable darkness.

CHAPTER TWENTY-THREE

I awoke to the sunshine blazing through a window. The curtains were open. Nina lay by my side, curled away from me, the blankets pulled up to her ears. My head ached dully. I sat on the edge of the bed. This was Nina's apartment. At some point during last night's delirium I had shed my tuxedo; like flotsam from a shipwreck, items snagged on the rocky coast of Nina boudoir. Nina's red dress was also there, hanging over the back of a chair, a shed skin. Also, I had apparently collected Thorn from my place. He perked up his ears, but left his narrow face resting on his paws; his lithe form stretched on a Persian rug at the foot of the bed, tail wagging to greet me.

I stumbled like a sailor to the bathroom and drank for a long time from the sink tap. Thorn appeared in the doorway, looking concerned. The room shifted at sea under my feet.

"I'll live," I told him.

He answered with a small whimper. He wanted to go outside. What time was it?

Nina had no clocks. How could anyone function with no clocks?

I washed my face but tried not to view my reflection. I feared I looked as bad as I felt.

When I came back out, Nina hadn't moved. I gathered my clothes and dug for my pocket watch. A quarter to twelve. Poor Thorn had been holding it a while. The thought of putting my tuxedo back on repelled me. It smelled of sweat, wine, smoke, and musky incense. Had we burned incense at the gallery house? I couldn't remember doing that. But I couldn't remember much of anything after Balthazarr's bloody rite. Certainly not coming home. Or the end of the party, for all that it mattered. I felt as though I'd been drugged, or the way I did as a child emerging from a case of the measles. Drained, depleted. Luckily, I kept some clothes in Nina's closet. I found pants, a flannel shirt. I retrieved my cigarette case and shut the curtains before slipping out. Nina snored, a soft burring sound. The gray room put me in mind of a zoo.

Thorn's leash was on the counter. Nothing appeared disordered in the apartment. It was in strange contrast to my state of mind, which felt uncannily dislodged, and vaguely guilty of something, though of what I couldn't say. Here were our shoes and an empty bottle on the floor.

I took the dog out to do his business. I dropped the bottle in the trash.

Fortunately, the weather had warmed. A sulfurous fog loomed over the water. Dampness clung to me like pond slime. I lit a smoke and squinted at the sun, glaring diamond-sharp in the sky. Thorn snuffled at the ground. I unhooked his leash, and he appreciated the freedom, trotting around the apartment house's backyard toward the riverbank but never straying out of my sight. God, my head hurt.

"Alden, hey Alden," a voice said to me from the fence at the far end of the yard.

I turned, seeing no one.

"Alden, over here." The fence on that side of the property was made of tall pickets. The slot between two of the pickets was darker than the others. It was a person standing on the other side, blocking out the light. I saw them pressing their face tight against the boards.

An eye blinked.

"Calvin, is that you?" I started to walk over to the fence.

"Stay there."

"Why? Where have you been? We've waited for you. You've taken your damned time showing up."

"What did you do last night?"

"What?"

"You heard me. What did you do last night, Alden? At the Sea Captain's?"

I took another step.

"Don't come any closer, or I'll go." The eye blinked again. It was bloodshot, red.

"We went to a gallery party. Things might've gotten a bit out of hand. I can't remember." The gong ringing. Pan flutes, vibrating harps. Balthazarr's arms outstretched.

The flash of teeth. A smile filled the gap. The husky rasp of a man laughing.

"A bloodletting. Yes? You gave them your blood to taste?"

"Calvin, come around and let me see you. Nina and I, we want to talk to you."

"Talk, talk. No! No more talk. You must kill her, Alden. Before she kills you."

Why did he sound so stilted and strange?

I threw my cigarette away. I glanced around for Thorn but couldn't spy him anywhere. "I don't know what you're going on about. Is this a joke? Now, you've helped us, so I'm giving you the benefit of the doubt here. But if you say anything like you just did again, I don't know what I'll do to you." I marched up to the fence.

The eye stared. It backed away. A metallic flash glittered in the air above our heads. He threw something over the fence to me. It twirled, landed at my feet. A knife. Nothing fancy, the kind of blade they used to gut fish at the docks.

"You go on and kill her, Alden. She's not real."

"Why are you saying this?" I picked up the knife. The handle felt dirty. My head hurt. I saw the figure behind the fence shift. A shrug? He'd be lucky if I didn't cut him first.

"No reason," he said. The dry husky laugh again. "I'm telling her the same thing."

There was a sound like flags flapping in the wind, like big yellow flames in a bonfire.

The gargoyle exploded into the air. He flew straight up to the roof and perched there.

He swiveled his head, looking at me, and then, hanging upside-down from the roof's edge, he tried to see in the window of Nina's bedroom. "Bastard, you closed the curtains." I was too stunned to speak. My feet rooted to the grass.

Letting go of the roof, he spun and pumped his skin wings, swooping down. I ducked.

The gargoyle laughed, slicing into the fog over the river.

The fog boiled behind him.

Thorn barked from the river's edge. The thing that was not

Calvin had disappeared. I looked up at Nina's window. Was he there too, like he'd said? Impossible. *"I'm telling her the same thing."*

I called my dog and raced back inside the mansion.

Skipping stairs and shouting, "Nina! Nina!"

I threw open the door and ran to the bedroom. The sheets were a tangled mess. She wasn't there. My God, I thought. They've taken her! Thorn dashed past me and into the bathroom. He bumped the door open with his nose and slipped in. A single sharp bark.

"Thorn! Privacy please, you sly old dog."

It was Nina's voice, muffled but unmistakable. My heart leaped in my chest.

I crossed the room in two strides and pushed past the door.

"It's a party now," she said. "Shut the door. I feel a draft." Nina lay up to her chin in steaming hot water. She'd filled the clawfoot tub as high as it would go without overflowing. She'd slicked back her wet hair, and her cigarette holder was clamped between her teeth. There was an ashtray on the floor beside the tub and a snifter of what looked like cognac.

Thorn rested his head on the rim of the tub.

"Don't even think of joining me, Thorn." Nina petted his snout with her drippy hand. "Darling, do tell me that's not a knife you're brandishing." She looked at me with mild concern.

I stared at the weapon the gargoyle had tossed over the fence. I was gripping it so tightly my fingers were changing colors. I put it on the sink. The rust-speckled steel, its edge shining like wet silver paint. I ushered Thorn from the room and closed the door.

"Did anyone visit you?" I asked.

"Besides Thorny?"

"I'm not joking. Has someone been up here talking to you?"

"Quiet down. You're killing my head. Of course no one's been up here. What's gotten into you?" She closed her eyes, reclining against the back of the tub. A damp hand removed the cigarette holder; she tapped ashes toward the ashtray on the floor. "Hand me my brandy, would you? Don't judge. Hair of the dog, as they say."

I stepped nearer to the bathtub, starting to bend over for the glass, when I paused.

"Do you have a knife?"

"Alden, you just put one on the sink. What do you need a knife for?" She yawned. One of her hands dangled over the tub, a foot above her glass, but the other remained hidden under the murky, milky jade water. I smelled sweet pine bath salts. The bathroom tropical with steam. Wisps floated in the air, mixing with her cigarette smoke. I was sweating.

The gargoyle's words echoed in my brain. *"I'm telling her the same thing."*

Had the demon given her a knife? Did he suggest she murder *me* because I wasn't real? How did he know about last night? And about Balthazarr's blood ritual?

I inched forward, attempting to see through the bathwater. It was impossible.

Nina's eyes remained closed. She clenched the cigarette holder between her lips.

"Quite a party," she said, smirking. "You certainly enjoyed yourself."

"Yes… I'm having trouble recalling how things ended."

"What a pity. You were having the time of your life." She let out a low growl from the back of her throat. "My finger still hurts.

Will you kiss it for me?" She extended her middle finger, the one she'd pricked on the nail over the blood bowl. "Pretty please?"

I moved closer, never taking my eyes off the surface of the jade-colored water. "My memories grow fuzzy after Balthazarr's rite."

"Really? You seemed fine. You were talking to everyone. Balthazarr's enthusiasm over your paintings boosted your confidence to new heights. He's quite the character, isn't he?"

"What was your impression of the great Surrealist?"

I leaned against the tub at an angle slightly behind her. If she were going to stab me with a knife secreted in the water, she'd have to twist around to do it. I thought I might be able to back away and defend myself with the ashtray, if need be. Not hurt her but deflect the attack. Would she obey the gargoyle? I hadn't. I wasn't sure of anything. Not even Nina.

"Ummm. He's handsome and *very* charismatic. It's all part of his act, I should imagine. I've noticed him buzzing around the Colony but never met him properly." She shifted in the tub. Her pink skin squeaked against the porcelain-coated cast iron. I startled, but she didn't notice. Her eyes were heavily lidded. "Though come to think of it, I actually might have seen him before. Much earlier…"

"You saw Balthazarr before last night's party? Really? Where?"

"He was with Court, I think. Maybe coming out of his apartment? Or when I visited South Church. All I remember is a tall man with a black beard split at the bottom. *He's striking,* I thought. It might've been the day when you and I first met. Isn't *that* funny to think about?"

How could that be? Unless Balthazarr somehow projected himself across the ocean. Or he was lying about his arrival in the country. Or both. I crouched behind the tub, watching.

"What are you doing back there?" She lifted her head and sat up, craning to look at me over her naked shoulder. "Have you gone batty? Did the champagne do it?"

"That second round did taste strange," I said. "A chemical aftertaste, chalkiness."

"I'm kidding. *God.* Hand me the cognac, will you?"

"Let me see your hands first. Both hands." I stood, my back to the tile wall.

My request amused her, despite her current post-celebratory suffering. She took her hands out of the water. They were steaming, as if she'd crawled fresh from a hell mouth. She flipped her cigarette into the ashtray on the floor. She maneuvered around, so now she was half-kneeling, half curling on her haunches in the bathtub. It was a good position to spring at me. A wave sloshed over the side and doused her cigarette. She smelled like the pine woods. A forest creature I'd encountered in a fable. A wood nymph to enchant me. Her body was gleaming. I could count the nubs of her spine down to the waterline.

"Here are my hands," she said. "Now what should I do?"

"Is anything hidden under the water?"

"Practically everything." Her long arm reached for the cognac. She gulped it down.

"I'm not playing games here."

"You *are*, you silly boy. But I like this game. Keep going."

"There was something in my champagne. That's why I can't remember anything."

"You think I slipped you a mickey?" She pantomimed dropping something in her glass. Acting on the assumption that I was being playful. None of this was to be taken seriously.

Lovers' games.

That's what we were doing. Or she was pretending to think so.

I wouldn't have objected, except I'd met a monster outside at this very hour, in broad daylight, and he'd told me to kill my lover. I was dizzy. My head hurt where the night watchman had bashed me. The fog on the river that swallowed the gargoyle – I felt like I had some of it trapped inside my skull, like smoke blown inside a bottle and corked. Hazy, I was hazy.

"What happened after the lights went out? You remember, don't you?" I said.

She nodded. "Balthazarr must've had someone switch the power off to the house. It was a performance. Surely you realize that." I could see her playfulness ebbing. She wondered if I was serious. "He tried out a bit of hocus pocus. For mood. To bring the Colony closer together. No different than fraternity initiations. Secret handshakes. Clubby foolishness."

Nina pulsed her fingers at me like the fronds of a sea anemone. Trying to recapture the mischievous mood she'd felt before. She refused to acknowledge anything real had happened last night. I wished I could believe that too. But I couldn't. Everything can't be imaginary.

"My tuxedo stinks from incense. Tell me it doesn't. When did they burn incense?"

"I will not sniff your tuxedo. C'mon, my Oak Tree. Let's take a bath and get clean."

She shifted and another wave slopped noisily over the tub.

I jumped back, snatching the knife from the sink.

"Stay away!" I shouted.

Her jaw fell open. Her anger arrived in a rush. "Don't you pull a knife on me! Are you crazy? Look at yourself!" She pointed to the mirror.

I turned to witness my frightened face. Eyes bulging. Me, in the fogged-over lookingglass, clutching a brutal blade. In horror, I threw the knife away.

"What am I doing?" My lungs were heaving, my throat constricted as I struggled for a breath. "Why can't I remember anything after Balthazarr drank the blood? It's a void in my mind."

Nina rose from the bathtub. No weapon. She reached for a towel and wrapped it around her torso.

She put her arms around my chest. "Poor baby, you *are* scared. Of me?" She laughed, astonished at that. "Easy now, easy…"

"I love you, Nina."

"I love you too." She hugged me.

I shivered in the overheated bathroom.

"Maybe you've come down with something." She put her lips to my forehead. "You're burning."

We walked into the bedroom.

I lay on the bed, my head in Nina's lap. "Tell me what you remember of last night. After Balthazarr drank the bowl of blood."

"Someone turned the lights out. It was only for effect. Like a magic show. We all knew it wasn't real. A minute or two later, the lights switched on again. People clapped. Balthazarr took a bow. He'd done some trick with the floor, too. I don't know, it was like charcoal outlines of his shoes. They'd been burned into the wood. If he was hoping people would be shocked at that, it didn't work. They hardly paid any attention. You noticed them. The burn marks, or whatever he'd done to fake them. You said you saw him do the same thing in Spain."

I had seen them in Spain. But last night was still lost. "Did he say anything to me?"

"He called you a clever man." Nina combed her fingers through my hair.

"I think I was drugged. I didn't drink enough booze to knock me out."

Nina considered what I had said. "You were drinking quite a lot after the second round of champagne. But I suppose you might've been given something against your will. There are cacti that grow in Mexico, and vines from the Amazon in Peru, that cause hallucinations. Or opium might do it. It's possible…"

"When I went to take Thorn out this morning, I saw the gargoyle. He was behind a fence in the yard. And he gave me that knife. He told me to kill you." I made a fist. I was trembling with rage. "That you weren't real. He said he told you the same thing. To kill me…"

"You saw the gargoyle again?" She was shocked. "I'd almost convinced myself that never happened. That we dreamed it. No one told me to do anything, Alden."

We stayed in bed, silent. I wasn't asleep. When I turned my face to look at Nina, she was awake too, smiling down at me like the statue of a goddess. Serene, yet powerful.

"Did you see Balthazarr before last night? Are you sure of it?"

She shook her head. "No, not sure. But you saying you felt like you were drugged has me thinking. I wonder if they all were. The Galinka sisters. Udo Ganz. Dr Silva. That drifter in the boxcar with his throat cut, and even Clark Abernathy. If the killer, or killers, drugged them first, then it might've been easier to manipulate them like they did. I wonder if someone was trying some drug out on you. To see what would happen."

"A test?"

"Yes. A test. Or a preparation. I didn't tell you before. But I found out new facts about the murder victims. They all came from wealthy, aristocratic families. Oh, they didn't necessarily have mountains of cash now. For some it was in their lineage. The Galinka sisters were the granddaughters of a Russian princess. Dr Silva's family is one of the wealthiest in Rio de Janeiro. Udo Ganz's father owns an emerald mine in South Africa. The drifter was the one who didn't fit the pattern. That's because the police didn't know who he was. Well, his relatives showed up at the county morgue last week to claim his body. They're royal blood from Luxembourg, of all places. Clark's family is new American money. Rich people like us, Alden. We're the ones getting murdered."

CHAPTER TWENTY-FOUR

The next day Nina decided we needed a car. My father owned three Rolls-Royce automobiles. His favorite was a Silver Ghost, the only car he ever drove himself. Asking him for it was laughably out of the question. He also had a Phantom, reserved for special trips, and a smaller Twenty that Roland used to chauffer Mother around to appointments.

I paid my father an early morning visit. It was best to catch him at the end of his breakfast. His mood slid downhill as the day progressed, from irritation to aggravation.

"May I borrow the Twenty?" I asked.

My father's eyebrows lifted. A dramatic display for him. "What for?"

"I have a new girlfriend. I'd like to show her around town."

The corner of his mouth twitched. This was a smile.

"Mother said she won't be needing Roland to take her anywhere."

Father sat at his enormous desk, tapping his fingers on the mahogany. Deciding.

"It had better come back the way it leaves," he said, finally.

"Thank you."

Father put on his spectacles and rustled his newspaper.

I was dismissed.

Nina practically ran to the curb. A handful of curious bystanders gathered outside the Colony to gawk when I pulled up. I got out to meet her on the sidewalk. Nina bypassed me, walked around to the driver's side, climbing behind the wheel. She patted the other seat. "Get in."

"I cannot allow you to drive Wilfred's car."

"He'll never know. Will he?" She dared me to deny her.

"Fine." I got in. "Let's not have a wreck. If we do, make sure I die."

Nina drove fast. The roads were slick from a recent dusting of snow. I felt the Twenty lose traction a few times, but Nina always corrected the car. She had no patience, I was learning. Rush into everything. Catch up on the details as you go. Don't talk yourself out of risk. Find the limits, race up to the line, see if you might be able to push things out a little farther, or in deeper.

I won't lie and tell you she didn't excite me.

Life since Nina had more color. Bigger ups and downs. It was a thrill ride, to be sure.

Speaking of thrills, I reached into my pocket and removed an item wrapped in a rag.

I opened the cloth.

A gun.

Nina glanced down at it. Then looked back at the road. The car accelerated.

After the gargoyle's second appearance, Nina managed to wear me down about visiting the Black Cave to search for more clues. Not hearing from Calvin sealed the deal. I insisted we didn't have enough protection to go near the bootleggers' camp by ourselves. Nina disagreed but didn't argue. One night, she went out for a walk while I was asleep and came home with a pistol. She'd bought it at the Clover Club. "It's a Colt 1903 Pocket Hammerless. Compact. Holds seven rounds." She was quite proud of herself for having procured it.

"Are you serious?" I asked, sitting up in bed. I'd awakened at the sound of the door.

"You said we needed protection. Here it is."

"Who sold it to you?"

"What difference does it make?" She aimed the semiautomatic around the apartment.

The next day we took turns drawing the weapon, blowing bottles off stumps, in a vacant lot along the river. We were no marksmen, but in a jam, we might get off a few shots.

Now, riding beside Nina, I rechecked the magazine. Tucked the gun into my waistband. In case we ran into trouble. Which we certainly would.

Now that we were mobile, we didn't have to worry about walking everywhere in the freezing January cold. After a bit of poking around on lanes that dead-ended at the river, we found the one that led to the bootleggers' camp. Better to let them see us coming from a ways off with the sun in the sky, I thought. We didn't need them feeling any jumpier than they were going to be already. Pine branches hid the entrance to the camp road. We passed it a few times before I noticed the long gap running back into the trees. Nina pulled over, and I dragged the branches out of the way. Once she drove in, I arranged them back the way they were. Farther up the old dirt road, we encountered a heavy log crossing our path. No way to drive over it. But together we managed to roll the log off the lane. Momentum carried it out of our hands and into the ditch. We drove on. The Miskatonic flashed through the bare trees to our left. I hadn't spotted any lookouts watching the road for trespassers. I almost wished I had. Then they might've turned us back around and sent us home.

"We're getting close," I said.

The Twenty rocked and skittered up and down the hills.

"I'll talk first," Nina said. "They'll be less suspicious of a woman."

"Don't bet on it. How do you explain us driving on their road?"

"We're from out of town. Honeymooners. We got lost."

"After we removed their camouflage and barriers?"

"They'll believe me. I can be terribly convincing." Her cheeks turned rosy in the cold.

"Remember, when we get there, we can ask about Calvin. If we don't see him, we try to find Freddie or Winston. But don't get out of the car. Any sign of danger, we leave," I said.

"Life is danger, Alden."

"I prefer mine moderated."

We reached the camp.

She hit the brakes.

Squirrels. Cardinals in the pine branches, flashing like torn red flags. Junk on the ground. Cigarette butts. Broken bottles. Empty cans of beans. Footprints chewed up the snow. Truck tire marks slashed the ground, as if a giant had been digging with his fingers, but none of the tracks were recent. They had ice in them. Quiet as a saint's confessional box, it was. Nobody home.

"Where did they go?" I said.

Nina opened her door.

I grabbed her arm. "We're not getting out. Remember?"

"That was if they were here. The bootleggers have cleared out, obviously." She pulled away from me. Her shoes made glassy, crackling noises on the crusty snow. I hadn't opened my door.

"Then why get out at all? Calvin's not here." The sight of the camp made my head start to ache. Perhaps it was psychosomatic, a physical recollection of my head injury and treatment. My temples throbbed.

She turned. The wind was picking up, snatching at her words. Her hand held her hat down, keeping it from blowing away. "I want to look for clues. If nobody's here, we can explore the cave." She walked on before I could object.

I bit my lip. "This is a mistake," I whispered. My fingers rested on the gun grip.

I climbed out and followed her.

Honestly, I was curious. Visions of the scene I witnessed in the Black Cave still showed up in my dreams most nights along with the night watchman's swinging bat. My ride in the Burdon's ice truck with the mackerel. It was all there in my head. Nothing burned as brightly as my memory of the green lights in the cave. Hooded figures finger-painting on bumpy cave walls, their buzzy voices chanting as they carried me up the steps.

"Wait for me," I shouted.

Nina paused inside the cave mouth, as if she were about to be swallowed.

"You have your lighter? Fire up my torch. I found one leaning against the wall. I want to go investigate back there." She pointed to the depths of the cave, past the places where I'd seen the barrels and crates stacked for deliveries. They were gone. You could see their impressions in the sandy soil. I lit her torch, and she held it over our heads. The copper pot stills were pushed farther inside than they had been. Maybe they were too heavy to bother moving.

"They left in a hurry. Didn't take all their equipment," I said.

The torch reflected in the copper.

"Nobody with a half a brain is going to sneak in here and mess with their stuff."

"What does that say about us?"

"We're only taking a look around," she said.

I tried to take the torch from her.

"Let me have the torch. You've got the gun," she said.

"We must stay together," I insisted. "I don't want either of us getting lost."

"Of course, darling. We're a team." She kissed my cheek.

Side by side we searched the underground hollow. Just as I recalled, the cave turned to the left and the floor angled downward, like a ramp. It was clear that previous explorers had removed several small and medium-sized rocks from the pathway, stacking them on either side of the passage. At the bottom of the ramp-like descent we reached a level surface, and soon discovered a large fragment which had broken from the ceiling in a collapse. It blocked our progress. This chunk of geologic debris resembled a toy top, or cone; its point smashed into the floor, eons ago. Nina's torchlight revealed a blank circle on the ceiling where the fragment had once hung. We had no choice but to climb over the obstacle. With a little extra effort, we overcame the impediment. What bothered me was that I had no memory of encountering this obstruction on my first trip down.

"You said there were steps." Nina probed the darkness ahead. "How far ahead?"

"Just a bit," I said. But I could've sworn we should have reached them already.

We continued to hunt for the stairway. The cave walls narrowed, not to the degree they inspired any claustrophobia or fear of entombment. However, like the top-shaped obstacle, I didn't recall this constriction of the passageway. No wider than a doorway, the walls had pressed in around us. The flow of air lessened, or perhaps I was breathing heavier.

"Why didn't you tell me it got this tight? Does it open again by the steps?"

"The steps are wide across." Had we somehow turned the wrong way? All of this appeared unfamiliar to me. Perhaps my damaged brain had ignored or erased this interval.

I didn't know.

"I see something," Nina said.

"The steps?" I felt a momentary rush of relief. I'd simply forgotten this tunnel portion.

"No. Not steps."

Thankfully, the stone corridor did open wider. The walls disappeared completely, and we entered an enormous cathedral-like space, with high, ribbed ceilings of wavy colored rock; dark blues and purples streaked upward in serpentine ribbons, like the bottoms of many velvet drapes. Others took on more fleshy colors, reminding me of clam gills or the undersides of mushrooms.

"This isn't the way I came before."

"But there was no place to turn. We walked the only way we could go." Nina stuck the torch out in front of her. Fiery flashes answered her movement in the dark ahead.

"What's that?" I whispered. "There's somebody out there." I drew the Colt. If anyone rushed at us, I planned to shoot them. I heard a moist glugging.

Nina raised her torch again.

The flashes multiplied in reply.

"How many are there?" she said, astonished.

"It might be that group I met. The hooded ones who carried me back to the cave mouth."

Nina raised and lowered her flame, quickly. She repeated the action. Then did it once more, but slowly. "I think I know what's happening." She took several long strides forward.

"Where are you going?" I bolted after her.

She stopped abruptly and threw her arm out to block me from going any farther.

"Careful," she said, lowering her torch. "We don't know how deep it is."

A huge glassy pool of obsidian water stretched before us as far as we could see. The lights were reflections of Nina's torch, mirrored on the rippling surface. Water? I had no memory of this! "What's making those wrinkles… those undulations in the pool? Is it fish?"

"What else could it be?" Nina crouched, splashing her fingertips in the shallows.

"Don't do that." I didn't want us attracting anything closer. I felt suddenly like prey.

"Why not? I thought you wanted to see if they're fish." She splashed some more.

"Don't." I touched her shoulder. The ripples moved rhythmically, making bigger wavelets. Muscular waves churned farther out; the source skulked beyond the limits of our light.

"Is it a big fish? Or an animal that lives down here?" she asked.

"I can't see anything. Stop it. We have to turn back."

Nina withdrew her fingers from the black water and stood up. She put one finger to the tip of her tongue. "Saltwater. It must be connected to the river and the ocean beyond."

Something thick and weighty wallowed below the surface. A pale bulge of belly, or was it dorsal? The bloated body rotated under the water, twirling a few feet from us. We backed up.

From the unseeable borders of the pool came a loud slapping and the dull thud of – well, of I don't know what… some creature cavorting in the underground reservoir. The merriment of it nauseated me. How can I explain other than to relate that I experienced an instant and powerful physical revulsion when I perceived the sound and its vile echo inhabiting the ancient chamber?

"We have to go," I said, urgently. I had the horrible sense of time running out.

She felt it too, because she did not hesitate to retreat from the lake's perimeter. When we had gone twenty yards, or it might've been more, we turned our backs to the pool and made a quick evacuation from the Black Cave. The narrow portion of the passage seemed narrower. Behind us, at a distance not terribly close, but not as far as would have made us comfortable, a wet smacking of meatiness on rock – I won't say stalked, but trailed us.

Nina scrambled over the cone-shaped fragment that resembled a toy top.

I stared into the dark. If the cause of the wet smacking suddenly appeared, I would kill it.

But nothing emerged.

I pocketed the gun and went over the top too.

At the base of the cave ramp, we allowed ourselves to experience a sense of reprieve from the strange perception of threat emanating from that dismal, sea-connected, jet-black lake. I clutched Nina's cool, sweaty hand. The air seemed less thick, breathing easier.

Too soon we felt safe.

For we had not taken more than three steps up the ramp when we discovered the corpse. How we didn't smell it beforehand defies easy explanation, since the body showed clear signs of advanced decomposition. A leaky, leathery, human bag wrapped in a shawl of struggling maggots. It exuded a green, black, and brown rainbow of liquids – a slow, rancid waterfall of putrefaction oozing down the slope. Whatever we had been spared of the odor now advanced upon us ferociously.

I retched.

Nina buried her mouth in her sleeve, gagging.

I have left for last the most shocking fact: the corpse had no head.

I bent over the remains, feeling fascinated and disgusted. But, ultimately, my curiosity won the day. I searched the cave in vain for a stick to prod the body. Instead, I was forced to use the tip of my shoe to nudge the cadaver's lower leg. "Hand me the torch, please."

"What for?" Nina asked, her voice dampened by the crook of her elbow.

"Please give it to me. I want to see something."

She passed me the flame. And for the second time in recent months, I employed firelight to identify Clark Abernathy's scarred knee. It was a positive match.

"This is Clark Abernathy's body," I said, confirming what I suspected.

I returned Nina's flame.

"How do you know?"

"He has a long scar on his leg. See the mark? I spotted the same cicatrix on the body in the observatory. Before it was hustled away. I knew it! I am not crazy! Clark was, and is, dead. Murdered. Beheaded. His life offered as a sacrifice. Something… stole his corpse from the observatory. The gargoyle! Of course! It flew him out the window before I could show the remains to Preston and Minnie. He's been hidden away somewhere. Somewhere cold. Because he'd have been more decayed than this if the body were left to rot naturally. No. They've iced him. Now they've dumped him down here like a sack of garbage." I felt a modicum of vindication.

"Who?"

"Who what?"

Nina lowered her arm from shielding her nose. "Who dumped Clark?"

"His murderers. The ones who've been killing Arkham's unfortunate elites. Clark may have learned something from the Galinka girl he met at the Clover Club. Maybe he saw something he shouldn't have. But I'm sure it's no coincidence."

"He wasn't here when we came down the ramp an hour ago."

We turned simultaneously to gaze up the ramp, toward the cave mouth. Though I heard nothing, I knew we were not alone. Threats ahead of us and behind.

The Colt Hammerless was in my hand once more.

Gingerly, we stepped around Clark. He'd been dragged. A trail of putrid fluids illustrated the way. We came to the turn that led to the cave entrance. It was a blind curve. Light from the outside brightened the passage, after the turn. Nina's torch shone on the cave walls where we paused to gather our nerves.

"If they're waiting for us, it'll be right around the corner," I whispered.

Nina nodded.

"You stick the torch out to distract them. I'll take a look," I said.

"Don't get killed." She squeezed my hand.

Nina stretched out her arm and waved the torch in front of us. We waited. The appearance of our flame triggered no response. But if they were being patient… I put my back to the cave wall. I started forward.

"Wait," Nina seized my shoulder.

"Wait for what?" My heart hammered in my chest.

"I don't know…"

"Neither do I." It was no use prolonging things.

I ducked my head, and the gun, around the junction.

No one. Nothing.

Together we proceeded to the cave mouth. No discernible footprints stood out from those already left in the sandy soil near the opening. The stains from transporting Clark's mushy carcass began at the ramp. His carrier had fled the scene.

"Alden, look at this."

Nina pushed her torchlight at the wall. It was where the barrels had been stacked the last time I visited.

"A new drawing!" I said, startled. Then disgust took over. "These marks have been made with Clark's… fluids."

"Oh, God." Nina covered her mouth. But she didn't look away.

The blackish greenish lines flowed over the stone, as if a

powerful grip had forced them out of Clark, using him like a tube of paint.

"Two ovals inside a cup. This was the first pictogram I saw, when Preston drew it in the sand with his foot back at Cannes."

"Over here," Nina said. "There's more. Words." She slid her light along the rocks.

I read the message out loud.

> ### WELCOME ALDEN
> ### NINA
> ### YOU OPEN THE GATE!

"*We* open the Gate?" Nina said. "Why would we do that?"

"They know we're looking for them. We must go. Now!"

Moving quickly, we retraced our steps back to Father's Rolls-Royce. I got behind the wheel and tried to start the engine. But it kept stalling out. Damn! I pounded the wheel. Nina took the Colt from me. "Be ready!" I said. Finally, the motor turned. I turned the Twenty around and sped away. Every tree trunk hid a monk to my mind, each cluster of evergreen branches provided a roost to a clay-faced gargoyle. It wouldn't have shocked me to see the net blob lumbering along the road.

I wasn't even sure if I planned to report Clark's body to the police. I didn't want to be involved. What if his body disappeared again before the cops got here to retrieve it? Would I be a suspect in his disappearance? No. I was going to keep my mouth shut. Nothing would help Clark anyway. I pressed the gas pedal. Did my best to steer clear of the potholes and deeper ruts.

"Look!" Nina shouted. She pointed the barrel of the Colt at the windshield. "Someone rolled the log back across the road."

I slowed the car. Was this a trap? Would snipers have us in their sights? A pair of sitting ducks parked in a Rolls-Royce on a lonesome back road. How long would it take anyone to discover our bullet-riddled bodies? Until springtime? I had no choice. Only forward.

I stopped the Twenty. My tires crushed the icy mud in front of the log.

"That's no log," I said.

I climbed out. Nina's door opened. She joined me at the bumper of the running car.

Exhaust swirled at our backs.

On the frozen ground. Two more bodies. Lying head to foot in a neat row.

Freddie and Winston.

Lying face-up in a mockery of silent repose. Arms folded across their chests. The only thing that betrayed their peace was the matching look of horror petrified on their faces.

Mouths locked wide in eternal screams.

Throats cut, ear to ear.

They might've been caught staring, gaping at the blank white sky, except...:

They had no eyes.

CHAPTER TWENTY-FIVE

I felt guilty for not burying them.

Nina and I carried Freddie and Winston over to the ditch where we'd rolled the log. We lowered the men into a trough of soft snow and covered them with pine boughs. Our conclusion was that whoever disposed of Clark in the cave had also killed Freddie and Winston. They were freshly deceased, their blood still warm when it ran from their terrible wounds through our fingers.

"Were they guarding the camp?" Nina asked.

"If they were, then whoever murdered them did it prior to our arrival. Freddie and Winston would've recognized us on the road. If we drove past their guard posts, they certainly would've caught up with us at the camp." I wiped Freddie's blood off my hands on the rag I'd brought for the Colt. Nina did the same. We threw the rag into the ditch.

Back home at the Colony apartments, I reconsidered calling the police. I'd leave an anonymous tip about the bodies in the woods and the cadaver inside the Black Cave. I picked up the phone.

Nina grabbed my hand. She convinced me not to call.

"Half the force is on the O'Bannion family's payroll. News will reach them eventually. When the boys don't report back, the bootlegging crew will check the camp. They'll find the bodies."

"I don't know. We hid them pretty well."

"They'll notice the log missing and look in the ditch. Trust me, Alden. The O'Bannion gang takes care of their own. No one's calling the cops. Not us, anyway."

She was worried about the police again. My call wouldn't help the dead.

Nina poured two whiskies and handed me one. "It's for the best. You don't want Freddie and Winston buried in some Potter's Field owned by the city of Arkham, do you?"

"I guess not." I polished off my drink, feeling it burn all the way down.

Nina played with her glass, rolling it between her palms. "Listen. I've been thinking. Clark's murder fits with the others. It matches the pattern. He's from the elite class, and that's who's being targeted. If the murders are rituals, maybe they're leading up to something bigger. First, they send out a call. To what? We don't know yet. Then the rites offer a kind of protection to the ones doing the killing. It can't be just one person doing it, either. It's too complicated. All those murders… physically it must be a group behind them. For whatever reason, this group attracts a spirit or entity, sends out a signal. If the entity is pleased, it bestows power on the offeror."

"I like what you're saying, except Freddie and Winston weren't elites. Freddie was a farm boy. They were… ordinary."

Nina exhaled and shook her head. "Their deaths weren't sacrificial. They were killed because they got in the way. The method wasn't ceremonial. They were simply dispatched. The only signal being sent was to you and me. Like that message on the cave wall."

"You think these men were killed because they helped us?"

"I'm afraid so." She looked sad but not defeated.

"It makes me sick to think it's my fault." It tore me up thinking those two guys had their throats cut over me. Dead in a cold ditch. If I hadn't snooped around, they'd be alive.

"You can't blame yourself."

"But I do." I finished my drink. "What about Calvin? Think he's alive?"

"I hope so. We have no reason to believe he's dead. In danger? Certainly."

So, in the end we didn't call the police. I saw no story of the killings in the city papers. As far as we knew, the dead men were still out there on the dirt road, under the pines.

I was in my apartment a few days later when someone knocked on my door. Nina and I had made a habit of locking our apartments. But we had keys to each other's places. Nina never knocked. I knew it couldn't be her. Besides, she was out tracking down a lead on the dancing Galinka sisters act and who hired them to work at the Clover Club. Nina thought maybe that's how they were selected to be sacrificed. She took the Rolls, which I hadn't bothered to return.

I lifted the Colt off my dresser, holding it behind my back as I answered the door. I opened it a crack and was surprised to see Minnie's cat eyes blinking at me.

"Hiya there, Alden. May I come in?"

I stepped back, tucking the gun into the small of my back.

Pulling out my shirt, I hoped she wouldn't notice the pistol.

"Funny seeing you here. Shouldn't you be out planning a wedding?"

Minnie walked in, in a rush. She threw off her hat and dropped her purse on my sofa, and then plopped herself there too. With a smooth scissor move, she slipped off both her shoes, pointing her silk-stockinged toes at the rug and flexing her tight calves while letting out a deep, exhausted-sounding moan. "Oh, Aldie, I'm so worried I don't know what to do. I didn't know who else to come to. Because if you can't help, I don't know where I'll go. Insane, probably. It's all too much. I can't take it. I absolutely can't, not like this."

She started crying. Not big heaving sobs, but shiny, bubbly tears like glass beads rolling down her cheeks. Her dimpled chin quivered.

"Minnie, dear, what's got you so upset? It can't be all that terrible, can it?"

Minnie looked at me, and her eyes flooded.

I sat beside her. She draped her arms around me. Her breath smelled of peppermints.

"I think Preston's in real trouble," she said. "We both are."

I was alarmed but didn't want her to see that. "I've known Preston a long time. Longer than I've known you. He's gotten into plenty of pickles. But I haven't seen one yet that he can't wriggle out of. Usually smelling like a prize rose."

I rubbed her back.

She scooted closer. Her forehead brushed my cheek. I felt her laughing. Not happy but laughing. That's a start, I figured. "Tell me what he's done."

Minnie sat back. But her face stayed near to mine. The last

time we were this close we were lovers, I thought. My heart tripped faster. I tried easing back and ran into the stiff arm of the couch. My gun did, anyway. So I moved up again.

"Ever got in your head that somebody you love has changed?" she said.

"That's why we broke up. Isn't it?"

"I don't mean that. I mean that the person you knew checked out, and somebody, a stranger, checked in. Preston is not himself. He looks like Preston. It sounds like his voice. But he's different. I can't explain it exactly how I want. He's Preston, but he's not Preston, too."

"I'm lost here, Minnie." I didn't want to dismiss her concerns. I'd noticed Preston changing too. A man under pressure, I thought. Slowly cracking. I'd chalked it up to wedding jitters. It sounded worse than that. "He hasn't called the wedding off, has he?"

"Called it off? No. He's actually moved it up! To March! Oh, I know he's hiding something from me. That's nothing new. We lie to each other. Small things, the way all couples do. I'm not talking about that." She wore poinsettia red lipstick, dark and artificial, but it looked good on her, a dramatic contrast to her complexion.

"He mentioned pushing up the date to me. But I thought that was a mutual decision?"

"It was. It *is*." Minnie seemed a woman bombarded by thoughts and emotions. "I'm not against getting married earlier than we planned. I love him. I think he loves me. It's just such a total turnaround. If anything, I would've guessed Preston wanted to delay the wedding. He was anxious. He told me so. Now it's just the opposite. He'll only say he wants us together sooner. But where did that idea come from? It's not like him. Preston puts things off. His father is the restless one. Lately, it's as if a stranger were wearing Preston's body as a disguise. The way he moves. The expressions on his face. They're off kilter." Minnie squeezed her tiny hands into tinier fists. "Oh, it's so frustrating. You think I'm crazy. A crazy woman who complains about her new man to her old man…"

"I'm your old man?"

She punched me lightly in the chest, right over my heart. "You know what I mean."

Minnie left her hand there. Her fingers spread and pressed against my shirt. She felt my heart pounding. How could she miss it? I held her wrist, gently moving her hand away.

"Men often don't know how to express their feelings. Might it be simple as that?"

"Don't you think women get nervous too? Is he the right man? Is this it?"

An idea dawned on me. "Are you having second thoughts, Minnie?"

She waited a few beats, thinking it over. "No," she said, with finality. "Preston and I are perfectly matched. Only, I want him back the way he was. Do you know what I think it is?"

"What?"

"It's not a what but a *who*." Minnie dipped her chin and aimed a lacquered nail at me.

"Who then?"

"Juan Hugo! He's the one that's changed him. The man's practically taken over our lives. He would've if I didn't stop him. Preston is under the man's spell. Worse than another woman."

"But Balthazarr spends all his time at the Colony. I've never seen Preston there." I was surprised to hear her mention the Surrealist's name. If Preston existed at one remove from New Colony, then Minnie was at least two away. How was a visiting painter having any impact whatsoever on her relationship?

"That's just it!" Minnie jumped from the sofa. "Is it always so dreadfully chilly in your rooms?"

"I hadn't noticed."

"Don't you have a bottle we can open?"

I frowned, confused. "Of alcohol?"

Minnie put her hands on her shapely hips. "Alden. I want a drink."

"Why didn't you just ask?"

"I just did. Give me a cigarette, sweetie. I'm going through difficulties."

I handed her my case and lighter and went to fetch a bottle of whiskey.

"*God!*" I heard her calling out. "Men are so literal. And they can be frightfully dull."

I returned with the bottle, handed it off to her, and went in search of glasses.

"Where is Preston off to constantly? I'll tell you. It's Balthazarr. Balthazarr at the Lodge with Carl Sanford and his pops for brandies. 'I'm out for a drive with Juan Hugo, love'. We're the two getting married. He needs to think about us. *Our* event. Especially if everything is happening sooner than we planned."

I guided Minnie back to the sofa. She snuggled against me.

"You're saying Balthazarr is influencing Preston in a negative way…"

"Yes, he is." I noticed Minnie's perfume. Loud and citrusy when it first touched the nose, then settling back into a warm blue vanilla scent. Elegant, sad. Silk sheets and hours alone. I wondered how life would turn out for her.

"Care to elaborate?" Without thinking, I saw my hand stroking her bare forearm, the light fuzz rising from my attention, an appearance of goosebumps. I noticed I had them too.

Minnie relaxed; her shoulders drooped like a hypnotist's volunteer.

"Preston moved the wedding because of him. He won't admit it. But I know that's the cause. He's got me to shift the party over to the Silver Gate Hotel."

"Balthazarr suggested that? Preston told me you were thinking about it the morning Juan Hugo arrived. Oh now, see there, he couldn't have put the idea into Preston's head."

"Well, I don't know how he did it. But he did. Like a Houdini trick or something…"

I was the one having doubts now. About Preston and Balthazarr. Was Preston under the man's influence to a degree I had not perceived? I felt a fool for missing it if it was true.

"Having the wedding at the Silver Gate *will* be so terrific," Minnie continued, unaware of my mental reevaluations. "I'm not complaining about the quality of things. Preston keeps telling me how bright our future is becoming with each new day."

The winter sun broke from the clouds and shone white on the floor of my apartment.

We watched it like our ancestors watched their fires. Mesmerized. Seeking meaning.

"He said that? Here I always thought you two had a bright future together."

"Me too…" Minnie topped off her glass. "It's like he's suddenly gotten a vision, or something, about not only the wedding. But about everything. As if he's made an investment and the payoff is coming in bigger than he expected. He sounds like one of those creepy old schemers. It's not that bad, really. Only… there's something else attached to it. A secret. A double event that he's not letting me in on. Saying it out loud sounds crazier than when it's murmuring on in my head."

Dread, when it arrives, is like a falling inward. I was falling now. My two friends…

Minnie curled against me. I felt a kind of exposure then; involuntary fear crept over me like sickness. I was afraid to touch her. Yet I did and said nothing about it.

"Is Preston in some sort of secret society?" I asked, shifting my inquiry.

Minnie lifted her head to look at me. "The Silver Lodge? That's more his father's thing."

"What about here at New Colony? Has he said anything curious related to that?"

Minnie blinked. I could tell she was reviewing conversations past. "I don't think so."

"I only ask because Juan Hugo is the big cheese at the Colony. People worship him. Hell, I do too. It's almost cult-like, the following he has." I gazed at the bright sun scouring the wooden boards. "He does these mock rituals. Stagecraft, I thought. A bit of showmanship. But in front of the right crowd the effects are entrancing. Preston might find he's charmed. Afterward he acts as though he's still under the influence of Balthazarr, his Master, so to speak." I did my best not to introduce to Minnie any of the panic that was growing inside me.

Minnie had enough worries.

She sat heavily against me; her eyes fluttered. I took her glass. When she spoke, the edges of her words were rounded off and softly slurred. "When we're alone together, Preston is not Preston. He smiles at me like he's pulled some awful trick. Like inside, he hates me."

"That sounds awful." I cared for Minnie. But in that moment, I wanted to flee.

"Tomorrow is Preston's bachelor party," Minnie said.

"I know. I'm going."

"Balthazarr is his new best man. Did Preston tell you? It was supposed to be Clark, but Clark has vanished. His family hired a private detective. They think he might be dead." Her head tipped back. Eyes closed.

My throat rippled. I could not speak.

"Be careful when you're out with them, Alden. I have the most awful premonition that something ghastly is going to happen and ruin all our lives."

Minnie started to snore.

The clouds hid the sun. The floor, the apartment and everything in it grayed out.

CHAPTER TWENTY-SIX

Hours later, I woke up alone in the dark on the sofa. Minnie was gone. I heard noises in the hall, a kind of scuffling, and two voices, tensed and rising in volume. I couldn't make out the words. After a moment of disorientation, I shook myself awake and lurched for the door, hoping Nina hadn't caught Minnie slipping out, still a little drunk and looking guilty as hell of something.

Nina was there.

But she wasn't arguing with Minnie.

The other person was a man I didn't recognize, dressed in pinstripes and a snapped down fedora. "Mind your own business, pal," he said to me. I smelled his whiskey breath, and his eyes were pink from drinking and smoking in illicit establishments. The bulge under his arm was hard to miss. But when he grabbed Nina's elbow, jerking her away from her door, I had no choice.

"She is my business," I said.

I decked him.

He was slow from over-indulging, or I got lucky, because I caught him right on the knockout button. The tough guy collapsed in a heap. I took away his weapon, and as I did, his eyelids fluttered. I hammered him with the pistol grip, sending him back to hoodlum dreamland.

"Did he hurt you?"

"Just what you saw," Nina said. "I told him I appreciated being escorted home, but our night was over. He didn't like that. I could've handled him. But thanks."

"Don't mention it."

I couldn't help but notice Nina was dressed for an evening of entertainment. She'd done herself up flapper style. Sequins and beaded fringe; her silks rustled when she moved. Her feet looked like she stepped in black tar and then dipped them in a sack of gold dust. She wore a feathery bandeau and enough pearls around her neck that any pearl diver finding her might retire. This wasn't Nina's usual look. She'd made a point of getting herself noticed tonight, and I guess it worked. "I tried to lose him at the door. He pushed his way in."

"What should we do with him?"

I decided to roll him downstairs. Out the front door. Then I dragged him by the heels across the lawn to the street where I dumped him in the gutter. "That poor suit!" I said to myself as I lit a smoke.

"Amigo! What are you doing outside with no jacket?"

Balthazarr crossed the street diagonally toward me. He wore a long black overcoat, and if he hadn't said anything, I never would've noticed him blending into the shadows.

"Taking out the trash."

Nina watched us from the doorway to the mansion. When she saw Balthazarr, she hurried down the steps to join us. "A guest overstayed his welcome."

"Rudeness is a crime I cannot forgive." Balthazarr asked us for a detailed account of what transpired. Nina told him. He acted impressed by my decisive action.

"It's all over," I said.

"I think not." Balthazarr picked up the goon and threw him over his shoulder.

"What are you doing?" I asked.

"Teaching a lesson in manly behavior."

Balthazarr marched through the Colony mansion's snowy side yard and out to the back. I was freezing in my shirtsleeves, but I went with him. Nina had never taken off her coat and she trailed after us, negotiating the icy grass in her gold-heeled pumps.

"I'm not defending this guy," I said. "He was drunk and stupid. But I took him out. I don't think he's going to be happy when he finds out I kept his gun. We can let him go."

Balthazarr remained silent. He carried the unconscious man lightly, as if the body weighed nothing. He wasn't even breathing hard. His powerful legs crashed through the frozen weeds that grew at the back border of the property. He stomped them down, heading to the river, only halting when he reached the bank. Steam curled from his mouth, as thick as white smoke. What was he going to do? He couldn't take the guy past the water.

The Miskatonic hadn't frozen over completely. Along its edges, cloudy lips of ice made long, smooth curves out into the black water. The man on Balthazarr's shoulder groaned. The artist stared across the river, unblinking. He murmured something, a prayer, in an alien tongue. I couldn't make out all the words. Only it wasn't Spanish.

"Wait!" Nina shouted.

But it was too late.

In a remarkable display of strength, the Spaniard lifted the unconscious hooligan's body straight over his head and threw him far out into the water, beyond the snow-covered shoreline. There was an explosion of water. The body sank. Balthazarr walked away from the river without looking back. I stared dumbfounded, waiting to see if the man might break the surface and begin thrashing about for a saving hand. I studied the bank for a stick, something I might use to hook him back to shore.

But the man never popped up.

"He killed him," Nina said. She couldn't believe what she'd witnessed.

I couldn't either. I refused to.

"The current has taken him downstream. He must have come up. Only we didn't see."

"That water is deadly. Throwing him in is as good as tossing him in a fire," she said.

Like a pyre, I thought. Like a ritual sacrifice.

We turned to the mansion. Balthazarr was already at the apartment house. He was singing to himself. A song of joy and exuberance, perhaps a drinking song, but not in Spanish. The language had a cloggy sound. Guttural, throaty. He belted it with gusto. Did he sing out, "*Yuyu-Vabadaa*?" I don't know. He may have. He really may have.

When we caught up with him, he was smiling. He ensnared us in his great woolly arms, pulling us tight. "You are my friends! New friends! I love Arkham in winter!"

"Juan Hugo, what did you do?" Nina asked, incredulous.

The painter looked back over his shoulder at the Miskatonic.

"I gave a gift."

"A gift?" Nina was having none of it. His flippant attitude caused her agitation to grow. "How can you care so little about human life? You murdered that man!"

Balthazarr drew his head back and howled with laughter.

"I think we'd better go back inside," I said to Nina. I didn't want to anger Balthazarr.

"Murder? Did I murder a gangster who tried to force his way into your home? This brute who could not control himself. You have sympathy for him? No, no." Balthazarr shook his head.

"You've gone too far, Juan Hugo. We don't condone murder here in Arkham," I said.

"Murder again. What is this talk of murder? Look around you, Alden. Nina. Your town is rife with crime. Its industries have at their very foundations the exploitation and violence of one class of people carried out upon another. Bones. This is a city built on bones. But I am only a visitor here. Yet, I am accused of doing what? Drowning a mongrel who attacked my friends?"

Nina pointed her finger at Balthazarr. "You won't get away with this. It's barbaric."

"I think you do not understand barbarism," he said. "You only think you do."

We started to walk away.

Balthazarr called out. "My friends! Do you see? There! Under the lamppost?"

Nina and I stopped, looking to the end of the block, where the river veered close to the road. The bank was terraced and lined with stone steps for fishermen to sit and cast their lines.

The shape of a man plodded into the circle of light. He was composed of shadows, really, little more than an animated mass, drizzling water onto the pavement, exuding tendrils of fog, and shivering so profoundly that his vibrations smudged his outer silhouette to an indistinct blur.

"He is alive! Your worries are for nothing!" Balthazarr laughed again, and he took up his gruff, rasping song; its hoarse refrain like croaking from a swamp, a phlegmy cough repeated and repeated. "Good night, amigos. You are softhearted. Dream, my dreamers. Dream!"

"Is that the man who walked you home?" I asked Nina. "Is he up from the river?"

"Too far to tell... but who else...?"

The shape at the end of the block shuffled off.

"Balthazarr is right. He taught the man a lesson. No one died. We can go to bed."

"He didn't know what would happen." Nina opened the front door.

"Nothing happened."

Nina mounted the stairway to our floor. At the top of the stairs, she paused.

"Something did happen," she said.

Without inviting me in, she passed over her threshold, shutting the door behind her.

I went into my room and fell into bed, asleep with my clothes on, right until morning.

CHAPTER TWENTY-SEVEN

"I have to go. You said so yourself. Preston needs a friend to steer him from trouble." I stood at the mirror in my bedroom, tying my bowtie. The darkness had come on quickly. Black velvet night pressed its face to my window; a thin beard of ice spilled frostily over the sill.

Nina was adamant. "I've changed my mind. You're more important to me than Preston ever was. And remember, I know him as well as you do, or better. He's quite resourceful and responsible for his own actions. The situation's too dangerous. We saw what Balthazarr was capable of yesterday. The man's unpredictable. You can't say what will happen tonight. You can't, because you don't know."

I went over to the bed where she was reclining and kissed her. "That is precisely why I must be there. To protect Preston from unforeseeable events." I hadn't told Nina about Minnie's visit or her disturbing report on the recent changes in her fiancé. I was more worried about my old friend than I was letting on. Sharing that with Nina would only cement her determination to keep me at home. Preston needed my support. "I predict that several foolish men will drink too much alcohol, speak boldly, and smoke too many cigars. They will grow weary of each other's company because they are not so young as they once were. The end."

Nina rose from the bed, brushing me back.

"I don't like it. But it's your decision." Her coldness conveyed utter disapproval.

I combed my hair, watching Nina in the mirror, in the doorway, slowly receding.

I finished grooming. Yet I stayed where I was, my eyes locked on Nina's reflection. She opened her mouth about to speak. "Please save your arguments," I said. "I'm going."

A flash of red-hot anger. "Go on, then! It's you who'll regret not listening." She stormed out. Her heels clicked as she crossed my bedroom, not slowing down as she entered my studio. Soon she would be gone. Out the door. I turned and ran after her.

"Wait! Nina!"

Her hand rested on the doorknob. She was staring at the wood panels, the ghostly message the gargoyle had left for us, though it was barely visible in the lamplight. She saw it.

"I'll find you when I get home," I said. "If that's what you want me to do."

Without another word she left me standing there.

I went into the closet and fetched my overcoat, leather gloves, and black bowler.

A long chilly night awaited me.

I took a cab to Independence Square.

I wasted no time entering the park. The brutal temperatures inspired me to keep moving. The park shelters occasional unsavory characters after dark. I quickly recognized the loiterers hanging around Founder's Rock at near midnight, polluting the air with expensive tobacco smoke. My fellow partiers *pour la nuit*.

"There you are, Oakesy!" Preston said around his imported Havana.

"Let me have a look at you," I said, sounding more worried than I had intended.

Preston made a strange face and held out a silver flask. A tad gaunt, dark around the eyes, but his skin was flushed with drink. Overall, he did not appear as a man bedeviled.

"You need to catch up," he said. By the proof of his breath and wobble in his steps, he was speaking the truth. He slugged me boyishly in the upper arm. He and Minnie were very fond of administering a light pummeling during conversation. I pictured them aged in the Fairmont mansion, having abandoned language entirely, relying on biffs and thwacks.

"Who's on board with us tonight? Connors and Read? Bug-eye Westy? Did you wrangle Thurlow, Shattuck, and Nettleton? I fear a reunion with that gang might kill me off for good."

But, as it turned out, I had no worries. None of the old gang made it to Preston's bachelor party. Had they drifted away only to have their shoes filled by New Colonists? Not including myself, I counted six Colonists in tonight's group. I'd never seen Preston with any of them before now. From the far side of Founder's Rock emerged the caped, top-hatted Juan Hugo. He was walking with a cane, not because he needed it, but for the effect; his stick was blackthorn, its knob might have been a natural bulbous peculiarity, but it seemed carved and cycloptic.

"A few days ago, I read in the newspaper that my countryman Ramón Franco crossed the Atlantic in an airplane. From Spain to South America in less than two and a half days. Imagine what the Conquistadors would have done if they had airplanes. Our world is shrinking fast, *mis amigos*. Getting smaller each day. Soon it will implode violently, like a massive star. Where do you go when there is nowhere to run? When it collapses, where will you be?" he said.

"I'll be good and drunk." Preston tipped back his flask. It was empty. He tapped the last drops of whiskey into his mouth then capped the flask before chucking it into the bushes.

"Hey, that was silver! Wasn't it?"

The Colonist who had spoken was named Devereaux. He wrote Dadaist-inspired poetry, cutting up epic poems – *Beowulf* and Dante's *Divine Comedy* were favorites – mixing in local newspaper advertisements, and reassembling the random fragments into blocks of text, out of which he removed every other vowel. He performed these aloud. His aim, he said, was to destroy language. He complained his task was impossible. Although, I thought he did a pretty decent job.

"Damn my silver! I've twenty-nine more at home!" Preston shouted.

Balthazarr rubbed his bare hand on the Founder's Rock, looking at the sky.

"Isn't it cold?" a painter named Fowler asked, crouching at his feet.

The Surrealist studied the oblong stone dedicated to Arkham's *original* colonists.

"Not to me, it isn't. The menhir boils with energy surging from the earth's core."

"That's frostbite you're feeling," I said.

As Balthazarr watched me, his rubbery mouth pulled into a

clownish grin. Shadows filled the hollows of his face. He was a handsome man, but a grotesque animation enlivened his sneer, or perhaps it was the spotty electric lighting in the park. Glass shards from multiple damaged lamps littered the pavement. Vandals, I guessed. Ruffians. Nothing more sinister than that. Was I trying to convince myself? Or did every detail hint at a hidden threat?

"I am going to die tonight." Preston's tone startled me, forcing me to regard him with genuine unease. He pointed at the ground. "I will literally freeze right where I am standing."

"Where to next, Mr Balthazarr?" It was the other painter who tagged along with Fowler. Jeremy Whipple. He died not too long after that night. After sailing to Australia to paint scenes of farming life, he fell under a Sundigger cultivator.

"La Bella Luna," Balthazarr chewed on the words, biting into succulent fruit.

"La Bella Luna!" Preston yelled.

Nine well-dressed men of the city intoned his mantra.

I was too sober to enjoy our parade up Garrison Street. It was a relief to reach our destination. The warmth inside La Bella Luna seemed overmuch, a tropical contrast to the tundra of the park. Preferable, but soon I was sweating, my forehead beaded. The Italian bistro was unpopulated at this late hour. I hadn't realized we were planning to dine. My companions, apart from Preston and Balthazarr, appeared equally puzzled. Balthazarr tapped his stick on the podium, summoning a slouching concierge who counted out nine menus.

"Allow me," Preston said.

Balthazarr acquiesced, letting one of Arkham's native sons take the lead.

"Marco! It is Marco, isn't it?" Preston asked.

The concierge inclined his head a fraction of an inch in acknowledgment.

"Marco, can you serve a private party of our size? Downstairs?" Preston flashed a playful gaze back at us.

"We are crowded at the moment, sir," Marco said. "Maybe if you come back later."

I gawked at the empty tables.

Then I smirked as the reality of the exchange dawned on me.

"I always have a table waiting for me *downstairs*." Preston added a theatrical wink.

"Right this way, sir. Please follow me." Marco put the menus back.

We trailed him through the bistro, its walls papered with gold velvet *fleurs-de-lis*. Past the kitchen entrance was a second door, hidden behind the corner. Marco opened it, revealing a wooden stairway and strains of live jazz piano rising from below.

Preston tipped Marco. We descended into the passage.

"Tell them Marco said to let you in," the concierge called down after us.

At the bottom of the steps: a steel barrier. A spy hatch slid open in the center of it.

Preston repeated the concierge's words.

Bolts were thrown. A roar of music escaped as we were admitted.

"Welcome to the Clover Club, boys." A towering redhead in headdress greeted us. She had arachnid eyelashes, large hands, and a six-shooter on her hip. "No weapons permitted. Check your pieces here. Lie to me, you'll regret it. Ooh, I like your beard, hon."

The hostess stood nose to nose with Balthazarr and tweaked his chin whiskers.

"You are a very tall woman," Balthazarr said, blushing.

"I'm from Texas. Everything's big in Texas. What about your stick? Got a sword inside?"

"No, madam. It is natural solid wood."

The hostess held out her palm. Balthazarr laid the cane across it. She checked the stick for concealed blades, then returned it. "You coldcock anybody, we'll use that thing to break your legs. Understand? This here's a peaceable joint. We don't like shenanigans."

Balthazarr's eyes grew large in mock terror. He pretended to quake.

The lower level of La Bella Luna housed a speakeasy in full swing at midnight. Brick walls, part of the building's original foundation, contained most of the noise; the opulent dark green draperies, hanging ceiling to floor around the club, smothered the rest. Adorned with silver palms, the stage glowed in the center of the main room. A jazz band was playing. The same band that played at Preston and Minnie's party at the observatory. The piano player began to sing of lost love and memories best left undisturbed.

"Get a load of this place!" Whipple's head swiveled left and right.

Fowler nudged him with an elbow. "Act like you've been here before."

"But I haven't. Have you?"

Fowler shook his head and pointed to a row of archways at the back, their openings partially concealed with clacking strings of multicolored glass beads. Men and women parted the curtains, heading in and out, offering glimpses of felt-covered tables, card players, and spinning roulette wheels. "The high-rollers must hang out in there. I'd like a peek."

"Go on, fellas. Make yourselves comfortable. Oakesy and I will find a table. Come back when you're good and ready. Here's some seed money." Preston peeled off bills from a stack of crisp green lettuce. "Let's see who's lucky tonight."

Fowler, Whipple, and Devereaux headed for the card room. The other three New Colonists, whose names are not important, grabbed their allowances and advanced like a line of windup automatons to the club's poker tables, where they leave our story, never to return.

Balthazarr, Preston, and I ambled over to the bar in the corner.

Preston bought three whiskies. Balthazarr made a beeline for an empty table. A bull wearing a tuxedo stopped him, informing him that table was reserved, and he needed to look elsewhere. Balthazarr apologized but never broke eye contact with the bouncer.

"There's a table," I said. "Those people are leaving." I grabbed a chair, sat down.

"That's Naomi O'Bannion's table you tried to steal, Juan Hugo. Strictly off limits," Preston said, sliding into a seat nestled between Balthazarr and me.

I recognized Naomi's name from the bootleggers' camp. Winston had mentioned her talking to Freddie in the ice truck, while I was rolling around with mackerel. My mind flashed to the ditch, on their eyeless faces gaping at the stars through the pine needles.

"Who is O'Bannion?" Balthazarr asked, sipping his bootleg drink.

"Her family sells vice in this city. Naomi's fiancé is Peter Clover. This is his place."

"Ah, so that goon is her goon." Balthazarr was still watching the club muscleman.

"Somebody's making a killing tonight. The place is packed," I said.

"Alden's never been here," Preston said. "But Minnie and I love it. The club really swings. You wouldn't believe what we've seen happen down here. Crazy things."

"I'd believe it." I looked at Balthazarr. He turned to meet my gaze. Raised his glass. Did Preston know about his friend's temper?

Preston waved to a cigarette girl.

She saw him and smiled, sashaying our way. Everyone in the room noticed her. Short brassy curls and dancer's legs, her sparkly red and gold skirt bounced with each step. That didn't completely explain the attention. There was an energy in her, bright and infectious, you knew she'd have a husky laugh and brains to match her sassy looks. She might be a cigarette girl tonight. She wouldn't be for long. The world had big plans for her. She did too. When she arrived at our table, a sea of faces directed themselves to our table. There might as well have been a spotlight on her. She waved her hand in a practiced motion over her tray of goods. "What'll you have, gentlemen? Cigarettes, chewing gum, candy. A flower for a lady."

"Do you have cigars?" Balthazarr said.

"I sure do. How many?" Her gold pillbox hat tilted on her head so it made you worry it might slip off. You wanted to catch it before it fell. But she knew what she was doing. It stayed put. Her eyes were dark like buckwheat honey; her skin held a misty golden shimmer.

"One will do." Balthazarr pressed coins into her palm.

"I'll take a pack of cigarettes. Those right there with the dromedary." Preston pointed. "Say, do you know if they have any champagne tonight?"

"Is it your birthday?"

"No, I'm getting married."

"What a lucky lady."

Preston took the cigarette pack from her, letting his fingers graze her wrist.

She pushed out her lower lip. "You might ask Glenda about the champagne. She's the girl in the Egyptian getup."

"Thanks," Preston said. "Keep the change."

She looked at the bill he gave her. "Thank you!"

Heads turned as she passed by.

The lights came down so the room was almost black. After that, the jazz played even louder. People crowded the dancefloor. Others shimmied wherever they were, at the tables – or on top of them – pressed against the bar rail, even the most hardcore gamblers couldn't help but tap their toes to the drums and bass.

Preston got his bottle of champagne. It tasted like ice-cold liquid money.

As the night wore on, we hardly left our seats. I felt my face growing numb. Devereaux stopped by for a drink, reporting that Whipple and Fowler were winning at baccarat. He'd lost his last few bets and was taking a break to change his luck. He went off into the dark confusion of bodies to talk to a girl at the bar. He appeared ashen and either he'd had a drink poured over him or he'd broken out in a drenching sweat. In the men's room I met him again. He was hunched over a sink, coughing or sobbing. When I asked what was wrong, he waved me away. Somebody's night had taken a bad turn. Whipple and Fowler did win some money. But Fowler drew the ire of a Russian aristocrat at the baccarat table, and the Slav challenged him to a duel. Fowler laughed in reply, setting the man off, and the Slav exploded, clawing at Fowler's face, getting both men tossed from the club. Whipple agreed to take Fowler to the hospital for sutures.

Despite the lateness, or earliness, of the hour, the crowd only swelled to greater numbers. Lights brightened and went low again. At some point, without my noticing, the musical act changed, a woman was singing, but I had trouble making sense of her words. It was like one of Devereaux's poems, a jumble, with vowels missing or added in, ululations that didn't seem like jazz at all but a spiritless cry from centuries and continents away. Nothing energetic, only pain. I even thought I heard her sing something like, "Yuyu, Yuyu."

But I was drunk by then and doubting my own ears.

The singer announced they were taking a break. I was surprised to see Balthazarr standing in the shadows on the stage. The house manager came up to the microphone.

"We've got a real treat in store for you tonight. Who likes magic?"

The intoxicated crowd cheered.

The manager hushed them. "Easy now, my celebrants. I give you Balthazarr the Magnificent!"

I poked Preston. He shrugged and blinked, glassy eyed at the circle of light on stage.

Balthazarr approached the microphone. He had his black cane and a gleam in his smile. "I will need two assistants from the audience." He shaded his eyes as he pretended to seek in the crowd for volunteers. For all our carousing, he seemed as sober as a hatchetwielding teetotaler. I could barely keep from toppling out of my chair. What was he doing?

"I hope he doesn't pick us. I don't think I can walk," I said.

Preston put his head down on the table.

"You… and you, sir. Yes, you. Please, everyone. Encourage the fine gentleman." Balthazarr began clapping. The audience joined him with vigorous applause.

Preston looked up in a panic. But Balthazarr hadn't chosen us.

The cigarette girl and the bullish goon in a tuxedo stepped into Balthazarr's light.

"Thank you. Now, I need everyone to concentrate on the top of my walking stick. Look at it. Empty your minds of thoughts, logic, and reason. Think only of a depthless void."

"That shouldn't be too hard for–" a heckler tried to interrupt.

"Silence!" Balthazarr's command quieted the man, and the rest of room as well. The gambling rooms had emptied. No dealers dealt cards, no dice rolled, every wheel ceased its spin. People were transfixed on the stage. Every eye focused on the Surrealist.

"Stand next to each other. Very good." He guided the girl and the goon together.

From behind the two, Balthazarr lifted his stick overhead. The cycloptic handle was too far away from the table for me to pick out any detail, or really to see it at all.

Yet I did.

I saw the wood-carved eye, the lidless orb no bigger than an ordinary glass marble – it glowed, and I looked at it as if it were right before my face, a few inches away, burning and wide open. How was this possible? I blinked, but nothing changed. The eye burned into me.

"This is an illusion called *The Two Keys*. I am the Locksmith, if you will. They are the keys." The crowd chuckled nervously. "I use them to unlock … ! What? What do you see?"

The silence continued. I heard not a breath being drawn, not a crinkle of clothing.

Nothing.

I was somehow seeing everything on stage in perfect clarity. I was at the same time staring into that wood pit, that unpeeled lidless orb, the cyclops Balthazarr raised into the air.

"Do you see it? Answer me!"

"We see it!" My lips moved. I felt the involuntary spasm of my vocal cords, the vibration of words formed in my throat and mouth, my teeth and tongue and lips, but without my control.

Everyone in the room had spoken simultaneously. Our voices speaking as one.

"Do you see a doorway opening, perhaps?" Balthazarr said.

"We see it!"

The orb expanded. It was like looking into a telescope. Stars, galaxies, dusts and gases. Nebulae. The cosmos. An immense shape swam across the vastness. Both dead and alive, for whom life had no meaning, death no consequence, it turned its intelligence toward the watchers.

Toward *us*.

On the stage, a long, looping tendril dropped from the murky ceiling. Then another and another. Dozens of them. They danced and interwove their lengths. One bundled cluster of thick, vine-like appendages braided themselves together and coiled around the cigarette girl with her tilted pillbox hat and her brassy curls, her sparkly red and gold skirt and her stockinged legs. The other tendrils entwined and tightened around the stocky neck of the tough bruiser beside her.

"Beholder from Beyond, God of Dimensions Unimagined, Lord and Servant of None and Nothing, I call to Yuyu! Take this Man and Woman. Falling Star! Un-Sun, be born!"

"Falling Star! Un-Sun, be born!" every person in the Clover Club repeated.

The conjured cords snapped tight around the two volunteers and lifted them off their feet, carrying them high out over the crowd. Transfixed, we watched as they began to choke.

The man's legs kicked. He grabbed at the coils cinching taut, closing his airways.

The cigarette girl twitched, her whole body encased in a bone-crushing vise. I wanted to react but could not. I felt at a distance from myself. An observer. A disembodied eye.

Behind Balthazarr, as if projected on the wall, a vision of the cosmos swirled. Inside that deeply dizzying vision, the immensity that pulsed and swam, came closer.

Closer.

Balthazarr's body became a blur, vibrating with the Thing invading dimensions.

Colors beyond our visible spectrum of light radiated. But I could see them! Patterns overlapped. Ribbons and wavy bars of shifting fluorescence. Scribblings, blooms, and radiances like ink drops falling into dark water. I rubbed my burning eyes. Panic erupted from within me. The deeper I gazed into the wall, the deeper I was able to see. I peered out over vast distances, across the universe, agape, awestruck at its endlessness. While, at the same time, the objects floating before me were being x-rayed by unseen, increasingly powerful machines, exposing their underlying structures and the essential building blocks of all creation. Dizzyingly, my perception zoomed in and out. My brain felt pulped. My senses stretched past reasonable limits.

Others were experiencing it too, a stomach-churning cosmogonic seasickness.

The immense void loomed.

Then it roared. I have never listened to a dragon's roar, but this one also breathed fire.

The crowd suddenly awakened from their communal trance.

Men and women screamed. A gun went off. The club guards drew their weapons and began shooting haphazardly, without targets, at the stage. Bystanders were struck down in the barrage of gunfire. A stampede for the door started without warning. Clubgoers trampled one another. They tore at anyone they perceived in their way, blocking their escape. From what?

They couldn't name it. From fear. The spiking blood-rush of pure, insanity-inducing fear. It didn't matter who they were outside the club. Outlaws, judges, and regular joes. Jazz lovers, flappers, or busboys. Rich or poor, society page veterans or everyday citizens out for a night in the city of Arkham. Everyone was included.

They all picked the wrong night, the wrong place to be.

CHAPTER TWENTY-EIGHT

I don't remember going outside. Preston and I somehow fought our way through the river of Clover Club customers flooding out of La Bella Luna's doors. When the rush to exit through the restaurant momentarily screeched to a standstill – after a clumsy, sozzled couple tripped and went sprawling over the threshold – a frustrated group of men picked up La Bella Luna's choicest table and tossed it through the plate glass window. Shards sprayed onto the sidewalk. Marco the concierge looked on, mystified.

I couldn't tell if I was leading Preston or he was leading me. We seemed to switch back and forth, one of us supporting the other who lagged behind, physically and mentally exhausted, our minds hindered by too much hooch and champagne and lingering visions of impossible geometries, the abysmal field of swirling objects conjured on the Clover Club's brick back wall.

I must've blacked out briefly. I remember grabbing hold of Preston's hand and hauling him down the block, dodging away from the police cars and paddy wagons racing to the club. We cut through an alley and hopped a fence, delirious with dread and a case of uncontrollable nervous laughter. Shadows darted past us. Ghostly human-sized smudges hastened down gloomy avenues, their features appeared partly erased; pencil sketches of people, quick facsimiles, running amok. Were these the other Cloverites fleeing a scene that got too hot?

It must've been so.

I was covered in cold sweat.

Preston gasped. His ribs rattled with spasms.

I was about to ask him what he saw at the club when a sliver of the void must have caught up with me, because the next thing I knew I was sitting with my back against the hard, weathered contours of Founder's Rock, noticing my sock and my wriggling toes. "Hey, would you look at that?" We were still holding hands. I shook our conjoined fist. "I lost a shoe somewhere in the melee."

"You lost a shoe, but you gained a glimpse into something beyond."

It wasn't Preston's hand I was holding.

"How did you get out? You started the whole damned thing!" I let go.

Balthazarr held up his empty palms, defensive of my accusation. "What did I do?"

"Are you kidding me? People died back there!" I glanced around the side of the rock. Then I got up. Not a black Oxford wingtip in sight. My shoeless foot was freezing on the cobbled path.

Balthazarr waved for me to sit next to him. "I did a magic trick. An illusion."

"You call that a trick? No way, Juan Hugo. Pardon me, but that was not hocus pocus."

"Hypnotism. I put the audience in a trance. And you saw what you wanted to see. Somebody panicked and started shooting.

That club was filled with drunken gangsters. Don't blame me."
Balthazarr was taking slugs from a bottle of champagne.

"Where'd Preston go?"

"Home. His driver picked him up. You don't remember?"

"It's almost as if I were drugged. This has happened to me
several times in the last few months. Maybe I have a problem
with my brain. My toes are turning to ice. End to end I'm falling
to pieces." I sat, crossing my ankle over my knee and massaging
my numb foot. Spain and the Colony's Winter Show. It had
happened to me again. A brain fog. Confusion.

"Let me see," Balthazarr said, passing me the champagne bottle.

"What? My foot?"

He nodded. Before I could object, he pinched the toe of my
sock and pulled it off. Then his rough sculptor's hands began
to knead at my chilled flesh. I expected to feel something like
shock or embarrassment, at the least an awkwardness from
the physical contact. But it felt marvelous. Instant warmth, an
almost ecstatic relaxation. Tension was leaving my body through
the sole of my foot. Balthazarr removed my other shoe and sock,
without my stopping him. Two men in the park after hours, one
undressing the other. There was an aura of social impropriety,
but despite the incredible strangeness of this unexpected act, it
didn't strike me as weird. I was like a patient seeing his physician.
I wouldn't have wanted to explain that to the police. But they
were otherwise occupied this night.

I tipped the bottle, closing my eyes. Balthazarr's soothing
voice surrounded me.

"My friend, Luis Buñuel, is a film director. He is also a
hypnotist. He claims that motion pictures are a form of
hypnotism. He writes that he is working on a picture in France.

His boss tells him, 'Luis, you seem rather surrealist. Beware of surrealists, they are crazy people'. Do you think that's true, Alden? Are we like the unfortunates who live across the street?" Balthazarr gestured to Arkham Asylum, the hospital lit up like a haunted ruin. Were the massive gray cobwebs in the windows spirits or patients? The moon attracted them like bugs.

"I don't know what you are," I said.

"I am you. We are the same thing."

"Who is Yuyu-Va'badaa?" I blurted out. "I'm not sure I'm saying that right."

Balthazarr smiled. "It sounds like your own invention. I like it. Baby talk. A word the Dadaists might've come up with."

"It isn't. I heard it in Spain. And around Arkham, at the Colony. Now again at the Clover Club. All places you've been, coincidentally." I watched him for signs of recognition.

The Spaniard shrugged. "Maybe it comes from your imagination. I cannot say."

"I'm not making it up." Was he calling me crazy? A person who hears voices.

"If you were… is there anything wrong with that?" He stood, stretched. Letting out a gaping, cavernous yawn. "We must get you home before you doubt your sanity, eh? I will telephone for a cab." Balthazarr marched off across the street to the asylum. Taking the steps two at a time, rap-rapping loudly on the doors. I was certain they would turn him away. But they didn't. They let him inside. Minutes later he reemerged. "Your cab is on its way. I'm walking back to the Silver Gate. The air does me good. Ah, look, your ride is already here."

A black cab slid to the curb. Shining, insectile. The driver: gloomy and lumpen.

I got in. Balthazarr murmured something to the cabbie. His voice buzzing in my ears.

As the car was about to pull away, I touched the cabbie's shoulder. "Wait."

I leaned out of the window. Balthazarr watched me, amused.

"Why don't you live at the Colony with us, Juan Hugo?"

He considered my question. His eyes gleamed like smoky brown gemstones.

"Because, Alden, *mi amigo*, gods dwell apart from their followers."

I sat there, unable to tell if he was being serious.

His caped figure turned, melting away into shadows and river fog.

I told the driver to take me home.

Upstairs, I hesitated outside my apartment. I looked at Nina's door. I wondered if she was still awake. Would she be angry with me still? If I woke her up, would I make things worse?

I decided to take the risk. I needed to tell her what happened at the Clover Club, everything I'd seen and heard. My conversation with Balthazarr. I needed her to tell me I wasn't losing my mind.

As I knocked on her door, it swung open.

Nina would never go to sleep and leave her door unlocked. I felt panic rising in me.

"Nina!" I called out, rushing inside. I raced room to room. Empty, empty, empty.

Her bed was made. She hadn't gone to sleep there. But her purse was in the kitchen. Cash in her wallet. Her apartment hadn't been broken into by thieves. Nothing was missing.

Except Nina.

I did a slower, more thorough search. My head was full of bootleg alcohol and fear.

On the floor, by the edge of her bed: a broken pearl necklace. The pearls scattered. Were those scuff marks scratched into the floor? Had she been physically dragged away?

Kidnapped?

Too fast now, images flickered through my mind. The gargoyle. All the cases of those missing and murdered Arkhamites: Dr Silva, the Galinkas, Ganz and the boxcar drifter…

Headless Clark…

Would Nina be another name among the missing? Or worse?

The next phase of the ritual: another sacrificial elite. Was Nina's theory correct?

I tried to think… Think, Alden… I could almost hear her coaching me along.

Look for clues.

But where? What was I even looking for?

I went through Nina's closets, her dresser and nightstand. In the drawer of her writing desk I found what I needed. A reporter's notebook. I'd never seen her with it, but she must've taken it along when she went out alone. Jotting more notes after she got home.

I flipped the cover.

Blank. Not a single scribbled word. Why keep it in her desk if she didn't use it?

Damn it!

Wait. Caught in the spirals at the top were fringes of pages that had been torn out. Why would she tear pages out of her private notebook? She wouldn't. But someone else might. I held the notebook under her desk lamp. I saw impressions of handwriting pressed into the paper. I rummaged in the desk and found a pencil. I rubbed the pencil back and forth over the impressions, until the words of the last page she wrote became, mostly, readable. It was the same thing I'd done to copy the gargoyle's message off the door. Here I knew the author. I recognized Nina's handwriting. These were *her* words.

> *out last night to dig up info (Galinka sisters) Found who*
> *hired them to dance at the CC. The girls were popular!!!*
> *Had avid fan turned up some nights. After shows, they*
> *sat with man. Alone, private. He took them out. Where?*
> *Unknown. Not far away. In town. Maybe Clark???*
> *Not Clark. Descript all wrong.*
> *Tall, handsome, beard. Accent?*
> *Man bought gifts. Dresses, jewelry, etc. Paintings!!!*
> *JHB???!!! Who else? But was months ago. How did he?*

Balthazarr in Arkham, months before he said he arrived. Was it possible? It was only Preston and Juan Hugo himself who told me when he'd gotten into town. The bottom half of the page was spottier. Not all the words transferred through from the ripped-out page.

> *Black Cave. Underground lake. Unvisited Isle. Docks.*
> *Hospitals and Hotels!!!?*
> *Arkham police too dangerous – infiltrate every aspect*
> *Must tell A Smarten up. Watch out especially for*
> *be playing games with us. Don't trust N. Colonists. Spying –*
> *listen through walls – the mail*
> *They do rituals. Not everyone but… Will ask more ???s*

P&M in deep. P suspected but – unknowingly controlled
them puppets
JHB again 2PLACES AT ONCE?
Tell A it has to be

I reread the page a dozen times, then I read it some more. What did I see?

Nina listed locations of strange activity in Arkham. The cave, the pool we found there. The island where the sisters were burned. The docks where the bootleggers operated and where the net blob pursued me. Dr Silva was hanged outside a hospital. What about hotels? Balthazarr's current address was at the Silver Gate and it might be the new location of Preston and Minnie's wedding. Then came Nina's constant worries about the police. Here's where the gaps started to take a toll. "*Infiltrate every aspect*" could mean the police or it could mean someone else. But who? The murderers? I didn't know. "*Must tell A. Smarten up.*" I assumed I was "A." Who did I need to "*watch out*" for? Perhaps the answer lay in the next line. The New Colonists. Playing games, spying, eavesdropping…

"*They do rituals. Not everyone but…* " But mostly everyone. The Colonists couldn't be trusted. We lived among them. Nina was going to ask more questions. Of whom exactly?

I didn't have any suspects in the Colony itself. But *P* and *M* had to be Preston and Minnie. Our friends. Well, my friends at least. Nina didn't know Minnie. Preston was her ex.

Preston "*suspected*" something. Who were the "*puppets*" she mentioned? The Colonists? Nina and me? Or none of the above. It was too damned vague.

Too many pieces were still missing.

Juan Hugo Balthazarr in two places at once. What could that possibly mean? Did he control the *"puppets"*? The gargoyle leapt into my mind, wings flapping, laughing in my face.

Nina was gone. Who took her away? There was no obvious solution.

"Tell A it has to be…"

It didn't have to be! Not if I could help it.

I ran back downstairs and outside, seeing if I could find more evidence of Nina's kidnapping. A piece of clothing. A footprint. Blood in the grass. No, not that. Because I was certain she'd been taken against her will. I knew it in my gut. In my heart too. While I was out partying at the Clover Club with Preston and Balthazarr, witnessing God knows what taking place on that stage, someone or something crept into the Colony mansion and stole Nina.

The sky was still dead black. The only color came from factory smokestacks and the flash of early-rising gulls searching for breakfast scraps.

I was trembling.

What *had* I witnessed at the Clover Club? Was it a feat of hypnotism like Balthazarr said? It felt more real than a magician's parlor trick gone awry.

Or was it a preview of a cosmic catastrophe? Dimensional collapse? The cigarette girl in her pillbox hat. Did she die? Had Balthazarr murdered two people in a room full of witnesses and walked away?

What was my role in all this?

Nina. I had to find her.

Nina…

CHAPTER TWENTY-NINE

Following the events that transpired at the Clover Club, I went to the newsstand daily and bought the *Advertiser*, hoping to read a report of the incident. I wanted to know what the police uncovered, the number of victims, names of those who were arrested, and what explanation the authorities provided for the calamity. But there was nothing. Only a local business article relating that La Bella Luna bistro was closed temporarily for remodeling.

It was baffling.

How could such damage and human turmoil be ignored? It had to be a cover-up. Nina's suspicions concerning the police explained how these odd deaths might be kept hidden from the public. Now I believed she'd been correct all along. Here was the proof.

I couldn't go to the police about her disappearance. No. I was convinced they wouldn't help me. Talking to them might lead to false charges against me. Who knew who pulled the strings in Arkham? I'd thought I did, but I was wrong. I didn't want to end up in jail.

At least two people died in the Clover Club. I saw it happen. With my own eyes.

Balthazarr said he hypnotized the crowd, including me. But Nina didn't trust him. And now I didn't. He'd made me doubt myself. I couldn't easily shake off that feeling either.

Self-doubt hounded me. I was paralyzed by the idea that anything I attempted would be destined to fail. How *could* I find Nina? I stayed close to home at first, hoping she'd turn up. That I'd been mistaken about her leaving against her will. She'd taken a trip. That's all.

She did not miraculously reappear.

I walked the streets of Arkham looking for her. What else could I do? I didn't trust my New Colony neighbors any more. Preston and Minnie were nowhere to be found. When I stopped by the Fairmont house, the family butler told me Preston was not at home. He was out of the country, in fact. Beyond contact at the moment.

"Out of the country? Doing what?"

"Traveling."

"Traveling?" I sneered, obviously unsatisfied with that answer. Unwilling to leave.

"Perhaps he is working out details for his wedding. The date is officially changed."

"Changed to when?" I asked, confused and insulted that I hadn't been informed. I was still in the wedding party, wasn't I? An old friend, a confidante. Or so I had been led to think.

"March, sir. Saturday the 27th," he said, one hand on the door, already closing it.

I stuck my foot in. "Are you sure?"

"Quite sure. The event is scheduled at the Silver Gate Hotel."

"I'd like to talk to Mr Fairmont. Please tell him to call me as soon as possible."

"Very well, sir. Good day." He shut the door in my face.

To pass the time and distract myself, I painted, my work diving deeper into surrealist territories. I painted with oils exclusively during this period. A large vertical canvas depicted the gargoyle soaring skyward from behind the rickety wooden fence. His proffered knife twirling in the air, as the viewer's feet (my feet) stayed planted in the yard, the foggy Miskatonic to our left. Another canvas, horizontal, showed a panorama of the Black Cave's subterranean lake, a pale sea monster disturbing its sable depths. But my greatest project during this burst of creative energy was a triptych of the Clover Club. The three panels captured phases of the ritual I witnessed. Balthazarr himself at the microphone. The floating bodies of the cigarette girl and the goon. And, lastly, the transfigured brick wall leading to an imaginary world of threat and terrors.

Without knowing it at the time, I had just painted myself into the history of Surrealist visionaries. I was one of them now. But, in the moment, I was emptying my mind as it continually refilled with hallucinatory images, a relentless parade of dreams that invaded me daily, nightly.

January became February; February leaked into March.

One afternoon that felt more like a memory of winter than the promise of springtime, I ventured out from my studio, returning to the docks. It was reckless. I felt desperate, foolhardy. My latest work endowed me with a sense of immortality, and at the same time I yearned for something to break my world, even if the broken thing knocking inside it was me.

At the corner of the last dock, I was surprised to find Christophe and his little red wagon, roasting chestnuts, stirring them with a long spoon on his charcoal grill.

"One bag," I said.

The one-eyed former soldier recognized me immediately.

"Haven't seen you in a while." He scooped up the hot chestnuts into a paper bag.

"I've been around. Isn't it late for chestnuts?"

Christophe shrugged. "It's never too late if I have customers."

We stood there watching longshoremen unloading cargo from a ship. The air was cold, but you could sense the pressure of a coming change, a new season in the offing, the passing of time like smoke from Christophe's grill floating, disappearing.

"I've been looking for my friend, Nina."

Nina, Nina. She was never far from my thoughts.

"Isn't that what you were doing the first time we met? Looking for the same girl?"

I smiled. "You're right. I was."

"And I introduced you to Calvin."

"You did."

"He was just here," Christophe said.

My heart jumped. "When?"

"Oh, maybe a minute ago. I sold him a bag. He went walking down that way. Where are you running to? Are you crazy? You dropped your bag." Christophe pointed with his spoon to the chestnuts I spilled on the gravel.

I was running after Calvin. I went in the direction Christophe pointed.

But I saw no one.

I kept going.

I came to an intersection and scanned the cross street both ways. There!

The easy-flowing walk of a man of slender build. He wore a heavy overcoat and a dark wool stocking hat. He was smoking a cigarette, and in his fist was a rolled-down paper bag. I chased after him.

"Calvin!"

The man turned as I descended on him. It was Calvin Wright. He looked shocked to see me. I grabbed him by both shoulders. The cigarette fell from his mouth.

"I found you," I said. At last, a chance! Did he know the whereabouts of Nina?

"Alden! I'm working for the same people. We have a ship coming in tonight."

"Where is she? Where is Nina?"

Calvin acted as if he didn't understand my question. He rested his hands on my wrists until I released him. He looked at me with pity. "I don't know where Nina is. I haven't seen her since that day we were at the camp when you were hit so badly in the head. Are you feeling… better?"

I laughed bitterly.

Calvin shook his head, worriedly. "The O'Bannions broke up the camp on the Miskatonic. The cops were onto us. The gang moved me up to Canada for a while. The other end of the operation. I helped bringing shipments down to the states. I got back a week ago."

I hung my head in disbelief. "Freddie and Winston are dead."

"I know. A rival crew caught them out at the camp."

"No, no. That's wrong. We think the Colonists killed them."

Calvin stepped back. "The Colonists?" His hand went into his coat pocket. I wondered if he had a knife. Was he with them? I didn't know what to believe any more.

"Nina and I went down into the Black Cave. They were dumping Clark's body…"

"Who's Clark?" He took another step away from me. Wary, perhaps even frightened.

"He was my friend. It isn't important. You're telling me you haven't seen Nina since the day that watchman cracked me over the head with his bat?" My temples were pounding.

"That's right."

"My God. Where is she? Where could she be?" I said to myself, walking away.

Calvin tried to get me to go to a diner with him. He wanted to calm me down, to find out what I knew about Balthazarr, the Colony, and the Clover Club. I refused to go.

"I have to find Nina," I said. "No one is helping me."

"That's what we'll do, you and I together. First, you need to get control of yourself."

"Where's that warehouse?" My mind raced. "You told us it was around here. The place where Dunphy did his stone-carving." My hands balled up; all my muscles clenched. I had to do something, anything. It felt like my skeleton wanted to free itself from my flesh.

"It's up the street. But that was months ago. I don't expect they've kept anything."

We went up the street and, no, they hadn't kept anything. Because where the warehouse once stood was now a vacant lot filled with the charred rubble of a building.

"I hadn't heard about a fire," Calvin said, at a loss.

"No. How could you? Thank you for your time." I tried to leave.

"Wait. Let me walk with you. I'll get us smokes. We can talk." Calvin ducked into a shop to buy cigarettes, and I left. Turning quickly around corners. But I didn't go home. I wandered the streets of the city, thinking, trying not to despair, failing miserably.

The other Colonists shunned me now. I didn't want to talk to them. Or even see them. Life in New Colony had become terribly, awfully ordinary. Nina's disappearance was accepted, a tasty piece of communal gossip that faded and was replaced by more recent news. It drove me mad. I only stayed in case she came home. If only she were still here…

I had to find answers. So I decided to go where the answers were most likely to be.

To do what I'd dreaded doing for so long.

I had to see Balthazarr.

Balthazarr had taken up residence in the penthouse suite at the Silver Gate. He lived and worked on the top floor, with a view of the entire city available to him. I showed up at the hotel one afternoon, while cold March rain slashed the hotel façade. I asked at the hotel desk for them to ring Balthazarr's suite. I knew the artist had a reputation for sleeping late, but he'd be awake by now. In effect, I imagined he knew I was coming down to the hour, maybe even the minute I called on him.

"Mr Balthazarr says you should come right up. Elevators are across the lobby."

"Thank you."

The old guy operating the elevator greeted me cheerily.

"Good morning, sir!"

"Good morning."

"Oh, sir, don't I know it. I know it in my heart. Every morning is a good one."

What a peculiar man, I thought. Happy in his work. Ignorant of the dangers lurking.

He transported me up to the penthouse.

"To your left. Enjoy your visit. Once you stay here, you'll never go anywhere else."

I thanked the old man and watched the doors close on his grinning face. I walked the long hallway. The carpet was plush. The wallpaper geometric and modern. I felt as though I were inside a work of art. An artificial facsimile. Fake. Unreal. What is real? How can one know? At the end of the hallway, the door stood ajar. I was peeking in when I heard him.

"Welcome, Alden. It has been too long. Please, don't be shy."

I pushed the door open. I didn't see anyone. The main room of the suite was a tremendous mess. No maid had cleaned in here for weeks. Balthazarr transformed the rooms into a version of his home studio from Spain. Paints, canvases, brushes soaking in muddycolored jars. Beautiful wreckage wherever the eye landed. Someone had attempted to spread several drop cloths on the furniture and carpeting. They'd been moved and shifted around so that whatever protection they had offered was now nil. I found the bathroom. Empty. The sink was running. I turned the faucet off. Balthazarr's untidy, vacant bedroom. Cushions arranged on the floor. The bed stripped. The nightstand covered with drippy, melted candles and bottles of varying design. It reminded me of the floor tiles of South Church. But I tried not to look too hard. I didn't need distraction or to feel more uneasy. Wet roof. Dunphy falling.

Where did Balthazarr sleep?

I had concluded he must be hiding from me, when I felt his hand touch my shoulder.

"Ahh!"

"Sorry, did I frighten you? I am enjoying a cup of herbal tea. Would you like some?"

He offered his teacup for me to smell.

It was pungent, musky. I couldn't imagine drinking it.

"No, thank you."

"As you wish." He was dressed in a flowing silk kaftan of pale yellow. A medley of other colors had been splashed and dried across its surface over the years, so that it was like a modern Balthazarr canvas he wore. "Let's sit and talk. Not for too long. I have work to do."

I joined him on a pair of oversized ottomans in the middle of the room. All the curtains had been taken down. I had a dizzying sense of pitching over the end of the building as I looked out. Rain slithering on the glass. Shapes in the clouds. Billowing, gray, opaque.

"I'll get right to it," I said. "Where's Nina?" *JHB? Who else? Two places at once.*

"Ha! You're asking me? I thought she was your girlfriend."

"Do you know?" An edginess slid into my voice. I sound crazy, I thought.

"I'm sure she'll come back to you when she is ready. But I see you are serious and in pain. I am sorry I cannot help you. How is your painting going? Doing anything interesting?"

"I've had a productive few months." My surge of pride bothered me.

"Excellent. The Colony has been good to you, no?"

"They don't talk to me any more."

"Talk is not the only way to communicate. You are making art. That's what's important."

He sipped his horrible tea. I could smell it on his breath, like rotten flowers.

"What is going on in Arkham?" I asked. "Why are you really here? Don't lie to me."

"There are no lies. Only stories… pictures… our fantasies."

I shifted on my cushion. I could not find a comfortable position. My muscles ached. I had a new headache sprouting. "I know what happened at the Clover Club wasn't simply a case of hypnotism. You did something… something real…"

"We manufacture reality. Make it new every day on the assembly line of a shared consciousness. But truth is what *I* dream it is. There is no such thing as a fiction. My dreams are as real as their bricks. I am going to use my dreams to smash the windows of this world. Look around you. It is a dead universe we struggle to survive in, Alden. A graveyard only capable of breeding more graves. They will fill the earth with death. But not I. Balthazarr wants no part of their scheming. I am a destroyer and a creator. I annihilate death and replace it with my art."

He looked totally serene as he told me this. My spine was twisted, stiffening. "You are trying to break reality." I mopped my forehead. The suite was humid as a greenhouse.

"That's one way of putting it. Ask yourself, whose reality? Not mine, I guarantee you that. Politicians, generals, and businessmen conceived this reality. I reject it. I demand a revolution. Artists, dreamers, and the so-called mad people will have their chance. Reality must be broken." He finished his tea, placing the cup on the floor. He fluffed out his tunic.

"Is that what your paintings do?"

"Paintings? Yes, but they are so much more. Your thinking is too small. We must be big to triumph in these days of modern wonders. Live boldly." He spread his arms out.

"I'm a painter. I might even be a surrealist like you. 'Live boldly'. What does that even mean?" I loosened my tie. My head throbbed. I felt the veins under my skin, netting my skull.

"It is about time. Paintings, novels, sculpture, poetry, films… any work wrought by the mind and human hands. Once we conquer time, everything becomes meaningless. My life's work is digging an escape tunnel out from this dimension, my reality prison cell. My knuckles are bloody from tunneling out of their sterile world. When I go out, I'm leaving the Gate open for whatever haunts the other dimension to come in. It is of no concern to me! Come with me, Alden. Let's break out together. Everything is death except for dreams. We are artists. You work for my dreams. I work for yours. Together, we become the future. Our work will live for eternity. There isn't much time left."

I took off my jacket and folded it across my knees. Outside the windows, the distant grayed buildings appeared to be warping. "The night of Preston's party, when we were alone in Independence Park, you asked me if I thought you were crazy. I still don't know how to answer that question."

"Fair enough. That is how you choose to interpret me. I am too busy to be a critic."

"What comes next? What is your best reasonable alternative?"

The question bored Balthazarr. "If reason gave us this, what good is reason? Don't you want to see something new? Even if it's nothing? I have no plan. Perhaps we shall try chaos. If there is no order, then everyone has the power of a god. Do you want that too?"

"I've heard enough." I got up, nearly losing my balance. I caught myself teetering.

"You have everything you need to decide. I hope you make a wise choice."

Without answering him, or saying goodbye, I turned and left the suite. The elevator operator was waiting for me at the end of the hallway. His empty smile stretched wide like a mask. His blank eyes never blinking. I left the hotel, but the feeling of vertigo and the aroma of Balthazarr's tea lingered.

CHAPTER THIRTY

Preston called me the next day. He had decided to join his parents down at their winter home in West Palm Beach. They built a place there during the war, when the Mediterranean became inhospitably treacherous. The Florida land boom was over; real estate prices were dropping, but the Fairmonts had enough cash and diversity in their investments to ride things out. Preston had planned to travel south for some sun and leisure after his bachelor party, but I was stunned when I heard him say he'd left town by train the very next day. Doubly surprising was the news that Minnie left with him. Why hadn't they sent any word to me?

"Oakesy, we need to tell you something. It's terribly embarrassing. Shameful, really."

"What is it?"

"We've called off the wedding," he said. His voice was jarring. A hoarse croak.

"Called it off. I've only just learned the date was changed. Why on earth…?" It was beyond belief. I'd come home from Europe. For this! If not for them, Nina might still be…

"I'd rather not go into particulars. Father advised me to cool things off. Let's say it's postponed. Less grim, don't you think?" Preston sounded so far away. Not the other end of the country, the end of the galaxy.

I gazed out my window, combing my fingers though my hair. The Miskatonic ran fast with runoff. There were things floating in the water. Bloated, mottled. Rolling like fat barrels.

"Is anyone sick?" I asked. My mouth felt dry. I licked my lips, papery and cracked.

"No." Preston echoed as if he'd fallen down a deep well. "I can't talk much longer."

"Did you know Nina's gone missing? Since the night of your bachelor party…"

"Not Nina too." He gasped. His words bounced off the walls of that murky well. I heard a deep, gravelly voice in the background. His father? Or someone else? A cacophony of other voices suddenly interrupted us, talking all at once.

"Preston? Preston are you there?" I pressed the handset hard to my ear.

"Get away." That's what I thought I heard him say. I can't be certain. Not of what I heard or who said it. Too much static on the line, then the connection was cut off. Dead. I hung up.

The following morning two letters arrived in my mailbox. One was from Preston and Minnie, their apologies and a notice of the cancellation of their ceremony.

The other was an invitation.

The honor of your presence is requested
at Juan Hugo Balthazarr's Masquerade
In the Main Room
At the Silver Gate Hotel

Masks are required
Midnight, March 27th, 1926

The date and location were identical to Preston and Minnie's aborted wedding.

The time was later, of course.

The days leading up to Balthazarr's masquerade ball passed in a blur. From Oakwood, I received a delivery: my tuxedo and a note from Ro wishing me good times. New Colony was a hive of activity. Colonists who had shunned me in the months since Nina's departure now showed a renewed camaraderie and friendliness in the hallways and walking on the grounds. I wrapped up my finished paintings for storage, and Roland was kind enough to pick them up and take them to the house for me, in case anything unexpected happened. I told him I was worried about a leaking roof. He knew better but didn't ask questions. I wasn't sure what was going to happen. I wanted my work salvaged in any case. I worked too hard to lose it all.

I busied myself with a final piece that I planned to unveil at the ball. It was something I'd never attempted before, an arts and crafts project. Glue, paper, an elastic string.

The day before the party I happened to see Balthazarr mixing with Colonists on the front lawn of the mansion. His piercing gaze locked on me as soon as I exited the building.

I walked right up to him.

He extricated himself from his conversation. The crowd moved off to give us privacy.

"I got your reply. I am immensely pleased you are attending my event," he said.

"I had a chance to think about what you said to me that day at your penthouse. Well, I've made up my mind. I'm following you."

"Excellent, excellent. See you at the Silver Gate."

I don't think he believed me. But that didn't matter.

The night of the ball, I put on my tux and took out my arts and crafts project to study it one last time. It was a full-face mask. I'd made it myself from papier mâché, glue, and paint. I put the mask on and checked my reflection in the mirror. It wasn't perfect, but it suited my purpose. I thought about writing a letter to Mother and Father. You know, if things didn't work out. But what would I possibly say? Would they believe me? In the end I decided against it. What would last, would last. All else was destined to be forgotten, lost in time.

One final thing.

I opened the drawer of my dresser. I moved aside my undershirts. I still had the gun I'd lifted off the tough guy in the hallway, the man Balthazarr tossed in the river. I wasn't sure if he was dead or alive, that bully who went for a swim into the icy, onyx Miskatonic. What we saw dripping on the banks that night might've been him, or it might've easily been a monster made of nets and rats. Either way, I had his gun. I checked the bullets. Then I tucked it into the small of my back and covered it with my jacket.

I was ready.

I drove the Rolls-Royce to the hotel, parked it out front where everyone could see me.

The Silver Gate was a real beauty. That night she looked white and shiny like an ocean liner, or a huge stone cliff covered with snow and ice. Maybe, from a certain angle, she looked like a wedding cake covered in diamonds. She sparkled to beat the band.

Outside, the night air was fresh and clean. It would be a good night for sleeping.

Inside, they'd filled the lobby with roses. Explosions of red everywhere you turned.

I saw Colonists loitering in the lobby, smoking. They already had their masks on.

"Hiya, Alden! Where's your mask?"

I held up a paper bag. "Got it right here. See you inside."

Balthazarr's ball was in the Silver Gate's main room. I hadn't felt anything unusual the other times I entered the hotel. But I felt something now. A low, steady vibration humming from the structure itself, as if it were a tuning fork. I wondered how long ago the wheels of this scheme started turning, because Balthazarr and his Colonists weren't acting alone in this. They were in the final phase of a long-range plan. This was the last ritual in a string of others. Was it global? Who knew how far the tendrils reached? But whatever entity they had been calling to across dimensions, sending out their blood-soaked signals... Whatever they called it... Yuyu-Va'badaa or the Un-Sun... the Falling Star... that shapeless void careening through space and time had been drawing nearer to Earth, and tonight, finally, they hoped it would arrive in glory. The Gate would open. They didn't even try to hide it. The Silver Gate. I bet they had a good laugh at that. Hiding in plain sight, biding their time. As patient as they were deadly.

The doors to the main room were shut. Masked sentinels guarded them.

"You need to put on your mask," one said to me. It was Portia's voice, our downstairs neighbor, the sculptress who replaced Courtland Dunphy. Did she know how they killed him?

I removed my mask from the paper bag and put it on.

Portia drew in a sharp breath.

"Can you dispose of this for me?" I asked.

She took the bag but said nothing.

I opened the doors and went inside.

I could see why they wanted to keep outsiders from seeing the ballroom. They had removed all the tables and chairs. There was no bar, no banquet. Only the gleaming marble floor. From the ceiling hung lit chandeliers; tall black candles in wrought iron stands stood around the perimeter of the room, their wicks unburnt. The floor itself was the real stunner. Elaborate glyphs covered every available inch of tile. It must've taken them hours to create it, I thought. A small army of artists at work, following a mathematically precise occult diagram that was magnificently intricate. What was the purpose of this design?

It wasn't a map of any known universe.

I don't know what it was, to be honest. A symbol, or series of interlocking symbols, drawn on the floor is my best guess. In some places, the lines were poured in powders – rusty auburns, gray-speckled blacks, and bone whites. Brushstrokes of gold, silver, and red traced angles and spirals. At the center was a perfect circle. Within it, a falling star, the same symbol I'd seen before, dripped in wax at South Church and carved into Dunphy's apartment door.

Here, it appeared to be burned on the marble.

If a visitor wandered into this room by mistake and didn't look down, or notice the lack of furniture and refreshments, they might've thought it was just a bizarrely themed party. The attendees gathered in small conversational groups, smoking cigarettes, gossiping, killing time until things got swinging. *I* was the most shocking part of the night so far.

It was my mask.

Many of the masked chose to hide their eyes only, but I wore a full-face disguise.

I'd done my best to get the features right, but the dead giveaway was my long, forked beard. I used hair clippings from a barbershop. Oh, I was too short and slim to be mistaken for the actual Balthazarr. But at a distance, especially in profile, a quick glance might lead someone to think I was the sorcerer, the Twister of the Coil. It was disrespectful, my mocking their leader. At worst, the mask was blasphemous.

Balthazarr hadn't made an appearance yet. That was who they were all waiting for.

Well, one of the things they were waiting for, anyway.

The chandeliers dimmed. The candles were lit. Music – a thin, eerie wailing of strings from an instrument I could not identify, and whose player remained concealed – began. *Ah, the show is starting.* I made a path to the middle, on the rim of the circle. The crowd parted before me. The sentinels entered, securing the doors behind them with chains and padlocks. A group of busy Colonists passed out robes. The masqueraders cloaked up.

Someone handed me a robe. The garment was celestial blue.

"I expected black," I said.

No one responded to my remark. I slipped the robe on.

Juan Hugo Balthazarr knew how to make an entrance. Not from the background or some curtained wing off stage. No. He simply arrived inside the circle. Perhaps we were all hypnotized already. He glided among us, a moving blind spot. I don't know how he did it.

He was not the focus of my attention.

Because Balthazarr did not arrive alone.

Nina stood at his side.

I could not breathe. My torso experienced a temporary paralysis. Worrying I might lose consciousness and sabotage my mission, I struck my fist against my chest. Slowly, I inhaled. Had she succumbed to the allure of this cult? She was too good, too strong. But there was no denying her standing there assisting Balthazarr. His companion in this sorcerous rite.

Wisps of fragrant smoke floated in the room, scribbling up from bronze censers.

Balthazarr raised his hands overhead.

"New Colonists, allies, and benefactors... Welcome to the end of the world!"

The crowd cheered.

"This is a new day, the last day. We call to the Un-Sun, the Falling Star. We open the Gate for Yuyu-Va'bdaa. The old ways of reason, order, and logic are no more. We hunger for chaos and thirst for insanity, so that we may lose the burden of our servitude and be free from the dungeon of laws, rules, and commandments. Lies are true. We are our own gods."

The masked congregants fell to their knees.

All except for me.

I stood there, wearing Balthazarr's face.

My plan was to shoot him, to empty my pistol into his chest. An artistic statement as well as an assassination. What was more surreal than Balthazarr killing Balthazarr? But I hadn't expected Nina to be there. I was willing to take a chance with my personal escape from the scene. Her survival was another matter. Through the eyeholes of my mask I tried to make sense of her. She didn't seem to recognize me. How would she? All the people wore robes, and no part of my true face showed. Nina wasn't looking at anyone, just staring straight out. Her pupils were dilated. Entranced, that much I judged for certain, perhaps they'd drugged her. When did they catch her that night? How? It didn't matter, not now.

I made a gambit to play along with the ritual for now.

"Unmask yourself, Alden," Balthazarr said.

I obeyed.

Pain licked my fingertips. The mask was on fire. I dropped it to the floor and watched the paper curl and whiten to ash.

Nina's wrists were crossed under the sleeves of her robe. When she drew them apart, I saw she held the cycloptic cane Balthazarr had used to orchestrate the ritual at the Clover Club. She raised the diabolic stick into the air.

"Balthazarr! Yuyu-Va'bdaa!" she cried.

"Nina! Yuyu-Va'bdaa!" Balthazarr replied.

"Balthazarr! Nina! Yuyu-Va'bdaa!" the kneeling supplicants repeated.

"*Ebuma chtenff*! *Gnaiih goka gotha gof'nn*!" Nina said, slamming the tip of the wooden ritualistic instrument into the floor. The outer boundaries of the ballroom drifted away. The candles became pinpricks of starlight. A darkness enshrouded us. Slowly, a pale greenish hue tainted the surrounding air.

No, Nina, no…

How was this woman my Nina?

She always ran ahead, I thought. Sometimes ahead, there is a trap.

Balthazarr pointed at me. I was pulled into the circle as if a rope were cinched around my body, and I could not resist its urgent tugging. Balthazarr wore his robe from Spain; the mirrors and shards of broken glass glittered, a galaxy in motion, breaking down, tumbling into oblivion.

"Where do I stand?" I asked him. My will was slipping. The puppet master pulled my strings. I was determined to fight him. But it was so much easier not to fight…

Balthazarr pointed to a glyph drawn on the marble, a cup with an oval balanced inside. "You are the final sacrifice," he said to me. "The First Key."

"And what is she?" I asked.

"I am the Bride," Nina answered. "The Second Key."

"Whose bride?" I asked.

Neither of them said a word.

A roar came from not far off. Its volume grew stronger until my eardrums ached.

The same roar I'd heard in the Clover Club. The fire-breather, the voice of a dragon flying through space to consume our human race. To swallow us like a moistened crumb.

Nina raised the cyclops stick. Its lidless eye glowed, an orb containing galaxies.

"This is the ritual. I am the Sorcerer," Balthazarr said. "We are at the dawning of a new sun, never witnessed before by impotent human eyes, a sun that burns without light, that consumes all. I, the Twister of the Coil, open the Gate! Do you see it? Do you see?"

"We see!" the supplicants answered.

Our circle tilted on its axis – a disk floating free in outer space. The masqueraders clung to their own geometric platform as it lifted and fell, crest to trough, again and again, riding on a cosmic sea. Mirages materialized in the zone above us. Each vision a tableau of one of Arkham's recent ritual murders. Dr Silva swinging from a lamppost, her pockets stuffed with witchweed. Udo Ganz unzipped of his tattooed skin. The Galinka sisters kicking their dancers' legs as they burned on a pyre. The tramp bleeding outside a boxcar. Dunphy clutching a gargoyle horn as he plummeted toward the ground. Clark's naked, headless corpse splayed beneath a telescope pointed at the stars...

Somewhere outside of linear time, the murders were still happening, *would always be happening* in a continuous, never-ending loop.

They flashed like lighthouse signals to Yuyu-Va'bdaa as it navigated the cosmos.

I saw the murders for what they were: impersonal, cold as a mechanism, tumblers in a lock, but also lights, like candles, stationed along a dark path.

They led to the Gate and they opened it, too.

Smoke-like tendrils began to form out of Balthazarr's body. An array gathered around his head and as they solidified, they fashioned themselves into a spiked crown. From his hand sprung a long, three-pronged fork with which he stirred the air.

"Beholder from Beyond, God of Dimensions Unimagined, Lord and Servant of None and Nothing, I call to you! Take this Man as a final sacrifice of the last ritual. This Woman is your eternal Bride. Falling Star, Fall Here! Un-Sun, be born! Yuyu-Va'bdaa, come to us!"

"Be born!" the worshippers called out, even as turbulence rocked their platform and tossed numbers of them screaming into the ether. "Come to us! Yuyu-Va'bdaa!"

I drew my pistol and, pointing it squarely at Balthazarr, I pulled the trigger.

The trigger did not move. The weapon scorched my hand. I smelled hot metal and my burning flesh. Balthazarr's piercing eyes transformed into pits of swirling kaleidoscopic colors. The pistol glowed orange. Furnace-hot. My skin sizzled. The gun turning to liquid.

I screamed.

"Fool! I offered you the opportunity of a lifetime. Beyond any lifetime!" Balthazarr flicked his wrist, and the molten metal scattered. A glob landed on my cheek, searing into my cheekbone. A thick tentacle of ectoplasmic fog snapped out of the Surrealist's ribcage and looped around my throat, strangling me. A vile energy passed through him, entangling me.

As I choked, my fingers dug into the viscous substance.

"Chaos is the new order!" he shouted. "Lose your sanity! Abandon old logic. Yuyu-Va'bdaa shatters time. There is no future. No past. Now is All! See it! We are with Yuyu!"

Stars exploded in my eyes.

Not real stars, but the blood vessels in my head. I was dying. My body crushed. I would not follow Balthazarr. No one would. After the Gate opened, it would be death.

Only death.

In the dimming light of my receding consciousness, I reached out to feel the sleeve of Nina's robe. I could not see, but I could feel. Was that her hand touching mine? Yes! But she could not hold onto me. Nor I hold fast to her. Our fingers lost their grip. Soon our sanity would follow. I clutched the material of her robe in my fist. Then it too pulled away from me.

Gone, she's gone.

I am too.

Nina did not make a sound. The silence was worse. I called and called, "Nina!"

No reply came.

Only a whirling of winds greater than any earthly storm. And the roar of Yuyu.

My vision zeroed down to a tight tunnel.

In that tunnel with me was the face of Balthazarr, huge and triumphant, victorious. His grimacing mouth fell open. The noose around my neck slackened. Blood rushed into my starved brain. I struggled to see what was happening in front of me. Balthazarr spun his arms wildly, striking out at nothing. A flash of quick movement. A tall woman, the woman I knew.

Nina backed away from him.

He clutched at his neck. The tendrils looping from his body evaporated.

The handle of Nina's Frosolone stiletto protruded from the hood of his robe. She had stabbed him sideways, slicing through meat and bone. The slender blade transected his spinal cord. Strings cut, the Spaniard crumpled. His face transformed to a mask of total disbelief.

But what of her? Was it too late? My heart flooded with sudden hope of our survival.

"Nina!" My words lost amid a constant roar.

The void – arrested at the threshold!

The Gate split open. It was, and is, impossible to describe. Call it a dilation between dimensions. A tearing of the veil between our reality and an otherness. An evanescent portal.

It started to close. To seal itself like a cosmic wound clotted with stars.

Full of stars.

I strained with every muscle fiber to reach her. She took a step toward me, but a powerful funnel of air was sucking inward – a cosmic inhalation drawing everything to the Gate and the lightless immensity perching on the brink of universes. Balthazarr tumbled, flipping end over end, into the vanishing gap. Nina watched him go. She had saved me. She held out her hand for me to take. "Now, Alden." Fear seized me instead. Controlling me. Thoughts of the Gate and what lay beyond it: an unbounded chasm. Endless nothingness.

So, I am ashamed to admit I hesitated. A fraction of a second. No more.

Then I lunged for her. But it was too late. I was too late.

I watched the Gate take her.

It closed.

Back inside, the ballroom was chaos. The room was dark. I crawled on the floor, over bodies, dead and dying. The candles had fallen over, most of them extinguishing themselves.

But not every candle.

I found the doors. Locked. I smashed at the padlocks with my fists. I was too weak, my hands too soft. My eyes had trouble seeing things. I turned to the chasm of the ballroom, the moans of the injured, the giggling gibberish of those driven utterly insane by what they had witnessed. I groped for an iron candle stand. I ripped a burning candle from its holder and threw it at the wall. Taking the stand, I smashed open the lock. The doors flung wide.

"Alden! Is that you?"

Calvin caught me as I pitched forward. Behind me, the wall

where I threw the candle started to burn, a wavering curtain of flame. "We need to get out of here now," he said.

"Nina."

"Where is she?"

He pulled me upright.

I bolted back inside the ballroom, yelling her name, the smoke thick and poisonous.

The Silver Gate feeding itself, and everyone still inside, to the inferno.

CHAPTER THIRTY-ONE

Van Nortwick put down his pencil and massaged his tired hand. He reached for the last bottle of ginger ale and tilted it against his lips, but found it empty.

"That's quite a story, Mr Oakes." He was going to write it up. It would make the paper. But he wasn't sure how much of it he believed.

"We're out of cigarettes, Andy. I think that means it's time to stop."

The painter leaned against the dresser. He'd left the sofa hours ago, complaining that his bad leg felt stiff. He paced around the hotel room as he talked, settling back on the window ledge or propping himself up on the furniture, like he was doing now.

"You never told me what happened to your leg," Van Nortwick said.

"Ceiling collapse. Not in the ballroom but the lobby. A beam hit me. I thought that might be the end, but I managed to wriggle free. A fracture, they said at the hospital. But I limped outside. That's when the fireman tackled me. My jacket was burning. I mentioned this to you already. Don't want to start repeating myself. Anyway, I'm healed up. My body is."

The reporter picked up his pencil again, tapping it on his notepad.

"Preston Fairmont and Minnie Devane…?" Van Nortwick's pencil stirred.

"They went traveling for a while. Sent me postcards from around the world. Preston felt guilty for leaving town, but he needed to escape. He saved himself. And Minnie too. I don't blame him." Alden pushed off the dresser, walked to the window. "I saw it in the papers that his father died. I can only imagine the pressure Preston's under now." Gray rain fell steadily.

"Well, thank you for your time. You've certainly given me a lot to digest."

Alden turned to him, smiling thinly.

"You think I made it up."

Van Nortwick shrugged. "It's not my place to judge. I gather facts, write them down in neat columns the way my editor likes. It's up to our readers to decide what they think."

Alden nodded. "Care to try an experiment?"

The reporter paused, considering the offer.

"For the benefit of your readers, of course. It'll be easy," Alden said.

"Sure, Mr Oakes. You've been generous with me. I can do that."

The artist looked at the window again. Then, as if he'd come to a decision, he swiveled around and positioned himself in front of the hotel room's only mirror. "Come stand behind me, Andy, over my shoulder here, and look into the glass."

Skeptically, Van Nortwick rose and joined Alden at the mirror.

"How's this?" he said.

"Perfect," Alden said. "Now, concentrate on our reflections."

Van Nortwick did his best, focusing on the room as it was doubled in the glass.

After a long minute, Alden met his gaze. "Well, see anything? Besides the two of us."

Van Nortwick stared hard. Then, shaking his head, he stepped to one side.

"Sorry, Mr Oakes," he said.

"That's fine. I'll give you credit for trying. Good luck with your story." Alden started packing his gin, shaker, and glasses into his red crocodile suitcase. When he finished, he drew out the necklace he wore. Van Nortwick saw there were two keys on the necklace. Alden locked the case. The reporter prepared to go. At the door, they exchanged goodbyes.

"Have fun at the gala," Van Nortwick said, stepping out of the suite into the hall.

They shook hands. The reporter startled for a moment at the rough scar tissue. How had he been burned? In an accident of some sort? Or it might be self-inflicted, he thought.

Probably the hotel blaze. He was lucky to have survived.

Alden was smiling wanly as he shut the door.

Have fun at the gala. How stupid can I possibly be? Van Nortwick chastised himself as he rode down in the elevator with the creepy old operator outfitted like an organ grinder's monkey. Alden Oakes might be as crazy as people said. But after a tragedy like the Silver Gate fire, who wouldn't be traumatized? He didn't need to be told to have fun reliving the experience. Stupid.

Van Nortwick lingered in the lobby. It wasn't that Oakes

hadn't given him enough for a good story. Just the opposite. He'd given too much. How was he going to turn all that talk into a clever bit of journalism? Van Nortwick bought a pack of cigarettes from the hotel newsstand. He was watching the rain, hoping it would let up so he wouldn't get completely soaked walking back to the *Arkham Advertiser* offices, when he spotted Alden emerging from the elevator. The artist had a small satchel over his shoulder. He headed straight back toward the event rooms.

Van Nortwick followed him.

He was going into the newly renovated ballroom, the heart of the tragedy, and the location of tonight's party. Van Nortwick waited for as long as it took him to finish his smoke, then he crushed out the butt in a standing ashtray and went inside.

The room was mostly dark. He searched for the painter but found no trace of him.

"Back here," Alden said.

In a far corner of the great room, the painter sat cross-legged on the floor. His satchel was open, and a small array of paint jars and brushes were arranged beside him.

He was painting on the wall. The outline of the image was the size of a person.

"Start at the bottom and work your way up. That's how I'm doing it." Alden smiled.

"Some people would call that vandalism," Van Nortwick said.

"Everyone's a critic. But you're right about one thing. No one will be happy if they catch me doing this. I'll be quick, though. I've been practicing." He'd moved into a crouch, then up on his knees. His brushstrokes were fast and sure. It *was* a person he was painting.

"It's a woman."

"It's Nina," Alden said.

"*Portrait of a Lady*?"

"*Portrait of a Lady in Another Dimension*. Will you hand me the red, please?"

Van Nortwick passed him the paint.

"And that brush there. Don't worry, you're not my accomplice. I take full responsibility."

"I suppose an Alden Oakes original is worth a lot of money these days."

"The hotel couldn't afford me if I charged them." Alden was standing, leaning forward. He'd almost finished the painting of the woman, of Nina. Full of motion, stylized. She wasn't wearing a robe but a red dress. Her head was tipped back slightly, chin up, the hint of knowing smile barely perceptible on her lips. "I see Balthazarr in reflections, but he is not alone. Nina is there, too. I don't know if they are even aware of each other. They never interact. I think their spectral figures are like a double exposure, two overlapping images combined in the same photograph. I've studied the images. Balthazarr's paintings. Others I've found in my research that I'm sure are connected to their rituals. I've painted them over and over. Balthazarr's way isn't the only way to open a gate, you see."

Van Nortwick didn't see now, just as he hadn't when he looked deeply into the mirror over Alden's shoulder, but he wasn't going to interfere.

"Why did she have the blade with her, if she was a believer and follower of Balthazarr? Think about it, Andy." Alden put the final touches on his portrait. "She was still my Nina. I don't know who took her the night I went to Preston's party. It was either the Colonists, or maybe Juan Hugo himself. If Nina was right, he could project himself in two places at once. It doesn't matter now. The past is past, they say. I'm not sure I totally agree."

"You want to bring her back?"

"Not exactly. You'd better stand back over there. I can't predict everything that might happen next."

Andy started to move away to where the painter had directed him.

"Wait! I forgot something." Alden slipped the necklace from around his collar. "The gold one opens my gin case. It's yours. Here's my room key so you can fetch it afterward." He fished the hotel key out of his pocket.

Van Nortwick looked at the pair of keys on the necklace.

"What's this other key for?"

"Get back a bit farther. Farther. There. That should do it." Alden pushed his art supplies away from the portrait. He looked at Van Nortwick. "I failed Nina. As the Gate pulled her through, I hesitated. I lacked courage." A haggard smile, resolved, etched in pain.

He reached into his satchel and pulled out a pair of thick iron shackles.

"Houdini's handcuffs," Van Nortwick said. What did the artist have in mind?

Some magic trick of his own design? He hoped the result wouldn't be too awkward. Or sad. That would be even worse. To watch a fragile mind breaking in front of you. If that happened, Van Nortwick decided, right then and there, he wouldn't put it in his story.

Alden wasn't paying attention to him any more. He was reciting words in a strange guttural language, chanting in a singsong cadence. Van Nortwick was too far away to make out the exact phrases, but they would've made no sense to him.

The wall.

The portrait of Nina pulsed. Then it shone and rippled like the surface of a sunlit pond. Van Nortwick dropped the necklace on the floor. His mouth hung open like a fish thrown on the dock. It was truly supernatural! He felt hugely excited and terrified at the same time. If this were happening, then what other parts of Alden Oakes' tale were true? Could it be accurate in every detail? Van Nortwick's mind was boggled. He staggered. The world was not what he thought it was. It was deeper and darker.

And so much more.

Nina Tarrington reached out to Alden.

This time he clearly wasn't going to let fear get the best of him. Alden snapped one cuff on Nina's wrist, and then he snapped the other on his own. He took a deep breath as they crossed over the threshold, disappearing together, forever, through the Gate.

ACKNOWLEDGMENTS

At Aconyte I'd like to thank Marc Gascoigne, my most excellent publisher, for the opportunity to work on this exciting and rewarding adventure. I owe a special debt of gratitude to my editor, Lottie Llewelyn-Wells, for her keen eye, brilliant insights, and crystal clarity in all matters. And thanks to the whole talented Aconyte Team for their dedication, hard work, and support.

Thanks to Asmodee Entertainment, Fantasy Flight Games, and *Arkham Horror* for the world.

Lastly, I wish to thank my wife, Lisa, and my children, Emma and Quinn. Without their love this book would not exist.

Return to the Depths of Madness

An international thief of esoteric artifacts stumbles onto a nightmarish cult in 1920s New England in this chilling tale of cosmic dread.

When a movie director shoots his silent horror masterpiece in eerie Arkham, moving pictures become crawling nightmares.

As lost artifacts are found, dark incantations infest the minds of Miskatonic University students with supernatural horrors.

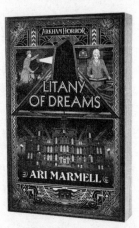

Venture into a land of duty and warfare, with Legend of the Five Rings

The mountainous border dividing the empire of Rokugan from the dark Shadowlands is perilous. Discovering a mythical city amid the blizzard-swept peaks offers heroes an opportunity to prove their honor, but risks exposing the empire to demonic invasion.

Meet Daidoji Shin, a charming and indolent Crane Clan aristocrat. When he's dragged away from a life of decadence, he and his samurai body-guard discover a talent for detection, and uncover a murderous web of conspiracies in the Emerald Empire.

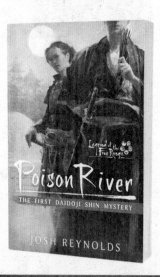